Henry Tilley

Eastern Europe and Western Asia

Political and social sketches on Russia, Greece, and Syria in 1861-2-3

Henry Tilley

Eastern Europe and Western Asia
Political and social sketches on Russia, Greece, and Syria in 1861-2-3

ISBN/EAN: 9783744752145

Printed in Europe, USA, Canada, Australia, Japan

Cover: Foto ©Andreas Hilbeck / pixelio.de

More available books at **www.hansebooks.com**

EASTERN EUROPE AND WESTERN ASIA

POLITICAL AND SOCIAL SKETCHES

ON

RUSSIA, GREECE, AND SYRIA

IN

1861-2-3

BY

HENRY ARTHUR TILLEY

LONDON
LONGMAN, GREEN, LONGMAN, ROBERTS, & GREEN
1864

TO

ALFRED HENRY BARFORD

B.A., F.R.G.S., F.L.S.

THESE SKETCHES ARE INSCRIBED

AS

A SOUVENIR OF MANY YEARS' FRIENDSHIP

BY

THE AUTHOR

PREFACE.

IN the following pages the author has attempted to throw some light on the character of a country and the institutions of a people which are little understood in the West of Europe, and, consequently, subject to frequent misrepresentations. A residence of some years among the Russians has afforded him many opportunities of enquiries and research into the national character and history, and of observing the various reforms which have lately been introduced into Russian institutions. An account of these will be found in the third, fourth, and fifth chapters.

One chapter is especially devoted to the consideration of the much-vexed Polish question.

The three chapters on Greece treat of the state of that country, and of the character displayed by the Greeks, both before and during the Revolution; while the chapter on Syria contains the author's experience in the Lebanon and at Damascus, at a time immediately following the Christian massacres.

With a sense of duty towards the public he addresses, the author has endeavoured to combine a spirit of justice and impartiality towards those of whom he writes; and, if by his remarks an error be corrected or a prejudice removed, his main object in writing will have been attained.

LONDON: *February* 18, 1864.

CONTENTS.

a

CHAPTER VIII.

CHAPTER IX.

CHAPTER X.

CHAPTER XI.

CHAPTER XII.

CHAPTER XIII.

CHAPTER XIV.

ILLUSTRATIONS.

EASTERN EUROPE ᴀɴᴅ WESTERN ASIA.

CHAPTER I.

ST. PETERSBURG AND MOSCOW.

Leave England—Copenhagen—Blowing-up of a Russian Man-
of-War—Miraculous Escape—Port Baltic—Reval—Cronstadt—
The Baltic Fleet—Entrance to St. Petersburg—Unhealthiness of
the City—Its Attractions to a Stranger—Society—Garibaldi and
the Russian Ladies—Popular Change during the present Reign—
Contrast between the Public Monuments of St. Petersburg and
Moscow—Fortress of St. Peter and St. Paul—Story of the Princess
Tarakanov—From St. Petersburg to Moscow—Sketch of the
Kremlin and its Historical Memorials—Muscovite Illustrations of
a Future State.

ON returning in 1860 from a voyage of circumnavi-
gation on board the Russian corvette ' Rynda,'
I received an invitation to embark on board a large
frigate then in Plymouth Harbour on its way to the
Mediterranean. Having had a glance at all those
ancient, transplanted, or nascent civilisations which
I described in my former work,* I was nothing loth to
visit the more classic shores of that sea which bounded
the great nations of antiquity. Through the kindness
of Admiral Popov, with whom I had made the last

* *Japan, the Amoor, and the Pacific.* Smith, Elder & Co. Cornhill,
1861.

voyage, it was arranged that I should first accompany him to St. Petersburg, and thence proceed overland by the Black Sea to the coast of Syria, whither the frigate had sailed in all haste on account of the massacres at Damascus. By so doing, I should be enabled to see something of Russia and the Russians at home, and as I could now speak their language, the arrangement was the more agreeable to me.

The summer was fast fading into autumn, when the squadron of three ships left Cherbourg on their return to Russia. A strong S.W. wind bore us swiftly through the Channel and the German Ocean, and on the third day, the coast of Norway and the old town of Christian-sand hove in sight. In another day, we were at anchor before the city of Copenhagen, where we stayed just long enough to examine the museum and masterpieces of Thorvaldsen, the curious old palace, and the port where the old wooden navy of Denmark was rotting under its sheds.

The day after leaving Copenhagen, we were the horror-stricken witnesses of an awful calamity. The gunboat 'Plastoon' had been four years in the Pacific, and its officers only the day before had been rejoicing at the prospect that a few more hours would see them in their native land and among their kindred. All the vessels were going merrily along under reefed top-sails, when a puff of smoke was seen to proceed from the 'Plastoon,' which was fortunately the most leeward of the three ships. At first we supposed she had fired

a gun; but as the smoke cleared away, we saw that
her foremast was gone, that the yards and sails of the
other two masts were hanging in disorder, and that
her forecastle was so inclined, that the bowsprit seemed
under water. In a moment, the dreadful truth broke
upon us; her magazine had exploded, and the ship
was fast settling down. The excitement of the moment
was intense—my own eager attention was fixed during
the few intervening seconds with equal anxiety on the
sinking ship, and on our preparations for bearing down
on her and lowering the boats. But long before our
ship could wear, the gun-boat was no longer to be seen.
Up to the last moment, I could distinctly see with my
spyglass the scared features of those on board—some
rushing from one point to another, others on their
knees and with their arms raised to heaven. On our
own vessel meanwhile, a young midshipman was in an
agony of despair for his eldest brother, who, at that
very moment, was clinging to a ring in the side of the
sinking vessel, unconscious of the entreaties of his
messmates, who cried to him to let go his hold. He
clung on desperately, and was borne down with the
ship. In about a minute from the explosion, the
vessel, having righted herself for an instant, settled
quickly down, and the horizon was unbroken where her
tapering masts and expanded sails had just before
been seen. The corvettes and their boats were on the
spot a few minutes afterwards; but there were only

a few blackened timbers, some boats bottom upwards, and quantities of splinters and dust floating in the still eddying waters. About thirty officers and men out of a crew of 120 were picked up, some dreadfully scorched by the explosion, or wounded by nails in the broken timbers to which they had been clinging. During that one minute between the explosion and the foundering, those who were on deck had cut away the lashings of the boats, or thrown themselves overboard with the first buoyant object which came to hand. One almost miraculous escape shows how great mental excitement may suddenly and unconsciously overcome physical incapacity.

The doctor of the gunboat was lying disabled from paralysis in his berth, when the sea poured in at the gaping breach caused by the explosion. Although he had not moved without assistance for weeks, he now managed, unaided, to crawl up the ladder to the deck, from which he threw himself into the sea, and, supported by the crutch which he happened to have in his hand, remained there without motion till we picked him up. At the same time three officers, strong young men, went down, as they were sleeping in their cabins. This was the second dreadful disaster which had happened during the last three years to Russian men-of-war in almost the same spot. In 1858, a line-of-battle ship, called the 'Lefort,' had left Reval with a number of officers and their families on board, the whole amounting to 800 persons. While tacking, a squall caught her, and she capsized and sank immediately. Although she was sailing in squadron, and other vessels passed over the same spot a few minutes afterwards, not a body or fragment of wreck was to be seen.

In the case of the 'Plastoon,' all that the survivors could tell us was, that they were cleaning out the magazine, but that the fires had all been extinguished and the usual precautions taken : beyond this, all was conjecture. To forward these painful tidings to the Government and to the friends of the drowned, the Admiral put into Port Baltic the next morning.

This port, situated about forty miles from Reval, is a rather spacious bay, protected by an old and half-finished breakwater, and is a common resort for the Russian Baltic squadron. Thence an officer was sent to Reval with despatches, and I accompanied him to see something of the country; the corvettes coming round the next day. Reval of late years has become the fashionable watering-place for the society of Moscow and St. Petersburg. It is surrounded by a pretty, undulating country; the adjoining Catharinenthal is dotted with the 'châlets' of the resident nobility or visitors, and contains the palace of the Empress Catharine II. and a small wooden house once inhabited by Peter the Great, the furniture and other articles used by him being religiously preserved in their places as relics.

On leaving Reval, the ships proceeded to Cronstadt. On their arrival they were inspected by the Grand Duke Constantine, and in a few days afterwards were reviewed by the Emperor. Nearly all vessels returning from foreign stations are thus honoured by an imperial visit, when the Emperor orders some manœuvres, thanks the officers and crew, and on leaving generally makes a signal, ordering a reward in money to be distributed among the latter. A few days afterwards the ships were paid off, when the men either received a long leave of absence or were housed in barracks on shore, as is the custom in the Russian navy.

Cronstadt possesses no object of interest for any but professional men. There is, indeed, a small wooden house which Peter the Great built, now the summer residence of the governor; and another still smaller, the model of the house which he inhabited at Saardam. Both are in the Summer Garden, and beyond these there is nothing to be seen but forts, ships, factories, and uniforms.

The foundation and support of a fleet in the Baltic Sea has, like every other undertaking in the north of Russia, been a difficult matter, involving an arduous war against nature ever since Peter, with a lead in his hand, sounded the Channel from Petersburg to Cronstadt. The outlet of the Neva into the Gulf of Finland has only nine feet depth of water; and, as even line-of-battle ships drawing double that depth are built in St. Petersburg, they have to be transported with immense labour in large floating iron docks to Cronstadt, where they are fitted out. In this manner I saw the last new line-of-battle ship, the 'Imperator Nicholai,' brought down the Gulf, and a large frigate carried up to St. Petersburg for repairs. Since the Crimean war, the Russian fleet has undergone a thorough change. Most of the surviving seamen of the Black Sea fleet were transferred to the Baltic; and a new set of screw ships has replaced those of the old system. The strength of the steam navy in the Baltic in 1862 may be given as follows; three 3-deckers, seven 2-deckers, fifteen screw or paddle frigates, between thirty and forty large corvettes and despatch boats, besides a flotilla of small steamers and gunboats.* Except a few built in England and America, all these were constructed in the dockyards of Finland, at St. Petersburg, or at Nicholaëv in the Black Sea.

As St. Petersburg and Moscow have been at length united to the west by railroads, few travellers will now arrive at the former city by the Neva. Yet the view

* All the old line-of-battle ships were sunk in the Northern passage of the Gulf during the preparations for war in the spring of 1863. Their place has been supplied by iron-clad ships, or, rather, batteries, one of which, the 'Pervenetz,' was built in England, the rest in Russia. These batteries, admirably adapted for the defence of a harbour or coast, are totally unfit for rough sea service. The 'Pervenetz' ran some danger of foundering on her passage from the Thames to Cronstadt. There are, altogether, five of these to be completed in the spring, besides eighteen rams of smaller size, but mounted with the largest metal.

of the city, as the steamer approaches, is very pretty, with the golden cupola of St. Isaac's Cathedral and the slim spires of the Admiralty and fortress churches in the distance towering above the flat on which the city is built. But if the entrance to the Neva is pleasing to the eye, it is not always so to the nose. The smell of the so-called Russian leather may be agreeable when made into pocket-books and other useful articles, but the stench of its preparation, which floats on the air from the different tanneries at the mouth of the river, is overpowering.

St. Petersburg is a city of palaces, barracks, and sheds, which, if situated between the 40th and 50th parallels of latitude, would be the finest of modern European towns. As it is, it is an anomaly which Folly has raised at an enormous sacrifice, but which it is now Wisdom to uphold. The time may, indeed, come when, as many prophesy, it will sink into the morass from which it was reared; but that time is far distant. In spite of the disadvantages of its situation, St. Petersburg, owing to the increasing civilisation of the country, and the facilities of intercommunication, is more and more bound up with the interests of the Russian people.

The foundations of this city were laid, as all know, at an enormous cost of human life: immense sums of money were lavished in raising its public buildings, and every now and then the city is half swept away by floods or consumed by fire; while anything less hard than granite rots in the damps and snows of very few winters. But all this is as nothing to the perpetual wear and tear of human life experienced every year in this struggle of humanity with resisting nature. During the ten years, from 1852 to 1862, the deaths in St. Petersburg have exceeded the births in the most favourable year by 3,000; in the most unhealthy (1855), by 10,000. The severity of the climate alone can scarcely account for this. The great drawback to the health of St. Petersburg is the absence of all drainage. The land on which the city is built is so low and marshy, the frost in winter so severe and prolonged, that any system of underground drainage seems to be impossible. A certain portion of the filth of the city might, indeed, be carried off by the river; but its waters, now drunk by the whole population, would be polluted, and the narrow passage leading into the gulf blocked up in a very short time. Hence the accumulations of sewerage, found in the centre of every family, are constantly sending forth pestiferous gases. As these sinks of filth are disturbed nearly every night throughout the year, the atmosphere for a verst around is reeking with contamination. Typhus is, therefore, an endemic, and the cholera is every now and then fearfully active among such an inviting congregation as the inhabitants of St. Petersburg. One of these days it may make such havoc among them, that some means will be taken to provide a better system for cleansing the city.

St. Petersburg is not very attractive in autumn to those who seek pleasure in society and amusement. All the world is then out of town, in the islands, at Peterhov, Oranienbaum, Tsarskoe Selo, Paulovsk, or Reval. But the palaces, museums, and churches, with their metallic riches and grotesque art, are enough to excite the interest if not the admiration of visitors. In October the town assumes a little liveliness—the Nevsky Prospect, as the Regent Street of St. Petersburg is called, becomes tolerably filled during the afternoon, and a fine day will even draw out a little beauty and elegance for a walk in the summer gardens. But to see or know anything of St. Petersburg the stranger must be there in the winter. Two operas, a French theatre, the best ballet in the world, the delights of the omnibus box and first row of stalls, splendid sledges with fur-muffled beauties, a clear sky and the thermometer 20 degrees below zero, will all help the tourist to pass the time quickly. But if he has anywhere read of meetings in the summer gardens, where rich merchants' wives bring their daughters for exhibition and offer them with some tens of thousands of roubles for a penniless or ruined officer of high rank or family to pick and choose from, let him banish such ideas from his thoughts. Some good old woman is now the go-between, and these affairs are arranged in private.

Thanks to the friendship of some of my late companions, my time was passed very agreeably. Living for a month or two in the home of one and making occasional visits to the houses of others, I received such kindness as makes travelling a pleasure, and the remembrance of it a regret. When a stranger once becomes thoroughly intimate in Russian society there is none in Europe more pleasant or more free from absurd etiquette.

During my stay in St. Petersburg two subjects occupied all minds, and were the almost exclusive topics of conversation—the Emancipation of the Serfs and Garibaldi. The enthusiasm for the latter pervaded barrack and boudoir, his name was in every mouth, his photograph in every hand, the most exaggerated anecdotes were related and greedily read about him. The ladies, as in all other countries, were his chief advocates; for the Russian ladies have the most exalted ideas of patriotism and liberty, and admire rebellion even to stimulating it. At a later period all this enthusiasm for Garibaldi and the Italian cause centred itself on home affairs, and many of the fair sex became the most zealous partizans of the Liberals, wearing badges distinctive of their principles—a freak which brought some of them into trouble.

I had been accustomed to hear so much of the rigid mode of public life prescribed by the Emperor Nicholas that I could not but be struck by the change which had already taken place since his death. Whereas all public feeling was then held under strict control, it was evident now that the Russian people had a will, desires, and intelligence of its own.   Nowhere was this change more sensibly manifested than in the Imperial theatres.   Formerly no expression of applause or disapprobation was allowed in these places of amusement, but now in the Grand theatre might be heard noisy cheers, hissing, hooting, and stamping of feet, as the enthusiasm, party spirit, or patience of the upper audience was touched. One incident which occurred just as I left St. Petersburg will especially show how the people were beginning to feel their strength.   At the interment of the celebrated comic actor, Mortinov, when the people were dragging the funeral car to the cemetery, amid thousands of spectators with heads uncovered, the Commander of the gens d'armerie made his appearance on horseback, with his helmet on his head.   He was immediately mobbed and compelled to doff his helmet. Under Nicholas it was as much as the people dared to do to look at such a personage as the Chief of the gens d'armerie, much less force him to bow to their desires.   A Russian gentleman who had just returned from a forced visit to the Caucasus asked me how long the Emperor Nicholas had been dead—

'About five years.'

'Nonsense!' he replied, 'at least five hundred, if you calculate by the change which has already taken place in the country.' *

* During a second visit to St. Petersburg, in the summer of 1863, the

One of the great privileges of travel is to read the history of a country, illustrated in its monuments and museums; and there is perhaps no history so well illustrated as that of Russia in its capitals of Moscow and St. Petersburg. In Moscow are the early and thoroughly national records of the land; in St. Petersburg is seen the transformation and the striking out in a new path. The traveller should always pay a visit to Moscow before St. Petersburg. The Oriental character of the former city will give force to the contrast presented by the wooden isba of Peter the Great, the splendid Hermitage of Catharine the Second, the Palace where the foul murder of Paul was accomplished,* and the Palace Square of 1825 celebrity. The mosque-like and grotesque churches of Moscow will challenge comparison with the beautiful church of Our Lady of

change, I remarked, was still more decided. People freely discussed politics in public places of resort, the press had a bolder and more dignified tone, and hardly any part of the foreign newspapers was obliterated by the censor; even the police intruded still less on the amusements of the people. Altogether, there seemed to be more freedom of action, with greater expansion of thought and boldness of sentiment, than before.

* This palace is now a school of engineers. The room where Paul was murdered was till lately nailed up. The Emperor Alexander, the other day paying a visit to the school, asked why that door was closed, and paying no attention to the confused excuses of the reply of those around him, ordered the door to be forced, and he passed through the room. Since this time it has been used by the students like any other chamber of the establishment.

Kazan, or the gorgeous cathedral of St. Isaac, with its monoliths of Finland granite, its rich interior, where gold, silver, and jewels glitter among columns of marble, lapislazuli, and malachite; and where huge gates in bronze portray the deeds of Alexander Nevsky and other heroes, who, having in a dark age exhibited talents and virtues above their fellows, have been dubbed saints by a too admiring posterity. Let the stranger stroll through the picture gallery in the Hermitage. Among the portraits which hang high on its walls there is a series of Tsars who might well pass for Grand Llamas or for the first-born of the sun and moon; close to these is a portrait in the French costume of the end of the 17th century, followed by another series in modern uniforms or wide-spreading hoops.* In one glance is seen the immediate change from Oriental stagnation and semi-barbarism to European progress and civilisation. Whether the bounds between Europe and Asia should be at the Ural or the Niemen was decided by the young genius of Peter, and the city which bears his name and the progress which his descendants have made during two centuries are the living proofs of his genius.†

* This is in the room called the Petrovsky Gallery.

† The character of Peter and the acts of his reign have lately been thoroughly sifted by Russian historians, having at their disposal all the archives of the times. Much new matter has been brought forward, but only to confirm what was already known, viz. that he was a man who well understood his times; an extraordinary genius, but a passionate and brutal despot.

As, in more despotic times, London had its Prison-tower and Paris its Bastille, so, surrounded by the waters of the Neva, St. Petersburg has its Petropaulovsky Krepost. In the church within its walls are the simple tombs of its Emperors and Empresses, with one exception, from Peter to Nicholas. There also is religiously preserved that broad-beamed boat, built after the fashion of the 17th century, which Peter constructed and navigated with his own hands, and which has received the name of the Father of the Russian Fleet.

From this fortress the signal for opening the navigation of the river is given in spring by firing of cannon, when the Governor is the first person to cross. But it is chiefly when the west wind drives the waters of the Gulf of Finland into the river that all eyes are turned towards it. The signal of red flags and the booming of cannon from the fortress proclaims the increasing danger of inundation. Of the many floods which have ravaged the city the most disastrous were those of 1777 and 1825, when the waters rose respectively 10 feet 7 inches and 13 feet 7 inches. In the former, in a low cell of the fortress, perished the young Princess Tarakanov, whose story, as related by some writers, is the saddest that can be found in the annals of secret history.

The Empress Elizabeth, the daughter of Peter the Great, had secretly married her favourite, Razumovsky, after she had raised him to high rank in the army and made him Ataman of Little Russia.   From this union were born two sons and a daughter, who received the name of Tarakanov.   The sons died before their mother.   Just before the first partition of Poland, a plot, of which Prince Radzivil was the head, was formed for the abduction of the young Princess, then about 15 years old, to make her an instrument for the dethronement of Catharine, and perhaps to satisfy some hopes of personal ambition on the side of the Prince.   The guardians of the young Elizabeth—for so she was called, after her mother—were bought over, and she was removed, first to Poland and afterwards to Italy. Catharine immediately confiscated the immense estates of the Prince, who, reduced to poverty, promised to abandon his projects if his property were restored.

On returning to Russia he left the young Tarakanov at Rome, under the guardianship of her governess. Thither Alexis Orlov, ready for any deed at the behest of his Sovereign, proceeded, in order, by fair means or foul, to bring the young girl back to Russia.   With a Neapolitan named Rivas, he arrived in Rome, where Rivas, having introduced himself to the Princess, informed her of the interest she excited in Russia. When better acquainted, he let her know that he was only the messenger of Alexis Orlov, who, tired of the tyranny of Catharine, offered to place her on the throne of her grandfather, if she would accept him as her husband. The young girl, already somewhat schooled in ambition by her former protector, accepted the proposal with gratitude. Orlov presented himself and soon acquired great influence over her. After strangling an Emperor it was nothing for him to ruin a defenceless girl. They were secretly married according to the rites of the Greek Church by two adventurers, one dressed as a priest and the other as a lawyer. After this mockery the pair removed to a palace at Pisa, in order, as Orlov told his victim, to await the breaking out of the Revolution in Russia; in reality to be in a better position for carrying out his atrocious scheme.

The opportunity came a short time after the naval battle of Tschesmé, where ten Russian ships under the flag of Orlov, but in reality commanded by the Scots in the Russian service, Admiral Elphinstone and Captains Greig and Dugdale, defeated and burnt fifteen Turkish ships. . A squadron, under the command of the two first officers, now put into Leghorn, when Orlov, pretending that he must visit them, easily persuaded his wife to accompany him to that place, where she was received into the house of the English consul. At Leghorn the young girl seems to have created a sensation, which was destined to increase as the shameful plot unfolded. Orlov without much difficulty persuaded her to visit the ships. A boat decorated with flags bore her on board; with her were the wives of the English consul and of Admiral Greig, who, it is to be hoped, were not privy to the plot.   An arm-chair was let down from the rigging, and the princess was hoisted on board. But no sooner was she in the cabin, than the unfortunate girl realised the whole truth of the shameful comedy which had been played around her.   She was confined below; some accounts say that she was even placed in irons.   In vain she implored the pity and invoked the pretended love of her barbarous husband.   The ship sailed, and on her arrival in St. Petersburg she was put in secret confinement in the fortress of St. Peter and Paul, where she lingered nearly six years, until, smothered by the rising waters of the river, she died the victim of a political necessity.*

Winter had already begun to whiten the housetops when I left St. Petersburg, and took the train for Moscow.   All my acquaintances assured me that I should steal a march on the bad weather, and find in the South, during the month of October, sunny skies and gentle breezes.   The time occupied in passing between the two cities is twenty hours.   My journey thither was rendered more agreeable by meeting with a family returning from their travels.   The renewal of our acquaintance in Moscow led to an invitation to visit their estate in the south of Russia.

---

* This girl is said by some to have been an adventuress put forward as the daughter of Elizabeth.   Still, her mock marriage with Orlov and her miserable death remain as facts.   Her history must necessarily remain a matter of dispute until it shall please the Government to open the State Paper Office to the inspection and criticisms of some future Soloviev;—a time, it would seem, not far distant.

In this remote part of the world, the hospitality of old times has not yet taken its flight heavenward, and letters of introduction are not indispensable for obtaining admission into society. Unfortunately the aspect of the country, the climate, and the complete want of accommodation, offer little inducement to those who travel only for pleasure or amusement. For those who brave inconveniences for the sake of instruction a tour in the interior of Russia and an impartial examination of the character and habits of the people would furnish an interest not to be surpassed elsewhere. No country in Europe is so little known or so much misrepresented. The railways now in construction may, however, attract future travellers, especially if the comforts of Western civilisation be provided for them in the towns through which they pass. But this is not the case at present.

In the Kremlin, the Acropolis of Moscow, the visitors may find all that is national in Russian manners and customs. There he may see the traces of all that is interesting in her history, from the time when the genius and intrigues of one of her princes gained her a pre-eminence over the other vassal States,* down to the ever memorable expedition of Napoleon. Nearly every

* The Tartars were bad administrators, and, contenting themselves with the homage and tribute of their vassals, left the administration in the hands of the natives. The Princes of Moscow received from the Grand Khan the right of collecting this tribute, and hence their influence over the other States.

object which there meets the eye is connected with some episode of her history prior to the epoch of Peter the Great, that is, of Muscovite history.

There is the celebrated *Krasnaya Ploschad*, or Red Place, the forum, at different epochs, of popular liberty, of anarchy, and despotism—in the midst of which are the statues raised in honour of a prince and a butcher, who roused up their countrymen to drive out the Poles in 1613.   There are its churches of grotesque architecture, where, beneath candelabras, lamps, and censers, jewelled crosses, Icons with frames of gilded and curiously-wrought silver, and caskets of sacred dust and bones, are the tombs of her most famous men.   There rests the celebrated Dimitri, surnamed the Donskoi, the first but ineffectual conqueror of the Tartars ; there sleeps the not less famous Ivan, who first took the title of Grand Prince of all the Russias after their final conquest. There, too, is another Ivan, whose mad barbarity has acquired for him the name of *Grosnie* (the Terrible), and who died the death of a Herod, after he had played the farce of turning monk, in imitation of the Emperor Charles V.*   The first of the Romanovs also lies there, with Peter II. the last of the male line of that family and the only one of the Emperors not buried in the

* A palace of some interest to Englishmen is still to be seen in Moscow, built by this tzar for the reception of our Princess Elizabeth, whose hand he had sought in marriage. Ivan was about as much the uxorious despot as the Princess's father. He had, altogether, seven wives.

new city. From the churches let the tourist turn to
its palaces and museums. In the Imperial Palace, from
the noble halls which are dedicated to the modern
orders of Russian knighthood, a few steps will lead into
the vaulted and arabesqued interiors of the half Asiatic
tsars. In the museums the eye wanders in amazement
over thrones, sceptres, *derjavas* (orbs ornamented by a
cross), and crowns of jewels; over endless rows of coats
of armour, swords, and grotesque weapons of almost
every Asiatic people; from flags of conquered nations
now incorporated into the colossal empire, to other
objects more simple and time-worn, the sight of which
may provoke much more serious contemplation than
gold and silver. There may be seen the litter which
bore Charles XII. at the battle of Poltava; the double
throne on which sat the two childish tsars, Peter and
his brother Alexis, with the recess behind it from which
their clever and wily sister Sophia prompted their
replies during important receptions; boxes containing
codes and constitutions fallen into disuse or abruptly
abrogated. One especially attracted my attention. It
was a brass box, used as a door weight, which, I was
told, contained the late Polish constitution granted by
the Emperor Alexander I. and taken away by his
brother. Lastly, there are the costly and curious
official walking-sticks of the tsars and patriarchs, none
of which are half so interesting as the stout and knotted
clubs of Peter the Great. Having examined these, let

the stranger take a look at the grotesque paintings over the portals of some of the churches. Among them he will find one especially contrived to strike any poor sinner with horror at the fate reserved for him. The subject is ' The Separation of the Sheep from the Goats ' —at least, so I read it. The beatified sheep are safely folded up in one corner quite in the background. The Devil, *sic in mundo*, has the foreground to himself. Portrayed in the most popular manner, with erect ears, long tail, and grinning teeth, he is seated between the fangs of an enormous dragon, and, harpooning one after another the awe-stricken sinners, he shoves them down the monster's throat. Looking over the parapet a few yards off, over one of the most curious panoramas in the world, the half-European half-Oriental city, dotted over with some hundreds of golden-domed or green-roofed churches, the reader will no doubt hope, as I hoped, that more merciful doctrines are there taught on a future state than in this pictorial sermon on eternity.

CHAPTER II.

RUSSIA'S RISE AND SOCIAL ORGANISATION.

Russia and the United States contrasted—Russia often misrepre-
sented—Rise and Aggrandisement of Russia—Peter the Great—
Catharine the Second—Increase of Population—Orthodox Russia
—Social Status of the Empire—The Russian Nobility—Russian
Princes—The Hereditary Nobles—Nobility of the Tchin—Their
Character—The Tchin—Tchinovniks—Merchants of the Three
Guilds—Their Habits and Character—Disposition to Trade in
the Character of Russians—Low Social Standing of Traders—
Russian Clergy—The Black or Monastic, and the White or Secular
Clergy—Their Position and Character—Celibacy and Monogamy
—Dissent in Russia—The Staroveri—Doukobortzi—Molokani—
The Skopsi—Begouni, or Russian Mormons.

NAPOLEON III. in the 'Idées Napoléoniennes,' published in his days of exile, remarked that there
were only two well-governed peoples in the world, viz:
those of Russia and the United States of America.
Doubtless his later experience has led him to change
that opinion. As good working specimens of an ultra
autocracy and an ultra democracy, they did not perhaps show the disease which was undermining them.
Both these model Governments, now shaken to their
very foundations, are in a degree exchanging their
characters—Russia, while her whole society is being
transformed, advances slowly towards civil freedom;

the United States of America seem to be making gigantic strides towards despotism. If apparently the best-governed, they were certainly the worst-administered of States. In America, the civil servants sold their votes for places, which they lost on a change of ministry, or only preserved by political apostacy; while in Russia, according to all its writers, an overbearing bureaucracy, master of its corrupt position, conspired to preserve its privileges, and placed barriers in the way of every good measure of the Government. What becomes of that trite saying of the French Emperor, *on peut gouverner de loin, il faut administrer de près*, when the administration of any country is so conducted? This corruption was the very excuse for the great centralising system of the Tzar Nicholas, who mistrusted everybody and everything not under his immediate control.

No two countries, however, merit more attention at the present time than Russia and America. No nation, in proportion to its numbers and its strength, is, I believe, so little known as the former. Any atrocity or absurdity which is told or printed of Russians, is received without the slightest criticism. I remember a year or two ago reading in a newspaper at Buenos Ayres, that many Russians were still cannibals. A Frenchman, who, from his position, should have been an educated man, asked me seriously if the Russians were Christians. More lately at Turin, I overheard the conversation of a group of gentlemen, who believed that the frigate on board of which I was then serving, had proceeded to sea from the neighbouring port of Villa Franca, in order to shoot eight men, and give the *knout* to some hundred more, for the slight offence of having out-stayed their leave.* The opinions about Russia and the Russians generally, are founded on what may have been their condition a century ago, when, as Macaulay relates, princes dropped jewels and vermin wherever they passed;† when sensitive and delicate

* Here is another tale, taken at hazard from an English newspaper in December 1863. Whoever believes such a tale must have a wonderful amount of credulity or prejudice: 'A correspondent informs us that after the engagement in the Palatinate of Prasnysz, in which the Polish leader, Lenzica, perished, several Polish prisoners were brought to Mlawa, to the Russian commandant, Bogdanowicz. This officer, having perceived a boy of sixteen among the prisoners, had him brought before him, addressed him in insulting terms, and flourished his sword about his head. The boy, meanwhile, stood unmoved, and looked boldly in the eyes of his persecutor, who foamed at the mouth with rage. "You Polish vagabond! You Catholic hangdog! So you are frightened, are you?" he exclaimed. To this the boy quietly answered, that he had not feared him on the field of battle, and did not fear him now. "You do not fear me! We shall see;" and with another flourish of his sword the savage cut off the boy's head, which dashed against the wall. The body stood for a moment with the hand raised, and then fell on the blood-stained ground by the side of the head, Bogdanowicz, meanwhile, taking a pull at his brandy flask. This terrible deed was witnessed by several persons who were in the room at the time.' This is only one tale out of a thousand, which have been spread abroad by Polish agents for rousing the indignation of Europe. That the Russians have been merciless in their severities on many occasions, I have not the least doubt, but at least nine-tenths of the atrocities attributed to them have been pure inventions, or the grossest exaggerations of facts.

† *Critical and Historical Essays.* Madame D'Arblay.

women were publicly flogged in the capital; when
serfs were sold by auction like negroes; when Russians
drank train oil out of the street lamps; and when a
whip, the chief article in a marriage basket, was used
to enforce conjugal obedience. In the present volume,
my wish is to place before the reader materials which
may help him to form an opinion for himself. Many
arbitrary acts of cruelty, and abuses of authority are,
no doubt, still committed, as they always will be, when
men have irresponsible power; but from the change of
policy in the Government, and the increasing force of
public opinion, they are happily becoming more rare.
Although there is much in Russians and in their institutions which, from difference of education, I cannot
admire, still I have no reason for not being impartial.
I am not presumptuous enough to denounce sweepingly
institutions, which wise men have considered appropriate to a world in which they lived; nor unjust
enough to anathematise a whole people, because their
training has not elevated them to the same level as
our own.

I propose, therefore, to give a short sketch of the
rise of Russia to an important place among nations;
of the organisation of Russian society; of the various
reforms which have lately taken place, or are about
to be instituted; and of the causes and results of that
great struggle between Russia and Poland, with one
phase of which we are contemporaries.

The history of Russia carries us back to several small groups of men belonging to the Sclavonic race, who, feeling their way into the future, became, through mutual jealousies, a prey to invading hordes of barbarians, truly named the flails of God. We see them receiving and bearing for generations the fatal mark then stamped upon them; freeing themselves, after many vain struggles, by the force of an innate and a superior genius, aided by the natural decay of the prestige of their oppressors—collecting their elements of strength in one spot, and establishing a nucleus of nationality in Moscow. This small State beginning at length to feel its strength, and having to choose between a worn-out and a new system, found in Peter the Great a master-spirit to shape its destinies—a compound of genius and rude humanity, whose ideas were all of the former, whose actions were all of the latter. Adopting on the one side that civilisation which was necessary to its existence; stretching forth the other hand over wide wastes of barbarism: from the ice of the pole to the warm and genial regions of the south, the new empire soon comprised climates of which the reindeer and the dromedary are the emblems. After less than 200 years, the tenth part of the world's space has been in some measure moulded into an homogeneous empire, and has taken its place in the great commonwealth of European nations. The aim of its despotic Government during the last 160 years, but especially under the late Emperor, has been to amalgamate the various elements of an incongruous mass into an harmonious whole—and, with the exception of Poland and the Caucasus, it has succeeded. But following the fate of nations, no sooner does a nationality become firmly established, than, strong in its longings, it aspires to self-government, and rises up against the power which fostered it.

Peter the Great began his career with an army of about fifty men under western discipline, a fleet consisting of an open boat built by himself with the aid of a Dutch carpenter, a people numbering less than ten millions, and a revenue amounting to not more than 215,000*l.* in English money. At the peace of Nystadt in 1721, he had added the so-called Baltic provinces, the frontier provinces of Persia and Turkey, and the whole of Northern Asia as far as the peninsula of Kamchatka, to his empire. He then possessed an army of 220,000 men, a fleet of thirty ships of the line with innumerable smaller vessels, a revenue increased twelvefold, and nearly five millions more subjects. Lastly, a beautiful city, reared from a swamp, to which the white sails of commerce already began to crowd, was left as a monument of his genius and of his barbarity.

From his death in 1725 to the accession of Catharine II. was a period rather of consolidation than of conquest. Russia was received among European nations; her alliance was eagerly sought, and to obtain it her ministers were bribed by all the chief Powers;* foreign potentates flattered and coaxed her self-love, and her troops made their first excursion into central Europe.

With Catharine again came the passion for conquest by arms or by intrigue. Poland, long torn and weakened by internal feuds, was dismembered. The country of the Cossacks and Tartars bordering the Black Sea and the Crimea were added to the empire. Immense tracts of land were taken from Persia and even from the distant frontiers of China. Christian Georgia, harassed on one side by the Turks, on the other by the Persians, ceded itself to Russia in 1783, and became finally embodied in the mass. Our own century has seen her troops on the shores of the Mediterranean and the Alantic; the present generation has witnessed her mighty struggle with allied Europe, which, at length, put its veto on further encroachments. In the empire itself a war with a handful of mountaineers, which has spent blood and treasure for the last fifty years and is not yet finished, together with the revolutions and continued intractability of Poland, that thorn in the side of Russia, has alone interrupted the internal economy. When Peter died the population of Russia was only fourteen mil-

* Bestujev, the Chancellor of Elizabeth, received hundreds of thousands of pounds from the English Government to promote the English interest in Russia, and annul that of France and Austria.—See *La Cour de Russie il y a Cent Ans. Dépêches des Ambassadeurs Anglais et Français.*

lions; on the accession of Catharine it amounted to nineteen millions. Her conquests, with the natural increase of population, made the number thirty-six millions on her death. Since that time, without any important conquests, it has doubled itself, and a natural increase is going on of more than half a million per annum.

The present population of Russia in Europe is over sixty-one millions,* and unlike most other parts of the East, where religion far outweighs nationality, in Russia for Russia, in Poland for Poland, the two are closely allied. (Of these the orthodox Russians present a compact body of fifty-three millions, speaking the same language, kneeling at the same altar, united by the two strongest ties which can bind men together.)

The social status of Russia Proper with the Baltic provinces may be seen from the following table, women and children of course included : —

The hereditary or personal nobility, the latter including all persons having a tchin or rank in the service—the privileged class   .   .   .   2·36 per cent
Merchants of the three guilds; the class called

---

* In 1860 the population of Russia was 61,380,043
       „   „   of Poland „   4,840,466
       „   „   of Finland „   1,672,032
Of all these 80 per cent. are of the Orthodox Creed.
       „   11 per cent.   „   Roman Catholics.
       „   5 per cent.   „   Protestants.
the rest Jews, Mahometans, and Bhuddists.

Meschani, being the *bourgeoisie* of other countries
—all paying a trade or a capitation tax . . 5·86 per cent.
The army and navy . . . . . . 3·78 ,,
The clergy and those connected with the churches ·95 ,,
Peasants, workmen, &c. . . . . . 72·27 ,,
Strangers and others whose social position is un-
defined . . . . 1·21 ,,
86·43 ,,
Leaving for Poland, Finland, and the Caucasus . 13·57 ,,
100·00 ,,

The reform of Peter the Great completely crushed the political influence of the old boyards of the tzars by the creation of the tchin, which rendered nobility personal to all who held one. Their material power remained, however, immense in the provinces, as they possessed fully half the *souls*, or serfs, of the empire, and until lately many of them kept up almost a court in their old city of Moscow, much like the Legitimists in the Faubourg St. Germain, and long maintained the bitterest animosity towards the reigning house of Holstein-Romanov. There is hardly a name of any one of these old families which has not at different times during the last 150 years been found enrolled in some conspiracy for recovering their political privileges of former days. They were emphatically called the Muscovite party in distinction from the Petersburg or German party, in whose hands lay really all the power of the State. The distinction is, however, now more apparent than real. The extremes are, no doubt, at daggers drawn; but the moderates on either side, more bending in their views, have become woven one into the other by the same social and political interests. The terms Muscovite and German must now be considered as exploded names which have been replaced by the more appropriate epithets of Conservative and Liberal. During the last year or two the hereditary nobility of Russia must be classed with the latter; for in their district and provincial assemblies they have been the most active in trying to effect some modification in the government of the country—a modification which would give their own class an increase of political power.

The oldest families are those who can trace their descent from the Varangian princes, Rurik, Sinav, and Ascold, and number, if I mistake not, only thirty-nine names. With the union of Lithuania, and of the Tartar, the Georgian, and other Caucasian provinces to Russia, their chief men were incorporated with the Russian nobility, preserving their titles. It is owing to this and to the absence of primogeniture in Russia, that there are such swarms of Russian princes. The Gargarins and Galitzins have become almost a proverb from their numbers. Of the latter there are no less than 120 members, bearing the title of kniaz or prince. Descendants of many of the most ancient of Russian families have fallen into complete poverty, and now belong to the lowest social status of the free population.

Besides this nobility of long descent, all holders of a tchin above the fifth class, all who have the Cross of St. Vladimir, and, I believe, one or two other orders, have the privilege of being considered nobles hereditary. These titles of nobility vary much in value. Age and purity of descent furnish a supreme criterion among the old aristocracy.* Those nobles whose patents have been conferred by the Emperors, or who have acquired them from their tchin, rank according to seniority of creation; and, in certain books, called 'Class Books,' are registered the dates of creation of all nobility, whether the old or the new. All who feel any special interest in the Russian nobility will do well to consult the work of Prince Peter Dolgoroukov, entitled 'Les Principales Familles de la Russie.' I will here cite the judgment of a Russian on his own countrymen and class:* 'The higher class,' says M. Gerebtzov, 'has quite departed from the national type; it is ruled by egotism, personal ambition and formalism; its sentiment of charity exists only in high-sounding phrases. In a moral point of view this class is in order inverse to its social standing; it has not preserved any bond of ideas, customs, creed, or moral feeling with the people, but forms a distinct race of itself. It has abjured all profound belief in

---

* The famous *Velvet Book*, containing the origin and descent of the old Russian nobility, was first compiled in 1682, and first published in 1787.

† *Histoire de la Civilisation en Russie*, par Gerebtzov.

orthodox Christianity, and has tried to replace it with the philosophy of the eighteenth century, which has filtered through all its members.' This severe criticism is somewhat softened by an acknowledgment that the Russian nobility can offer a great number of worthy exceptions, and that the cause of his condemnation must be looked for in the constant influx of nobles introduced by the tchin, and in the wide difference which is to be found in their moral and intellectual education—which so far is true.

The word *tchin* denotes the rank of all servants of the State, whether in the army, navy, civil service, or church. It is an institution little understood in Western Europe. As established by Peter there were sixteen steps, which were afterwards reduced to fourteen, each of which decides the social standing of the bearer in any service by a comparison with the corresponding military rank. Beginning at No. 14, in which are found ensigns, clerks and deacons, it comprises all the intermediate ranks up to No. 2, where are found generals and admirals—No. 1 being reserved for the metropolitans, marshals, and chancellors of the empire. A priest or navy lieutenant is thus equal to a captain in the army; an archimandrite, a privy councillor, or a post captain, to a colonel; an archbishop, or a rear-admiral, to a lieutenant-general, and so on. Admission into this hierarchy is obtained by length of service (like rising from the ranks in our army), or by a course of study and the diploma of the university or military school, by which the lower grades of the tchin are avoided. This somewhat corresponds to our competitive examinations. Particular titles are appropriated to certain grades of tchin-rank. Thus, from Nos. 14 to 9, an officer or civil servant is only styled 'Your Honour;' from 8 to 6, 'Your High Honour.' No. 5 is 'High-born;' in Nos. 4 and 3, it is 'Your Excellence;' Nos. 2 and 1, 'Your High Excellence.'

The clerical ranks of the tchin have also their own titles.

All these titles are strictly observed in writing, and when an inferior addresses a superior.

The word *tchinovnik*, in a broad sense, means the holder of a tchin or rank in the service, but is restricted to civil servants only. The very word has become a reproach in the mouths of all who are not themselves tchinovniks, and the most celebrated Russian writers have striven to expose the vicious organisation of the tchin—the venality, pride, and vanity of its members. As the distribution of these ranks is often vested in the higher members of the tchinal ladder, a degrading servility has been fostered, which caused Dolgoroukov to remark that all tchinovniks, to get on in the world, must have, if not talents, a very flexible spine.

'Who is the Devil, father?' asked the son of a moujik. 'The chief of the tchinovniks, my little son,' was the father's reply. It will show the manner in which the tchinovnik is regarded by the peasant. There is hardly a merchant in Russia who cannot illustrate the insolence or tantalising indifference of some tchinovnik, who has put forward objections, and interposed delay to every demand of signature or service, until propitiated by the accustomed gift. Complaint, and still more prosecution, would be of little avail in such cases. An offensive and defensive alliance exists throughout all the ranks of the service, from the lowest *employé* to his chief. This *esprit de corps* renders the administrative body in Russia the most conservative of any class, and of course opposed to any reforms affecting their material well-being. The more arbitrary the Government, the better the tchinovniks thrive, more especially that class which comes into immediate contact with the people, as the police, law officers, &c. The great tolerance allowed to Sectarians was a great calamity to them; but their severest trial has been the abolition of the *otkoup*, or farming of the brandy, as its abuse was one of their richest sources of revenue. Old tchinovniks pronounce all the intended reforms of the present reign impracticable, and it is not to be expected that they will be very hearty in furthering their execution. But younger men of more liberal ideas will by degrees replace these, and then the tchin must collapse altogether. Perhaps if a ukase were to appear forbidding all classes below the fifth to wear breeches, as is the case in Japan, it might have the effect of hastening its disuse.

The small middle class in Russia comprises (1) the merchants of the three guilds, who pay a trade tax on a stated capital, and enjoy certain privileges, such as exemption from corporal punishment, military service, &c.; and (2) the *meschanstvo*, or *petite bourgeoisie*, who, like the peasantry, pay the poll-tax to the Government.

The merchants, beyond the indirect influence of their money, have no voice in the Government, although they possess certain municipal rights, conferred on them by Catharine II. and her successors. They are the most national part of the Russian people. Still wearing the national dress and beard, they live in a retired manner, eat *tschee* and drink *quass*, dream about the Devil, and send for a priest to exorcise him, besides retaining various other habits of former times. To see them in perfection, the stranger should stroll about the *Ketai Gorod* of Moscow, and watch them drinking their dozen cups of tea out of a glass, which they hold between the extended fingers of one hand, while they have in the other a piece of sugar, which they nibble between every sip of their favourite beverage.

A peep into the interiors of those blinded houses which are in the outskirts of Moscow is more curious still. The master of the house is probably a Russ of the old school—polite, but cowed; his wife, a fat good-natured dame, dressed in rich furs, with a painted face, and loaded with jewels. There is probably a son who has just returned from the lorettes and lansquenet of Paris, and in whom the old leaven will now and then appear from between the cracks of his varnish; or a daughter, often pretty, but spoiled, whose only dream is to fall into the arms of some offering swain, who will lead her out into a world of which she has as yet had only a few glimpses. Formerly all Russian women were kept in close seclusion, and marriages were made up by an old woman, whose trade it became. These dames do not play a less prominent part in such matters, even since exhibition of the daughters of the merchants in the Summer Garden at St. Petersburg has fallen into disuse.

Of these three guilds, only the first two can enter into foreign trade. As a rule, the merchants of Russia are parsimonious, while fond of display. Active in business, but very cautious and deficient in enterprise, they rarely incur any risks. 'The trading class in Russia,' says M. Aksakov, in contrasting the merchants of Great and Little Russia, 'form a type of themselves; their wives may also be distinguished from other Russian women. The merchant of Great Russia unites in a wonderful degree the love of moving about, and of having an established home; a passion for money, and a proneness to spend it. He does not shut up his capital in an ancient chest, but puts it in circulation, either to increase his business, or provide himself with comforts, and lead an easy life. He is fond of horses, loves to parade himself and family in fine carriages and trappings, and builds solid stone houses, which, though not always picturesque, help, as he believes, to beautify his native city.* Along all the high roads which connect the different towns of the Ukrain, where fairs are held, the postmasters and postboys await with impatience the arrival of the "Moscow merchants," and their grandeur and liberal drink-money remain a subject of conversation long after they have passed. The Little Russian merchant is, on the contrary, stingy, and makes himself out to be always poor. . . . There is the same difference in their manner of transacting business. The Little Russian always fixes his price, although it may be far above the worth of the article, and, sell or not, he sticks to it. The Great Russian knows immediately, by the dress, manner, and speech of his customer, if he can ask double the price he has already set upon his wares. Yet even then he can often sell so cheap, that the Little Russian, who has paid high for his goods, thinks him a fool. In fact, the Little Russians have no such disposition to commerce as their northern brethren, and thus the chief trade of all the Russian fairs is in the hands of the latter. The Little Russ sells only for ready money ; the whole trade of Great Russia is based on an enormous and hazardous credit, which frequent

* One of the finest private houses in St. Petersburg was built by a rich merchant, who intended it to rival the splendid new palace of the Grand Duke Michael, which is close beside it.

bankruptcies cannot shake. The non-credit giving merchant contents himself with a very small though certain gain; but it is obvious that, without a spirit of enterprise and a little keen daring, no great results can be expected in trade.'

Out of 180,000 registered traders, many thousands were till lately serfs, paying the *obrok*, or tribute to their proprietors. Among all the lower classes there is, in Russia as in China, an extraordinary disposition to barter, and the number of little shops and stalls in the streets and about the *dvors* of the large towns reminds one much of similar scenes in Singapore or Shanghae. Besides the regular licensed traders, there are thousands of petty hawkers in the villages, whom it would be impossible to register. As many privileges are attached to the three guilds, one of the most important being exemption from military service, private persons whose yearly purchases may be very trifling, frequently take out a patent for trading in order to share this privilege. Hundreds of men, doing a large trade, can neither read nor write; but a good memory and a counting machine, like those in general use throughout Asia, supply all deficiencies. If Russia considered her true interest in the various projects of reform, she should immediately tear down the absurd barriers which prevent men of education from entering into the ranks of her traders, that the merchant trading in millions, a farmer or a manufacturer, need not feel himself below the puniest *podparuchik,* or college secretary, in uniform, who swaggers before him. If a constitution is to be firmly established in Russia, such a class must be called into existence, with education enough to understand its position, and dignity and energy enough to act up to it.

It is well known that the Russian like the Greek clergy are divided into two orders, the black or monastic, and the white or secular clergy—both being under the spiritual authority of the Metropolitans of St. Petersburg, Moscow, and Kiev. The black clergy are superior in education and social standing to the other order—and from these alone are chosen the dignitaries of the Church. Some of their monasteries are exceedingly rich; but it must be remembered that an inexhaustible source of revenue is derived from their ministering to the superstitions of the people. Saints' bones, wonderful virgins, and ingenious miracles attract the faithful to their convents as a magnet attracts steel filings. A few years ago the finding and canonising of saints' bones became so common in many parts of Russia, that the Emperor Nicholas was obliged to make his voice heard, and, as Head of the Church, to declare that there were quite enough saints already discovered, without inventing any more.

The secular clergy, on the other hand, are extremely poor, with the exception of a few who are attached to churches in the large towns. The village priests are very little above the level of the peasants, from whom they are taken, being generally as lazy, dirty, and drunken as they.   All the clergy are paid by the Holy Synod, except in the monasteries, which are mostly self-supporting.   A large source of Church revenue in Russia is from voluntary offerings, and the sale of wax candles. Any traveller in Russia may always see innumerable small candles burning in the churches or the little chapels in the streets, and the devout peasants buying them at a stall close by.   Moneys derived from these sources are funded, and from them the clergy are paid their pittance. This, with a little aid received from the parishioners, and, in the provinces, by their own agricultural labour, just enables them to live.   Both orders of the clergy are incorporated in the tchin, and for grave offences— though such are generally hushed up among themselves for fear of scandal—they are liable to be unfrocked and sent to serve as soldiers in the Caucasus or on the frontier.

The black clergy are doomed to celibacy, while the white or secular clergy marry only once, not from any love of the principle of monogamy, but by the laws of the Holy Synod.   They generally take their wives from the daughters of other priests, and inherit thereby the living of the father; often, on their becoming widowers, they are forced by their superiors to become monks. It has been remarked by Madame Doria D'Istria that the clergy are much sought after by Russian girls from the idea that, being unable to marry a second time, they are more likely to take better care of their wives and keep them alive as long as possible.   A great object of ambition with them is to obtain an admission for their sons into the monkish orders; and until the present time the whole clergy forms a caste, not easily to be entered by those who are unconnected with it.   But their low social position, their scanty material advantages, and the restraint to which they are liable, prevent any great encroachments on the part of the higher classes.

Besides Orthodoxy (as by law established) and the Roman Catholic and Protestant creeds, there exist many Sectarians in Russia, called *Raskolniki*, the chief of which are the Staroveri or old believers, who number more than ten millions.   Their origin is this: When the Patriarch Nikon revised the Sclavonic translation of the Holy Scriptures, his act was considered as a sacrilege by many, who continued to follow their old rites and to read the original translations.   After a time they became divided into two classes: some without priests, others having their hierarchy, with a patriarch at the head.   The greater part of the merchants and middle classes in Russia belong to those Staroveri. During the reign of Nicholas they were much interfered with by the Government, though seldom exposed to actual persecution, for they paid the police well in order to be left in peace.   In the present reign they are as perfectly free as the members of the regular Church, and exemplify the truth of the political axiom

—that the most perfect tolerance produces the most loyal of subjects.*   As a secret sect the Staroveri are a curious subject of study.   They appear to have a large written religious code peculiar to themselves, which they preserve in secret places known only to the initiated.   If the Government meddled with them, it was not so much because they mingled politics with religion—though persecution would surely lead them to do so—but because the exercise of their customs was an infraction of the civil laws of the empire.   Among these are some very peculiar practices relating to marriage and the disposal of their dead; moreover they count it a virtue to harbour all debtors, deserters, and malefactors, who are sure to find hospitable refuge and concealment among the Raskolniki.

Besides these respectable Sectarians there are in Russia several sects of fanatics, some harmless, others most mischievous to society.   Among these may be named the *Doukobortsi,* or *those who strive with the Spirit,* who profess to renounce all the pomps and vanities of this wicked world, and so abstain from female society altogether.   Another sect are the *Molokani,* so called from the word *Moloko,* milk.   These abstain from all animal food and have their peculiar religious rites.   A more fanatical set of men and

---

* This was shown in the summer of 1863, when the most loyal addresses and the largest collection of money sent to the Emperor came from the Staroveri.

women are the *Skopsi*, or eunuchs, who are found in small societies all over Russia, and who make a propagand among soldiers, sailors, and peasants, persuading them to submit to a shameful mutilation. If any of these are discovered their sentence is invariably hard labour in the mines of Siberia for life. Lastly, there is a sect called the *Begouni*, or 'Runners,' who abjure marriage, government, or property, and live in complete communism; in fact they are a kind of Russian Mormons, whose place of worship is an Agapemone.

CHAPTER III.

REVOLUTION AND REFORM IN RUSSIA.

Repression of Public Feeling under the Emperor Nicholas—
Former Popular Government in Russia—Elective Tsars—The
Zemskoe Sobor—Rise of Absolute Government—Attempts of
the Nobility to regain their Power, under Ann, Catharine, and
Alexander—The 25th December, 1825—The Emperor Nicholas—
Spread of Revolution in Europe, and afterwards in Russia—
Necessity for Reform—Secret Literature and Societies in Russia
in the Reign of Alexander I. and Nicholas—The Kolokol or Bell,
and M. Herzen—Its Influence in Russia, and the Causes of its
Decline—Prince Peter Dolgoroukov and the Pravdievie—Russian
Travellers—Forbidden Literature—The 'Velikie Russ'—How
Circulated—Saint Techon—The Editor of the 'Velikie Russ'
Exiled—The University of St. Petersburg—Admiral Putiatin—
The Sunday Schools—The Provincial Assemblies of the Nobility
in 1862.

BEHIND a ponderous machinery of piles and beams,
the dammed-up waters of a river may appear calm
and unruffled, but the removal of a slight wedge—it may
be by the hand of a child—seals the fate of the whole
structure. If no channel be already formed, the
rushing waters soon form one for themselves; if the
channel be too narrow, they run wild on every side.
Russia, and especially Poland, for a long time, re-
sembled such a reservoir. The Emperor Nicholas was
the wedge of the dam which, for thirty years, had

arrested the wishes of the Russian and Polish peoples. No sooner had the hand of death removed this obstacle than the pent-up stream rushed forth. By a wise discretion, it has been in some degree guided into a hastily-prepared channel. The effort to gather the waters once more within their original bounds would be as vain as the attempt to recall the effects of the last seven years in Russia. The old machinery may be reconstructed, but these seven years, with all their faults, must be numbered as years of progress. The wishes so long pent-up in the breasts of Russians were for reasonable liberty of individual thought and action, for an impartial administration of law, for equality of civil rights, and for a more responsible Government. These are, no doubt, inestimable blessings ; but the paramount consideration was that of a strong Government. The great difficulty in Russia is to reconcile the two.

Throughout the early history of Russia, down to the reign of Peter the Great, we cannot lose sight of the share taken by the people in the conduct of public affairs. Nearly every Russian writer of the present day is especially careful to reiterate this truth, and impress it on the public mind. The burghers of Novgorod and Kiev long defended their privileges against the encroachments of the descendants of Rurik, and the name of Martha, the *Posadnitza*, or Mayoress of Novgorod, who defended her city against the centralising ambition of Moscow and its tsars, is just now in great favour with the Russians. When Moscow, after the final defeat of the Tartars, gathered around her the other States, the Russian people, as they might then be called, bore no small part in public affairs. The *Krasnaya Ploschad* in the old walled town was the Pnyx of the people of Moscow. Here the first Tsar of Russia convoked an assembly from all the land. Here Boris Goudonov was elected as the head of the State, and here, on the death of that great man, and after the Poles were driven from the country, a Parliament chose the first of the Romanovs. In the charter which he then subscribed, it was written that he should, without introducing any change, govern according to the old laws— that he should neither establish new laws, nor make war or peace nor impose taxes— nor estrange the Crown lands—nor sign the death-warrant of any subject without the consent of a Parliament. ‘The Tsar has commanded, and the Boyards have consented’ is the form which headed all public acts. This form continued only while the country had no large standing army. When this was established, liberty died away in Russia, as in most other States of Europe. We are further told that Ivan IV. convoked the deputies of all the land from all classes, to sit with the Boyards and higher clergy, to make laws and sift important political questions. ‘According to usage,’ says a Russian historian, ‘the consent of the people was necessary to confirm the election of the young Peter, on the Red Place of Moscow.' The Sclavonic *mire*, or commune, was in itself the very germ of self-government; and the guilds of the *Gosti*, the provincial assemblies, and lastly the *Zemskoe Sobor*,* were all popular meetings for the public weal. The *Zemskoe Sobor* was, indeed, the Imperial Parliament of the time, in which the Boyards and chief clergy sat in their own right, with delegates from the communes of the peasantry, from the guilds of the *Gosti*, and the corporations of the towns. In it the right and the liberty of discussion seem to have been more or less kept up, and its decisions, with one or two exceptions, appear to have been carried out by the Executive.

The reforms of Peter the Great, his formation of a standing army, his conquests, the creation of the tchin, the forcing of European, and especially of German habits on the people, obliterated all traces of former liberty, and divided the nation into two great parties, the oppressed, and the oppressors who, in their turn, were submitted to many vexations. On one side, the working classes were kept brutalised, and in a state little better than slavery; on the other hand, the

---

* *Zemskoe Sobor* or *Douma.*—*Zemla*, in Russian, means the land, soil, country; *sobor*, assembly; *douma*, council—Assembly or council of the land. The word *Gost* means foreign merchant; not necessarily of foreign origin, but coming from another part of the country to the dvors, or bazaars of the large towns, where they ultimately settled.

privileged class, among whom was portioned out the result of their labours, hustled one another in the hurry of personal ambition up the sixteen steps of the ladder of the tchin, each grade of which gave a greater share in the partition. A small intermediate class remained, the merchants and others, but these were mostly ignorant men, absorbed in the acquirement of wealth, or the enjoyment of it, and, though necessarily protected by the State, destitute of all political rights, and altogether insignificant. It was scarcely possible that one of the people could rise from his caste to a superior one, except by some act of despotic favour, such as raised Menschikov, the pie-boy, or Demidov, the blacksmith, to notice and power; or by the still less worthy influence of the bed-chamber, to which many families owe their origin in Russia, as in other countries. The army, indeed, sometimes brought forward its intelligent members to the lower ranks of the tchin, but they seldom mounted higher.

Meanwhile the old nobility, whose political power had been crushed by the new German regime, and who would not coalesce with it, lived retired and sullen, but awed and depressed. One great attempt was, indeed, made by them (when Ann, Duchess of Courland, was invited to be Empress) to restrain the power of their Sovereign, and regain their former influence; but their aim was only to govern themselves in the manner of a Venetian or Polish oligarchy. They were made to pay dearly for their rashness, in the indignities heaped on them by Biren, the favourite of Ann. The name of the people was invoked only to favour the views of the Empress's party, as it is now used in semi-despotic countries to cloak some extraordinary act of absolutism. But the old nobility, which since that time had become accustomed to the new order of things, is now again making its voice heard, in its provincial and district assemblies, in favour of a new constitutional Government.

Many changes, legislative and administrative, were enacted under Catharine II. but they did not much affect the real condition of the people. The privileged class increased its privileges, chief among which was an exemption from corporal punishment (i. e. they had to be degraded first), a favour granted by Peter III. when in a maudlin fit (1762). The Emperor Alexander, besides improving greatly the condition of the peasantry, during some years even dreamed of a constitution, and an extension of civil and social liberty to his subjects; but the spirit of revolution, which had been the nursling of his grandmother, appalled him in the end, and he shrunk back to become the corner-stone of the Holy Alliance.

The 25th of December 1825, was the result of his tantalising coquetry with constitutional government, and the confusion which existed in people's minds concerning the succession gave the liberal party some hopes of a favourable issue to their undertaking. Their plan was to form a provisional government, whose duty it should be to convoke a national assembly, in order to draw up a charter of rights and select a sovereign. Through the indecision of the conspirators and the personal courage of the Grand Duke Nicholas the plot failed, and executions and banishments were the fate of the chief men among them. One of them, Prince Troubetzkoi, the admirable devotion of whose wife, in following her husband to Siberia, was a noble contrast to his own pusillanimity, only lately returned from exile, and at the time of my first visit was living retired in Moscow, where he died in 1861.

The portrait of the Emperor Nicholas has yet to be drawn. He, at least, was consistent in his thoughts and actions, which were to centre all power in himself. As his fine person rose above the hosts of his Guards, the great observed of all observers, so his spirit exercised marvellous influence over Russia and over Europe. Strong men trembled, weak men lost the use of their faculties in his presence. Honest men respected while they blamed, knaves feared while they deceived him. Liberalism was not to be expected from such a nature. A band of ministers imbued with his ideas, a legion of secret police, and the red chalk of his censors, combined to crush the appearance of it. Yet, according to his own stern ideas and despite the arbitrary exercise of power, the improvement of his people, and the national aggrandisement, was the absorbing aim of his life. Some future Russian historian may have to tell, how, in the inscrutable designs of Providence, the stern training which he gave his people were causes leading to a happier issue.

The Revolution, begotten in the seventeenth century, sprung into life at the end of the eighteenth in a deluge of blood, which soaked into every soil of Europe. It has been constantly springing up again during the nineteenth, sometimes under the mild and pleasing aspect of reform, at others in the hideous shape of riot and destruction. As against the ogres and giants of fable arose knights sworn to exterminate them, so in Europe sprang up princes, who, with their ministers, conspired to crush the hydra of revolution. Their crusade against it was severe; but it has been ineffectual. Barred towers, deep and loathsome dungeons, moral anguish, added to physical torture; the *knout* and the mines; solitary executions, or wholesale fusillades—all were brought to bear against it. The mystery which often enshrouded it, the strange forms which it assumed, the dread with which its proximity filled its antagonists, confounded one kind of revolution with another. The innocent and the guilty, patriotic reformers and mischievous socialists, too often shared the same fate. The result we all know. The Holy Alliance, with its secondary meetings, its congresses without number as without effect, were answered by fresh outbreaks and reprisals. Thrones have been cast down, and their possessors forced to seek shelter elsewhere. But Reform, the good genius of Revolution, made good its way, overcoming all obstacles, and even insinuating itself into favour with its oppressors, who turned it to their own glory and the progress of their country.

The remoteness and inertness of Russia, aided by the jealous watchfulness of the Government, long withstood its influence. But the spark fell on it at last, and, after long smouldering, broke out into a general flame. Times were changed; reforms became a necessity; and the necessity made itself felt in a manner not to be mistaken. It was a happy instinct which led the Emperor Alexander to put himself in time at the head of such a movement, and impelled his ministers to help him in directing it. Had they not done so, the people would have brought down the whole fabric of Government upon their heads, and the horrors of revolution would have been in inverse proportion to the apathy and general inertness of the rude but patient Russian people.

There was a need not of partial, but of radical reforms, affecting the most weighty interests of a State, the settlement of which has hardly in any country been accomplished without bloodshed. But in Russia such reforms can scarcely be followed by the same results or success as elsewhere. A servile imitation of the institutions of another people is seldom attended with any harmonious working. The complaint of a great part of the Russian people is, that they have had forced on them a system of German administration and government which was not congenial to the country and could not take root in it, which has only been kept up by the overpowering force of circumstances, but which must now be purged of the abuses which have crept into it.

If a constitution similar to that of Great Britain were introduced into Russia, it would be a monstrous absurdity. A constitution, like the laws of a people, to be thoroughly effective, must proceed from the people, and must grow up with it. Whether Russia obtain a constitution or not, the reforms which are now on the point of being introduced justify a hope that those enormities which were sometimes darkly heard of from that country can never be repeated. The long-cherished arbitrary ideas of one class, the venality and lax morality of another, and the general ignorance of the people, cannot soon be eradicated or amended. But the present is only the seed-time of better things; the harvest must be judged of hereafter.

Intimately bound up with the question of reform in Russia, is the history of its secret societies and its secret literature. In all countries these are the forerunners of revolution. In our own country, after the second Parliament of Charles I. an abundance of revolutionary writings was scattered along the roads and streets. Sealed and anonymous letters, addressed to the chief men of the counties, were found hanging on bushes or furtively dropped in shops: all giving warning that a time was fast approaching when ' such a work was to be wrought in England as never was the like, and which would be for our good.' * Such, or nearly such, has been the plan pursued in Russia for some time past; and it has baffled the researches of a vigilant and expert secret police—an institution which England was not blessed with.

Already in the reign of Alexander I. the movement began. So prevalent and rampant was the liberalism of the young officers who returned to Russia after their great Western campaign, that one of their old generals was heard to remark 'it would be better for the Emperor to have his army overwhelmed in the Baltic, than that they should return to spread their ideas at home.' The truth of his words soon became evident in the many secret societies which sprang up in Russia from 1816 to 1825. In these were enrolled the names of some of the highest Russian families, with those of others to whom personal talent was then opening a career. Among them were the well-known names of Muraviev, Troubetzkoi, Tourguenev, Orlov, Obolenski, Naritchkin, Glinka, Pestel and others. A great deal of sublime but impossible ideology was, in their plans, mixed up with projects of assassination and changes of dynasty. The well-known military revolt in 1825 and the partial risings in the south were the results of all their plottings. Many secret societies had formerly been allowed

---

* *Life and Reign of Charles I.* by D'Israeli.

in Russia, but as they were naturally enough used for political purposes, a ukase put a stop to them in 1822, when every official was required to take an oath that he had dropped all connection with any of them.

In spite of the repressive measures of the Emperor Nicholas, these movements still went on, though more secretly. The evidence of them oozed out in a hundred different ways. Poets, the creators of history, liberty, and progress, continued to sing—Pushkin, Gogol, Lermontov, Polijaiev, and many others; and though their political poems could not be published, they were not the less secretly passed from hand to hand, or less eagerly read because they were prohibited. At last some of them reached the highest personage of the State, who, considering nearly all literature useless, if not mischievous, was not very likely to be charmed with effusions which satirised his august person and the institutions which he was bent on consolidating. Graver men, professors of science and polite learning, took up the theme, and gave a form to what poets had vaguely outlined. Young enthusiasts were ever ready to carry out their theories, as they were in 1849. But the time was ill-chosen : an unflinching head and arm swayed the destinies of the nation, and poets, professors, and patriots went one of two roads—to the mines of Siberia, or the defiles of the Caucasus.

At last Nicholas died. The tight reins were a little relaxed. Poets, professors, and patriots returned from their exile, where their opinions had only received a deeper tinge from restraint. Those who then could not or would not submit to the censor's pencil, or confine their advanced ideas among a select acquaintance, either returned to their old abodes, or became exiles in Western Europe. Among the latter two men deserve particular attention, on account of the influence which they have exercised on current affairs—M. Herzen and Prince Peter Dolgoroukov, both literary men, both editors of newspapers in the Russian language, advocating more or less advanced opinions.

M. Herzen, or, as he is generally known under the pseudonym of Iskander, emigrated on his return from exile, and established a newspaper called the 'Kolokol,' or Bell, in London. To this he afterwards added a yearly publication called the 'Polarnaa Svésdá' (Polar Star), and an occasional supplement called 'Pod Sud' (under judgment), which exposed various iniquities in the administration of justice. M. Herzen is also the author of some political works, or novels having a political tendency, and has the reputation of being a man of high intellect but of somewhat socialist opinions. His 'Kolokol' soon created an extraordinary sensation in all Russian circles, as abuse after abuse was laid bare, as acts of the Government were criticised, and numerous incidents of corrupt official life exposed. His correspondents were found not only in every goubernie of Russia, but in Irkutsk, and even that

Ultima Thule of all the Russias, Nicholaievsk at the mouth of the Amoor river. Although, as may be supposed, most of them were anonymous, still, from the information they sent, many must have been men occupying high positions either about the court or in the administration.

Bundles of these newspapers were smuggled into Russia in all possible ways. Though seldom found, they were known to pass from hand to hand, till everybody read them. M. Herzen's influence became immense; his name spread into remote provinces of the empire, and was whispered in a mysterious manner from the lips of men who could hardly read. A peasant in a remote village asked me who Iskander was. In St. Petersburg a shoemaker begged me to give him his address, in order that he might write a letter to the 'Kolokol,' and expose certain creditors who were dilatory in paying their bills. In fact, writing to the 'Kolokol' became an idea in Russia like writing to the 'Times' in England. There is little doubt that to its determined exposure of abuses and its constant attacks on many arbitrary acts of individuals Russia owes some of the wholesome reforms which are now taking place. It has, however, of late somewhat lost caste, from its having been made the vehicle of many personal and groundless attacks. As its correspondence is anonymous, a wide field was open for the indulgence of personal malice. One instance came under my own notice.   A letter appeared in 1861 in the 'Kolokol,' accusing Admiral Shestakov with having, on board his flag-ship, inflicted corporal punishment on a midshipman.   Such an accusation naturally caused much excitement in St. Petersburg among persons connected with the navy, and no little astonishment and disgust, when read, as it was soon afterwards, on board his frigate.   It had evidently been sent with a malicious intention, for the writer must have been perfectly aware that no admiral in the service dare commit such an action now, even if he did not know that Admiral Shestakov was just one of those men who are opposed to corporal punishment altogether.   The only colour for such an accusation was, that the midshipman in question had been put under an easy arrest for a few days for some act of misconduct.   One or two such attacks, with the evident bias of the 'Kolokol' to doctrines which even liberal men consider highly dangerous, has had the effect of estranging from it the confidence of many of its former admirers.   Its editor is, however, always willing to do the *amende honorable*, and to publish all communications which may be addressed in defence.*

* At the present moment, August 1863, the *Kolokol* has almost entirely lost its influence in Russia.   Nobody any longer questions his neighbour as to the contents of the *Kolokol*.   There are three reasons to account for this.   The first has been already given.   The second is that the Government, no longer making its existence a mystery, permits extracts from it, and answers to it, to appear in the Russian press.   The

Prince Peter Dolgoroukov, a cousin of the Chief of the Secret Police, successively passed through all the phases of Russian liberalism. He served, spoke too freely, was exiled, and afterwards emigrated. Recalled to Russia after the publication of his 'Vérité sur la Russie,' he refused to obey the order. He then started a newspaper called 'Pravdievie' (Truth), with the intention of advocating a constitutional Government. Till lately this paper was published in Leipsic, although it has since been replaced by another journal of somewhat different name. The influence of the 'Pravdievie' was much less than that of the 'Kolokol,' owing, perhaps, to the famous trial which lately took place in Paris between Prince Worontzov and the editor, when evidence came out not at all in favour of the veracity of the latter.

These two journals, with a host of other publications forbidden in Russia, are circulated all over Europe, wherever a few Russians are found together. Along the frontier, at the baths of Germany, at Nice or Athens, as in Paris and Leipsic, they strike the eye of the travelling Russian from the shop windows. Thousands of revolutionary proclamations addressed to the youth of Russia, to officers and men of the army and navy, exciting them to sedition, also flow from the presses of

third reason, and the most fatal, is that M. Herzen is no longer considered, as before, a Russian patriot, on account of his siding, in the present dispute, with the Poles, whose pretensions, in the belief of the Russians, involve a dismemberment of their country.

London and Leipsic ; and their ideas, sown in a soil of only superficial cultivation but of hot productiveness, have brought many a young man who offered himself as their apostle to the casemates of a fortress or a dreary banishment.

It is only during the last few years that Russians of any except the higher classes have had permission to travel. The cost of a passport during the reign of Nicholas was alone sufficient to deter many from applying for what would probably have been refused. Of the many young men who were then sent to complete their education in German Universities fully half found their foreign training a curse to them on their return. Men of powerful minds became imbued with a political ideology which they found impossible to maintain in their own country and under their own institutions. Many felt bitterly the sudden contrast from Western European life to the deserts of Siberia. The names of hundreds could be mentioned who, possessed of all the talent and adornment which make life respectable and glorious elsewhere, found those talents simply hurtful in the land in which they were born. In advance of the society in which they were called to live, they will in a happier future be enrolled among the army of martyrs who have suffered for the misfortune of being half a century in advance of their fellow-countrymen.

When with the new reign greater liberty of travel was accorded, thousands rushed towards the West. With the greater part this liberty would naturally be exercised at first in running wild among the pleasures and luxuries which more genial climes and a cheaper civilisation afforded, in catching up crude and extreme ideas, and revelling in a literature which had for them a mysterious charm because it was proscribed at home. Some, attracted by the liberal principles of other countries, but, without tracing them back to the laws and character of a people, applied them too hastily to their own land, and took on themselves the task of disseminating them. Others, not content with reading alone, must see and converse with the authors of what they read, must have their photographs, and, in the revolutionary atmosphere of Leicester Square, greedily snapped at many a hook which was baited with such tempting words as Liberty, Fraternity, Communism, Republic.

The year 1861 was a fruitful year for secret literature in the interior of the empire, but chiefly at St. Petersburg. One publication especially created an extraordinary sensation. It was called the 'Velikie Russ' (Great Russian), and was edited by a young man named Michailov. The whole police of the capital were long puzzled to find either editor, printer, or disseminators. Copies of it were strewn about the streets at night, or openly left at the doors of houses: and the connivance with which it was everywhere received must be some evidence of the state of public feeling. Its contents revealed the existence of revolutionary clubs all over the country, with a secret committee in the capital. The members of these seemed to be pretty equally divided into two parties. The one was the ubiquitous republican party, whom nothing less would satisfy than the overthrow of the present dynasty and a complete change in the Government. The other was the constitutional party, who wished only to set bounds to the power of the Sovereign, and to effect a reform in the laws and administration. Thus divided in their views, the leading liberals, in the last published number of the ' Velikie Russ,' counselled a general plan of committees throughout the country ¯in communication with the secret club in St. Petersburg, in order secretly to draw up and obtain signatures for a petition to the Emperor. A formula, setting forth grievances, was added to serve as a model for the petition. The chief items of this formula were complaints of the unsatisfactory manner in which the Emancipation was being carried out; of bureaucratic influence; of the state of the finances, and the constant depreciation of paper money. It urged that the retention of Poland was the chief cause of Russia's internal weakness, as it required an enormous army to keep down the Poles, and that in a manner which was barbarous, besides costing millions of treasure, thus hurting the material prosperity and national honour of the Russian people. It went on to say that as the Emperor then stood he had to struggle with abuses of every description, against which he was completely powerless: The address concluded by praying the Emperor to convoke a parliament in one of the capitals, to draw up a constitution for Russia, and another in Warsaw for Poland.

Among the divers manners in which this newspaper and other revolutionary pamphlets were circulated, one is highly amusing. About two centuries ago there lived somewhere near Moscow a holy bishop called *Techon,** who literally followed the Christian injunction of giving all his goods to feed the poor. He died and was buried; but left a name not to be forgotten among the simple peasantry, whose fathers had shared his bounty. During the perplexities of the Emancipation, it became necessary, by some striking example, to clinch the faith and rivet the religious obedience of the peasantry. So Techon's bones were dug up, and solemnly canonised by the Holy Synod: and, as is every day the case in Russia, miracles were soon performed on the faithful.

Techon's success was immense. Pilgrims came from all corners of the orthodox empire to kiss his crumbling bones, and even the Emperor, during his journey south in 1861, did them the honour of a solemn visit. The exemplary life of the saint was published in St. Petersburg. It passed, of course, in an easy manner, the ordeal of the censor, and had an enormous

---

* Commonly called Techon Zadonskoi, from the name of his monastery. His theological letters are well known.

sale. Thousands of copies, in covers illumined by a portrait of the holy man and other sacred but grotesque figures, were sold at the book-stalls in the gateways of the city. A most praiseworthy inclination for pious literature was evinced by the public of the capital, which could not fail to be remarked with pleasure. At last the truth came out. It was a wolf in sheep's clothing. Under poor Techon's skin were discovered revolutionary writings of the worst description, and the real saint soon ceased to attract the public.

At last Michailov, the editor of the 'Velikie Russ,' was caught and exiled to Siberia. His deportation, however, only gave a further opportunity for the manifestation of public feeling. Thousands of his photographs were sold. Subscriptions were opened. The ladies' secret liberal societies (for they had theirs also) exerted themselves, as women only can. Concerts and soirées littéraires were given for *poor unfortunate literary men.* A carriage was presented to him for his journey, with a valuable set of furs to keep him warm in his Siberian exile. Even on his arrival in Tobolsk he met with further demonstrations of sympathy, not only from exiles who had preceded him, but from public functionaries—an act which caused the Government to send thither a commission to enquire into the matter.

About the same time occurred those disturbances

which led to the closing of the universities. As in most other countries where the tongue and pen are under control, these were found to be the very wasp's nest of Liberalism. Professors were there who clothed political axioms in the garb of fable, or dressed up some event in earlier history as a satire on the present time and its events. Students applauded or hissed, as the substance of the lecture or the political bias of the lecturer coincided with their own views. At last, during the Emperor's visit in the south, a dispute arose between the students and the authorities of the university of St. Petersburg, which determined Admiral Putiatin, the Minister of Public Instruction and Morals, to take the wasp's nest and root out all the grubs of infection. This was very clumsily performed by the troops. The dispersed professors and students went buzzing angrily all over the country, and, of course, propagating their opinions, which good policy might have kept confined between the bounds of the university. Poor Admiral Putiatin got dreadfully stung in the action, and, no doubt, regretted that he had changed salt water and plain sailing for the intricate navigation and constant luffing of a ministerial bureau. As is known, the universities remained for a long time closed ; and a hasty act, which nearly drove the extreme Liberal party into open rebellion, was only remedied on the Emperor's return by the retirement of the admiral and the appointment in his place of M. Golovnin, who had the reputation of being a Liberal, and whose first act was to reopen the universities and soften the rigour of literary censure.

The Sunday schools which had been established for the purpose of giving instruction to artisans and others engaged during the week, were also closed at the same time. It was found that political doctrines and the rights of man were taught to the scholars at the same time as A. B. V. D. In this affair were found implicated one or two personages high in favour at Court, a fact from which we may divine the source of certain intimate communications which appeared from time to time in the ' Kolokol.'

Early in 1862 took place in certain governments of Russia the usual triennial meetings of the nobility to choose their president or marshal. These assemblies of the nobility, which were held in every district, with a general one for the province, were founded by Catharine, but never possessed any political power. Their business was confined to local administration, to appointing the public functionaries for the district or government, and to arranging or deciding all disputes between the proprietors and their peasantry. But in this year they assumed somewhat different responsibilities. At St. Petersburg, Moscow, Toula, Novgorod, Smolensk, and Tver they converted their halls into something like a parliament, in which the two parties, Liberal and Conservative, young and old

Russia, came face to face. At all these places the members soon threw aside their usual subjects of discussion, and broached the ticklish topic of reform. At St. Petersburg, under the very eye of the Court, the two parties were pretty equally divided. At Moscow, however, the Liberals had the upper hand, and a petition to the Emperor was proposed, voted, and drawn up, praying for local self-government, a thorough reform in the administration of the laws, liberty of the press, the immediate and final settlement of the Emancipation question, the publication of the budget, and a parliament of all the estates of the land. The same petitions were sent up from the other assemblies; but Toula went farther than the others in the liberal tendency of its address. To the last-named petition alone did the Government deign any notice at the time; and the answer to this address was a party of gens d'armes, who carried off thirteen of its chief subscribers to the fortress of St. Petersburg, where they were confined for a short time. Yet the year did not pass away without the appearance of some more favourable effect to these serious and solemn demonstrations of the feeling of the nation.*

---

* The Polish Insurrection, by absorbing the attention of the country, doubtless explains the interruption of these agitations. When that question is settled, we shall probably see them renewed, if the Government have not fully carried out its reforming programme.

CHAPTER IV.

THE MILLENNIAL BIRTHDAY OF RUSSIA, 1862.[*]

Monument at Old Novgorod—The Six Epochs of Russian History —Russia's Influence on the World in the Past—Her Aspirations for the Future—Railways and Telegraphs, the Missionaries of Civilisation—Reforms in Russia—Their probable Effect—The Budgets—The *Otkoup* or Brandy Farming—Statistics of Russian Finance—Reform in the Administration of Justice—Russian Law —Its Abuses—Immovable Judges—Advocates—A Jury—Russian Law of Habeas Corpus—Great Difficulty of Introducing Reforms—Abolition of Barbarous Punishments—Flogging—The Russian Army—Freedom of the Press—Laws concerning it— Popular Education in Russia —Religious Liberty—Less Meddling in Private Affairs of Subjects—A Constitution for Russia—Constitution *versus* Autocracy—Reasons for and against a Constitution in Russia—Agitations of the Nobility—Difficulties in the Way—Programme of Russian Government—Conditions for securing the Benefit of Reforms already given.

IN the month of August 1862 the Tsar celebrated the millennial birthday of the Russian monarchy in the old city of Novgorod. On the monument there consecrated as a memorial of that day are inscribed the names of nearly all those men of whom Russians are

[*] This is, of course, a popular fiction. In 862, the Scandinavian princes came to Novgorod, and thence spread on to Kiev and other centres of population. But the country cannot be said to have had either government or history before the reign of Ivan III. about A.D. 1445.

proud. Its form is that of a bell, surmounted by a
Greek cross. On it are exhibited six groups of cele-
brated men, representing the six epochs of Russian
history. The chief figure in the first group is Rurik,
the Varangian chieftain, A.D. 862.* The second cen-
tral figure is that of Wladimir, who introduced the
Christian faith from Constantinople, A.D. 988. The
third, that of Dimitri, the Donskoi, who defeated the
Tartars at the battle of *Koulikouvo*, on the Don,
A.D. 1380. In the fourth group is Ivan III. Prince of
Moscow. The central figure of the fifth is that of Michael
Romanov, the first of that family elected tsar by the
Boyards and people, A.D. 1613. In the last is that of
Peter the Great. The secondary figures are those of
various heroes, martyrs, saints, poets, and generals who
have figured in Russian history up to the present times.

‘A thousand years in the eye of the Lord are but a
moment,’ sang the wise King David; but it is nevertheless a long time for the childhood and youth of a
people. It may be said that Russia has produced no
one great national genius, who has exercised any
influence on the world at large. As is the case with all
young peoples, the real genius of the nation has been
shown in poetry. The rest of its literature may be
called exotic. What is to be the result of the next

* A curious dispute has lately been going on among learned Russians,
many of whom maintain that he was not, as is generally supposed, a
Scandinavian, but that he came from Lithuania.

century or two, now that the body is fully grown? Will it play a noble part?—or will its acts and thoughts be only faint struggles for prolonging a diseased existence? Till now her career has been that of a young savage, doing all to increase his physical development, and roaming far and wide to extend his hunting-grounds. That object has now been gained. Russia has advanced to the shores of two oceans. She has a vast network of internal waters, some of the most fruitful lands, some of the richest and most varied mines in the world. She possesses the means of all prosperity, and her only need is that the people may be trained to take proper advantage of them.

Moscow and St. Petersburg have been connected by railways with the cities of the west, and the wires of the telegraph have been laid down to the remote capitals of the celestial empire. Railways and telegraphs are the arteries and nerves which must bring all mankind into unison. Russia is at last joined by them to Western Europe, and the sympathy of union will never permit a repetition of the tyrannical and sometimes barbarous deeds of a former age.

In judging of reforms in Russia we must not compare them too closely with the more perfect institutions of other countries. Our duty is to measure them by the changes for the better in Russia itself. The chief reforms which have received the sanction of the Emperor up to the present time are the emancipation of the serfs, the publication of the national receipts and expenditure, the substitution of an excise for the *otkoup*, or farming of the brandy or vodka, certain reforms in the administration of justice, modifications in the severity of punishments, and a greater liberty in local administrations. Others equally important are being considered, embracing finance, the army and navy, the public press, &c. &c.

Throughout the year 1862 the ministers and generals brought up in the political school of the last reign, one after another resigned their functions, and their places were filled by new men, who felt that a great change was impending, and that it behoved the Government to do something to meet the demands of the country. Despotic governments have often before sought to quiet the hungry dogs of Liberalism with choice and tempting morsels. But the times were now too critical for such dealing, and men's minds too highly excited to take promises for facts. Though the reforms which have been granted may appear trifling to those who live in a more liberally organised society, for Russia they are immense; and though they will certainly be more perfect on paper than they can be in practice, still, flagrant abuse of authority must be detected, and if not punished, will be at least so stigmatised by public opinion as to deter others from offending in like manner.

I have reserved for a special chapter the consideration

of the emancipation of the serfs, and the character and state of the Russian peasantry.

Imperfect copies of the budgets of 1859 and 1860 were surreptitiously obtained from a correspondent of the 'Kolokol,' and published in that paper. The Government, yielding to strong public opinion, published that of 1862 in its official gazette; and the details of finance may now be examined in Russia as in any other country. At the same time, many retrenchments in the expenditure of public money were ordered, especially in all that concerned the members of the Imperial family, their extraordinary allowances, and the celebration of their saints' days.

One of the most beneficial of the reforms already accomplished is the substitution of an excise for the old system of farming the vodka, or corn brandy, to individuals. This system was a great cause of demoralisation both in the public officials and the common people. Drunkenness is one of the greatest curses of the Russians: but its encouragement became a political necessity, for by no other means could so large a sum be brought into the revenue. The importance of this Government monopoly may be appreciated, when it is said that the farming of the vodka produced 123,000,000 roubles a year to the State, or about two-fifths of its whole income.*

* The income of the Russian Government for 1862 was as follows, in round numbers:—

The corruption to which the *otkoup* gave rise (such as the adulteration of the spirit and the bribing of inspectors and police of all grades) has been for years exposed in almost every work in Russia. The new system of excise is said to work well, and a slight increase is perceptible in the revenue. The number of grog shops is greater; the vodka sold is cheaper and of better quality; and the tchinovnik would seem at present the only sufferer by the change, if the chief consumers of the vodka could be excepted. But unfortunately drunkenness has increased among the lower classes in proportion to the diminution of price and the improvement in the quality of the spirit.

The greatest need of reform lay in the administration of justice. No country in Europe had a more perfect

---

The poll and other personal taxes levied on the people, the privileged class paying no direct taxes . . . . . . 55¼ millions of roubles.

Produce of woods and mines . . . . 11¾ ,, ,,

Excise and customs, salt tax and other indirect taxes, of which the vodka alone produced 123 millions . . . . . 198½ ,, ,,

Railroads, Post-office, government lands, and various other sources . . . . 30 ,, ,,

Interest on Mortgages . . . . 14½ ,, ,,

311 ,, ,,

Of this sum 106½ millions were required for the army alone; 54¼ millions for interest of national debt; 20½ for the navy; 8 millions for the court; 26¾ millions for the finance department; and the rest for the usual working of the other administrations.—*St. Petersburg Mesiatseslov, or Calendar for* 1863.

written code than Russia; but nowhere perhaps has the practice been so little in accordance with the theory. Pinned on to every law were half a dozen ukases or orders changing or abrogating it, so that a decision could be given and maintained either way. Into this code, drawn from the ancient laws and reformed by Peter the Great, Catharine introduced other laws from Western Europe, and the work of consolidation was completed by the Emperor Nicholas in 1830. If its administration has not been always pure, it was certainly not the fault of the different emperors, who, though superior to the laws they made, wished to have them binding on all classes of their subjects. The reason must be sought elsewhere. The members of the Executive, often badly paid, but with expensive habits, yielded to a system of bribery which extended throughout every branch of the public service. The secrecy which accompanies such transactions in other countries is a proof of public morality. In Russia bribery became open and shameless, and was looked on as matter of course. Crimes could be hushed up, a lawsuit gained, the eyes of a police inspector closed, and things *utterly impossible* quickly executed by the timely administration of *bzadki*, varying according to the importance of the affair or the rank of the receiver, from a silver *grivnik* (ten copecks) to a bank note for a thousand roubles.

The forms of law procedure furnished an opening for

all abuses. Every case, criminal or civil, was heard with closed doors. The depositions were given in writing. From these judgment was formed and sentence pronounced, and thus the proceedings ran to an indefinite length of time which a bribe alone could shorten. The secret police had an unlimited power of arrest, and, in minor cases, of punishment. They were thus the terror of the innocent as well as of the guilty, both of whom were only too glad to ransom themselves, the one from a deserved punishment, the other from an impending accusation. The new acts, by which judges will be immovable and will receive a higher salary, the institution of a jury, the pleading of advocates on both sides (a new class in Russia), oral evidence in open courts, and its publication in the newspapers, an immediate and decisive verdict of condemnation or of acquittal in place of a verdict of *not proven*—all afford, if manfully carried out, sufficient guarantees for the greater security of the subject. Added to these is a law in some measure resembling our *habeas corpus*, whereby any person arrested on any charge must be brought within twenty-four hours for examination before a magistrate, and in every district a proprietor has been appointed with powers answering to those of our justices of the peace. The secret police are no longer to have the power of arbitrary punishment. All civil processes are to be public, the necessary papers are to be furnished to the counsel on either side, and every pretext is taken away for spinning out a trial, in order to bleed both parties to the utmost.*

Such are the wholesome changes ordained by the legislative section of the Imperial chancery. It will be a more difficult task to cleanse the Augean stables of Russian administration, to root out the love of arbitrary power, and purify the morality of some tens of thousands of functionaries. New professions have to be called into existence. To plead as an advocate requires long and special study ; and to promote this object faculties have been lately established in the Russian Universities, while the fine law library of the late Count Speransky at St. Petersburg has been thrown open to students.

Public education must be fostered for years before an institution like that of a jury can be properly under-stood or appreciated. Even then, judges, pleaders, and a jury may be made the instruments of the worst of all despotisms—a despotism which has the sanction of the law to cover it. English history furnishes some melancholy examples. In ordinary criminal and civil cases a Government is seldom interested in tampering with justice. But in political trials public opinion is generally favourable to the prisoner and adverse to the Government. It would seem, therefore, of less consequence that the reforms already mentioned are not to apply to cases of treason, where in general they are most needed.

* These new laws are to come into force from the year 1864, unless the Polish insurrection delays their promulgation for a short time.

Altogether, though these reforms cannot soon become solid institutions, yet, if carried out even imperfectly for a time, they must prove an inestimable benefit to a people who have so long been the victims of caste and of arbitrary power.

Barbarous and debasing modes of punishment seem also coming to an end in Russia. That horrid instrument called the *knout,* which, by a fiction of clemency, was inflicted instead of the penalty of death, though a few strokes of it properly applied generally had the same effect, was already abolished in 1845. Corporal punishment seems on the point of being abolished altogether, in spite of the unctuous opposition of Philarete, the patriarch of Moscow, who, a supposed Liberal under Nicholas, drew from the New Testament an apology for whipping and for its necessity under the present Emperor. The following reasons for its abolition were lately put forward in the report of the Minister of the Interior to the Emperor: 'That corporal punishment does not exist in other countries, and that its use is not warranted either by the habits of the people or by the frequency of crime in Russia; * that such punishments offend public morality, and, instead of acting as a warning, rouse only a feeling of pity, in which horror of the crime is lost; that this is especially true of the

---

* It is a curious coincidence, that while the question of abolishing corporal punishments was being mooted in Russia, many members of the British legislature were desirous of re-introducing it into English law.

punishment of women; and, lastly, that crime has been lessened, since milder sentences have replaced the more barbarous punishments formerly inflicted.'

Corporal punishment for women has therefore been abolished altogether; while for men its infliction has been rendered less cruel, nor can it be inflicted at all unless sanctioned by a legal sentence. The law no longer justifies proprietors in beating their peasants, masters in chastising their servants, or the police in flogging their uncondemned prisoners. It is probable that the severe military punishment of running the gauntlet between two rows of soldiers armed with sticks will also give place to some other, to act more as an example, with less of torture. As it is, commanders in the Russian service are restrained from severely flogging their men, except by sentence of a court-martial.

Reforms in the military and naval services have long been talked of; but of their nature or extent little is yet known. Enough, however, has come to light during the last few years to show that a serious disaffection existed in the army, both among officers and men. Revolutionary writings, circulated widely in various regiments, found readers not only among the wild and headstrong youth, but even among some of the superior and more sober officers. The events which took place in repressing certain disturbances in the south of Russia in 1861, and a letter published in the 'Kolokol,' in October 1862, are examples of this. The officers of the Russian services are patriotic in the highest degree, and, though the younger members are apt to be led away by political ideas, they are not in the least revolutionary. The soldier, doubly attached by religion and tradition to the person of the Emperor, is simply dissatisfied with his lot as a soldier, and listens willingly, therefore, to any plan which he thinks can alleviate it. But it must not be supposed, as a certain part of the ultra-press wishes it to be believed, that he is given to sedition and ready to take part in a revolution against his Emperor. He wants only to be better fed, better clothed, and, more than all, to be permitted to return soon to his village and live quietly. In most countries, in which a conscription is in force, the term of service varies from eight to three years. In Russia it was formerly 25 years, but now it is only 15. During this time the soldier is hardly paid at all, and, if his colonel be corrupt, he is badly fed and clothed, so that he is only too glad to earn a few copecks by odd jobs, when not on duty. At the end of his term of service he returns to settle in his native village, which he had quitted as a young recruit; but generally he comes back only to find his parents and connections in their graves, and to resume among strangers a life for which he has long lost the habit. If he is wounded or disabled, his pension barely suffices to keep life within him, even in the cheapest part of Russia. During the present reign his condition has been much improved. The conscription has made no call on the youth of the country since the last war;[*] it now falls more equally on all classes; while, during his period of service, the comforts of the soldier have been increased and his punishments mollified.

Another subject which has occupied much attention in Russia for some time past, is the freedom of the press. This freedom, however, seems still far distant. A greater license has certainly been allowed, the censure moderated, and liberty given to reply to radical literature published in Germany and England.

The necessity for granting this liberty was overpowering. Every educated man in Russia read the secret prints from foreign countries, but he had generally judgment enough to distinguish the wheat from the chaff. The youth of the country, more than ever politically inclined, also read them, and often nothing else; for in the public press at home, hardly any notice was taken of the ' Kolokol ' and the ' Pravdolubievie,' and if ever the home papers replied to any matter found in those journals, the control which was known to be exercised over them, neutralised any wholesome influence [†] which they might otherwise have exercised. But it must be remembered that, in the matter of

* Until the late preparations for war called forth a conscription of ten in a thousand. August 1863.

† See last chapter.

education, Russia is unlike any other country in Europe. Out of more than sixty millions, fifty millions can neither read nor write; certainly not five millions take interest in political news, and perhaps not more than 100,000 men have education enough to found their judgment of things on facts, and not on newspaper criticism. ' On an average,' says M. Gerebtzov, in his 'History of Civilisation in Russia,' ' only 1 in 8 can read and write; in some goubernie, there is not one in a hundred who can read.'* That some form of control is necessary to prevent revolutionary and profane ideas from becoming a source of mischief among ignorant men, no one, who thinks sincerely, can deny. General education must precede a freedom of the press; if it be the effect of it, it will receive the im-

---

* Till lately, the only instruction received by children of the lower classes from their ignorant village clergy was confined to the Sclavonic Church Liturgy and the principles of morality, with anecdotes and traditions of the Elders, which were learnt by heart. There were also a few schools under the direction of the different administrations, such as the Ministry of the Imperial Domains, &c. But since 1859 the Ministry of Public Instruction has organised a system of national schools throughout the country. The difficulties in the way of popular education in Russia are far greater than in any country of Western Europe, and cannot be overcome unless the Government interferes, supplying the buildings and teachers, and compelling the attendance of the young. In some districts schools are already established; but they are attended only in winter, and then, owing to the rigorous climate and the dwellings being scattered over so large a space, the attendance is necessarily scanty.

pression of its teachings; and that such impression may be not hurtful to the well-being of the State, some control must be exercised.

The changes in the laws concerning the press will make the censure partly preventive, partly penal. Most works, the contents of which are not likely to give umbrage to the Government, may be published without preliminary censure, the authors and publishers being liable to prosecution for any illegal matter which they may contain. The periodicals which fall under this head will, like the press in France, receive so many warnings before they are prosecuted. But for most of the newspapers and political works the censure will remain preventive as before, and that, by the wish of the editors themselves, who prefer the preventive censure to the risk of a prosecution, which may be directed by private animosity, or which it might be necessary to hush up by a large bribe.

Russian orthodoxy, though not very liberal in its dogmas or in its laws where men of other creeds are concerned, is yet tolerant on the whole. But the Emperor Nicholas, in his rage for centralisation and uniformity, had also a mania for converting his subjects, which has happily subsided during the present reign. In his lifetime the various Raskolniki, as Dissenters or Sectarians are called in Russia, had to pay the police well to be allowed to practise their rites in secret. Many a good Jew was turned into a bad Christian, or an indifferent Lutheran into a very hypocritical orthodox. The most cruel measures were put in force to convert the Uniates and Catholics of the Polish frontier to the national orthodox Church—measures which, unhappily, were only a retaliation on the conduct of Polish proprietors and Jesuit priests towards members of the Greek Church. Those unfortunate pariahs of Europe, and especially of Poland, the Jews, are at length also admitted to be men, and allowed civil rights. Looked upon as traitors, some of them actually became so, and it was only a year or two before the last war, that the whole Jewish population was ejected from Sevastopol. As far as civil equality goes, the Jews possess it throughout all the Russias, but their social equality is still far distant.

Altogether, that meddling in the private affairs of subjects, which we naturally look for at the hands of a so-called paternal Government, is fast dying out in Russia. For example, the late Emperor was fond of forcing all his youth into Government schools and colleges, to be trained in the way he thought they ought to go. Parents were frowned at, if not reprimanded, who preferred private or home education for their children in tender years, although, to judge by many examples which have come under my own notice, persons educated under their parents' eye, while not inferior intellectually, are certainly morally superior to those who have grown up under the lax morality and deadening routine of these public schools.

There remains the subject of a constitution, which many educated Russians eagerly desire, and many not less earnestly deprecate. As theories of government, both the autocratic and constitutional forms have each their merits and their faults. If the latter is the safest, an autocracy is more prompt and decisive in its action. The traveller must remark the quickness in diplomacy, the compactness of huge armies, the order and regularity with which public works are carried out; but, though he admire, he need not envy. A despotic Government cannot, in our times, be a lasting one. When Madame de Staël told the Emperor Alexander I. that his character was a constitution in itself, his answer was, 'I am only a happy chance.' The remark and the reply embody the good and evil of all despotic Governments. The loyal and humane character of the Emperor Alexander II. is a guarantee for the time being. But who can answer for the future rulers? Where an innate sense of justice does not exist in the mind of an absolute prince, there remains no other check to the abuse of authority than the fear of assassination, or the horrors of a revolution which convulses all society.

That the Russians are fit for a constitution few Englishmen probably will deny. The people are ignorant;

the roads are bad; the principles of the leading men
waver with the circumstances which surround them;
there are abuses and corruptions of all sorts to be got
rid of. But the Russian people are patient, loyal, and
patriotic, and under a rough and semi-barbarous appearance they possess much sound common sense. The communal system, under which the greater part of them are
born and bred, is the very nursery of self-government.
At present their wishes are confined to the proper
execution of their just laws, the permission to manage
their own local affairs, and protection against the
rapacity and ill-treatment of Imperial favourites, of the
official or proprietor, with whom they have to do.
They understand no more of a constitution than they
know how to fly, and would probably be quite opposed
to it, if they thought it was to weaken the power of
the Emperor, to whom they have been accustomed to
look as a last resource in their troubles. During the
revolution in St. Petersburg and the south of Russia
in 1825, the ringleaders, to rouse the enthusiasm of their
followers, shouted ' Hurrah for Constantine and Constitoutsia!' The men did not understand, and remained
silent. ' Constitoutsia! who's she?' they said, ' is she
the Grand Duke's wife?'

The wish for a constitution is confined to the million
or two of educated, ambitious, and restless Russian and
Polish nobles and students; and there is certainly
among them enough talent, science, and principle to

carry on to the benefit and honour of the country such a machine of government. But one insuperable difficulty intervenes in the host of interested and talented supporters of an established despotism, backed by an army of three quarters of a million of men. A forced constitution under such circumstances is scarcely to be thought of. Even if acquired, it would probably go the road of other famous European constitutions. The people would neither have the time nor the chance of any organisation in its defence, while the army, if it interferes against one prince, becomes too often a tool in the hands of his successor. Where a ruler has directly or indirectly uncontrolled power of the public money to pay or reward a standing army and talented supporters, a so-called constitution is a farce, and it is better to call things by their right names and say *autocrat* at once.

Some hopes were, however, cherished by many Russians, that the present Tsar purposed to surrender many imperial prerogatives, and ' octroyer ' as the French call it, a sort of constitution. This appeared the more likely when certain Government newspapers published formulas of the different constitutions of Europe. But this was, probably, only a sop thrown out to appease the longings of the moment. Whatever may be the opinions and intentions of the Emperor, it would seem to be quite against the views of the Grand Duke Constantine, who, for his station, is certainly one of the most progressive men in Russia, and also against the convictions of very many educated men who have studied the wants of their country. Their idea seems to be that the country would not be benefited at present by curtailing the prerogatives of the Emperor, owing to the vast extent of the empire, the variety of its nationalities, the absence of an educated middle class, but chiefly perhaps, also, from a fear that the class whose talents and ambitions would then come into play, might, with their newly-acquired power, prove intractable and turbulent; and further, that those prerogatives are absolutely necessary to carry out intended reforms in a quiet manner, without *endangering the foundations of society. My own conclusion, so far as I am able to form a judgment by personal observation and by much that has been written, is, that while the Emperor will continue an autocrat,* with his ministers, his chancery, and senate, as consulting and legislative bodies, his Government will take the lead in carrying the country through a series of reforms, some of which have been already accomplished; that without interference from the central power a certain local self-government will be conceded; and that on western models a system of national education will be organised to pave the way for future reforms; that the

* The Russian word is Samoderjetz, the etymology of which is precisely the same as the Greek word 'Autocrates'—he who governs by himself.

press will enjoy greater liberty. At the same time, the Government seems to be averse to a parliament elected by the country, which is naturally enough desired by all who, from their position, would be called to take part in such an assembly.

If all these reforms are successfully carried out, a new era will have commenced for Russia with the anniversary of her thousandth birthday, and when they have reached a stage of prescription, she will be in a better position to obtain and to benefit by the acquirement of a more popular government. To hasten that happy time every patriotic Russian should strive, as far as may be in his power, to carry out and consolidate the reforms which have just been granted by promoting agriculture and other forms of industry, and by residing more among those whose labour is the wealth of a country, instead of deeming it the *summum bonum* of life to pass frivolously through it in the garb of a soldier or a tchinovnik. He must no longer look on trade and commerce as either derogatory to a gentleman or too mean an occupation for a man of education, but, on the contrary, as the chief means of advancing the prosperity of his fatherland, of promoting the liberty of its people and a kindlier feeling towards the stranger. He must remember that they can never have these effects if they are abandoned to men who are at once ignorant and despised almost as much as the traders and mechanics of China or Japan. Lastly, it should be the

object of all who have in any way the command over
their fellow-men, to promote their education in all
useful and practical knowledge; in the conviction that
public opinion and the good common sense of the mass
are now more powerful weapons than sword and cannon
for effecting happy revolutions.*

* A ukase sanctioning the formation of provincial and municipal
assemblies has just been promulgated. *January* 1864.

CHAPTER V.

THE EMANCIPATION OF THE SERFS.

The Emancipation a Credit to all Classes in Russia—Serfdom not Ancient in Russia—Its Origin—Slaves and Serfs—Serfdom Abolished, and Re-established by Godounov and Romanov—Peter the Great confirms it—Public Grants of Land, with Serfs attached, under Peter, Catharine, and Paul—The Crown Serfs and those of Private Proprietors—Three Denominations of Serfs—Their Position and Duties—Causes of their Misery—Duties of a Proprietor—The Land belonged to the Serfs—The Russian *Mire*, or Commune—The Artel, or Working Men's Association—Character of the *Mire*—Anecdotes—Pro and Con. of the Communal System of Labour—The Obrok Serfs—The Obrok System of Cultivation—The Semi-Emancipation of 1862—The Dvorovye, or Personal Serfs—Sufferings of the Proprietors—Their Character and Habits—Difficulties of Emancipation—The 3rd March, 1863—The Emancipation completed, except on the Polish Frontier—The final Arrangements—How the Land is paid for—Communal Courts—Effects of Emancipation—Character and Habits of the Russian Peasantry—Whipping—Religion and Patriotic Feelings of the Lower Classes in Russia—Holy Russia—The Peasant as a Soldier or Sailor—Anecdote—Social Traits and prevailing Vices—Cost of Living in Russia—Opinion of a Russian Landowner on the Emancipation—How the Russian People is judged in Western Europe.

WHATEVER may be the future course of the Emperor Alexander II. the emancipation of the serfs must remain the chief and most glorious act of his reign. But although he has nobly directed the movement, still the self-sacrifice of the proprietors and the patient forbearance of the people in their newly-acquired power have been such as to win for them all credit from those who know how great has been the loss of money on one side, how great the provocation to avenge old injuries on the other.

The early history of nearly all the Sclavonic peoples of Europe is involved in no slight uncertainty. But although the accounts of Polish and Russian historians are inconsistent, there is on the whole little doubt that as early as the seventh century there were many families of this race, living under a half-patriarchal, half-democratic polity, of which the most powerful ruled afterwards at Novgorod in the north and Kiev in the south. The burghers of these towns seem to have carried on an extensive caravan trade in furs, amber, &c. with savage tribes on one side and with the luxurious but decaying civilisation of the Byzantine empire on the other. With the arrival of Rurik and his followers, A.D. 862, were first introduced the germs of feudalism and serfdom. Yet it would appear that, during all those dark years of anarchy and blood which followed the great irruptions of barbarians into Western Europe — while Charlemagne was conquering and consolidating his vast empire, and his descendants were parcelling it out and making slaves of its peoples, down to the time of the Mongol conquest of Russia — the only slaves in that country were either prisoners of war, debtors, or those who voluntarily sold themselves into slavery. During this epoch, A.D. 990, Christianity was introduced from Constantinople, and its influence, great wherever it took root, became singularly powerful over the mystical disposition of the Sclavonic races, and helped them in a great measure to support the coming burden from the crushing weight of which they have been only just set free. Speaking of the Tartar dominion, Russian historians are accustomed to extol their countrymen as martyrs who saved Europe at the price of their national existence. With more truth it might be said that the senseless feuds and constant rivalry of their rulers well-nigh brought Europe itself to ruin.

Under Mongol rule the peasant was first bound to the soil, in order to facilitate the collection of the tribute then levied on the whole population. When this yoke was removed, he became again more or less free to remove from one district to another, as desire or necessity might prompt him. The slaves, as before, were bought and sold apart from the land. The system of the Tartars was reimposed by Boris Godounov, as an act of policy to rally the large proprietors around his throne. In the disorders which followed his death it again fell into disuse, and the final establishment of serfdom was reserved for Michael Romanov, acting under the advice of his father, the patriarch Philarete, for the same State reasons which influenced Godounov. Many privileges and immunities were, however, still left to the peasant, now a serf. He could not be sold away

from the land on which he was born, and of which he
considered himself as the proprietor, although he himself was the property of his landlord. He could not be
put to forced labour, but cultivated his land and paid
over a portion of the produce to his landlord, one-third
or one-half, according to circumstances. He was also
free from military service, which was considered too
noble for hinds, and reserved for a special class.* But
all these privileges vanished, one after the other. The proprietor soon abused his powers; Peter the Great wanted
soldiers; and it was only in the reign of Nicholas that
the secret sale of human beings apart from land was
quite done away with.

When the Great Reformer of Russia re-established
the poll-tax, and numbered his people for the purposes
of recruitment, he confirmed and aggravated the condition of the serf. In the lists of population then made
out, the personal slave and soil-bound serf were mixed
up together, and such confusion followed that it soon
became impossible to distinguish the two classes. As
the empire enlarged its bounds, serfdom was introduced
into all those countries (as of the Cossacks, &c.), the
rural populations of which had hitherto been free.
But a certain distinction could still be made among the
peasants and slaves thus condemned to a common
serfdom. The serfs of the Crown lands were still

* The serfdom in Japan at the present day seems to have much of
this character.

distinct from those of private owners. The former, paying their yearly contribution to the Government for the land they occupied, were in comparison free men; at all events, they were not subject to the petty tyranny of a poor but extravagant master. But from the time of Peter the Great to that of the Emperor Paul, the tsars carried out the odious system of bestowing Crown lands, together with the serfs attached to them, as rewards to generals or statesmen, or as presents to favourites. Examples of this had, indeed, been given before, when the States-General in Moscow (1613) gave Crown lands to Minime, the butcher of Novgorod, and to Prince Pojarsky, for their services in driving out the Poles from their native city; but these instances were rare. Menschikov, the favourite of Peter the Great, could travel, it was said, from Riga on the Baltic to Derbend on the Persian frontier, and sleep every night on his own estates. At the age of thirteen he was a poor boy, selling rolls in the Kremlin; when he died he possessed 150,000 families, or about 500,000 peasants. Catharine II. bestowed millions of serfs on the nobility, whose favour she wished to gain, as well as on her fortunate lovers. Of these the Orlovs received 45,000 souls; Potemkin no less than 37,000. Her son Paul, following her example without her reasons and necessities, went beyond her in counting off lands containing upwards of 2,000,000 of souls for the use and profit of the Imperial family. The

Emperor Alexander discontinued the system, and would have abolished serfdom altogether throughout his empire, as he had done in the Baltic provinces (1816-20), if his firmness had been equal to his humanity.

The 42,000,000 of serfs in Russia might be divided in round numbers as follow:—20,000,000 of Crown serfs, 2,000,000 on the Imperial domains, and 20,000,000 under private proprietors. The emancipation of the former, of course, could take place without difficulty, the serfs being simply made tenants of the Crown until they could ransom their land on certain fixed conditions. The emancipation of the rest involved intricate interests, which required all the patience of the Government, proprietor, and peasant to bring to a satisfactory settlement.

When the day named for the emancipation arrived (March 3, 1862), the arrangements were far from complete; and, though serfdom then came nominally and legally to an end, it was in reality retained for another year, in order to reconcile many diversities of interest and opinion.

Serfs might be classed under three denominations :— First, the agricultural serfs, who tilled their land, and either paid their proprietor the *obrok*, or gave him their labour ; secondly, those who pursued any other occupation away from the estate and paid the *obrok* or tribute to their masters, much as is the case with hired slaves in South America ; and, thirdly, the *dvorovyé*, court, or domestic servants. The lot of the former varied with the existence or the absence of the *mire* or commune.

The extent and value of all estates were estimated by the number of souls, i. e. peasants, upon them. If the proprietor farmed his own land, his peasants were obliged to work for him three days a week all the year round. This term was established by law but continually evaded. Some proprietors made the peasant work four, five, or even six days a week during the busy times of seed-sowing and harvest, so that he had little time to cultivate his own plot; and in winter all field labour is impossible. Villages and estates where this slave-driving was in force might always be distinguished by the filth and misery of the peasantry. These were generally found on the estates of small proprietors, of retired *tchinovniks* and *parvenus,* whose debts or whose desire for keeping up appearances served as an excuse for squeezing the unfortunate peasantry to the utmost. A proprietor, who had many times travelled the length and breadth of Russia, told me, that whenever he passed through a village more than usually poor and dirty, with the enclosures badly cultivated and the *isbas* in a state of dilapidation, the answer to enquiries on the subject invariably was, that the *paméschik* or landlord made his peasants work six days a week, and that they had no time for attending to their own affairs. On one or two occasions during my journey through Russia, I put the same questions and received the same reply. These small proprietors of from twenty to fifty souls have been the greatest sufferers by the change. To many the loss of at least three-fourths of their land has been utter ruin. Where the number of the peasants is in too great a proportion to the extent of their land, the money . which they receive would be immediately swallowed up to pay off the mortgage with which most of them were burdened. A fund called the Emancipation Fund was established to relieve the small proprietors of twenty-one serfs or under, who have thus been reduced to great difficulties.

Many wise proprietors, when the subject first took a serious aspect, voluntarily emancipated their personal serfs and made private arrangements with those who possessed their land. A friend of mine, an officer in the navy, when his peasants came, according to old custom, to congratulate him on his return from a long voyage, addressed them seriously on the coming change, and told them that they would soon be independent of his control. With one voice they cried out that they did not wish to be free. Indeed, under an easy and humane master, serfs were almost as much a burden as a profit. They had no other cares than that of labour; and the *paméschik* was bound to them by many ties. He paid their taxes; if their *isba* or hut was burnt down, he gave timber to rebuild it; if the horse, cow, or pig died, he must replace it; if sickness was in the family, he found doctor and medicines; if the harvest was bad, he had to feed them; if they were naked, he must clothe them. In a word, in all their wants they looked up to their *paméschik* for assistance and advice. It is true, this was all charged against them by the proprietor; but the serf was lazy, and was generally deeply in debt. All such proprietors, who behaved to their serfs with real humanity, will find in the emancipation, when the first loss has been got over, a release from many anxieties and much extraordinary expenditure. As the arrangement between them and their serfs has been effected with equity and good feeling, their future relations will be those of respect on the one side and of friendly interest on the other. Men, whose ideas were narrower or whose property was heavily mortgaged, had no alternative but to submit. Few could venture openly to plead the cause of serfdom; for, when once the serfs heard the word emancipation, they were not to be put off any more, and they would not be free without land. 'God gave our forefathers the land to till,' was the logic of the Russian peasant. 'We are the children, the land is therefore ours. The Tsar is God's representative; him and those whom he sets over us we will serve, but the country, the soil is ours.' Such a feeling as this among the peasants was a powerful lever in the hands of Government, and a sword of Damocles hanging over the heads of repugnant proprietors.

RUSSIAN COMMUNAL LIFE. AN 'ARTEL'.

The *mire* * or commune—one of the curious institutions of the Russian people, though not peculiar to them—still retains all its old vitality. Individuality is completely lost in the mass. Not only in agriculture but in commerce and handicraft the Russian lower orders exhibit the same proneness to possess in common. Mr. Mill, I believe, somewhere remarks, that as civilisation advances, men more readily give up their individuality, and act in masses. This disposition is manifest through the whole history of Russia. The Russian people are eminently gregarious in their instincts and occupations, and soon become lost if left to their own individual resources. If a Russian peasant leave or be banished from his village commune to seek his fortune elsewhere; if he become a soldier or a sailor, the same instinct of communism remains with him. In the regiment or on board ship a sort of commune is soon formed among those who are of the same village, district, or *goubernia*. If the peasant become a tailor, cobbler, smith, *isvoschik* or coachman, or takes to any other trade, he soon forms with others an association called, in Russian, *Artel*, or enters into one already formed; and this society in Russia answers the purpose of working men's associations, the order of Odd Fellows, Druids, &c. in England.

* *Mire* in Russian means the 'World.'—The Commune is, indeed, a little world in itself.

For the same reason the Russian peasant seldom emigrates willingly.

Where this *mir* or commune exists, as in Great and White Russias, the mass of land is held by it and cultivated in common, a certain portion of the produce being paid over to the proprietor or so much labour being given as an equivalent for it. The land is measured and portioned out among the different families which form the commune, according to its quality and convenience of situation. There is a public granary, where corn is stored up in case of dearth; there is a communal bath, a communal well, and a communal bull. If the wealth increase, a re-division is made: each male child receives his share on arriving at majority; and a habit of industry is kept up among its members, although it is of course accompanied by a spirit of narrow-minded conservatism. If a member wishes to quit the commune he can do so, but he cannot be re-admitted except by general consent. Besides possessing property in the commune, he can also hold some independently. Every village commune is presided over by its *starost* or elder, who acts as a magistrate, and from whose decision appeal is seldom allowed. A union of several village communes forms a superior commune, which meets to deliberate on the general good, and occasions have not been wanting in their history when they have protested against wrongs and injustice, shown a firm face, and in the end established their rights.

The following anecdote will show how this *mire* or commune is woven into all the habits of Russians. A large emigration took place a few years ago from over-crowded districts to the waste but fertile lands which border the Volga. Every family received a large piece of land with certain privileges. The minister of the Imperial domains soon afterwards visited the new settlement. He found the peasants perfectly satisfied with their lot, with one exception—they had no commune, and prayed the minister to allow it to be established. ' Without the commune,' they urged, ' the justice and equality with which the land had been distributed would soon be troubled. One family would increase faster than another, and so become poorer; another family would remain the same or even decrease, and so become richer than the others : whence would arise all sorts of dissensions and disorder.'

In another instance the lands of a certain commune were required for Government purposes, and its members ordered away to other lands at a short notice. The commune assembled, talked over the matter, and the result was a protest to the Emperor Nicholas, who admitted the justice of the demand, and ordered that the peasants should be left where they were.

Under this institution two-thirds of the Russian

peasantry are born and live. Much has been said and written during the last year or two on the wisdom of continuing or abolishing it. The chief accusations brought against it as a system are—that it is the relic of a barbarous age, unsuited to present civilisation, and deadening individual energy; that, as all men in the *mire* are not equally capable, the progress of one is retarded by the insufficiency of another; that time lost in consultations, which might be more profitably spent in action, leads to lazy and apathetic habits; that the commune often keeps in its body men whose capabilities might find better and more useful employment out of it; and, lastly, that its spirit of stubborn conservatism is a barrier to all improvement either in the peasants themselves or in their mode of agriculture. On the other hand, its advocates not only deny these charges, but insist that it is so deeply rooted in the habits of the people as to be, in practice, indispensable, and that, in order to carry out any good system of national education, the commune, by keeping many families together, is invaluable. It is a happy sign for the welfare of Russia, that her writers, no longer wasting their talents in introducing an exotic literature from France and England, give their attention to the internal condition of their own country and whatever may lead to its improvement.

The surplus serfs on an estate hired themselves out and paid to their proprietors a tribute called *obrok*.

These *obrok* serfs were generally found among the domestic servants in the towns, as coachmen, postboys, vendors of small wares, and as workmen in factories. Many of the small shopkeepers about the different *dvors* or bazaars of St. Petersburg and Moscow were *obrok* serfs. Several had raised themselves to the position of merchants, amassed wealth, and purchased their freedom. One serf, it is said, offered a million roubles to his proprietor for his freedom, and was refused, the proud noble declaring that he would relish the luxury of having a millionnaire serf. The same nobleman possessed a serf who, having attracted the attention of an Italian artist by his fine voice, was taken by his patron to Italy; whence he returned to Russia with an Italianised name. But he was still a serf, and, though his master would not take the *obrok* from him, he was compelled to attend on certain occasions, when the Prince gave a great dinner, to charm the guests by his singing.

As a great part of the proprietors were absentees during many months of the year, their estates were cultivated on the *obrok* system. The peasants under the *starost* or chief man, and sometimes controlled by an agent of the proprietor, undertook the entire management of the estate, whether under the communal system of Great Russia or that of separate farms, as in the Ukrain. The proprietor furnished nothing but seed. The peasants ploughed, dunged, sowed, and gathered in their harvest with their own implements, took the produce to market and sold it, and paid over to the *paméschik* or his agent a portion of the profits, generally from one-fourth to one-third, and kept the rest themselves. But in these cases they had to bear all risks from fire, tempests, or disease among themselves or their cattle.

The new laws chiefly touched those peasants who actually possessed land, whether held by manual or horse labour or by paying *obrok*. The right to the soil was the chief difficulty to be overcome. Every male adult peasant had a right to his *isba* and a plot of land on the estate, partly arable, partly grass, of about eight acres, but often less in valuable districts, though that quantity was fixed as the medium by the Government. For this land he paid an equivalent, either in labour, money, or kind; and for the future he will pay the same, under a somewhat different arrangement.

Where the commune exists it will re-imburse the proprietor. In other parts of the country, where the land is divided into hereditary farms, each peasant will receive about the same area of land, which he must ransom at once or by degrees from the proprietor, or from the Government who advances the money for him. In cases where there is no actual possession of land, where the estate is too small for the number of serfs, the peasant, after the two years of forced service, i. e. after March 3, 1863, can pass on to Crown lands, where he will receive wood from the Government for building an *isba*, and a sum of money to commence life with.

Peasants paying the *obrok* could, during the two years of probation, arrange with their landlords to capitalise their *obrok* at the rate of six per cent. or five per cent. in some districts. Artisans, small dealers, domestic servants, and others who exercised any calling and paid their *obrok*, continued to do so until 1863, but during that time the master could neither recall him from his employment or increase his *obrok*.

The *dvorovyé* or personal servant became simply free on March 3, 1863, and henceforward will get his living as he can. Numbers of them immediately inscribed their names as *meschani*, in order to exercise some petty commerce. During the following month more than 4,000 inscribed their names in the commune of Cronstadt alone, not necessarily to reside there, but because the tax of that town was trifling compared with the tax of the capital. The emancipation of this class will be a great relief to many masters and mistresses, who can thus get rid of half their lazy, lounging, and unprofitable servants. In many families these personal serfs were a thorough and permanent nuisance. They considered themselves as much bound to their masters as their agricultural fellows considered themselves bound to the land. Lounging about the mats when the master was at home, snoring on the velvet arm-chair when he was absent, the Russian servant has been often painted by foreigners. With all his peculiarities and dirty habits, he was generally honest and affectionate. Feeling himself one of the family, he took an interest in it as such ; always said *nash*, 'our,' when speaking of the property of his master, and sometimes, in minor matters, such as with the *vodka* bottle, hair-brush, or such like, carried his ideas of communism into practice. I know families who have tried to get rid of drunken, dishonest, lazy, or dirty servants ;—who have beaten them, put them in prison, sent them miles away—in vain. They would soon wander back, with the sagacity of dogs in keeping to their old masters, would blubber out their promises of amendment, and take up their old stations again. A Russian proprietor will now be free from all these encumbrances, and in place of half a dozen lazy fellows whom he only fed, he can take one good servant to do double the work of six; only he must pay him his due wages.

A measure like this emancipation could not of course be carried through without great difficulty and loss both to individuals and the nation, especially as theories of still more important changes were mixed up with it. Yet March 3, 1862, passed by without any disturbances, although the delay discontented both proprietor and peasant. The former wished to be rid at once of his uncertain position: the peasant, nominally freed, had to remain a forced labourer for twelve months more.

Later in the year its effects began to be severely felt by many. Incomes were reduced one half; thousands of families who had lived in affluence in the capitals were obliged to retire to their diminished estates or to foreign countries. Families living abroad found themselves suddenly without their incomes, and hastened back to remedy the evil by their presence. On many estates the peasants *struck*, and would do no work, or just what they pleased, causing total loss or great waste to the crops on which the incomes of the proprietors in great part depended. Yet after all, good must come out of the evil. The peasant and the absentee landlord had been too long strangers to each other. The proprietor must soon from necessity live more on his estate, and his presence and example must lead to the improvement of his tenantry.

At last the eventful day, March 3, 1863, arrived. It was also the anniversary of the Emperor's accession. The peace of the country was not in the least disturbed, and the efforts of the revolutionary party failed before the obstinate good sense and immobility of the Russian rural classes. From that day the serfs in all the Russias became free. And this freedom means, that he will have the liberty of his movements, of his labour, and the full enjoyments of the fruit earned by the sweat of his brow; he can marry whom and when he pleases; he can no longer be beaten, banished to Siberia, or carried off to the ranks of the army in some province distant from his village, at the will of a cruel or capricious master. Henceforth he is the master of his own land if he can pay for it, or a tenant of the Crown or of the proprietor according to circumstances, until he can do so; he cannot be punished without the sanction of a magistrate, and is only subject to the lawful call of the conscription.

By the end of the same month ninety-five per cent. of all the serfs in Russia had become free; 8,642,909 men and their families began a new kind of life, and of these 1,195,715 had already paid for their land and become proprietors themselves. The only districts where the arrangements were not completed were in Lithuania and on the Polish frontier, where the unsettled state of society owing to the Polish insurrection and the intrigues of the small proprietors had retarded their accomplishment.

Here the Government intervened with a high hand. A ukas of March 13 ordered the immediate completion of the emancipation. If not carried out before May 1 by amicable arrangement it was to be forcibly brought to a close by the Government, which would then indemnify the proprietor in full, leaving the peasants to pay the *obrok* to the Government until they are able to reimburse the principal.

A few words will explain to the reader the terms of the final arrangements. Up to March 3 the affair was left to the proprietor and peasants to settle in a friendly manner, and, as is seen, with tolerable success. Only, in case of the obstinacy of either party, a law was passed for every district according to its special wants, by which the price to be paid for the land and the term of payment were fixed. In giving the summary of this law and the bases on which it was fixed, I take a district of which I had the particulars; but it must be remembered that both the quantity of land given and the price paid for it varied according to situation, fertility, and the means of transport. In this district every male adult peasant receives his isba with its little enclosure free, besides three dessiatins,* more or less, of mixed arable and meadow land, for which at some time or another he must pay at the rate of fifty roubles per dessiatin, in all, 150 roubles silver, or about 24*l.* English money. If he pay this, he is at once a proprietor; if he be unable to do so (which is generally the case), he must pay rent to the proprietor at six per cent. per annum until the Government have paid the principal for him. In this case the Government pays 120 out of the 150 roubles, leaving the peasant to pay the remaining thirty roubles himself to the proprietor, as by agreement between them. The sum advanced by the State, with the interest, must be repaid during a term extending over forty-nine years. But, as the Government was unable to find so large a sum at once, bonds, bearing interest at

* 1 dessiatin = 2.699 acres English.

five per cent. were issued, a series of which are to be drawn and cancelled every month.*   When the serfs were in excess of the land on any estate, the proprietor was required to* give up two-thirds of the land to his peasants, and to retain the other third, the surplus peasants being removed to Government lands.

On certain large estates cultivated on the *obrok* system, things are to remain as they are until the year 1865, when the distribution of three dessiatins, more or less, to each peasant must take place.   But during this time the *obrok* cannot be increased.   This in reality amounts simply to this, that the peasants remain tenants until that year.   In all these transactions, when the commune existed, as it does in most villages of Russia Proper, neither the Government on the one side, nor the *paméschik* on the other, has anything to do with the peasants themselves.   The head man or *starost* of the commune, after consulting his fellows, arranged all matters with the proprietors and Government, and will, for the future, pay the rent or instalments of the principal.   In the system of local self-government lately granted to the communes, a court has been established, called the Communal Court, for enforcing

---

* These bonds of 100 roubles, negotiable on the Exchange at St. Petersburg, at first fell very low, but, owing to some foreign speculation, rallied, and are now quoted at about 87 roubles (September 1863).   Those proprietors who were in immediate want of their money were great losers by disposing of them ou their first issue.

A 'KABAK' OR DRAM SHOP.

all the above stipulations, and for settling disputes between proprietor and tenant.

The effects of this eventful change upon the peasantry, for whose special benefit it has been carried through, cannot be thoroughly estimated for years to come; and until their whole social life shall have been reorganised and things find their level, there must necessarily be the greatest uncertainty. At present the people are too excited by a change which their common sense now tells them ought to have been accomplished years ago. During all this time they have been deceived into the belief that the state of serfdom was only in accordance with God's providence and the order of human life upon earth. The next few years will be the most critical period in the history of the country. They will witness the awakening from slumber to life — the transition from a state of deception to the light of truth. If these years should pass without disturbance, a wonderful change for the better will be seen in Russia, and many ignoble traits in the character of its people, the result of serfdom and social oppression, will be effaced.

Under Mongol rule the Sclave of Russia acquired that deep religious sentiment which is one of his characteristics, and which, though mechanical and superstitious, is free from bigotry. He is tolerably patient of other creeds, while he is fanatically attached to his own. Of a very forgiving disposition, he is rarely guilty of acts of violence, and then only when maddened by long tyranny or under the influence of drink. Never except at a time when they have been exasperated by years of brutal treatment have the peasants risen against their proprietors; but then their rage has been always fearful. Although ignorant, they are acute, and with a natural wit and humour are ready at repartee. Living a monotonous life in a monotonous country, they are for ever moving round and round in the same circle, and are by nature and habit strictly conservative. Their docility and obedience is that of sheep, whom a dog's bark will keep in the right path. It is true that their obedience has been as yet too often shown as the obedience of fear, enforced by the stick; and it is yet to be seen, since corporal punishment has been abolished, what moral means will effectually replace it. 'During my life,' says M. Koschelev in the 'Moscovsky Vedomost,' 'I have hired many thousand workmen for different purposes, and I must confess that the non-fulfillment of the agreement on the part of the workmen was not the rule but the exception. Yet I consider it my duty to add the following important fact:—my workmen were subject to corporal punishment. Twice I tried to do away with it, but was obliged to return to it by the repeated demands of my overseers. Certainly we had recourse to it as seldom as possible; yet, entirely without it, the taskmaster and *starosts* could not manage their people.'

The Russians are eminently a pastoral, agricultural,

and bartering race, and not at all the warlike people which they are sometimes supposed to be. Two powerful levers can alone raise in them anything like military enthusiasm. They must feel first that their religion or their country is in danger. Their patriotism is, indeed, one of their striking features, as indeed it is of all Sclavonic peoples. But for Russians these two sentiments have the greater force, because they look upon themselves as the only Sclavonic people who have succeeded in founding an empire of their own. Holy Russia is no empty word. When their country has been invaded, the Russian of every class has well known how to rise, and sacrifice self and property in its defence, as the Poles found even in the sixteenth century, as Charles XII. found at Poltava, as Napoleon found at Moscow and during his retreat. In all the wars of conquest against the Turks, stubborn religious enthusiasm often helped to gain the victory. This enthusiasm was invoked during the Crimean war to little purpose. But should the so-called reconstitution of Poland be attempted by a force which may menace orthodox provinces of Russian Poland, such as Kiev, the war would at once take the character of a crusade, and not only the peasants of those provinces, but all classes in Russia, would rise as a man for their defence. Although the Russian peasant, less from the hardships of the service than from the repugnance of his nature, detests military life, still, when once he is enrolled and under strict discipline, his very ignorance, stubbornness, and blind obedience make of his class, directed by able officers, one of the most formidable armies in the world.

For the same reason that he hates being a soldier or a sailor, and dreads Siberia, the Russian seldom or never deserts his colours, as he knows that such a step would banish him from his village home as inevitably as exile to the Amoor. Deserters from the Russian army or navy are nearly all Jews or Poles, who find among their fellows in foreign countries associations ready formed, into which they can enter, with a home and assistance until they are able to provide for themselves. That this seldom happens with a pure orthodox Russ, the following incident will help to show :—Going ashore one morning a few years ago at Nangasaki, we were startled, as we passed a Dutch vessel at anchor in the bay, by a splash in the water, and cries for help from a man who was swimming towards our boat. We took him in, and learnt that he was one of three Russians, who, with several Poles, had been decoyed to desert the year before at Hong-Kong. The Russians soon found themselves alone, ill-treated by their new skipper, and without that mutual support to which they had been accustomed. Suffering from home-sickness, they determined to risk all the terrors which they knew to be in store for them, and took the first opportunity of giving themselves up. A boat was immediately sent to demand

Schedovsky, del.
Hanhart, lith.

the other two Russians, who were confined below on board the Dutchman, and they were immediately given up. Fortunately they found in Admiral Popov a lenient commander, who thought they had been punished enough by the consequences of their act.

In their personal habits the Russian peasantry are indolent, dirty, and careless. Though a Saturday seldom passes without the *moujik* seething in a steam bath, yet, as he puts on his dirty sheep-skins immediately afterwards, the beneficial effect of the bath is not perceived. Their *isbas* are seldom clean in the interior, and the heat of the large stone on which they lie in winter attracts all the vermin of the neighbourhood.

Drunkenness is one of the chief vices of all the lower orders in Russia, though they are seldom quarrelsome in their cups. In their social habits they are very good-natured and hospitable, though rough; and, to cover a multitude of faults, they show no little charitable and kindly feeling one towards the other.

If left quite to himself, the Russian peasant, like the Celt in Ireland, will work just enough to supply his wants, and no more. It is true that, hitherto, he has had few inducements to better his condition. He will cultivate a little buckwheat for his *kasha*,* a plot of

---

* *Kasha*, the grain of buckwheat, boiled and eaten like rice in the East, or made into cakes, forms, with *tschee* or cabbage soup, the favourite food of the Russian peasantry. Not that they do not get more

cabbages for his *tschee*; the sale of a pig, calf, or an odd job, will provide him with *vodka* and tobacco; sheep-skins supply his clothing, which he makes up for himself, and which serve his wife and children after him. It has been feared by some that immediate emancipation might have the effect of making the Russian peasant too much like his fellow in the west of Ireland. Not accustomed to have any demands made on him except by his proprietor, he will at first be at a loss in managing his own affairs. But this very necessity ought 'to have the effect of rousing him from his apathy and of calling forth all his energies.

In concluding this sketch of the Russian peasant, I avail myself of the judgment and opinions of a large landowner, which, grounded on the experience of twenty years, seems truthful, and may serve to explain many topics on which I have only lightly touched. ' My estates,' says Mr. Koschelev, ' contain several solid food, as the following table of a peasant's monthly cost in a cheap government will show :—

Rye-meal, 2 puds, or 80 lbs.	2, 00	roubles
Kasha, 2 measures at 35 copecks	70	,,
Beef, 9 lbs. at 7 ,,	63	,,
Linseed-oil, 1½ lbs. at 20 ,,	30	,,
Salt, 2 lbs. at 5½ ,,	11	,,
Cooking	25	,,
	3, 99	,,

These figures represent the old depreciated paper roubles, worth only one-third of a rouble silver. Paper roubles are now at about five per cent. discount only. The 3 roubles 99 copecks equal 4*s*. English money.

thousand souls. I inherited them from various proprietors, some of whom had been careful, some careless of the weal of their peasants. As they came under my control, I could immediately perceive that the well-being of the peasants was in an order inverse to the care which had been taken of them by their former masters. In a short time those about whom their proprietors had never troubled themselves soon improved their circumstances, both communal and private, when they were made to manage their affairs themselves. On the other hand, those who had been accustomed to look up to their *paméschik* in every little matter—who could neither buy or sell without his advice or consent—who could not stray from their village—whose marriages must even be arranged by him and celebrated at his own house — were for a long time unable to order an independent household. I had ten times more trouble with these than all the rest who had lived under absentee or careless landlords. Thanks to God, and to my resolution not to meddle in the private or communal affairs of my people, their condition has become much improved! Tumble-down huts are becoming rare (I make them pay for their wood); the corn magazines of the commune are well stocked; there are not so many drunkards among them; in a word, I am convinced that I am indebted for these improvements to my not troubling myself about their private affairs.

' This care or meddling on the part of the proprietor,

now becoming more rare, was not so much from a movement of charity or any appreciation of the duties of a proprietor, as from a stern necessity. The rapid spread of agriculture, the partial exhaustion of the soil, the need of a more careful husbandry, the difficulty of transport from the place of production to the place of consumption or export, the extension of cattle-breeding, the establishment of various industrial works — were all causes which made labourers more scarce, and the proprietor more desirous of keeping them in leading-strings. Having seen so many examples of this, I have come to the conclusion that the peasant, free to dispose of his own labour, and no longer looking exclusively to his proprietor for subsistence, will be the best founder of his own prosperity.'

To Western Europe the Russian people are almost unknown, seldom awakening any interest, and never meeting with any confidence or sympathy. Often judged of from absurd rumours, they are misunderstood, over-valued, and not unfrequently feared, when sensation writers dwell on the probabilities of another barbarian invasion, in which the Russians are to play the first part. This dread must be traced to the ambition of their Government, and to the mistrust with which its acts are regarded by other Governments. But it is unfair to estimate a people like the Russians by the acts of their Government. It is unjust to judge them by a standard which may serve as a fit test under very different circumstances. Allowance must be made for their peculiar position, for the influence of their climate and soil, for their previous experience and training, first under the Tartars, and then under despotic and sometimes cruel masters. Custine was highly unjust towards the Russian people, of whose character and language he knew nothing, and of whom he only saw enough to find out their bad qualities, which lie exposed on the surface. If we choose to write about the weaknesses of human nature, a book may soon be filled; but theories and prejudices are bad guides for anyone who wishes to arrive at a just conclusion.

CHAPTER VI.

THE INTERIOR OF RUSSIA AND THE FAIRS OF THE UKRAIN.

The *Podorójnaa*—Modes of Travelling in Russia—The *Tarantas*—The *Teléga*—What a *Poputchik* is—My first *Poputchik*—A rich Virgin—Incidents of the Road—Pleasures of travelling *Pericladnoi*—Roads—Post-horses—Stations—Tea-drinking—Character of Interior of Russia—The Corn Lands—Difficulties of Transport—Cost of Living—Proposed Railroad from Moscow to Sevastopol—Aspect of Russian Towns and Villages—*Isbas* of Peasantry—Belgorod and its Churches—Kharkov—Hotel Accommodation in the Interior of Russia—Universities of Russia—Fairs of the Ukrain—The *Isvoschik* of Great Russia—The *Tchumaki*—Mode of Trading—The Jews—Karaimi—The Pedlars—Their Artels—The *Orpheni*—The *Sloboshanen*—Trade of these Fairs—Contrast of the Great Russians or Muscovites and the Little Russians or Cossacks.

BEFORE leaving St. Petersburg I had provided myself with that important paper, called a *podorójnaa*, without which it is impossible to obtain horses or travel in the interior of Russia. As I had heard much of the inconveniences endured by private travellers from the whims and exactions of postmasters, who are generally as overbearing towards a merchant or a private person as they are servile to anyone in a uniform of high rank or with an order on his breast, I had obtained a Government pass, in order to get horses immediately at all the stations. The officer who gave it wished me to understand that an ordinary one would suffice, as matters were now so well arranged; but I had received too many warnings to take all he said for granted, and insisted on a Government pass, which carried me without any trouble to my destination, and saved me, besides, many little expenses on the road.

All the places in the diligence for Kharkov from Moscow were taken for some ten days in advance; but for this I did not much care, as I was in no great hurry to get over the ground. The only other available conveyances were a *tarantas* (a sort of hooded carriage, which must be purchased or hired, slung on poles instead of springs, but admirably suited to the bad roads of Russia); or the *teléga* (an open springless cart with two ropes and a sack of straw for a seat, but which costs nothing at all). This mode of travelling is called in Russia *pericladnoi* or shifting, because the passenger is turned from one *teléga* to another at every station.

Not wishing to travel 800 miles alone, I strolled down to the post-station to ask for a *poputchik* or travelling companion. In Russia, where the distances are immense between the towns, and public conveyances so few, a travelling companion is generally sought, and notices for such are posted up in the post-stations. Merchants especially who are pressed for time are always anxious to meet with a *poputchik* armed with a Government *prodorójnaa*, as they are thereby insured against delay, and various exactions from the postmasters, who sometimes have not a horse in the stable, until they have pressed the hand of the traveller. To travel, therefore, with an officer or a *tchinovnik* the merchant is sometimes willing to pay the whole expense of the horses, besides giving the use of his carriage. During my journey south I had *poput-chiks* of divers grades—here a farmer, there a merchant, a sore-footed soldier and sailor whom I picked up on the road, and a Georgian returning to Tiflis.

On reaching the post-station I was told that a certain person having his own carriage would leave Moscow in two hours for Orel. I immediately sought out my gentleman, whom I found to be the intendant of Prince M——, and it was soon arranged that I should share his *tarantas* and the expense of the horses. As my *impedimenta*, when travelling, never gave me much trouble, I was ready to his time, and at 4 o'clock in the afternoon, after a parting glass of champagne, the *yamshik* cried ' C' Bogom ' to his three horses, and we darted through the streets. At one of the gates of the Ketai Gerod in the Kremlin, where a small chapel contains a miraculous image of the Virgin, thronged day and night by the faithful, our carriage stopped for a few minutes, while my companion went in to kiss the image, pay a short devotion, and burn a candle for the prosperity of our voyage.

This little incident in the beginning of our journey

gave me some insight into the character of my fellow-traveller.   He was evidently a Russ of the most national and orthodox type.   When we got fairly out of the city, he let me know that the Virgin to whom he had just paid a visit was one of the holiest and richest of all Russia; so rich, indeed, that she had been known to come to the assistance of the Government in a time of need, when a little ready cash was very acceptable.   So we travelled on together through the night, stopping for an hour at every third station, ordering a *somovar*, and making tea, my companion drinking six glasses to my one.   The next day we arrived at Toula, the seat of the iron manufacture of Russia, and famous for its guns and sword blades, *somovars*, and other working in metals, in imitation of the old Damascene and Oriental arts.

Although my *poputchik* was a man of coarse exterior and of the simplest education, he possessed a fund of common sense and practical knowledge, especially in all that concerned the agriculture of the country, He had heard of the 'Kolokol' and M. Herzen, and wanted me to give him all information about them, but at that time I knew as little of either as he did, During the three days we remained together, I could not help remarking his piety or superstition, whichever the reader may judge it to be.   We never passed a church but he crossed himself; not a beggar implored alms but the *tarantas* was stopped to give a few *copecks*. There could be no doubt about this latter virtue. Among no other people have I remarked so much charity and alms-giving as among the national classes of Russia. At Orel we parted, he proceeding by a cross road to the estates of his employer, I continuing my journey alone in a *teléga* for want of some better conveyance.

Oh ye happy travellers in first-class railway carriages! ye learned writers in the 'Lancet' on the influence of railroads on health, who make long phrases about the want of elasticity! make a journey in the interior of Russia for a few hundred versts in a *teléga*, and then describe its influence on the human body. He who has mounted for the first time and ridden fifty miles on a bad-trotting horse, and remembers the symptoms which appeared about the second day afterwards, may form some idea of the pleasures of travelling in the *teléga*! The nerves are stretched up to snapping-point, and then become relaxed with a jerk, which seems to make every part of the body change place, and requires the strongest exertions of the muscles to preserve a balance. But, as with everything else in this world which cannot be avoided, the traveller gets accustomed even to a *teléga*.

Between Moscow and Kharkov the road is macadamised, a chaussée, as they call such roads in Russia. Other roads of the same kind start from this centre to Poland on the one side, to Irkutsk on the other; to

Vladimir and Nijni Novgorod, &c. The cross roads and others not made are generally well beaten tracks, even and passable enough in fine weather, or with a sledge when snow is on the ground, but axle-deep in mud and almost impassable in wet weather and after a thaw. On most of the highways the post-horses are furnished by the peasants who live near the *stansie* or stations, and as there is a little competition among them, the lines are well served. In other districts where the horses are Government property, great difficulty sometimes is found in procuring them, as the postmaster will always keep back his best horses on the chance that a general or other great man may pass that way. The cost of horses is very small, varying from one and a half to five *copecks* each horse per verst, according to locality; the number of horses to be furnished is written on the *podorójnaa*, but it is varied according to season, the kind of vehicle, and the number of passengers. Sometimes, however, the postmaster, according as his horses have much work or not, will only give you the number marked on the pass—these hardly sufficing to drag you through the mud; or he will force on you more than your carriage requires, in order to make use of his horses. Frequent disputes thus arise; but as the regulations admit an interpretation, the traveller has to submit at last. I was once witness to a scene between an ensign and the *starost* of the station, who insisted on putting three horses to a *teléga* in which were three persons. The poor *starost*, who was perfectly right, was fearfully abused and beaten with the fist about the face, but the wrathful officer had to give in at last. As I was never unwilling to take an extra horse when forced on me, although the two allowed by the post regulations were more than enough, I got on very well. The horses are small, strong, and hardy beasts, and a promise of a double *za vodka* to the *yamshik* if he did the fifteen or seventeen versts of a monotonous road within the hour, carried me quickly on my way. Crying 'C' Bogom,' or ' God be with you,' to his horses, off they would start, and an occasional *pst*, or a *bour-r-r* sound made by a vibration of the lips was enough to keep them in full gallop to the next station. At every station is a book chained to the table, in which complaints are entered by travellers, and I often amused myself during the few minutes of delay in looking over them. But the postmaster takes good care to keep out of sight the name of anyone whose complaint would be likely to attract notice. As these stations are often at a great distance from towns where any inn-accommodation is to be found, chambers are provided in which a traveller may rest, if he be so inclined; but with few exceptions they are so dirty that few make a longer halt than they are obliged. A *somovar* of hot water is always provided for a few *copecks* to make tea, of which the traveller should carry his own supply. No one who has not travelled in Russia can imagine the luxury and the relief from fatigue which a glass of good tea can give: it is true, it is the only luxury which he must expect in the interior of Russia.

The surface of European Russia presents three distinct aspects,—the vast northern forests of larch and pine, which extend into Lithuania and Poland; the rich and black grounds of the interior, stretching southward to the steppes: and, lastly, the steppes themselves, always woodless, often without water, and in many places forming salt marshes.   Covered from spring to the end of summer with thick vegetation and flowers of a hundred different hues, they are as pleasing to the eye as they are monotonous and dreary in autumn and winter.   Although the land is exceedingly rich, it is only on and near the rivers, which flow sluggishly through them, that there is at all a dense population.   Every year, however, the wide space between the rivers is becoming settled.

The following table will show the division of Russian and Polish soil, taken from the statistics of Tengoborsky :—

Arable land . . . . . . *dessiatins* 90	millions
Cultivated meadow and steppe pasture land . . 110	,,
Woods and forests 180	,,
Barren land 120	,,
Forming a total of . . 500	,,

of *dessiatins*, each of which is about 2⅔ acres.

The great corn-growing districts are the Baltic and Polish provinces, whose outlet is Riga; the south-west

K

governments, whose port is Odessa; and the country around the Don and the Volga, whence the corn is conveyed to Taganrog and other ports of the Sea of Azov by coasting vessels, to be shipped to the ports of the Mediterranean.   Lastly, the country through which I was travelling presented, mile after mile, and day after day, one monotonous panorama of cornfields of rich black humus, as far as the eye can reach.   Unfortunately the price of transport sometimes amounts to six times the value of corn.   Russia alone produces more than 300,000,000 of *chetverks* * of grain, or 27,060,000 quarters, out of which she exports about one twenty-fifth part.   Any quantity might be produced if a market could be found for it.   At present, if more be grown above the wants of the country, the fall in the price on an abundant harvest would be so great, that the expenses of reaping and harvesting could hardly be covered by the sale.   In many districts where communication is especially difficult, most of the corn is bought up by the Government for distillation; or, where private distilleries are allowed, it is made into brandy at the remote farms to render it less bulky for transport. When the rivers are frozen up, which is the case for five months in the year, and when there is no snow for sledge transport, wagon transport is impossible, as much from the difficulties of nature as from its enor-

* A chetverk = 0·0902 quarters, English.

mous expense.   One or two great trunk railroads with good roads for cross communication can alone prevent the enormous waste of productive forces in Russia, and bring about greater equality in the prices of the necessities of life.   Corn and other produce, which cost one rouble on the spot of their production, have increased to ten or twelve times that value on arriving at the place of consumption or shipment.   In some provinces a family of three persons may be fairly fed and clothed for about eight shillings a month: in others that sum will hardly suffice for the same family during three days.*

All the towns in Russia which are the capitals of goubernia, with the exception of the most ancient, such as Kiev, Vladimir, &c., have one monotonous character. A triumphal arch is generally the entrance: a straggling collection of buildings then opens to view, which on nearer approach discovers wide and regular streets, with sometimes a few fine public buildings and churches.   Towns and villages alike cover immense

* In the summer of 1863 a concession was given by the Russian Government to an English Company for the railroad between Moscow and Sevastopol. The capital to be subscribed is to amount to twenty-three million pounds sterling, guaranteed at five per cent. interest by the Government; the line to be completed in six years. This line will pass through the richest part of Russia and some of the largest towns of the interior, such as Toula, Orel, Koursk, Kharkov, Ekaterinoslav, and from this latter city through the Perekop to Sevastopol, which is to become a commercial port of the first class. This railroad would soon absorb all the carrying trade of the many fairs of the Ukrain.

surfaces.* Droshkys are as necessary to get over the space in a small town (that is, small as to the number of its inhabitants), as they are to avoid the mud in bad weather. The villages and hamlets are mostly a collection of mud or wooden hovels, standing each in its small enclosure, with here and there a more solid-built house, conspicuous from its green-painted roof. In the huts of the Russian peasantry in some places the traveller might fancy himself in the west of Ireland. Groups of listless, lazy, and dirtily-clad men, women, and children hang about the doors in fine weather, among beasts of burden, agricultural implements and dung-hills, or lie promiscuously about the floor, or crowd together on the stove in winter. The pig has a free entry through the door, the fowls nestle on the rafters, and there are seldom any windows to admit light or fresh air. Some villages, however, present a more favourable appearance, and in a few isbas which I entered, I found cleanliness and comfort. This was especially the case in the steppes, where the climate and disposition of the inhabitants incline them to a more agreeable life. Nearly everywhere the character of the peasantry reflected the character of the proprietor.

Every straggling lot of huts called a village has its

---

* This is especially the case in the south and in Little Russia, of which it has been remarked by some Russian author, that the towns resemble villages and hamlets, while the villages and hamlets are like towns.

two or three churches. In one town through which I passed, called Belgorod, between Koursk and Kharkov, I counted the belfries and Byzantine porches of no less than fifteen churches, rising above the 200 huts and houses which formed the village. Church-building is still quite a rage in Russia, though less so than formerly. Ignorant but wealthy merchants, who have passed their lives in trickery and hard dealing, ease their consciences of a legion of peccadillos by building a church or presenting it with a set of bells when built. The Empress Elizabeth especially had this passion, and the many such monuments which she left behind her must be looked upon as what she considered her atonement for various sins which pricked her conscience, and their number may be estimated accordingly.

After two or three days' jolting in a telega, I was not sorry to take a short rest in the hotel at Kharkov, which was a fairly comfortable one for Russia; for, with the exception of those of St. Petersburg, Moscow, and Odessa, there are, properly speaking, no inns in Russia. At best they are caravanserais to receive the traveller and provide him shelter from the elements, and even for this he must pay dearly enough. In the towns of the interior a miserable room costs from two to four roubles silver (6s. to 12s.) a day. He can find something to eat if he be an old traveller and not too nice in appetite; but the tourist accustomed to a comfortable *salle à manger* and white-necked waiters would be driven to despair at the hospitality of a Russian inn. A really good dinner was in Russia to be had only in private houses. Among the good gastronomers of Moscow the guests are invited, an hour or so before dinner, to visit the kitchen and inspect the preparations. The fish may be seen swimming lively in a tank, and the fish picked out by any guest is placed before him at table a short time afterwards. One useful hint I may repeat, which applies equally to Russia or any out-of-the-way country. Be content with the usual meats of the country; take what is given, or, better still, cook for yourself; but on no account order your dinners unless you know the capabilities of the cook. So with what you drink; drink quass, vodka, tea, or water, but beware of ordering foreign wine! You will certainly get some if you do, for all wines can be produced in Russia: but, as with Professor Anderson's wonderful bottle, champagne, claret, port wine, or hock, flow from a common source.

The room into which I was shown at the hotel was a large bare space, with a bedstead, a Russian stove, and two chairs. The traveller generally brings his own bed-clothes with him, but in this hotel they provided them at my desire, adding an extra charge to the bill. As the servant-boy was making up the bed, I examined the sheets well. My reasons for doing so arose from an anecdote which I had heard of this very inn from an acquaintance. He had been sent, during the Crimean war, from Sevastopol to St. Petersburg, and, wishing to rest after three days' successive jolting, ordered the boy to put sheets on the bed, and to look to it that they were clean. As their appearance did not satisfy him, he said to the servant, 'Somebody has already slept on those sheets.' 'No, your honour; they are quite clean,' said the boy. 'It is a lie. Go and fetch thy master.' When the hotel-keeper made his entry, the officer addressed him thus : 'How is this ? I order clean sheets, and some one else has already slept in these.' 'Yes, your honour, but he was a general, and only slept in them once.'

This was said with such emphasis, as though the man could not possibly understand why a mere captain did not think it an honour to sleep between a pair of sheets in which so great a personage as a general had slept before him.

The interior of Russia is not a desirable place wherein to fall ill; my nature happily arranged itself so well that I could not have found a better place than Kharkov to work off a fever which I had caught somewhere on the road. Kharkov has a medical university, and in its able professor I found all that aid and kindness which are so grateful to a sick man. After I had been blistered and leeched (for which operations the barber's services are still called for in Russia), the head was relieved, and during the convalescence of a fortnight I had time to look round the town of Kharkov.

Besides being the chief town of the goubernia and the seat of one of the five Russian universities,* Kharkov is the central point of an extensive trade, and holds annually four large fairs, each lasting three weeks or a month. One of these was being held at the time of my visit. Nearly all the commerce of Little Russia and the Ukrain is carried on at these fairs, which are peculiar to this part of the country. In western lands fairs are fast falling into disuse before steamboats and railways, and in Russia they will share the same fate when that country is blessed with better means of transport.   In the goubernia of Kharkov there are no less than 425 fairs every year, and in the adjoining government of Poltava 372. As the Little Russians are not much given to commerce, almost all the trade is carried on by Muscovite merchants and Jews, who pass the greater part of the year in moving from one fair to another. It is an instructive and curious sight, in strolling through the streets of sheds, to watch the different types and manners of the dealers, the various carriers and their conveyances, from the *Isvos-chik* of Great Russia with his horses and telega to the *Tchumaki* with their droves of oxen, with which they pass to and fro over the monotonous steppes, bringing fish and salt, lamb-skins or foreign produce from the

* St. Petersburg, Moscow, Kiev, Kazan, and Kharkov, are the Universities of Russia Proper; Helsingfors is that of Finland; and Dorpat that of the Baltic Provinces.

Crimea to the different fairs of the interior. These old types will soon pass away from among the people, when the puffing engine rolls rapidly over the steppe, sweeping away the last traces of their calling.

'Soon,' says a Little Russian poet in a tone of melancholy regret, 'soon will the *Tchumak* with his traditions and popular song become a thing of the past; no more, with his sun-burnt face, his tarred shirt, a short pipe in his mouth, his bare head exposed to sun and wind, will he be seen strolling beside his patient oxen over the ash-coloured steppe, humming some melody as melancholy as the steppe itself, and as monotonous as the slow and measured tread of his beasts.'

Like all other labouring classes in Russia, these carriers form themselves into Artels, choose themselves a leader (*starost* in Great Russia, *ataman* in the steppes), and possess and enjoy all things in common during their journeys.

The manner in which trade is carried on at these fairs presents a curious picture of Russian life and trading habits. Nearly all transactions are by barter of native produce against manufactures or foreign produce; or by an extensive system of credit based on no capital or guarantee on the side of the retailers, but simply on the honest character of the purchaser. A merchant with money buys of the manufacturer at twelve or even eighteen months' credit, and immediately resells at six months' to another trader, when he discounts his own bills.* The Jews and hawkers next buy the wares, also on credit, and from their hands they are soon distributed over the country from Galicia to the Volga. If a misfortune should happen to any of them, the last thing a creditor does is to go to law, which would infallibly eat up all the assets. A private arrangement takes place, so much per cent. is paid, and, if the insolvent have the character of an honest man, he can immediately begin afresh on credit.

The regular retail shopkeepers, established in the towns and villages, form but a trifling part of the trading community. The wants of the country are commonly supplied through the Jews and pedlars. The Jew is the chief character in all petty mercantile transactions in Russia as in Poland, especially with imported articles. A traveller, in immediate want of anything, will be sure to get it through a Jew, and what is more, the Jew will surely hunt him out and remind him of his want. His industry and activity are greater in these countries than elsewhere, as he has greater impediments to fight against. From some of

---

* Bills of Exchange could, until lately, be drawn only by merchants of the first and second guilds: they are now becoming more common in business. To show how little they are made use of in Russian interior trade, it may be mentioned that in 1854 goods were sold on credit at these fairs to the amount of thirteen millions, of which only 850,000 roubles were represented by bills. Yet it would seem that bankruptcies are rare, and the losses generally insignificant compared to what is the case in other countries.

these fairs he is excluded altogether; credit is more sparingly given to him, but for this he does not much care, as he appreciates all the advantages of paying cash himself and giving credit to others. Where a Russian will turn over a rouble once, a Jew will turn it over ten times. As the Jews everywhere hold together, one rich Jew generally has a hundred poorer Jews dependent on him, who make up by their aptitude in business for their want of means.

Besides the regular Jews or Talmudists, there is another race of Semitic extraction, professing something like Judaism. They are called the Karaimi, and are mostly found in the Crimea and southern governments of Russia. They are all traders, and some of them are very rich. They have a good character for honesty and integrity, are dignified in their demeanour, scrupulously clean in their persons, and stand out in favourable contrast with the ordinary Jew in Russia, who is just the reverse. On this account, they are much more respected by the Russians. Their origin is shrouded in some mystery. They pretend to be a remnant of the Hebrew emigration after the first Babylonish Captivity, and affirm therefore that they had no hand in the blood of Christ. In their mode of life, they are quite oriental; their women are kept secluded, and their language is a mixture of Hebrew and Tartar.

But by far the greater part of the country trade is in

the hands of the pedlars. A party of six or seven forms an *artel*, elects an *ataman*, and then, having filled their baskets with small wares, such as needles, finger and ear rings, which every peasant woman or girl wears, the members hawk them through the villages, exchanging them for small quantities of raw produce, which they afterwards sell or exchange at the fairs, their usual place of meeting. Nothing is too trifling for them, a bunch of pig's bristles, a hank or two of flax, a pound or two of wax or tallow, a few skins;— they can always give in exchange some trifle which the peasants prize. The rag and bone merchants in England, who give crockery or plants to a thrifty housewife for her waste, will give some idea of these Russian pedlars.

One class of these hawkers is known by the name of Orpheni. Of these, nearly all come from the government of Vladimir, deal in goods of a higher value, and generally supply the proprietors with what they require. A still more extensive body are the *Sloboshanen* or *villagers*, from the government of Tchernigov, who visit, in their wanderings, the most remote parts of the empire. These are more popularly known as the basket-carriers, from their manner of carrying their wares. Some merchants employ as many as 200 or 300, divided into small bodies; each of which, under an agent, travels over certain districts. At stated times, they all meet to make up accounts with their

A FAIR OF THE UKRAIN, WITH GROUP OF MOSCOW MERCHANTS.

employers.   This trust placed in a large body of ignorant men is a striking proof of the general honesty of the people.

The fairs of the Ukrain are held in regular succession all the year round.   No sooner is one finished, than the agents of the great commercial houses pass on to the next town where a fair is to be held, followed by their carts and sledges loaded with merchandise.

The most frequented of all is that held at Kharkov on the 18th of January, the feast of the Three Kings.

As many as 200 little wooden huts are erected in the square, and a hundred thousand carts and sledges, with their horses and oxen, visit the town from all parts of Russia, bringing gold and jewels, furs and manufactures from Moscow; knives, *somovars*, and other hardware from Toula; caviar and dried fish from the Volga and the Don; salt, wine, and the beautiful black lamb-skins from the Crimea; and the produce of warmer climates from, Odessa and Riga.   There are also special fairs for wool at Kharkov and Póltava, which are always attended by the cloth merchants of Germany.   The sale of sheep skins is enormous. More than thirty millions are annually required for the *kaphtans* of the peasantry.   By the beginning of autumn, the series of fairs is over, and the carriers then obtain loads to return to their houses.   Of late years, most of the great Moscow merchants have established depôts at Kharkov as a central position, and, instead of

the migratory trade of these fairs, carry on a fixed
wholesale trade.   Hence, as railways extend, they
must gradually fall into disuse, with the exception of
fairs for wool, cattle, &c. &c.   It is estimated that
the business transacted at all these fairs at Kharkov,
amounts to more than twenty-two millions silver
roubles per annum.

In so extensive a country as Russia, the character
and habits of the people must vary widely in different
parts. The gloomy forests of pine and larch in the north
produce an impression on the inhabitants, for which
we look in vain in the Little Russ or Cossack of the
steppe, and *vice versâ.*   In my remarks I have chiefly
had in view the people of Old or Great Russia, as it is
called, of which Moscow and Novgorod are the centres.
Their history as a people, has always been more compact than that of the country which I was now entering
—Little Russia or the Ukrain,* and the steppes of the
Don.   Here, not only climate and locality, but popular
experience combine to give the natives a type different
from that of their brethren of the north.   The Little
Russ is the Italian of Russia; he loves his ease, and is

---

* 'Ukrain' is a Little Russian word, and means frontier or boundary.
The country formerly so called was the frontier between Great Russia
and Little Russia, and frequently shifted its limits.   The government
of Kharkov now bears that name.   But the term Ukrain seems to have
the signification of including all ancient Little Russia, and as such I use
it in the pages which follow.

content to gaze on his blue sky and monotonous landscapes in a *dolce far niente*, while he dreams over the past and indulges in vain speculations for the future. As obstinate but more lively, as poetically inclined, but with more of melancholy, more easily excited, but of greater mental activity, than the Sclave of the north, he may be at once distinguished from the latter in his occupations and likings. Unapt for business, he has allowed the Muscovites to usurp all the commerce of the country, and he looks with indifference and contempt on their astuteness and trickery, as they buy up his produce or sell him their wares. There is about him much less of that patient resignation which marks the native of Great Russia. He easily fires up at a sense of wrong; and, when he is excited by political or other theories, his manner changes in a moment from his usual placid melancholy to fierce gesticulations and fiery eloquence. The Little Russ generally enters the public service, chooses some liberal profession, cultivates his land or breeds stock, but seldom becomes a trader.

The personal habits of the lower classes of Great and Little Russia also differ in many respects. The Little Russ is perhaps the cleaner of the two. The merchant or peasant of the north is invariably known by his beard, which with him is as much a symbol of his rank in life, as it was formerly of his moral and religious character.* The Little Russ shaves all the hair off his face, with the exception of the moustache.

* This wearing the beard dates from the fifteenth century, and was ordered by the Holy Synod as a distinctive mark of morality, and all who shaved were excluded from the Church. Many unnatural vices had been introduced by the Tartars among the people, and persons addicted to them were known by their shaven faces. This accounts for the great opposition Peter the Great met with among the lower classes, when he made them shave off their beards.

CHAPTER VII.

POLAND *V.* RUSSIA AND RUSSIA *V.* POLAND.

The Poet Pushkin on the Polish Question—The Antagonism of
Poland and Russia dates from the Tenth Century—The Religion,
Alphabet, and Almanack of Poles and Russians—First Encroach-
ments of Poland on the Sclavonic Tribes of the East—Boleslaw's
Daughter—Poland and Russia in Fifteenth and Sixteenth Cen-
turies—Jadwiga i Jagiello—Lithuania has Conquered all the
Frontier Provinces of Russia—Union of Lithuania to Poland—
The Jesuits in Lithuania—Their Success—Congress of Brest—
Jesuit missionary zeal—The False Dimitri and Marina Mniszek
—The Poles in Moscow—James I. and Gustavus Adolphus in
the Affairs of Russia—Expulsion of the Poles from Moscow—
Rebellion of the Cossacks and their Secession from Poland
—The Zaporojia—Bogdan Khmelnitsky—Peter the Great the
Arbiter of Poland—His Reforms and German Organisation the
Cause of Poland's Downfall — Germanism *versus* Sclavism—
Poland under Alexander I.—Under Nicholas—His Despotic
Rule—Change of Policy under Alexander II.—The Poles thereby
Encouraged—Preparations for an Outbreak—The Grand Duke
Constantine in Warsaw—The Recruitment—The National Com-
mittee—Its Agents in Russia—The Hanging Gensdarmes—
Forced Loans—Its Reign at last became one of Terror—
Its Orders for Public Dressing and Behaviour—The Polish
Women—Their Character and Influence—A Church Demon-
stration—The Roman Catholic Church and the Priesthood—The
Literary Members of the Committee and the Polish Refugees
—Character of their Writings, and Remarks on them—The Poles
are as Bad as the Russians—The Mendacity of Reports spread
abroad—The Pretensions of the Poles—The Disputed Provinces
—Are they Polish or Russian in Language, Religion, or General

TO the foregoing chapter, which was written in 1862,
I had added a short account of the Polish element
in the west and south-west of Russia, in anticipation of the
outbreak which was then plainly looming in the distance.
The progress of the insurrection, a deeper acquaintance
with the history of the two countries, and some later
personal experience in the insurgent provinces, have led
me to treat the whole subject at greater length in a separate chapter. The overwhelming and contradictory mass
of material which has flooded the newspapers of Europe
for months past will not, I hope, have so thoroughly
disgusted the reader as to deter him from reading a
concise and (as I believe) correct and impartial
account of that great struggle between Russia and
Poland, of which the present insurrection may be the
closing scene.

The Russian poet Pushkin, during the insurrection of

1830, wrote his famous lines, which are on the lips of every Russian, beginning thus:

O chem shumete vui, narodnei vetie?

Why do you make a noise, O popular bard?
Why menace Russia with your anathemas?
What moves you so?   Is it the strife in Lithuania?
Be quiet! That is a dispute among Sclaves, among ourselves —
An old, a household strife, already weighed by fate—
A question which you never can decide.

And Pushkin said truly. The Polish question is a dispute among Sclaves, between Russians and Poles, a household quarrel which fate has decided in favour of the Russians. The causes of that dispute, and the means by which it was decided, I shall endeavour to explain in the following pages.

A slight knowledge of the history of either country will show that this antagonism is not an affair of to-day. It carries us back far into the haze of barbarism. Poland A.D. 965 took her religion and civilisation from the reviving West; Russia took hers a few years later from the declining Byzantine empire. Each nation adopted with equal earnestness, and retained with equal pertinacity, its respective creed and customs. The rivalry between Rome and Constantinople was reflected in the rivalry between the Western and the Eastern Sclaves. Poland, adhering in heart and soul to the West, adopted not only its religion but its institutions, its computation of time and its alphabet; Russia superstitiously embraced and retained all that belonged to the fatal conservatism of the East.* The effect was soon seen. Poland in the fifteenth century was powerful, united, and one of the chief states of Europe; Russia, split into discordant parts, had become the prey of hordes of migrating Tartars. At length, when something like a state became established among the Sclaves of the East, with Moscow for its capital, the struggle began in earnest between the Oriental Russians and the Western Poles—between Orthodoxy and Catholicism. The whole country between Moscow and Cracow, not having any well-defined natural frontier, became the theatre of a series of political and religious encroachments, which began in the twelfth century and have continued, with very short intervals of repose, down to the nineteenth.†

* I have often asked educated Russians why they do not assimilate their almanack and alphabet to those of Western countries. The answer was always the same—that such a change would be most impolitic, if not impossible to carry out ; that such a measure would inevitably cause riots everywhere, as the people would see in it a covert attempt to impose on them the Roman Catholic religion, which they abhor. They have not forgotten the wily attempts of the patriarch Nikon in the sixteenth century, when, in alliance with the Jesuits, he tried to play traitor to his Church, or the many attempts which have been made by the Poles to convert them. These religious convictions of the Russian people form the great strength of their nation, are a weapon of enormous power to the Government which fosters them, and would be its ruin if tampered with. Protestantism, never having made any attacks upon Orthodoxy, is little understood, and never alarms the people. This is one reason why Germans get on tolerably among the Russians. Romanism, on the other hand, is the great bugbear of the Russian orthodox peasant.

† See Karamzine, or the more modern Russian historian, Soloviev, Lelewel, or any other Polish histories, and compare their descriptions.

In the beginning of the eleventh century, when Boleslaw the Brave ruled the Polish Sclaves, the descendants of the Scandinavian chieftain Rurik were petty monarchs of those provinces, which afterwards formed part of the Polish Republic, such as the Ukrain, Ruthenia, Galicia, and Lithuania. Even in this period we begin to see the commencement of Polish influence on the Sclavonic peoples.

'The daughter of Boleslaw,' says the Polish historian Shainoka, 'was married to Sviatopolk, surnamed the *Okainie,** or the Cursed, son of Vladimir, Grand Prince of Kiev, and as she was accompanied to her future home by a Latin bishop, the seeds of Western civilisation and the Catholic religion were first introduced into Russia.' This influence brought on a civil war in Kiev, and the son-in-law of Boleslaw was forced to take refuge in Poland. After a time he was reinstated in his power by an army of Poles, who took and sacked Kiev. From this moment dates that influence and superiority of Poland in the western provinces of Russia which she maintained down to the middle of the seventeenth century.

In the fifteenth and sixteenth centuries Poland had become thoroughly imbued with the culture and religion of the West, and had become their champion in the East. The Eastern Sclaves were meanwhile crushed under the

---

* Okainie, from the word Kain or Cain. This Prince murdered all his brothers, and was cursed by his father Vladimir.

abominable rule of the Mongols. One by one the provinces governed by the descendants of Rurik fell to Poland. Galicia, or Red Russia, united itself to Poland under Casimir the Great. In order to extend their power still more in the East the magnates of Poland married Jadwiga, the daughter of Casimir, to Jagiello, the heathen prince of Lithuania, and a few years later that fine province, with all its Russian conquests, was joined, at the Union of Lublin in 1569, to Poland,* which thus extended its sway to Kiev and Smolensk, and further yet to Novgorod the Grand. Poland under the rule of the Jagellons was in the height of its glory; while the newly-formed state of Moscow, which had just been gathering round it the minor Sclavonic principalities and driving out the Tartars, seemed on the point of annihilation.

In 1562 the Jesuits first made their appearance in Lithuania to counteract the new Lutheran heresy, which was fast gaining ground in that province. In the Polish diet and people they found the heartiest helpers. Having thoroughly crushed out Protestantism, they turned all their subtlety and zeal for conversion against the Greek Church in the newly-annexed provinces, where the inhabitants were still Orthodox. Success so far crowned their efforts that many of the

* Kiev, Little Russia, or the Ukrain, Volhynia, and White Russia, had already been conquered and united to Lithuania by one of its princes in 1320.

Greek bishops of Lithuania and Ruthenia were brought to acknowledge the supremacy of the Pope (Congress of Brest, 1596); while at the same time they were allowed to retain all the dogmas and rites of the Greek Church. These took the name of Uniates, or the United Greek Church—a name which is still preserved, though most of them have been re-converted into Orthodoxy or Romanism. When the Jesuits had accomplished this, they extended their campaign into the Ukrain and even into Great Russia. Their progress at this moment was vastly aided by the anarchy in Moscow, which afforded both to the civil power and the Church the opportunity of nearly subjugating the Muscovites. Poland seemed for a moment on the point of treating Russia as Russia has since treated Poland. And as this period is the turning-point of the struggle between the two peoples, I shall briefly relate the fortunes of the Poles in Moscow.

During those mysterious years in Russian history which followed the death of Theodore, the last of the house of Rurik (1598), when Moscow was governed by the able Boris Godounov, a pretender was set up by the Poles, who was said to be Dimitri, the brother of Theodore, who had been murdered when a child, if not by the orders, at least by the partisans, of Godounov. This young pretender had been a groom in the service of a Polish *pan,* was educated and instructed in his part by the most able of masters, the Jesuits; was betrothed to the beautiful and ambitious Marina, who belonged to the powerful family of the Mniszeks, and at last openly put forward as the brother of the late Tsar. The Russian people, ever moved by the word of a man whom they consider their rightful Tsar, flocked by thousands to his standard, so that he was accompanied by a large army when he reached the gates of the Kremlin. Boris died from apoplexy, caused, it is stated, by the mortification of his position. His youthful son, whom he willed to succeed him, and his wife, whom he appointed regent, were soon afterwards strangled by the people, who opened their gates to the Pretender. The first false Dimitri, as he is called in history, made his solemn entry into the walled city, where he was rejoined by his bride. But their Polish and Catholic education soon shocked all the superstitions and prejudices of the Muscovites. They even celebrated their marriage on the eve of St. Nicholas, one of the most venerated of orthodox saints—a proceeding contrary to all the religious sentiments of the Russian people, who observe the eve of all feasts, Sundays, and fasts, with more reverence than they do the day itself. The consequence was a general rising of the people, which issued in the massacre of the Pretender and all his Poles, and the flight of his young wife. But Marina's life had been devoted to a cause, and not to any one instrument of that cause. Her ambition was soon consoled by her marriage with a second pretender of the same name, a mere brigand, to whom the confusion of the times offered some chance of success. A large army invaded the Muscovite territory, and the gates of the Kremlin were again opened to them, this time by treason. The indefatigable Marina, who had already got rid of her second husband and taken to herself a third, raised the Cossacks of the Ukrain to aid her in her schemes. But the Russians had been touched in the most tender part—they had been persuaded to accept an impostor as their lawful Tsar, and an attempt had been made to disturb their orthodoxy. The national spirit awoke in the person of a poor butcher of the rising town of Nijni Novgorod, whose fanatical patriotism, combined with a rude and powerful eloquence, brought about a general rising of the people. In this work he was powerfully aided by the more cultivated talents and military genius of Prince Dimitri Pojarsky, and by the anathemas of ten thousand ignorant but patriotic priests. After having occupied the city of Moscow for about five years, the Poles were driven. from the sacred city, when a general assembly of the Boyards and people elected Michael Romanov their Tsar.*

---

* It is mentioned in Russian annals, that James I., of England, sent a body of troops to Archangel, then the only port which Russia possessed, in order to assist the Muscovites against their Polish invaders, but when they arrived the Poles had already been driven from Moscow. Sweden also, at this time, aspired to make conquests in Russia. After the death

This expulsion of the Poles from Moscow was the turning-point of the struggle between Moscow and Cracow. Seventy years later the great revolt of the Cossacks and the secession of the Ukrain from Poland to Russia first portended the downfall of Poland. The Cossacks of this time were a barbarous and heroic people, with many of the qualities of their Scythian predecessors. Although nominally conquered by the Lithuanian princes, they were never thoroughly subdued. Their semi-independent history extended over 250 years, and the memory of that period is kept alive by the poetry of the people, which reminds them how their ancestors were by turns allies of the Poles against the Tartars, and then how in league with these they fought against Poland for the preservation of their civil and religious autonomy. In their great stronghold of the Zaporojia,* into which no woman

of Godounov, the inhabitants of Novgorod, which must still have been a powerful city, although greatly lowered by Ivan III., invited Philip, the brother of Gustavus Adolphus, to be their Tsar. After the election of Romanov, Gustavus avenged the apparent insult which had been offered to his family and the failure of his plans of aggrandisement by repeated invasions of Russia, which lasted till Peter the Great turned the tables on him and robbed his no less celebrated successor of some of the richest provinces of his kingdom. It is a curious subject of speculation, how the map of Eastern Europe would now be constructed if such a man as Peter had never existed.

* From *za*, behind, and *porog*, cataract, from its situation behind the falls of the Dnieper, just below the town of Ekaterinoslav. This Zaporojia was to the Cossacks what the Isle of Anglesea was to the Druids.

was ever admitted, their youth were trained to arms, their old men gave their counsels, and their *ataman* sent forth his orders. On the annexation of Lithuania to Poland the Cossacks had been made to receive a Polish political organisation, the Mecklenburg code of laws, and an army of Jesuits. Against these they rebelled long and stubbornly. Their *guidamaks* or minstrels spread throughout the land a vast plot to get rid of their oppressors, and on one occasion there was a massacre of the Poles throughout the Ukrain. At last a general rising took place under the famous Bogdan Khmelnitsky, a *cotnik* or captain, who, having been insulted by a Polish officer, fled to the Khan of the Crimea. He returned to the Zaporojia with an army of Tartars to deliver his country. The Poles were everywhere beaten, and the Ukrain again became independent. But the Cossacks, wholly given up to war, found themselves incapable of managing a civil government, and were obliged to make a choice between Moscow and Poland. Determined in their decision by religious motives, they united themselves to Great Russia or Moscow. A war naturally followed between this state and Poland, at the end of which, in 1686, the boundary between the two countries in the South was fixed at the Dnieper—a boundary which the Poles of the present day are anxious to restore. All that part of the Ukrain which remained on the right bank of the river, including Kiev, was treated as a conquered province, and portioned out among the Polish *panni,* whose descendants to this day consider themselves Poles, and who are continually agitating for a political union to the kingdom of Poland.   Little Russia, united to Moscow on the condition that all its privileges should be maintained, soon found that they were violated.   It received the same organisation as Great Russia; and against this the Cossacks equally rebelled.   Under Catherine II. their semi-independence was completely obliterated. They received an army of *tchinovniks,* and the peasants were bound to the soil.   Their religion alone remained inviolate.   Though one or two attempts to regain their independence have been made since their annexation to Russia, all difference is now nearly effaced, and the Ukrain is thoroughly Russian.

The great arbiter of the destinies of Poland as well as of Russia was Peter the Great.   St. Petersburg became the capital, and thenceforth commenced a new phase in the struggle.   That far-sighted man perceived the necessity of cutting off his people from the declining East, and adopting the progressive principles of the West.   When he had once accomplished this, the fate of heroic but discordant Poland could no longer be doubtful.   The annexation of the German Baltic provinces completely transformed Russia.   All the talent which they afforded, and all the restless intellect which could be collected from other parts of Europe, combined to establish Russia among European nations.   The successful campaign of Peter against Charles of Sweden annexed a large portion of the old *voyavodeship* of Kiev A.D. 1721.   The increasing anarchy of Poland soon afforded to the successors of Peter the opportunity of interfering in his internal affairs, until Catherine placed her old lover Poniatowski on the Polish throne, to be her instrument in the total subjugation of the country.   The three partitions which followed are well known (those of 1772, 1793, and 1797).   The whole of Old Poland was absorbed, with the exception of the Grand Duchy of Warsaw, with 4,000,000 of in-habitants, which was placed under the protection of Prussia.   This duchy, at the congress of Vienna, was constructed into a kingdom, with the Emperor of Russia as king, and endowed with a constitution which it lost after the great insurrection of 1830-31.*

The German element in Europe seems to have been created to prey on the other elements with which it

---

* The following table will show at a glance the repeated dismember-ments of the Polish State, and the share taken by Russia of the spoil:—

Secession of the Ukrain . . . . A.D.	1686
Part of *voyavodeship* of Kiev, after the Peace of Nystadt .	1721
Parts of White Russia and Lithuania, situated between the Dnieper, the Duna, and the Drusch, with half a million of inhabitants	1772
Volhynia, Podolia, rest of Kiev, and part of Lithuania, with 3¼ millions	1793
The rest of Lithuania, with 1¼ million	1795-7

Prussia, at the same time, took Posnania up to the shores of the Baltic, with the Grand Duchy of Warsaw; Austria took Galicia and Cracow.

came into contact.   Its influence has been omnipotent over Gaul or Celt, Latin or Sclavon.   The excitability of the latter could never long withstand the cool, calculating endurance which marks the character of the Teutonic race.   Bitter, therefore, has been the despair and indignation of the victims.   The conquest of Poland by Russia is, in my belief, owing entirely to the solid German organisation and direction which the Russian government assumed from the time of Peter the Great. Long before *Germanised* Russia began to retaliate on the east of Poland, the German contact had been fatal to the Sclaves on the west.   These peoples formerly inhabited all the lands east of the Oder, but they had been long ago swept away.   The Czecks, Dalmatians, and other Sclavonic tribes have for hundreds of years been under German domination.   Poland also in due season felt the corrosive element.   The Teutonic knights of the Baltic provinces, the Prussians in Posnania, the Austrians in the South, have crushed and stamped out the very germs of Sclavism.   The whole population, language, and institutions of those provinces have been Germanised, and Poland there may be said to be no longer anything but a name.*

If the Polish nationality has been anywhere unmolested, it is certainly in Russian Poland, where, despite all animosities of religion and prejudice as to Tartar-

---

* See Chapter VIII.—Germans in Russia.

Sclavonic blood, there is still more kindred feeling than there is between the Sclave and the German.   If Russia since 1772, instead of using the brute force of armies, had acted towards Poland after the Machiavellic fashion of Prussia and Austria, we should not be troubled now with Polish insurrections.

The Emperor Alexander I., who sympathised with the aristocratic and chivalric character of the Poles, wished to reconstruct a large kingdom of Poland, with not only a civil but a military autonomy. This idea was not only condemned by the Allied Powers at the Congress of Vienna, but brought down upon him the censures of his own statesmen — among others, of the historian Karamsine—who better understood the Polish feeling, which has always been the same. This was plainly shown in 1831. When Paskévitch was about to storm the Praga of Warsaw, he invited the Polish commander Krugoviecky to a conference, to arrange terms for a capitulation, and thus avoid bloodshed. Although pushed to extremes, the latter would listen to no terms which did not grant the restoration of the Poland of 1772. This tenacious clinging to an idea must be admired, although we may see its vanity. The greater part of those provinces for which the Poles are crying are no longer Polish in anything but the memory of a time long since passed away.

For nearly fifty years the kingdom of Poland and the Grand Duchy of Lithuania (for it is there that the

Polish and Catholic elements are strongest) have been governed by Russian viceroys and Russian troops. During the reign of Nicholas the harshest means were tried which can be tried to break the nationality of a people. For twenty-five years, after the bloodiest of insurrections had been put down with frightful severity and its leaders dispersed over Europe and Siberia, the hand of iron, which weighed heavily on Russia, crushed out in Poland every visible spark of life. A crusade was opened against its institutions and religion; its youth were taken away by thousands, and estranged from the sympathies of their childhood. Siberia or exile received all who opposed the things that were, and a fortress bristling with cannon was erected in its capital to awe those who remained. Poland was quiet and trembling, even when the rest of the world was in flames.

On the accession of the present Tsar, the Russian policy in Poland was completely changed. Confiscations and other harsh measures of the late reign were rescinded; patriots were recalled from exile; Poles were put into all good places of the administration; the council of the kingdom was composed of Poles; the Roman Catholic religion was no longer tampered with, and liberal promises of a further extension of national and popular government were held out, if the Poles would only show that such could be given with safety. In acting thus the Russian Government, with all its good intentions, committed the greatest blunder a government can commit — that of inconsistency. It went suddenly from an extreme of severity to the extreme of lenity. Its fault was not in not giving, but in giving unwisely. It gave too little or too much. It should either have kept things as they were—i.e. ruled Poland as a conquered province—or it should have given the Poles their complete independence. Only in one of these two ways can the Polish question be settled.

The Poles, when they found a little given, naturally endeavoured to take more. At all times of their independent history they were never famed for moderation as rulers or for tractability as subjects, and the reign of Nicholas had not improved them. Their national feeling and hopes, like herbage over which the flames have swept, sprang up more vigorous than ever. A vast and well-organised scheme of rebellion, in connection with the revolutionary and clerical clubs of Western Europe, spread over the country, and the word of a mysterious leader was only wanting to advance or retard the moment of outbreak. The Government again became alarmed; and once more reports of plots and of repressions, arrests, banishments, assassinations, and fusillades were heard of from Warsaw. Against the Russians, whether as merciless and cruel or humane and conciliating governors, a certain party of the people remained implacable.

The Government, however, without arresting its

intended reforms, still hoped to allay the spirit of revolt. The Grand Duke Constantine was sent to Warsaw with the generous intention of conciliating that unhappy country and gradually restoring to it that autonomy which it lost in 1831. All his actions show his desire to conciliate the Poles. He gave to his babe born in the country the name of a Polish saint; he made himself master of the Polish language, surrounded himself with Polish advisers; appointed Polish civil officers to all important posts; and became so Polonised himself as to excite the discontent of his own Government and countrymen; so that when, in September 1863, he returned to Russia, he was the most unpopular man in the country. Whatever may have been his private ideas, his government was a complete failure, while the anxiety of his position had whitened his head, and a coat of steel mail had hardly preserved him from assassination.

But the political crimes of the father were not so easily redeemed by the good intentions of the son. The conspiracy made head faster than he could check it. At last, when the insurrection was on the point of breaking out, the Government, to counteract or anticipate it, committed another great blunder by ordering an illegal recruitment, affecting chiefly those classes of the population which were known to be the most revolutionary.*

* This measure, the Russians say, was entirely decided by the Polish Council of State, at the head of which was the Marquis Wielopolsky,

The result only showed that the great principles of justice ought never to be violated, under any circumstances, by a Government in its dealings with a people. In Poland the measure, so far from having its intended effect, only hastened the crisis. The revolution commenced by a series of cold-blooded murders on sleeping soldiers, which naturally led to a fearful retaliation afterwards. The worst passions were unchained, and for months barbarities have been committed which would rival even those of Asiatic warfare. *

The very soul of the present insurrection has been the secret National Committee, backed, it is true, by every class of the community with the exception of the

while the Emperor twice refused his sanction, and only consented to it when hard pushed.

* In a copy of the instructions issued by the National Government, I find these words: 'In Spain children were trained to pick out the eyes of the enemy's horses with needles. At the inns, when French soldiers came, the mangers of the stables were rubbed with a preparation of arsenic. In uninhabited houses, eatables and drink containing opium and arsenic were left in the cupboards. From the pulpits priests preached such means as these to get rid of their country's oppressors, and all Europe clapped with applause. Why should they not be allowed now under similar circumstances? A national war, when it once begins, is in itself a war of extermination. Vengeance for the injustice and insults not only of the past, but of the present, and even of the future—vengeance for so much blood spilt in defence of our fatherland—honour as well as necessity, make it the duty of every Pole, without distinction of sex, age, or position, to employ every method to exterminate the enemy. And let every Pole remember, that the more he knows how to conceal his hatred the more dangerous he will be; and that in the success of every undertaking lies its justification.'

peasantry, who were forced on with the stream. Who were the members of this Committee, or where it held its sittings, nobody seemed to know. Prince Gortchakov hinted at the Palais Royal in Paris; many Russians believed it to be in the very Palace of Warsaw. Be this as it may, it is very certain that the old aristocratic families, like the Czartoriskys—the democratic literary men, like the Mickievicz—the men of action, like Langievicz and Mieroslawsky—were all connected with it in one plan against the Russians, however much they may have been squabbling among themselves. The 'Sclachters' or petty nobility of Poland, the *pans* or landowners of the old Polish provinces, were to a man its supporters. Refugees who had been in exile, earning their bread as shopkeepers, clerks, or professors, threw down their pens and books and returned, with unabated patriotism, to put themselves under its orders. Professors from their chairs, priests from their confessionals, inculcated obedience to its orders. Fully half the Polish servants of the Government in Poland or in Russia were among its agents. Its emissaries carried into the most remote parts its orders to those Poles who were in the Russian service. Disguised as Russian secret police, they made domiciliary visits in St. Petersburg and Cronstadt, so that the most rigorous passport system had to be enforced between those towns. The orders they brought to every officer assigned him some special duty. To assist the national cause, they must do the

Russians as much injury as possible in every practicable way.   Thus, at the beginning of the insurrection, quantities of arms and ammunition were smuggled through St. Petersburg into Poland.   In one factory in the Ural mountains, where Poles were employed in great numbers, all the valuable machinery was one day found to be useless.   If any Polish *employé* refused to obey these orders (and there were many who would not compound with their consciences, and either remained true to their allegiance or nobly threw up their commissions), he was sure to receive a warning to the effect that he must not forget he had property left in Poland, or, failing that, parents or a sister to answer for his disobedience.*

In Poland and Lithuania the reign of this Committee became at last a reign of terror to all who wished to be neutral.   The peasantry, it is known, kept aloof from the insurrection ; they hated their proprietors, and saw no chance of bettering their condition by fighting under their orders.   But the Committee appointed a leader to such and such a district, and the peasants had no choice but to take up a scythe or be hanged to the nearest

* Polish officers in Russia were thus placed in a deplorable situation. So many were found acting the traitor, that the Government mistrusted all.   Looked on with suspicion by the Government, they were treated as renegades by their own countrymen.   Many who received threatening letters revealed their contents to the authorities.   One letter, of which I had some knowledge, informed a young Polish officer that his parents and sister should pay the penalty of his disobedience to the orders of the National Government.

tree. The march of a rebel band was marked by the bodies of refractory peasants hanging from their own doors or from the posts of the telegraph. And, besides these, every Pole found serving the Russians met with the same fate if he had the misfortune to be taken prisoner and refused to join the insurgents.* It was this that often so exasperated the Russian soldiers, and led to the brutal reprisals which the Poles took care to spread abroad over Europe. Its police, known as the *hanging* gensdarmes, were spread all over the country, encouraging the patriotism, upbraiding the lukewarmness, or summarily punishing the disobedience of individuals. Loans, of which the independence of their fatherland was to be the security, were raised or extorted from the townspeople —and woe to him who refused! So great became its terrorism in one part of Poland, that the peasantry actually sent a deputation to Mouraviev to take them under his protection and free them from the incubus which oppressed them.

Neglecting none of those means which may rouse a people to enthusiasm, the orders of the National Committee touched even the intimacies of social life. It prescribed to men and women where they were to walk, and not to walk in Warsaw; how they were to behave in public; to the women how they were to wear mourning

---

* The Government permitted all Polish officers of regiments sent to Poland to remain behind; but many persisted in going, to show their loyalty and zeal.

and make political demonstrations in the churches; at another time, when mourning was forbidden by the authorities, that they were to dress in red; at another, time, and hardest of all, that they were to distinguish themselves from the Russian women by an absence of crinoline. But the part played by the women of Poland has been such as to merit the special attention of the reader.

The Polish women are distinguished by great physical beauty, heightened by all that art of manner which is so fascinating to the opposite sex, over whom they know and exert their power. In their mental qualities they are equal if not superior to the men, while their character partakes of all that mysticism and idealism which is common to both sexes.* High-flown in the love of their country, fanatical in their religion, the passion of the Polish women is in the glory of the one and the ascendency of the other. Over the men of her family and kindred her power is greater than in any country in Europe, and there is only one man before whom she bows her head and humbles her mind—and that man is her priest. Throughout every page of the history of her country the passionate and energetic nature of the Polish woman breaks out. Her character is well typified in the seventeenth century in the person of Marina Mniszek,

* It is an old saying, that among people of the Latin race, men and women are equal in their mental qualities : that, in the German race, the men are superior; in the Sclavonic, the women.

of whom I have already spoken. In 1770 the French commissioner of Louis XV. writes home to his master, 'that all capacity and energy in Poland have passed from the men to the women, who are occupied in action, while the men are leading the life of women.' It is the same in 1863. While the men are quarrelling as to the use of power, before that power is acquired, the woman, with all her exciting moral energy, is pushing forward to one goal—the independence of her country and the supremacy of her religion, for with her the two go together.

Already the infant on his mother's knees looks up with his extended eyes into her face, and sobs break from his little bosom, as she relates to him the story of the three partitions, the sufferings of his fathers, and the horrors of Russian domination. Weaned, so to speak, with patriotic maxims, he is ready, at a moment's notice, to fly to his country's call. As soon as the insurrection broke out, the Polish youth vanished altogether from the universities and schools, and it is sad to think what the fate of so many generous youths has been.

The influence of the Polish mother on her children is scarcely greater than the influence of the Polish wife on her husband. What man can long withstand the tears of supplication, the bursts of irony, the persuasions which are backed by caresses, when his heart is in the cause which the loved one advocates, though his reason may be against it? It is impossible to know how

many Poles or Russo-Poles have been brought over to
the insurgents by women.   But this is undoubted—that
wherever they brought their influence to bear, it was
never exerted in vain; and that women have been first
and foremost in supporting the National Government,
and bidding defiance to the enemy.*

While young and delicate women have been found,
mounting on horseback, handling lance and revolver,
and braving all the dangers and hardships of an ever-
changing camp; their influence has also been immense
in private, in spurring on the young to action, in re-
warding the heroism of some, in seducing the loyalty of
others.   In the depth of the forest or morass might
be found women, who had figured in the first society of
Paris or Warsaw, exciting those who were preparing for
an expedition by their eloquence, their prayers, and
their promises.   The seductions of women, indeed,
have only been part of the programme of the insurrection.   As such we must also consider their public
demonstrations in the churches.

Let the reader picture to himself a Catholic cathedral,
hung in black cloth, and, as worshippers, some thousand
women clothed in the deepest mourning, on their knees
before the altar, filling up the whole aisle.   Imagine
that some solemn mass is being intoned, that the organ

* For a fuller account of the influence of the Polish women on the
Insurrection, I refer the reader to an article which I contributed to
Fraser's Magazine for December 1863.

resounds through the arches to such words as these—
Dies iræ, dies illa; that the vast mass of worshippers
break out into sobbing and moaning, raising their hands
and eyes to heaven: remember that those women are
your mothers and sisters, that they are bemoaning the
captivity of your common fatherland, and supplicating
Heaven for its ultimate success and deliverance from
the hand of the oppressors—and you will have some
idea of the scenes which frequently took place in Warsaw
and Wilna. Do you think such a scene would not have
its effect on you? Add to this, that the Government
has declared its intention of stopping such proceedings
on the next occasion, and that your wives and sisters,
knowing this, persist in going. Would you not accompany them? When you see them trampled down by the
soldiers in the excitement of the *émeute*, should you not
be persuaded to make use of the pistol or dagger, which
you had been persuaded to put in your pocket in case of
necessity? Probably you would; and so did the Poles,
and by so doing, the women became instruments for
dragging on the men after them into the ranks of the
insurgents.

Even the little boarding-school girls were taught to
add their demonstrations to the general confusion, and
so increase the chances of success.

The great prompter of all these actions of the women
may be imagined sitting in the confessional. In no
country in Europe has the Roman Catholic religion

taken deeper root than in Poland. In nearly every country of Europe, it acts hand in hand with the civil power to curb the aspirations of the people. In Poland it is the strongest ally of the people against the Government, and from the Pope down to the meanest village priest the Catholic hierarchy has given more trouble to the Russians than all the pranks of the secret National Committee. Since the First Partition the clergy have been the most active in keeping alive—chiefly through the women—the idea of a glorious restoration of a free and Catholic Poland. They have supplied fuel to the smouldering fires of discontent, whenever the sun of tranquillity began to beam too brightly on that unhappy country. Their power may be easily understood, if for a moment we consider the strength which religion, combined with what the Irish are still pleased to call their oppressed nationality, even now gives to the priesthood in Ireland and America. In the kingdom of Poland the clergy may point at the Antichrist as well as at the tyrant.

What the women and priests have been to the National Government at home, that the literary members of the emigration have been abroad, from London to Constantinople, from Breslau to Madrid. For years Europe has been inundated with their pamphlets; while their writings have found insertion in half the newspapers and magazines of England and France. Is not the picture of the Polish refugee familiar to us all, as in pure French, or broken but not the less interesting English, he awakens the sympathy of woman's heart by the despair of his sufferings or the enthusiasm of his hopes? It is natural that we should sympathise with him and believe what he tells us of his oppressors. But such writings and narrations should be received with the greatest reserve as matter for history. It would be as unfair to write the history of the English Government and people from the outpourings of Irish emigrants in America, as to accept blindfold the character ascribed to Russians by the Poles. The whole burden of their doctrines may be summed up in a few phrases—that Poland has always represented the civilisation and liberalism of the West, while Russia has been the incarnation of Oriental despotism—that the west and south-west of Russia had been civilised and Polonised, and that there only were the true Ruthians or Russians—that the fifty millions of so-called Russian people are a contemptible mixture of Tartars, Calmuks, and Finns, with very little Sclavonic blood, and that they received the name of Russians by an ukas of Catharine II.—that the antagonism of Russia and Poland is one of the secrets of Divine Providence, the destiny of Russia being to weigh on the world, that of Poland to exterminate the oppressor.

These writings of the Polish refugees, together with their pretensions, have had a very bad effect on their cause, not only with the Government, but with the Russian people. This effect has more than counterbalanced any good they may have done by exciting the imagination or the sympathies of Western nations.

If we regard their mutual accusations, we shall find quite as much despotism and illiberality, and more of religious persecution, in Poland than in Russia. Quite as many barbarous deeds have been and are committed, and humanity has been quite as much outraged, on one side as on the other. But when Poland in her turn is persecuted, her cry goes forth at once for liberty, equality, and tolerance in belief. With the feelings of pity towards an injured person or people we are wont to mix up sentiments which are undeserved towards the one, while we exaggerate the evil deeds done on the other side. We should avoid either extreme. In all that concerns the real welfare of either Russians or Poles—the true aim of a government, and the bounden duty of a noble class—both sides have been alike unconscientious. The Poles had greater talents, and they abused them. Although they have been nearer to the focus of civilisation, and more able to profit by it, yet the condition of the Polish people is no better than that of the Russians: perhaps it is even worse. The peasantry have been as much oppressed by forced labour and feudalism under Polish *pans,* as any Russian serfs under the worst of *paméschiks.* The attempts to enforce a change of religion among the people of Ruthenia were equally disgraceful, whether made by wily Jesuits, or ignorant orthodox monks backed by the will of an Autocrat. Nor was the lawlessness of their Diet less injurious to the country than the despotism of the Russian Emperor or the palace revolutions of the nobility. In all their quarrels on paper, and in their reports of things done during the present struggle, the greatest mendacity has been employed to mislead the opinion of Western Europe, and no tidings could be relied on which came through Warsaw, Cracow, or Wilna, until the other version had been compared with them—and then the confusion was hopeless.

It is now generally known that the pretensions of the Poles are not confined to an independent kingdom of Poland with five or six millions of Catholic inhabitants, but extend to the restoration of Old Poland as before 1772. In this there is, however, nothing new. They were avowed when Kosciusko fought, during all the wars of Napoleon, in 1831 as in 1863. These pretensions present the greatest hindrance to their obtaining an independent Catholic Poland; otherwise, I believe that Russia, or at least its people, would be glad to wash their hands of Poland altogether, provided always that Poland remain independent, and be not annexed to Austria at any future period.

A few statements will serve to show the reader the present condition of these provinces, viz. Ruthenia, the Ukrain, and Lithuania.

There is no doubt that, in ancient times, such towns as Vladimir-Volinsky, Kiev, and Wilna, were the capitals of little principalities governed by the old Russian princes. It is true that the dates of such possessions are remote and barbarous; that the Tartar occupation of two centuries intervenes, at the end of which Poland was in possession of what had formerly been Russian ground. It is also true that these provinces owe their civilisation to Poland. But it is not less true that now, after nearly a century's re-possession, the conviction has entered into the very core of the Russian people, that the so-called dismemberment of Poland was only the reunion of scattered members to its kindred body, and that the *people* of those provinces are of the same blood and religion as themselves — a feeling shared by the people of those provinces.

In all these provinces taken together the Poles, or Polonised Russians, number about ten per cent. of the population. The Polish Catholic proprietor extends far east into Russia; the orthodox peasant far into Poland. But as all the wealth and education of the country are centred in this ten per cent., as their political and religious sentiments are all towards Poland, their wishes alone become current, and they are made to represent the 9,000,000 of inferiors, who detest their persons, their influence, and their religion. For two years prior to the, insurrection, the nobility of these provinces on several occasions petitioned the Emperor for political union to the kingdom of Poland.

But Polish emigrants deny that the peasantry of

these provinces are so patient under Russian rule or so earnest in their orthodoxy. The truth is, that their degraded state leaves them indifferent to which party they belong. But that they are not favourably disposed to the Polish cause and to Catholicism is evident from the efforts made among them by the clergy. ' Why do you not,' it is stated in a circular to the Polish proprietors—' why do not you, who are the lords and absolute masters of your peasantry, use the great means you have at your disposal, to Polonise the country? Let each of you take a few peasant children into your houses, and in the course of a few years they become true Poles and fervent Catholics. Afterwards give them their liberty and a piece of land, and they are for ever our friends and will powerfully serve our cause.' When such means are necessary to effect a change, little need be said of the real inclinations of the peasantry.

In the Ukrain and Kiev the people, to say the truth, will not be considered as either Russians or Poles. They are Little Russians. Their memory and legends recall the time when they were independent of both; their language they regard as neither Russian nor Polish; it is Little Russian. They can also boast a small literature of their own. The insurrection hardly touched these provinces, and what disturbances there were came from without, and were easily put down by the peasants themselves.

In Podolia, Volhynia, formerly part of Red Russia or

Galicia, the Polish element is rather more numerous. During the Polish insurrection of 1831, the Poles made every effort to raise the peasantry against the Russians, but without success. General Dverniki penetrated far into the provinces with a *corps d'armée,* but only a few proprietors joined his standard. The peasantry were everywhere apathetic. The same apathy is seen in the present insurrection. When any of the lying telegrams from Lemberg reported that Podolia or Volhynia had risen, anyone who knew those countries at all could check the information. The small proprietors who were Poles wished to rise, but could not prevail on their tenants to follow them; and if insurgents came from Galicia or the kingdom for the purpose of causing a rising, their attempts always failed. It would seem that the Poles have quite estranged from themselves the sympathy of the people who were once their subjects.

The only one of these provinces where the insurrection was really dangerous was Lithuania.* Here the Russian rule in former times was most evanescent, while the Lithuanian princes afterwards conquered half of Russia itself. Here, too, Poles and Catholics are far

---

* The reader will bear in mind that the spread of the insurrection has been in exact ratio to the Catholicism of the inhabitants. The following table will therefore show the extent of the insurrection, as well as the religious denomination of the people in the disputed provinces;

N

more numerous than in the other provinces.* No people in Europe are such fanatics as the lower classes in the northern part of Lithuania and Samogitia, but, fortunately for the Russians, their fanaticism is counterbalanced by their hatred of the Polish proprietors. In one month from the time when Mouraviev was appointed Governor of Lithuania, the insurrection was all but quelled. The means by which he effected this lead me to make a remark on that interference of the three Powers which ended so unsuccessfully.

Two of the six points demanded for the Poles the full liberty of their religion, and participation in the administration of the country. These demands were either made in excessive ignorance of the country, or the mistake was wilful. For the very fact that the Poles had both these was the great cause of success to

the Protestants being strictly neutral, and the Jews serving as much one party as the other :—

	Orthodox	Romanists	Protestants	Jews
Lithuania—				
Wilna . . .	188,567	610,428	897	80,123
Grodno . . .	487,009	267,560	5,351	95,434
Kovno . . .	29,596	834,863	36,892	101,337
Witerbsk . .	452,242	231,392	10,866	66,711
Minsk . . .	709,154	186,888	527	84,834
Mohilev . . .	727,743	41,736	346	114,870
Ruthenia—				
Volhynia . .	1,171,356	172,264	2,202	185,833
Podolia . . .	1,319,975	210,915	1,327	191,847
Kiev	1,621,928	76,150	51,253	225,074

—From the *Official Calendar of St. Petersburg for* 1863.

* In the kingdom of Poland nearly the whole population is Catholic.

the insurrection. It is hard to say that there was not full liberty of religion, when the priests could preach against the Russians from their pulpits, excite the multitude to rebellion, hang their churches in black, or arrange the vast demonstrations of women in mourning which were so powerful in stirring up the mass. If all persons employed by the administration had not been Poles, how would it have been possible to organise the movement so well, or to take away some millions of roubles from the national bank to pay the insurgent troops ? Not only in Poland, but throughout the whole Russian administration, civil and military, the Poles were found in such numbers as to become a cause of envy to their Russian comrades. The very fact that the Poles already had what their sympathisers asked the Russians to give them, accounts for the prolongation of the insurrection in the kingdom of Poland.

Mouraviev well knew this. As soon as he took possession of his Government, he struck at the very root of the insurrection by turning out all Poles who held official positions and replacing them by Germans or Russians. He imprisoned every priest who outstepped his duty in preaching, and would have hanged them all, had they not immediately desisted, for they knew his character well. He fined every woman who wore mourning without cause, and stopped the proceeding in a week. He made the proprietors pay ten per cent. of their incomes for the cost of putting down the insurrection which they had raised ; hanged or shot every insurgent chief, Polish deserter, or attempted assassin ; and in one month Lithuania was comparatively quiet. If the insurrection was to be put down, he adopted the only method of doing it, and he must go down to the grave with all the infamy which his position has entailed. It is, however, only just to say that it would be hard to prove any of those unnecessary barbarities which are imputed to him by Poles, such as flogging women or torturing prisoners, and which in Western Europe have put him on a par with Haynau, of immortal memory, or New Orleans Butler.

In Warsaw, meanwhile, the Grand Duke went to work in quite a different way. It is, of course, almost impossible to get at the true policy of his actions. But it is certain that that policy aimed at conciliating the Poles, and putting down the insurrection in the mildest way possible. But it was not the intention of the National Government to have it put down mildly. Their petty little kingdom of 5,000,000 alone was not worth fighting for : while they were in insurrection, it was worth while going in for the whole of Old Poland. This was the reason why the three propositions of the Powers met with so little gratitude from them. They had already what these asked ; they wanted something more, and saw some chance, in the uncertainty of the Russian Government and a European war, of getting what they wanted. Their position was still pretty good. The Government officials were all Poles, and their willing agents; the priests still did what they liked; the women went on with their demonstrations, in spite of many deaths among them; their friends from without were as liberal as ever, and the Russian Government not over vigorous in its measures. They could prolong the struggle, bide their time, and wait for Fortune or the French to come in and complete their deliverance.

Three months after the insurrection had been crushed in Lithuania, the struggle was as fierce as ever in the kingdom of Poland. But suddenly the Grand Duke was recalled. General Berg, his *locum-tenens*, immediately commenced the programme of Mouraviev, turned out all Polish officials, cut down the forests on each side of the railway, levied the accustomed contribution on the proprietors, and fined the women who wore mourning. That this policy will have the same effect iu Poland as in Lithuania is not at all doubtful. The real difficulties will only begin when the insurrection is quelled.

Meanwhile during this painful struggle all Europe has been looking on and judging either party. That a universal sympathy on the side of the mass should be shown for the cause of the weaker is happily one of the generous attributes of civilised human nature. But undoubtedly that sympathy and the interference of

Government to which it led has had an effect very different from that which the sympathisers intended. It has led the Poles to attempt what they can never complete, to break down barriers and dig chasms which can never be filled up, to indulge in speculations which cannot be realised. For the attempt of the Poles is to restore what no longer exists. The old provinces of Russian Poland are now no longer Polish except in the feelings of their aristocratic *pans*. Prussia and Austria, with true Machiavelian policy, have for years past been replacing the Polish by the German race in Posnania and Galicia. There remains the kingdom of Poland with all the Polish partisans in the neighbouring provinces— about 7,000,000 in all—to wage war against 53,000,000 of orthodox Russians, as fanatic as themselves in all that concerns religion or fatherland; to wrench from the solid sway of Prussia Posnania and East Prussia to the shores of the Baltic; to get Galicia from Austria, to whom every little bit of a heterogeneous empire becomes doubly dear as the chance of her losing it increases. If she has lately been acting the comedy of liberalism towards Poland, it is only from her antago- nism to Russia in the south-east of Europe, and her dread of Panslavism filtering in among the 17,000,000 of her population of Sclaves. Can Poland effect all this by her own unaided powers? It is almost an impossi- bility. She has already made two heroic attempts into which was thrown all the force of her mental and material power.   The present insurrection, although waged on a better plan, with energies more united, with vast assistance from without from revolutionary clubs, from the ultramontane clerical party, and from generous sympathisers, has once more shown the folly of pursuing an idea which it is impossible to realise without drenching the whole soil of Europe with blood.   To restore Poland as she was in the seventeenth century, is practically to reduce Russia and Prussia to what they then were also; and if any one supposes that this can be done without a war of extermination, he knows very little of human nature.

The only hope of Poland in carrying out her idea has been from England and France.   In England sympathy for Poland has become part of the education of youth. 'That Freedom shrieked when Kosciusko fell' is declaimed by every school-boy.   The charity of England towards Polish refugees has become a chronic virtue. Englishmen have always made their voice heard whenever the tidings of oppression and unjust acts committed against a subject race have reached their shores.   This is as it should be.   But while a natural sympathy is forcibly aroused, it is well that a selfish part remains to check its superabundance.   A war undertaken by England for the restoration of Old Poland would no doubt be a very chivalrous act, but she would have to pay for the honour by the tears of thousands of widows, the wails of thousands of orphans, the waste of millions of treasure, the increase of power in a jealous ally, and worse than all, the mortification of finding afterwards that the cause she supported was a rotten and an ungrateful one.

Fortunately the motives which govern English statesmen are the reverse of chivalrous, and though they make a little noise in deference to public opinion, they wisely abstain from entering upon a war of sentiment. In the struggles of Poland there is a poetical aspect, and there is the sober aspect of reality : the former will always win the sympathy of all the world ; the latter ought to prevent wise statesmen from hazarding themselves too far in her affairs.

With France it seemed more likely that sympathy would lead to armed intervention. Poland had always been an ally and friend of France. From among French princes the Poles once chose their elective king. A king of France had married into one of the great Polish families. France had always been the refuge of her dethroned kings and fugitive nobility. Just before the first partition the French Government alone tried, although in vain, to prop up the tumbling State. During the wars of Napoleon Polish and French troops fought side by side from Moscow to Madrid. The character of both peoples in many qualities is akin. The policy of the first Napoleon, so often expressed in his conversation at St. Helena, was to have erected a powerful Poland, with Ponia-

towsky as king, to intervene between Russia and
Germany. It was not inconsistent therefore with the
present imperial policy, so impregnated as it is with the
ideas of that great man, that a powerful Poland should
be established in the present day with Czartorysky as
sovereign. The erection of some such State as a check
to Russia on the west had been entertained by the
greatest of statesmen, especially by the first Napoleon.
With a powerful Poland in the east of Europe France
would acquire that supremacy in Europe which she lost by
the Congress of Vienna, and to regain which the French
Emperor has persistently striven, first in the Crimean
war, and secondly by the depression of Austria. A Polish
war would certainly have afforded him the opportunity
of treating Prussia in the same way, and of restoring
to France those frontiers which nature has given, but
which human policy denies her. In France also were
to be found elements of sympathy—elements fortunately
insignificant in England—united for one purpose from
two extremes—from the Ultramontane Catholic party,
and the Democratic and Socialist. The French Government, uncertain of the alliance of its neighbours and unwilling to commence action without them, managed the
French nation throughout the excitement about Poland,
as an experienced rider would guide his fiery steed. At
one moment shouts of sympathy and petitions for war
were permitted to the masses of generous Frenchmen;
at another they were reined in by the eloquent decla-

mation of that organ of the imperial mind, the minister without a portfolio, M. Billault; then, again, the press was uncurbed, the faubourgs excited, and the spirit of the nation raised to glory point, just as the chances of an armed intervention became more apparent.

It is impossible to know to what extent the French Government gave encouragement to the Polish insurgents. Prince Gortchakov was probably right in the delicate hints which he gave in his clever despatch to the minister in Paris. It is improbable that the Poles would have been so noisy without some direct encouragement, and quite impossible that they could have continued their struggles so long on the bare sympathy of other people. What the real policy of the French Government is, and what it may become hereafter, it is impossible to say. Spring may perhaps unfold it. Though one of the famous ideas is the duty of assisting oppressed nationalities, there is not so much Quixotism in it as is supposed. The idea must be backed by the prospect of some little corner of territory as a reward for its generosity. Now though Poland is too remote to offer such a prospect, Prussia is near to pay for her neighbour; but, as it is probable that other powers would not be well satisfied with the exchange, a war beginning in Poland might not impossibly end in Paris.

Before the breaking out of the insurrection much was heard of the sympathies of Russians for the Polish cause. This was quite true. All liberal Russians sympathised deeply with the Poles for their harsh treatment under the Emperor Nicholas. In 1861 and 1862 they were enthusiastic for Poland. The whole of young Russia was then yearning after a constitution. Poland was looked upon as a champion striving for national and civil liberty, and the idea in Russia was, that what was gained to Poland was gained to Russia also. 'If Poland gets a constitution, we shall soon get ours,' was the thought of half Russia, and sometimes loudly expressed. And indeed it is an absurdity to suppose that, if her constitution be restored to Poland, Russia will long remain without one.

Among the students in the Universities of Kiev and Kharkov, where liberal and revolutionary ideas would naturally form part' of their curriculum, Poland became the incarnation of an idea, the emblem of progress towards the fulfilment of many a cherished dream. While the Universities of St. Petersburg and Moscow were being turned inside out for hatching such ideas, it was not likely that the excitable Little Russians, with their vicinity to Poland, their constant intercourse with Poles, and the remembrance of their history so linked with that of Poland, would be unmoved by what was taking place in Poland. That country to them represented liberty, heroism, a constitution; but it was on the things represented and not on the representative that they centred their affections.

When, therefore, the pretensions of the Poles became known among the people in Russia; when it was seen that the object of their struggle was the re-conquest of the west and south-west of Russia; when their abuse of Russia and the Russians was read in the newspapers; those two fiery passions in the sluggish nature of the Russian peasant—patriotism and religion—were aroused, and the bitter hatred which had always existed between the Moscals and Lakhi was renewed. Kiev was a name that touched every Russian soul. 'The Poles want to take Kiev!' was sufficient to raise two millions of men for its defence.

While it was yet uncertain whether England and France would espouse the Polish cause by arms; while line of battle ships were being sunk and enormous cannon mounted to render the entrance to Cronstadt almost impregnable, addresses came pouring in to the Emperor from every Government and district in Russia, from the nobility, merchants, and the communes of the peasantry. * Those of the Staroveri

---

* I believe all these addresses were looked upon in the West as a sham to blind Europe. This was a great mistake. It is true no one put much faith in the sincerity of the address which Mouraviev got out of the Polish nobility of Lithuania. But in most parts of Russia the people took the initiative, and the Government and the press did no more than tickle the patriotism and fanaticism of the masses in order to prepare for coming events. Indeed, it needed only to listen for a moment

and the Molokani, sectarians lately persecuted by the Government, were among the most fervent. All offered their money and their persons for the defence of their country. The Cossacks of the Don and Ural, the most fanatic of orthodox, even the Calmucks and Tartars of the Asiatic Steppe were ready to set out on a word from the Emperor. Thus was furnished half a million of excellent light cavalry, armed, and costing the Government not a kopek. The Government had not had a conscription since the Crimean war. A levy 'of ten men per thousand was ordered, which would have raised the Russian regular army to a million and a half of men. And that army is at the present day one of the finest in Europe, both as regards the feelings of the troops and the perfectness of the weapons with which they are armed. I fully believe that, had a European war arisen for the restoration of Poland, that unhappy country would by this time have been totally annihilated, and that when with peace the work of reconstruction came, there would have been little

to the conversations of the lower classes, to see that even this was unnecessary. It was against the Poles first, and then against the French, that all their imprecations were levelled. Among the better classes there was a sober resolution, apart from all bravado, to meet the worst. Their feeling was—'Let England and France mind their own business; why should they do to us what they would not permit another power to do to them? If they attempt to force us, we will at least preserve our reputation as a great power, and resist to the last.' But I do not think that anyone anticipated that England would ever make the Polish question a *casus belli.*

left to reconstruct, so bitter would have been the rage and fanaticism of the Russian troops.

The serious question is, what to do with the Kingdom of Poland, as constituted by the Treaty of Vienna, when once the insurrection is put down? That Treaty affirmed to Russia all the provinces of the first partition; and, by being made the excuse for foreign intervention, their cession has been confirmed. Let these, therefore, be out of the question. As affairs now remain, Poland is an incubus to Russia which she cannot throw off without danger, or preserve without exhaustion, while it is a smouldering brand in the midst of Europe. What is to be done with it?

What is wanted by a very respectable minority of Poles, who know that they can expect no more from Russia, is a semi-independence, in which they may be governed by their own statesmen, and by laws made in a Polish Parliament, and in which the Roman Catholic Church shall be inviolate. They wish to see their banner with the white eagle unfurled above the citadel of Warsaw; to have their coin stamped with a national motto; in a word, to have their constitution restored to them, or such another given as would put Poland on an equality with the Grand Duchy of Finland.* But

---

* The Grand Duchy of Finland has now a constitution of its own, and the people are, on the whole, contented. Since their annexation to Russia, in 1809, we have been continually hearing of the desires of the Finns to be reunited to Sweden. A tour in Finland in the summer

to have such a constitution Poland must also have its own army, and it is vain to suppose that the Russian

of 1863 soon convinced me that this is not the case. Out of a population of 1,630,000 there are, perhaps, about 80,000 or 100,000 Swedish proprietors, who entertain the same desires with Polish proprietors in the Ukrain or Volhynia, and would naturally be glad to have Finland reunited to their mother country. On the other hand, the Finnish proprietors will all say to you, what one of the late deputies to the *Landtag* said to me : 'Finland is a very small country, and as it is impossible for us to be quite independent, we get the nearest approach to it from the Russian Government, which allows us to manage our own affairs as we please. We have our Landtag in our capital of Helsingfors, where the four Estates, the nobles, clergy, merchants, and peasants, meet to make our laws and impose taxes; we have our little army and fleet; our language and our religion are inviolate; the Russian service is open to our youth; and, what is more, as we are a very poor country, we have a rich protector to fall back upon for our corn supply in case of dearth. If we were reunited to Sweden, we should lose our individuality directly, and be what we were before, a province of Sweden sending our deputation to Stockholm; and, as Sweden is as poor a country as ours, we could get very little aid from her if we wanted any. We prefer the Emperor of Russia as our Grand Duke as long as he allows us to govern ourselves, and we must put up with having our fortunes linked with those of Russia. It is true we do not like to have the English fleet ravaging our shores and destroying our commerce; but the chance of that is not so great as the danger of having the Russians walking over the ice, if we were a Swedish province. We are a peaceable people, quite contented as we are, and do not want to be dragged into the quarrel.' Such, the tourist would find, is at present the general sentiment among the Finns; a conversation with Swedes would, of course, give him another impression. The Finns are in character the very opposite of the Poles. Their heavy phlegmatic good sense and superior civilisation attract the consideration of the Russian Government and the respect of the Russian people; and, altogether, the million and a half of Finns are as happy as Dutchmen.

A still greater mistake is made by those who lead the Western public

Government would ever allow this. For years Russia has worried the Porte to admit Christian Greeks into his army. If the Sultan were to comply, he would not remain six months in Europe. So, if Russia practised what she advises her neighbours to do, Poland would certainly soon use her force against Russia to carry out her grand idea of 1772.

But the great majority of Poles desire a complete severance from Russia. With the remembrance of their past greatness rankling in their minds, the desire is natural, and it might be gratified (if their aspirations did not extend from the Baltic to the Black Sea) by the formation of a small Catholic Poland of 5,000,000 or 6,000,000 of inhabitants, placed like Greece under the guarantee of all Europe, which would coalesce to resist all attacks made on it as to repress all attacks made by it. Whether this would be to the interest or happiness of the Poles is quite another affair. Many Poles think that it would not; for there are some peoples in Europe who have shown themselves quite

to suppose that the so-called Baltic Provinces of Russia, Liefland, Courland, Esthland, are only waiting a fit occasion to drop away from Russia. These provinces produce the most valued public servants of the Russian Government; they are, as I said before, the hotbed of Russian statesmen and generals, and their interests, pecuniary and social, are entirely bound up with those of Russia. There are, no doubt, elements of discontent, as there are everywhere else, but they are insignificant. Generally, Europe is persuaded that Russia is an empire of patchwork, ready to fall to pieces at the first great movement: my opinion is just the contrary, the greater the danger, the stronger Russia will become as a nation.

incapable of self-government, among which the Irish, the Greeks, and the Poles stand foremost. Their national character is too petulant, impulsive, and turbulent. Besides, Poland does not possess that well-regulated proportion of forces which is necessary to the well-being of a popular government. There are a few old aristocratic families jealous of each other; a talented democratic literary party opposed to the former; a horde of petty nobility with wishes beyònd their means; a middle class, of whom the greater part are Germans or else Jews—the latter socially *hors la loi*; and the *kholopi*, a peasantry the most ignorant and abject in Europe. Such a state would contain all the seeds of turbulence and disorder, very few of order and happiness. Past experience, it would appear, has failed to teach even her most influential men the beauty of concord in a nation which is striving, by moral as by physical means, to obtain its autonomy. Already during the present insurrection the jealousies of the leading men are apparent, and the enmity of Czartorysky and Mickievicz in the civil, of Langievicz and Mieroslawsky in the military department of the national government, give a warning of the confusion which may be caused by an independent Poland. Even if all . the parties were united, the threat to carry on the great crusade against Russia for the favourite idea of 1772 still remains.

Still, by one of these two methods only is it possible

to patch up a peace for the present — an independent
kingdom of Poland, which would probably be for years
in a state of semi-anarchy, or only united for the sake
of crusading against its neighbours,—or Poland constitutionally governed by Russia.   In the latter case
—and it is vain to expect anything else, however constitutionally the Russians may govern the Poles — the
history of Poland and Russia will be a repetition of
the history of Ireland and England, and the last we
shall hear of the Polish question will only be when
there remains not one single Catholic priest or one
single Polish woman in Poland.

CHAPTER VIII.

THE STEPPES OF SOUTHERN RUSSIA.

Introduction to my Second *Poputchik*—A Georgian Merchant—
Leave Kharkov—Uninteresting Journey—Conversations with my
Companion—Incidents on the Road —His Manners and Habits—
Invitation to Tiflis—Rostov, on the Don—The Country of the
Don Cossacks—Novotcherkask—Mineral Riches of the Country
Modern Ataman of Cossacks—Sports of the Steppes—Country
Life in Russia—Its Monotony—Amusements — Gambling—
Character of the Cossacks—Foreigners in Russia—the *Nemetz*
or German—Foreign Influence on Russia—Adventurers—Cele-
brated Germans—Germanism and Gallicism—Wisdom of Cathe-
rine II.—Germanism under the Emperor Nicholas—Antipathy
of German and Russian Character—The Germans without
Tact in their Dealings with other People—Opinion of Germans by a Russian — Russia Fifty Years behind Western
Europe.

A S I had no great wish to continue my journey to
the Don in a *teléga*, I caused a notice to be stuck
up in the post office that I wanted a *poputchik* who
had a good carriage and was journeying my way. But
day after day passed, and, as I was afraid of losing the
fine weather which then prevailed in the steppe, I at
last became impatient, and ordered horses and the old
teléga for the next morning, packed my traps, and
went to bed. About 12 o'clock I was awakened by
the servant of the inn, a dirty, dull, but good-natured

fellow, who had during my illness slept on the mat of my door like a watch-dog, ready to start up at the slightest call. He had without ceremony introduced three strangers into the room. When candles were lighted, I saw three tall figures in Circassian costume standing before my bed in a state of perplexity and uneasiness, as though they did not exactly understand in whose presence they were. As in Russia every man is judged by his uniform, epaulettes, or orders, it is somewhat puzzling when anyone is seen for the first time in his nightshirt or a bath. When they were seated around my bedside and had each lit a *paperos*, the speaker, a man about forty, told me he was a Georgian merchant returning from Moscow to his home near Tiflis, where he had a wife and family. Would I consent to have him for a *poputchik*? He had a comfortable carriage, and would arrange his time to suit my plans. We soon agreed (as usual in such cases) to share the expense of the post-horses. He would make all the arrangements, and would lay in a stock of provisions, as nothing was to be had on the road except eggs, cabbage soup, and *kasha.* Not being quite recovered, and fearing a relapse of fever, I stipulated that we should halt for a few hours now and then at any station where there was a tolerably clean sofa to lie down upon. To this he willingly consented, and then, with his two brother-merchants, took his departure, promising to call for me with the *tarantas* the next morning.

Punctually at 11 o'clock we started — myself, the Georgian, and his servant; and, rattling down and then up the steep of the ravine in which Kharkov is built, we were soon out on the naked steppe.. A few miles beyond we quitted the *chaussée* which goes on to Odessa, continuing our journey over the common road, which is nothing more than a track over the rolling steppe, with piles and posts planted at intervals on either side to guide the traveller when the snow lies deep on the waste. Woe betide him who swerves from these landmarks in the bitter colds of winter, when the keen north wind and snow-dust are sweeping over the shelterless plain! Many are the unfortunate *tchumaki*, or pedlars, whose well-preserved but stiffened bodies are uncovered by the thaws of spring!

The description of a journey over the steppes of Russia at the end of autumn would be as dull to the reader as the journey itself is to the traveller. Little is to be seen of the peasantry. They are huddled together in their reeking hovels, and the few who are encountered on the road, with boots half way up their bodies and sheep-skins muffling the other half, are neither picturesque nor otherwise attractive. The country, the weather, the sky, and the aspect of the people are all alike gloomy and monotonous.

My *poputchik* and I were soon on very good terms. He was a very fervent Christian, had a mass-book with him which he read every now and then aloud, and took great trouble in explaining to me the dogmas of his Armenian creed. His simplicity, good nature, and ignorance of the world made his conversation very amusing. He had heard that England was a very great and rich country, and wished much to go there. Did all the English understand Russian? We talked about the Circassians, who were dreadful robbers and heathens; about the Turks, towards whom he naturally had a most inveterate hatred; and about the *tchinovniks*, whom he hated and feared still more as he came into rather closer relations with them. He was evidently a man of the simplest character, passing through life in a comfortable though monotonous manner, making his periodical journeys between Tiflis and Moscow, pocketing his roubles, fearing God, and doing his duty to his neighbour and himself. A perfect man of peace, he had a great abhorrence of fire-arms; and, having the curiosity to examine a tiny revolver which I carried loaded in my pocket, he sent a bullet within a few inches of my head, nearly fainted at what he had done, fell on his knees in a fit of horror, and then, starting up, embraced me in another paroxysm of affection and joy at his deliverance from homicide. From that moment he treated me with redoubled attention, begging me only to draw the charges out of the revolver, which, he said, might go off by itself while we were in the carriage.

Before starting he had told me not to trouble myself

about provisions, as he had a large stock with him. But as, in travelling, I prefer a dry biscuit to the contents of another man's wallet about which there is the least suspicion, I had, of course, taken with me my own stores. When the servant spread the meal in the little room at one of the post-stations, I found that it consisted of wine, pressed, he said, from the grapes of his own vineyard, and cheese, made from the milk of his own goats, both of which his thrifty wife had packed up for him when he left his home a few weeks before. I need hardly say that the wine was undrinkable, owing to the careless way in which it had been made, and from the taste of the skins in which it had lain, while the stench of the goat's-milk cheese was nauseating. Nevertheless my friend ate and drank with considerable gusto; the viands reminded him, he said, of his home. The rest of his stores consisted of roasted fowls, sausages, and bread, wrapped up in old newspapers; besides a supply of tea and sugar, the only part of his wallet acceptable to me. Fortunately I was ill enough not to be able to eat, which was sufficient excuse for refusing without giving him pain. His manners at table were perfectly natural and unaffected. He mostly made use of his fingers to feed himself, while his knife was now and then called into requisition to clean his nails, and his fork to pick his teeth. Notwithstanding these and a few other little peculiarities, my Georgian companion showed much kind and generous feeling. He stopped wherever and as long as I pleased on the road, and more than once, when the fever returned, nursed me almost as tenderly as a woman could, humoured all my whims, and would have half killed me with Georgian household remedies if I had let him.　When we parted at Rostov on the Don, he pressed me to continue my journey with him to Tiflis, where he would introduce me to the society of his countrymen and women, that I might see and judge of their private life for myself. Such an opportunity of seeing something of the very secluded society of that country was one seldom offered to a traveller; but the lateness of the season compelled me, with much regret, to decline it.　On parting he embraced me with much fervour, prayed that God would accompany me, and proceeded on his journey.

Rostov on the right bank of the Don, a few miles from its sand-choked mouth, was one of the *kreposts* or forts, with a few surrounding houses, in the most ancient Russian times.　It is now a town of about 12,000 inhabitants, rambling, unpaved, of a very nondescript appearance, but with a highly increasing trade.　In the neighbourhood are many extensive slaughter-houses, where the cattle of the surrounding steppes are killed, and the flesh and skins salted and dried for export, much in the same manner as on the banks of the La Plata.

Having remained a day or two at Rostov, I passed over to Novotcherkask, the capital of the country of the Don Cossacks.　Hundreds of wagons drawn by a couple of oxen, and containing not more than half a ton of coals each, were toiling along the muddy and seamed road towards Rostov. Such is the inefficient mode of transport still used in this country! This anthracite coal, of which there are enormous fields around the Don, is hardly worked at all, and when brought to the ports cannot compete in price with English coal, which has been brought as ballast by ships coming to load with hides, tallow, and corn stuffs. The working of these coal mines ought to be a source of wealth to a country whose chief drawback is a want of wood. Besides coal, other valuable minerals are known in these parts, but the land-owners keep the existence of the mines as secret as possible. The reason is to be found in the constant interference of persons in authority, which would make them a source of much more vexation than profit.

The formerly famous position of *ataman* of the Cossacks has subsided into that of an ordinary governor-general of a province, who, however, still bears the old name.* When I paid him a visit I found him in full-dress uniform, stars, crosses, and orders ; in which dress all ministers, governors, and high officials transact business during the hours of office. Among the many amiable things he said, the kindest was the expression of a wish to get rid of me as soon as possible. He advised me, if I did not wish to lose the last boat that

* The heir-apparent of Russia, Nicholai Alexandrovitch, is now *ataman* of the Don Cossacks.

left Taganrog for Odessa, not to accept the hospitality which he would be so happy to offer me, and which others would press on me more closely. The advice was too good to be neglected, so after a couple of days among the Cossacks, I returned to Rostov, and thence journeyed on to Taganrog.

An abundance of sport in hunting and fishing was offered to me if I would wait until the snow fell or the frost set in. Two kinds of hunting are peculiar to the steppe. At the dawn of an early winter's day, the bustards or wild turkeys are roused from among the tall grass by the steed of the Cossack. As their wings are glued and numbed by the hoar frost, they trust to fleetness of foot to escape from their pursuers. Another amusement is to hunt the wolf of the steppe. The snow must be fresh fallen and a few inches deep. The huntsman is armed only with a whip, having a leaden bullet at the end of the thong. An exciting chase is afforded, but the wolf's shorter legs get fatigued in the snow and he cannot escape. A whirl of the bullet at last strikes him down.

Russia is by nature the dullest and most monotonous country in Europe. Even in St. Petersburg and Moscow half the world pass their time in a profound *ennui*, which can scarcely be chased away by rounds of convivial and boisterous excitement. In the interior it is worse, and it needs no little effort of mind in a rich proprietor to remain there many weeks together.

If he have intellect and occupation enough to make the
hours pass swiftly, in the fulfilment of duty or in study,
it is otherwise with the females of his family.   Distances are so great that there can be little interchange
of social visits; newspapers are stale before they reach
remote country houses. ' We are obliged,' says a Russian
writer, ' to have recourse to strong and frequent excitement, such as gambling, dancing, uproarious society,
the pleasures of the table, furious sledge-driving, to the
passionate language of the theatre, to constant locomo-
tion, and changes of scene.   Anything which can break
the monotony of a prisoner's existence is an imperious
necessity in Russia, and must be satisfied at any price,
to avoid the alternative of perishing from dulness,
weariness, and an indescribable consuming longing.'

I found this to be thoroughly the case at Novotcherkask.   Most of the officers had served their youth in
the capitals, and, now on the reserve, had but nominal
or occasional employment.   An hour or two sufficed
for the necessary business of the day; and then came
the cards.   Gambling is a passion which begins timidly
at the Atlantic, increases in force as it proceeds east-
ward, and reaches its climax in Shanghae or Pekin.
In Europe, a man will gamble away his movables and
immovables, and his reputation into the bargain; in
China a man's concubines and daughters go to pay a
gambling debt.   It is a marked passion among the
Cossacks.   These honorary members of the Russian

army have made one or two well-known excursions into the West during the wars of 1813–15 and the Hungarian campaign of 1849. In all, they were always very successful in paying themselves, so that a vast amount of treasure, gold and silver, jewels and rarities found its way to the villages of the Don and Volga. But such things seldom remain as heirlooms in the family of the fortunate warrior. The gambling propensities of the country cause a frequent change of possession, so that when there is no more ready cash, there is generally some silver goblet from an Alsacian church, or a set of jewels which formerly decked the person of an Hungarian dame, to be staked against an equivalent of roubles silver.

But, after all, the Cossacks are not half so black as their enemies have painted them. Though their very name has in France become a byword to express acts of ruthless violence, the visitor will find among their men and women some of the most generous and best educated in Russia.

In England, in the good old days of stage-coaches, when a smooth upper lip and chin were almost emblems of a person's respectability, any foreigner or stranger who was unfortunate enough to appear in a secluded district with much hair about his face, was immediately put down as a Frenchman. In the interior of Russia, every foreigner is a *Nemetz* or German. Of all the strangers who have sought their fortune in Russia the German has played the chief part, and excited the greatest antipathy. Around the Volga and Don are several colonies of agricultural Germans, some dating from the time of Catherine; yet until now there has been hardly any amalgamation among the two peoples. A few words on this foreign element in Russia, which for more than two hundred years has made its influence felt among the people, may, perhaps, be not without interest.

Long before the time of Peter the Great, a host of foreign adventurers found in the Russia of the *tsars* a field for their talents and ambition. Peter invited thousands to enter his service to help him in forcing his reforms on the Russian people. During his reign and that of his successors, not only Germans, but British, Dutch, Italian, Swiss, and Greek adventurers flocked to Russia. The British and Dutch were utilised in establishing a Russian navy; the Germans in forming the civil and military administrations, and training up a race of *tchinovniks*; the French, fleeing from persecution, became either milliners or diplomats; the Swiss, teachers of language and polite literature; while Italians and Greeks, with their usual elasticity, insinuated themselves into any service, from that of a *valet de chambre* to that of chancellor of the empire. In the Russian history of the last two centuries the names of at least one-third of the chief actors are of foreign extraction. Many of these names have been

Russified, by some affixed syllable, without destroying the trace of the original. Thus, when we read of Brunov and Cankrine, it must not be forgotten that their forefathers were Herrn Braun and Krebs.

When the Baltic and Finnish provinces were incorporated with Russia, an enormous field was at once opened to their nobility. The army, navy, and civil service soon became flooded with young Germans. The university of Dorpat sent forth its physicians, surgeons, and professors, who have ever since occupied the chief places in the public services and universities.

Among the celebrated foreigners who have played a prominent part during the last 150 years may be mentioned the famous Biren, the favourite of the Empress Anne, who, with the celebrated Münnich and Osterman, formed a triumvirate, against which all the national Russian party strove in vain. Bestujev, the famous minister of Elizabeth, is said to have belonged to a Scotch family, whose name was Best. The father of Count Panin, the minister of Catherine, was an Italian. Nesselrode was a Bavarian. Besides these, there are hundreds more of subordinate station, whose lives and actions have largely affected the national history.

In Russia, Germans found themselves under the powerful ægis of absolute sovereigns, whose slaves they became, while they made their masters their instruments. German discipline, German administration, German dress, periwigs, and powder, German ministers, generals, serjeants, kammerherrn, cooks, and lackeys, were all received and turned to good use The high-sounding titles of German etiquette—Wohlgeborner, Hochgeborner, Hofrath, Geheimrath, &c.,—were translated into Russian, and became distinctive titles of the *tchin*. So rooted became Germanism as a system during the early days of the empire, that all the French innovations of Elizabeth and Catherine could not check or change its stolid routine. That the omnipotence of foreigners of another religion and uncongenial habits was regarded with fierce jealousy by the proud nobility of Russia is not to be wondered at. They writhed and struggled and made vain attempts to regain what had once been theirs. The people were then, as they are now, ignorant and much-enduring, true to their traditions, their love towards their *tsar*, their religion, and their country. They naturally hated the Germans, and their hatred could now and then be made subservient to the purposes of personal ambition. While Peter III. was frivolously parading his Germanism, half worshipping Frederick of Prussia, reviewing his Holstein Guards, or rudely toying with Mademoiselle Woronzov, his unfaithful but talented spouse was on her knees before the altar of an orthodox church, kissing the dirty hand of some pope, or plotting between the caresses of Gregory Orlov or some other thoroughly Russian lover. The whole revolution which overthrew Peter III., and elevated a German princess to the throne of Russia, was half brought about by the pretended Russian feeling of Catherine, pitted against the Germanism of her husband.

Under the Emperor Nicholas, Germanism fell apparently into disgrace. The Emperor was in the hottest stage of his centralising fever, bent on Russifying and amalgamating into an orthodox whole the different breeds and creeds of his vast empire. Philoslavism was then also rampant in its Utopian theories. The national feeling, already half smothered under foreign encumbrances, was summoned from its recesses, and the Russian language, Russian dress, and Russian cooking were paraded as emblems of the revival. Germanism was at its lowest ebb. Only four men with German names were found near the Court. Hundreds in hot haste changed their names into *ëff* and *chëff* and *sky*. Their very names barred the advancement of men whose fathers came from the Baltic or the petty states of Germany. The cloud soon passed by, and Germanism regained its influence. But at the same time the Russian national character had passed into a more seemly phase. Its rich language was no longer considered good only for hinds; a spirit of enquiry was searching into the past, and extracting materials for imparting a greater impulse to the national feeling. The Russian element, left to itself, has during the last eight years made more progress than during the thirty which preceded them.

The antagonism between the German and Sclavonic character must always exist. The destiny of the German race has ever been to encroach on and subdue the Sclavonic. Long ago it overpowered, though it never could assimilate, the Czechs, the Hungarians, and the Poles. In Russia the contrary took place. The Russians have subjugated a portion of the German materially; the German has subjugated the Russian morally and mentally. The German is compensated for his defeat in the one by his victory in the other. All the antipathy of the two characters remains the same, and added to this antipathy is a jealousy which is not unnatural when two races of people are formed into one nation. The Russians are jealous because Germans and Poles monopolise the best places in the public service— for the Germans from their capabilities, the Poles from policy, are more often put forward than the Russians, who naturally abuse the Government for what they call its partiality, and feel a more intense dislike of the intruders.

In spite of all their sterling qualities the Germans find themselves disliked, whether in America, Greece, or Russia. The reason is a want of tact, which leads them to do all they can to increase the feeling of antagonism. In America, whole villages and towns are German, and only German; in Russia the German colonists of the South are now just what they were when they immigrated. The Germans who have sought their fortune in Russia have generally belonged to the better-informed class. Called for the avowed purpose of training the people into a new life, they have been more or less successful. Besides the mortification of feeling that they owe much to foreigners, the Russians are continually reminded of it by phrases which tell them with sufficient bluntness that their character is incapable of the higher phases of civilisation and art, and that foreigners are needed to supply the deficiency! However much Russians may despise the wholesale abuse of Custine and his school, the Germans, from their familiar acquaintance with Russia, know how to touch the most sensitive nerves, and awaken the bitterest feelings of dislike, which a difference of habits and character in the two people tends only to strengthen. The Russian is all giving, the German all receiving. The one is generous and impulsive, the other reserved and parsimonious. The Russian character is aspiring, reforming, and liberal; the German is the most conservative by habit, and from selfish motives averse to any change in the Government, by which their influence would be endangered. 'The Germans are capital fellows, while they are young,' said an angry Russian to me one day, ' but no sooner do they become generals, than they far surpass us in absolutism and tyranny. They are the cause of half the obloquy which is cast on Russian character abroad.' That a foreigner, after residing some time in Russia, would find much to condemn in Russian character and Russian institutions, I have already admitted;

but he would also find that they do not deserve those wholesale detractions which travellers copy out of one another's books, or which the Polish press is interested in diffusing among the people of Western Europe. The reason is that they are now passing through stages which the nations of Western Europe traversed half a century ago. In another fifty years that country may be as far advanced as England or Germany is now, while these countries, continuing their path of progress and well-being, may still have to reproach Russia for being behind *their* age.

CHAPTER IX.

THE BLACK SEA AND THE LEVANT.

Taganrog—Kertch—Emigration of Crimean Tartars—Southern
Coast of the Crimea—Sevastopol—A Storm—Black Sea Storms—
Catastrophe—A pretty Captain—'Where Ignorance is Bliss, 'tis
Folly to be Wise'—Odessa—Its Backwardness—Constantinople
—An Adventure of Travel—How to get a Divorce—A Marriage
—Scenes on Board a Russian Steamer in the Levant—Russian .
Pilgrims—The Mussulman Passengers—Rhodes—Anglomania of
a Russian Gentleman—Latakia and its Tobacco—Gulf of Scan-
deroon—Alexandrette—The Russian Frigate 'General Admiral.'

THE last boat of the season generally leaves Taganrog
about the end of October, before the closing of the
shallow sea of Azof by ice. Between that town and
Kertch the voyage lasts two days, many hours being
lost by touching at the corn ports of Mariopol, Bordi-
ansk, and Eisk, the inhabitants of which consist of
Russians, Tartars, Germans, Greeks, Armenians, Jews,
and even Maronites from Lebanon.

At Kertch, the junction for the traffic of the line of
the Caucasus, we remained another two days, during
which I was much interested by witnessing the embarkation of about 2,000 Tartars, emigrating to the
opposite coast in Asia Minor, where land had been
allotted them by the Turkish Government. The
Crimea had by this time become half emptied of its

Tartar population. Turkish missionaries had long exerted their influence to promote this emigration. Families sold off their cattle, land, and effects at the lowest prices, and hastened to get away. During the years 1860-1 land could be bought for a trifle, and was eagerly taken up by Russian speculators. Attempts were afterwards made to bring in colonies of Bulgarians and Little Russians, but they did not remain long, and much of the best land in the Crimea is consequently waste. As to the Tartars, the Russians were very glad to get rid of them. Though generally peaceable, their hostile behaviour during the occupation of the Crimea by the Allies, their well-known sympathy with Turks in religion and political desires, were sufficient reasons why the Russians were not sorry that the Tartars should no longer be in the Crimea, in the event of another war with Turkey and the Great Powers.

I had intended to go overland from Kertch to Sevastopol, to view the magnificent scenery of the south coast of the Crimea; but a return of fever and the commencement of winter compelled me to continue my voyage in the steamer. The mountain summits, already covered with snow, afforded, in the intervals of sunshine, a few glimpses of their grandeur. At Sevastopol, where the steamer remained only a few hours, I had just time to take a rapid glance at the ruined forts, the roofless and windowless barracks, and the battered buildings, most of which were in the same condition as at the close of the war. Hundreds of people were still daily employed in those situations where the battle had been thickest, in picking up the shot and fragments of bombs. Many bombs, found unexploded, sometimes burst in being rolled along, more than once causing loss of life. It was with the greatest regret that I was prevented from visiting the scenes of memorable battles in the grandest siege of human experience.

The passage from Sevastopol to Odessa, generally occupying only a few hours, took us two days, as we encountered one of those famous storms which are so frequent in the Black Sea. The worst of these blow from the NE. to the NW. On the coast of the Caucasus the wind called the *Bora* resembles, in a fiercer form, the Mistral of the Gulf of Lyons, or the famous Pampero of the South American coast. With an un-clouded sky, the wind rushes down with terrific force from the summits of the lofty range of mountains, and, lashing up the waves in a few minutes, carries the spray of their crests along with it in one continued mist. If a ship is in the way, its lower rigging, decks, and anchors are soon covered with ice, which grows steadily thicker. It becomes almost impossible to work the ship; the hawse-holes are choked with ice; the cables are immovable; the men, bleeding from the nose and nails, are incapable of action, and the only escape is to run before the wind southward, where, according to Russian navigators, on passing a certain line the temperature suddenly changes, and the wind abates. A few years ago, a large man-of-war schooner, at anchor in one of the bays on the coast, was caught by a *Bora*, and sank beneath the mass of water which congealed on its upper works. The officer, who was afterwards charged to raise her, told me that they found a gun loaded and pointed against the cable, as if the crew had vainly tried this device for breaking away the anchor in order to run ashore. The captain was found sitting in his arm-chair; the officers, wrapped in fur cloaks, were lying in their berths in the same position as when they fell asleep. This terrible catastrophe took place within a short distance of the shore, in full view of the crews of some vessels which had succeeded in running ashore, but who were prevented from giving any help. As we were in another part of the Black Sea, the storm which we encountered was of a different character. The air was darkened with snow-drift, and, although there was not much danger to a ship properly handled, the condition of our captain rendered the position anything but agreeable.

Fortunately there were few passengers, one only being a lady, and she possessed of much fortitude, or the confusion would have been unbearable. The captain, a Greek, as the barometer fell, had raised his courage with Hollands. When the storm increased, he sat down on cushions on the floor of the cabin, and, served by a ready attendant, tossed off glass after glass, until he had only just enough recollection to be mischievous. His second, a master in the navy, was fortunately a sober man; and the engineer, an Englishman, re-assured me by saying that there was still coal enough on board, by burning the dust, to last forty-eight hours. The worst, therefore, which could have happened, if the coal had all been spent, would have been to drive across the Black Sea to the Asiatic coast, for there was not a rag of canvas which would not have been blown to tatters in a moment. We could only guess at our speed, for there was not a serviceable log on board. But this did not so much matter, as the ship was going backwards a great part of the time. On the second midnight, the weather having cleared up a little, we had just found our whereabouts on the chart by comparisons of the lead, when our drunken captain woke up from a snooze, and, planting his finger on another point of the chart, ordered his second to set a course from that point. Luckily he was still too stupid to see his orders executed, or we should have made the land some fifty miles to the west of Odessa. As the wind continued to abate, we reached our destination some eighteen hours afterwards. On sighting the light-house the ridiculous almost banished the recollection of the terrific. Two colonels of infantry who during the passage had been groaning in their berths, came up on deck, and in their joy on nearing land threw their arms round the neck of our pretty captain, embraced him with tears in their eyes, and blessed him for having saved their lives and the lives of all on board. Surely if ignorance be ever bliss, it must have been so in this instance. It must, however, be admitted in fairness that this steamboat with its captain was an exception to what is generally found among the packets of the Russian Navigation Company. Most of them are well-found vessels, commanded by experienced officers of the Imperial navy, and as well furnished as the ships of the French or Austrian Companies.

When I landed in Odessa I was dropping with fever, and in that state fell among thieves, i. e. certain custom house officials, who, although we were from a Russian port, required us to go through formalities which occupied an hour or more before permitting our luggage to be landed. Despairing of ever getting to bed, I abandoned bag and baggage, and afterwards requested the master of the hotel to do what was necessary. Without this I believe I should never have got into Odessa nor out of it. For some thirty francs he released my baggage and got me permits &c. My personal experience of Odessa was from my bed-room window. After a week's unsuccessful torture by the doctors, I took the first opportunity of a few hours clear-headedness to run away from them, had myself carried on board a steamer going South, and was quite well before we arrived at Smyrna. I recommend this sudden change of climate as the surest remedy for getting rid of an obstinate remittent fever.

Odessa, the third city of the empire, is a disgrace to

it. In 1861 it was unlighted by gas, unpaved, and undrained. If it be wet weather, there is mud enough in the streets to drown a *droshky*. But this neglect must not be laid to the charge of the inhabitants: it is the fault of a government which until lately was constantly interfering with local administration. Many proposals had been made, and companies formed for lighting the city by gas, and for general improvements, but all had been rendered abortive by the intrigues of the higher authorities. Now that greater liberty in local administrations has been allowed in Russia, Odessa, it is to be hoped, will assume an appearance more befitting the chief commercial city of a large empire.*

In Constantinople I had just time and strength sufficient for a stroll through the bazaar. I shall spare the reader a description of our sail through the straits of the Golden Horn, of the plain of Troas, or of Sappho's isle. At Smyrna a romantic event which had long been preparing was brought to the usual finale of a marriage. As the episode is not an unusual one of Levantine society, I will hastily sketch the particulars.

Our cabin passengers on board the 'Chersonesus' were, a Russian prince,—one of a family swarm—who filled the modest post of agent to the Steamboat Company, two other Russian gentlemen, who were brothers, and myself. The younger of the two brothers was

---

* Many improvements have since been carried out. The city is already lighted with gas, and the streets are beginning to be paved.

afflicted with Anglomania, the greatest symptom of which was a hideous bulldog, which he took on shore at all the ports at which we touched to try him against the canine canaille which abound there. The elder brother, who was the hero of the history, attracted our attention by his deep despondency and restless demeanour. Having convinced myself that he was not mad, I could account for his behaviour only by assuming that he was in love. This was in truth the secret. The evening we arrived at Smyrna, a veiled lady came on board and took possession of the empty ladies' cabin. I questioned the brother, who only repeated ' que c'etait un ange,' and bade me wait and see the result. The next morning the other brother, taking me aside, confessed in a delightful confusion of words that he was going to marry the *angel* that day, and begged me to join the prince above-mentioned as witness of his marriage. Half an hour afterwards the Bishop of Smyrna, with his archimandrite, attended by six of his inferior clergy bearing their superior's robes and pipes, came on board, and was conducted into the cabin, where their attendants got ready the pipes, and the two dignitaries sat down to smoke their *chibouks*. Shortly afterwards two or three guests arrived, with one young lady to act as bridesmaid. The veiled bride, a pretty dark-eyed woman of about twenty, came forth from her cabin, when we all took our places around the table, and the ceremony began. As soon as the knot was tied, the

Bishop and clergy, followed by the husband and wife, and they by the rest of the guests, paraded round and round the table, while we pelted the happy couple with bonbons, of which a good supply stood on the table. This done, the bride's and bridegroom's health was drunk by all the company, the clergy smoked a few more pipes, and an hour afterwards we were steaming along the coast, with the bridal pair still on board.

Their previous history I only heard afterwards. The lady was a Jewess, the wife of a consul of one of the Great Powers at a large port of the Archipelago. Dissatisfied with her husband, she had made the acquaintance of the Russian commercial agent at the same place. Arrangements were made for a separate elopement, for a rendezvous at Smyrna, a forced divorce, and a new marriage. The gentleman was detained in Russia beyond the day named for the meeting, and thus his uncommon sadness during the passage was explained. The lady, followed, as it seemed, by her husband and his emissaries, arrived at Smyrna at the appointed time, and was kept in concealment for more than a week. The divorce had been a very short matter. Declaring herself a Christian, she was baptized into the holy orthodox Greek Church—a ceremony which cancelled her former marriage, as that Church does not recognise marriage between a Christian and a Jew. The saddest part of the business was that the woman, in abandoning her husband, had at the same time abandoned two little children. Nevertheless the Greek clergy, many of whom will do anything for money, gave their sanction, in the person of their bishop, to an act which they ought to have used all their influence to prevent. On meeting with the chief actors in this adventure a year afterwards, I had reason to fancy that they had already repented their folly. The most curious part of the story remains to be told. The first husband was looking down through the skylight into the cabin, and actually witnessed the marriage of his own wife to another man, and had not the power to interfere and stop the ceremony.

A trip on board a Russian steamer in Levantine waters presents a curious picture of mixed European life and Asiatic habits. The whole fore part of the ' Chersonesus ' was occupied by Russian and other Sclavonic peasants, dressed in their accustomed sheepskins, and accompanied by their village popes—all pilgrims to the Holy City. Thousands of the Russian peasantry perform the pilgrimage to Jerusalem every year, as the steamboat company is bound by its contract with the Government to carry such passengers at a very cheap rate. The cost from Odessa to Jerusalem and back again is less than 5l., a sum which every pilgrim easily regains, by laying out his little stock of money in Jerusalem in the purchase of beads, crosses, and other sanctified trifles cut in olive wood or agate, and reselling them on his return to his fellow-villagers, who were unable to make the journey. Before leaving Odessa these poor pilgrims are obliged to convince the authorities that they have enough money for their journey; and again, on landing at Jaffa, they are required to deposit a sufficient sum for their return in the hands of the Consul, lest they should spend all their money in Jerusalem. If these measures were not enforced, the Holy Land would soon be filled with devout paupers. The poor, long-bearded, pious, but very dirty *moujiks*, with their popes, who are in no wise superior in demeanour or cleanliness, make any shift and support any trial, in order to make the pilgrimage. At different hours of the day they might be seen gathered around their priest or some grey-bearded pilgrim, listening to a chapter of the Bible or to the relation of some wonderful miracles enacted on previous pilgrims.

In all their habits and ways these Russian peasants form a remarkable contrast to the Mussulman folk, to whom the after part of the deck is generally set apart for an abode. Here both sexes, scrupulously clean in their persons and dress, have with them all the comforts of their homes—soft mattresses and pillows, thick coverlets of cotton, and well-stored baskets of provisions. The women, half unveiled from negligence, look around, with their large eyes wild with surprise, on the novel scene in their monotonous lives—now peeping curiously down into the engine-room, pointing at the froth of waters in the vessel's wake, or clapping their little hands at the sight of some approaching vessel. At sunrise and sunset the most pious of the men would be seen prostrate on the deck, performing their devotion. Altogether the variety of figure, costume, and colour on board, the charm of the picturesque mountain shore on one side and the islands on the other, with the smooth azure sea and an unclouded sky, must render a run down this coast quite a treat to anyone accustomed only to the more sombre scenes of northern lands.

A halt of a few hours at Rhodes gave us time for a ramble on shore, during which a mortal combat took place between the Russian's bulldog and half the curs of the place, who attacked him in a body. The bulldog gallantly beat them off, nearly killing one and driving two others over the quay into the water, to the great astonishment of the Turkish spectators.

A stroll up the street of the famous knights, now nearly deserted and falling into ruins, a hasty visit to the citadel, which was destroyed a few years back by the explosion of an undiscovered magazine by lightning, occupied our time until the bell rang for the departure of the boat. The ports of Messina, Alexandrette, Latakia, Beyrout, and Jaffa are the remaining stations touched at before arriving at Alexandria. Of Latakia and its tobacco I may here say a few words, which may be not uninteresting to smokers.

The Syrian tobacco, known as *djebel* or tobacco of the mountain, is of excellent quality, which might, if the cultivation were more extended, compete with the production of American plantations in the European market.   At present the great market for it is Egypt, where it is much preferred to the Turkish tobacco of Cavalla or Salonika, especially that sort of *djebel* known in Europe under the name of *Latakia,* but which in the country has its particular name of *Abou Riha.*   Its peculiarity and celebrity are said to have arisen in the following manner.

In the year 1742 the mountain tribes around Latakia were in one of their periodical insurrections.   The crops of tobacco that season had been very abundant, and the farmers, being unable to dispose of it to the merchants of the coast, stowed the leaves away among the rafters of their huts, where it remained the whole winter. When order was re-established, this tobacco, blackened by the smoke, was sold at a low price, and exported to Egypt, its usual market.   A difference between the aroma and flavour of this tobacco and that of former imports so pleased the amateurs, that extensive orders were sent for more of the same quality.   Inquiries having been made among the mountaineers, it was found that the tobacco had acquired its dark colour and peculiar flavour from having been exposed so long to the smoke of a particular wood, a species of mountain oak, called by the natives *Ezer,* and extensively used by them as fuel during the winter. Experience afterwards showed that the best tobacco came from the dampest districts, that in a damp atmosphere the leaf became more thoroughly impregnated with the smoky flavour; and also that the higher the elevation of its growth, the better was the quality of the tobacco. Tobacco thus prepared now forms the chief item in the commerce of the port of Latakia, and brings in to the country a revenue of more than four millions of piastres. People once accustomed to smoke it always prefer it to every other; although at first trial the taste is repugnant to palates accustomed to Turkish or American tobacco. Very little of that tobacco sold as Latakia in London, is really such; the true sort may be easily recognised, from the quantity of nitre which it contains, and which constantly fizzes during the smoking.

The gulf of Alexandretta, or Scanderoon, extending far inland to the 'Gates of Syria' and the famous plain of Issus, separates Asia Minor from Syria. At the northern point, just beyond the spit of mud thrown out by the waters of the Gighoon, is the bay and now ruined settlement of Ayas, formerly a post of the Genoese. Here were assembled for winter quarters in 1860–1 the Russian fleet, forming, with several English and French men-of-war, the Syrian squadron drawn together by the late massacres in Lebanon. On arriving at the little town of Alexandretta on the southern or Syrian side of the gulf, I was fortunate enough to meet a party of Russian officers returning from Jerusalem, many of whom had been my companions during my former voyage round the world. The captain of the Chersonesus kindly offered to take us over the gulf, although it was at least forty miles out of his course; so that at two o'clock one morning in November 1860, I stepped for the first time on board the Russian frigate General Admiral.

CHAPTER X.

A WINTER WITH THE RUSSIANS IN SYRIA.

The Russian Squadron—Names now given to Russian Ships—
Interpretation of them—Old Acquaintances—Russian Naval
Officers—Life on Board a Russian Man-of-War—Sympathies of
the Russian Navy towards England—Admiral Shestakov and
his Wife—Russian Sailors—Their Character and Dispositions—
Their Piety—Religious Creed—Burial of a Mahometan Sailor—
Education of Sailors—Their Pay and Rations—The Scale fixed
by Peter the Great—Naval Punishments—Relaxed Discipline—
Celebration of Saints' Days on Board—Easter among Russians
—Theatrical Performances – Jonka—Customs of Russian Sailors
—The Bay of Ayas—Shooting—Excursions—Occupation of the
Turkomans—Cultivation of Cotton in Syria and Asia Minor
—Evil System of Taxation—The Circassian and Tartar Immi-
grants—Their Condition in Asia Minor.

THE small Russian squadron which had been sent in all
haste to the coast of Syria, as soon as the massacres
of the Christians in the Lebanon became known, consisted of four frigates and two or three smaller vessels under the command of Captain, afterwards Admiral, S——,
whose broad pennant was hoisted on board the General
Admiral. This large frigate of 70 guns had been built under his superintendence at New York as an experiment,
and had been named after the Grand Duke Constantine,
then High Admiral of Russia. Her armament and interior fittings had been arranged with all that art or

money could supply, and altogether she was a very noble vessel. The other frigates, whose names I give in order to explain their meanings, were the Gromoboi, Ilia Mourometz, Oleg, and Osliab. The Gromoboi, during the frequent intercourse between the English and Russian men-of-war at this time, had been changed by the seamen of the former—whose custom of turning all foreign words into some English word of similar sound is well known—into the Drummer Boy, which name the ship long afterwards preserved among the Russians themselves. The 'Gromoboi' was a legendary hero of North Russia, a kind of Russian Robin Hood. Ilia Mourometz, one of the old heroes of half fabulous times, was, according to the story, the son of a Bogatyr or knight of Kiev, and was carefully kept at home and educated by his mother until the age of thirty, when she sent him forth to seek for adventures. He was a man of extraordinary strength. During his journeys he came one day into a large wood, called Mourometz after a famous brigand, who was the terror of the surrounding country. He was generally known as the Solovyé, or Nightingale, because he whistled like that bird, only his voice was so powerful that it stunned and knocked down all who heard it. On seeing Ilia coming, the Solovyé fled for refuge into a large tree; but the Bogatyr tore up the tree by the roots and captured him alive. He afterwards brought him to Kiev and presented him to Knias Vladimir, who was anxious to hear the voice

of the brigand, although Ilia warned him that he would
be stunned by its vibration.   Finding his Prince determined, Ilia commanded his prisoner to whistle only half
voice; but the brigand, disobeying, began to sing with
full power, and the knight knocked out his brains with
his club.   From this adventure Ilia received the affix
of Mourometz.   Ballads about him are still familiar
among the Russian peasantry.   The name of Oleg is
better known as that of the brother-in-law of Rurik, and
regent of his empire during the minority of his son.   In
that capacity he marched with a band of his warriors
against Constantinople, which he put to ransom, besides
leaving the shield of his nephew nailed to one of its
gates in sign of conquest.   Osliab is the name of one of
those sturdy monks, who, by order of the famous saint
Sergius, formed a select band to fight against the Tartars.
By these Osliab, along with his brother monk Perisvét,
was killed at the battle of Koulikovo on the Don in
1380.   In the present day, and as a sign of the revival
of Russian national feeling, the names of their ancient
heroes may be read on the sterns of their men-of-war,
as on the commemoration monument lately set up at
Novgorod.

With many of the officers of these ships I had already
become acquainted during my previous voyage to
Japan or at the Amoor River.   Among them were
many young men whose fathers had made themselves a
name in the history of their country, either as navi-

gators or naval commanders, and who were following the same career thus auspiciously opened to them. For in Russia, owing to the direction given by Peter the Great to the whole administration, there still exists a sort of caste, by which the son in almost all professions follows the steps of his father, who after a term of service obtains many privileges, such as a gratuitous education for his sons in government colleges, with appointments for them afterwards. The sons of the white or secular clergy almost invariably become either priests or monks themselves. So in.the navy, though in a less degree, a name perpetuates itself in the service through generations. During my voyages on board of Russian ships, I became acquainted with bearers of many such names—Lazarev, the organiser of the Black Sea fleet before the war, and a Pacific explorer; Kovnilov and Nachimov, of Sinope, who commanded and were killed at Sevastopol; Krusenstern, Lütke, Lisiansky, Kotzebue, Bellingshausen, and others who are well known among all nations for their maritime discoveries. This descent of profession from father to son is not to be commended. The son too often follows it without ambition as he entered it without desire. But many of the liberal professions are shut off, owing to the lowness of their social standing, from the youth of Russia. Trade, if not considered exactly ignoble, does not confer the privilege and honour of a uniform or a pair of epaulettes. The Church is left for the peasants;

the medical profession is not popular, while the law is only just now calling into requisition private lawyers and advocates. The educated youth of Russia in the present day have to raise all these professions to the status which they deserve.

A short account of life on board a Russian man-of-war, during our wintering in the Bay of Ayas, may not be uninteresting to many English readers. In all that concerns the duties of the ship the same regulations exist as in the British or Dutch services, which were taken as models when Peter the Great and his successors invited over Englishmen and Dutchmen to organise their fleets. Although the executive or fleet officers, masters, surgeons, and engineers live and mess together, there exists, in spite of their apparent equality, the same real distinction which is perceived in other services. The members of the Russian naval service are in general as well-informed as any other class in Russia, and certainly more so than those of the military or civil service, if we except the diplomatic. For this they must thank their opportunity for travel, their knowledge of foreign languages, and literature; but chiefly their necessary contact with the natives of other lands. Most of the professional articles and works of hydrography which appear each month in the ' Morskoi Sbornik,' or Naval Magazine, are written by officers serving at home or abroad. Many make translations from English and French books relating to their professions;

while of late years, in nearly every ship on a foreign station, an Englishman instructs the young officers in the language and professional literature of the great sea-going people of the day.

It has often been said that the sympathies of educated Russians are on the side of France. The remark may apply to the generality of untravelled Russians, but it is not the case with the officers of the navy, whose sympathies, always decidedly English, sometimes assume the form of Anglomania. Experience has taught them to put confidence in Englishmen and in the work of English hands. During the time I was on board Russian ships I remarked that although they seldom lost an opportunity of exchanging civilities with English ships, such friendly visits seldom took place between French and Russians, either on board or ashore. Whether the restraint was on one side or the other, or mutual, their characters did not harmonise. Perhaps the Russians thought the French supercilious, or the French looked upon the Russians, in their favourite phrase, as thin-skinned Tartars; but one thing is certain, that no great cordiality existed between them.

Admiral Shestakov, who commanded the squadron, was an aide-de-camp of the Emperor, had spent some time in England, and afterwards in America, where he had superintended the building of some ships. One of the first men of his profession in Russia, he was admirably adapted to occupy a post, in which, during peace, diplomatic abilities are as much needed as nautical strategy. He had studied the naval systems of different nations, and his knowledge, directed by a liberal mind, had already introduced many reforms into the Russian naval service, and will no doubt be the means of introducing many more. Russian literature is indebted to him for a translation of James's 'Naval History of Great Britain;' as also for an interesting work on America and the Americans, called 'Mejdu Delom,' i.e. leisure hours. His wife was at this time living with him on board, there being no habitation on shore, except a few huts of the Turkomans. But afterwards at Athens, Smyrna, and Beyrout, her hospitable house and unfailing kindness rendered a stay in those places very agreeable; while, as a lady, she could introduce those who wished it to the society of those places.

The hardy mariners on the shores of the Baltic or the Black Sea may feel at home on the ocean, and make the sea their profession by choice, or remain on it afterwards for a living. But the Sclavonic peasant, taken from his isba in the forest or the steppe, may remain twenty years at sea without becoming a sailor at heart. He submits to his fate with the resignation peculiar to the Russian character. In his passive obedience he will face the raging wind on the vibrating yards or rigging of his ship, or follow his officer against a battery. But as soon as he is free to return to his pine forests or flowering steppe, no inducement of money or rank can keep him in a life which he abhors.   On foreign stations, where he has the means of purchasing enjoyments which he never had in his own country, his exclamation, accompanied with a sigh, is, 'Ach! kogda mui paideom domoi?'   'Ah! when shall we get home?'   Yet even his apathetic nature becomes brightened in his travels; he leaves his village and his country as he had lived in it, loutish, dirty, and apparently stupid.   In two years he acquires somewhat of that cleanliness, smartness, and peculiar gait which generally marks good seamen.   One quality, however, a Russian sailor never loses, and that is his piety and veneration for sacred things.   On rising from his hammock, before going to sleep, before and after each meal, he crosses himself many times and prostrates himself before the holy image which is to be found on the main deck of every Russian vessel.   Each man has also his cross or the effigy of his saint suspended round his neck, placed there by his mother or by some other cherished hand.   In every officer's cabin may be found a grotesque painting of the Virgin or patron saint of the occupier, with other pictures of a more mundane character, towards which his eye is perhaps more often turned.   The poor sailor, less exposed to such temptation, preserves his piety in all its simplicity, and the image of the Virgin on the main deck receives many a hard-earned kopek, offered by horny hands but thankful hearts.   After receiving their pay at the end of four months a collection is always made among the sailors, first for the Virgin, and afterwards for the barbers who shave them.

Among the crew of 700 men were many Catholics and Protestants, and a few Mahometans. The Catholics always attended church, confession, &c., when the ship was in port; the Protestants would also attend the service of their church, if convenient, or form a little assembly on Sunday for reading their Bible. The few Tartars on board were among the best of the crew. They went to Mosque, when the frigate was in the East. One of these died while we were at Beyrout, and his body, placed in a neat shell, was taken on shore and delivered over to the Mahometan priests. They immediately took the body from the coffin, stripped and washed it from all the abomination which it had contracted at the hands of the giaour. The grave-clothes were divided among the crowd, while the coffin was used by the little Arab urchins to paddle about the bay in.

Compared with the soldiers and sailors of other nations, few knew how to read, and still fewer how to write. Classes were formed, under the direction of the chaplain, for those who wished to learn. Books concerning their religion, on geography, and other subjects, mostly filled with heroic anecdotes from Russian story, and inculcating an obedient reverence to those in authority, were such as were chiefly seen in the hands of the sailors. The different Bible Societies of England and America either give or sell at a low price books in the Russian and Polish languages, which are eagerly sought for, when Russian men-of-war enter a British or American port. When on shore the Russian sailor, like those of other nations, considers it his duty to get drunk as soon as possible, only he goes to the greatest possible extreme, and becomes completely insensible. Total abstainers were, however, not uncommon; and these, though not always the best sailors, were generally the cleanest and smartest men, as they took in money the value of their daily allowance of grog.

Although the pay of a Russian sailor is next to nothing, yet the dietary scale on foreign stations is so liberal that he may, if he pleases, save much money during a voyage. It is said that Peter the Great himself established the scale of diet for his newly-formed fleet. Taking a sturdy beggar who had just reached St. Petersburg after a long journey, the tsar caused to be set before him *kasha*, peas, butter, salt beef, biscuits and *vodka*, and bade him eat his fill. The quantity consumed by the beggar was taken as a standard for the navy, and is still followed, with the exception of the quantity of *vodka*, for the beggar probably drank himself drunk. People who still think that Russians drink train oil by the pint and masticate tallow by the pound, would be surprised at the quantity of good butter served out to Russian sailors in all parts of the world, without regard to price. Another idea, which many people have, is that the knout is indiscriminately used in Russia. That dreadful instrument of punishment was never used except in cases where capital punishment or the galleys for life would be inflicted in other countries. The severest mode of military punishment, the running the gauntlet between two rows of soldiers armed with sticks, is still employed in the Austrian service, but has lately been abolished in the Russian. Within the last year (1863), the severity of military floggings has been much modified. Good-conduct men cannot be flogged at all— an officer can only inflict one dozen lashes with a rope's end, the captain four dozen, but for any greater number there must be the sentence of a courtmartial. As far as my own experience goes, during five years of travelling in Russian ships, I remember only five or six cases where more than fifty lashes were inflicted, and they were given for very grave offences against discipline and morals. Many Russian commanders complain that this diminution of corporal punishment is subversive of discipline; that no other efficient means can be substituted for it; that drunkenness, disobedience, theft, and bad morals increase as the use of the cord becomes more rare.

Feasts and anniversaries helped to while away the monotony of our stay. Saints' days in the Russian calendar are more numerous than the days of the year, though only the most important are observed. Then there were the fêtes of all the Imperial family; but these, by a recent order, are only to be observed for the chief members. The names' days of both officers and men were also feasted, and where it was possible, some little extra indulgence was allowed to the latter. The day celebrated by each person is not his own birthday, but the day of the patron saint whose name is taken. Thus on the feasts of SS. Alexander, Nicholas, Peter, or Paul, all who bear any one of those names keep festival. A huge cake, or rather loaf of sweet bread, filled with plums, graces the tea-table early in the morning. A monster *pirog* is a necessary part of the dinner. This pirog, or pie, stuffed with fish, rice, eggs, cabbage, carrots, and various other ingredients, is one of the really national dishes in Russia—much as plum pudding or mince pies in England. Easter, a great season for feasting, after the fast of the preceding week, is the best time to see a complete Russian spread. No sooner is the midnight mass finished on the eve of the Easter, and the ' Kristos voskres ' * with the accompanying kiss exchanged all round, than the company sits down, and for three days afterwards the viands remain on the table for the benefit of all visitors.

* Kristos voskres, 'Christ is risen.' A general kissing, with the above greeting, takes place immediately after the mass on Easter eve, when the clock strikes twelve. Friends salute one another in the same manner the first time they meet after Easter. A peasant meeting the Emperor would ' Kristos voskres ' him, and kiss him on the shoulder. The captain, first lieutenant, and other officers had to give and receive some hundreds of kisses on that day, according to the number of the crew.

During the winter, theatrical representations sometimes took place on board the ships. In these we were
assisted by the officers of the English ships lying with
us. One piece, 'The Revisor,' the masterpiece of Gogol,
was given twice. The intention of the author in this
play was to expose the bribery and peculation common
among all classes of Russian officials, from the governor
of the province down to the porter. Its unparalleled
success has, doubtless, done something to induce a
stricter probity among public servants. After the play
was finished, supper followed, and after this came the
jonka. For the information of amateurs I may mention that jonka, or Russian punch, is made in the
following manner. A loaf of sugar, q. s., placed across
the top of a large punch-bowl (or soup-tureen, if no
better vessel is to be had), well saturated with a bottle
or two of brandy, is set on fire, and allowed to drop
into the bowl below. A few lemons, a little spice, and
one bottle of rum, are put into the tureen, which, when
the sugar is melted, must be filled up with equal pro-
portions of champagne and Bordeaux, as fast as the
bottles can be uncorked. Not a drop of water enters
into the composition, and his must be a strong nature
who can venture beyond one tumbler. In all these
convivial meetings there is the utmost freedom and
equality, for the time, among all ranks of officers—more
so, I fancy, than would be allowed in other services.
Should the admiral, captain, or any superior officer, be

popular, as they were in the General Admiral, they were certain to become victims of the enthusiasm of the juniors, and receive from their arms three lusty tosses in the air. Once or twice the English captains, our guests, were treated to this honour, much, no doubt, to the delight of their middies present, as they saw their doughty superiors' heads making near acquaintance with the beams above. For many days, at Christmas and the New Year, the sailors made merry in their turn. Appropriately dressed up, they would act some impromptu comedy or drama from low Russian life. Some would recite long popular ballads about a brigand or fresh-water pirate of old times; and their powers of memory sometimes astonished me. In some of their exhibitions a bear and his keeper were sometimes the chief actors, and the aptitude of both in their respective parts excited roars of laughter in the bystanders. On New Year's day they also took advantage of the license of the season to chair or toss all their officers, an honour from which the latter could only escape by giving a dram of rum all round, or a donation in money.

The shores of the Bay of Ayas are formed by low alluvial lands, covered by a thick undergrowth of myrtle, wild thyme, and other odoriferous or flowering shrubs. At the distance of one mile from the sea is a low range of mountains, beyond which lies the large and fertile plain of Adana. The village of Ayas consists of only a few miserable mud huts, crowded together within the ruined walls of the old Genoese fortress, and inhabited by a dozen families of Turkomans, whose riches consist in flocks of sheep and goats, and coarse carpets woven from their fleeces. A wily Greek had pitched his tents at the landing-place, and opened shop for the supply of provisions to the ships. A dozen women and girls, refugees from the massacres of Damascus, had been brought over by another enterprising Greek, and found constant occupation in washing and ironing. The place was not altogether tempting for any long sojourn; but the climate was healthy in winter, the sky clear, the water wholesome, while the bay, sheltered from dangerous winds, had good holding-ground. For the sportsman there was unfailing amusement in fishing or shooting, and especially coursing, if he had the dogs. The low coast swarmed with partridges and hares; the streams had duck and other water-fowl in abundance; while in the little groves of gnarled and stunted oak and fir trees, along the swampy beds of the streams, were plenty of wild boar. The bounding roe or the startled gazelle often presented a full mark for the rifle bullet, but seldom got one—at least from our crack guns. The fantastic and unwieldy smooth-bore of the half-wild native chiefly supplied us with venison or wild pig.

As a horse is always and everywhere to be had in the East, we had opportunities of exploring the country in

all directions.   Two or three times I crossed the mountains to Adana, the largest town of the province.
Although, or, perhaps, because this part of Asia Minor
is little frequented by Europeans, we were everywhere
received with kindness by the uncouth Turkomans or
the more civilised proprietor, with one or other of
whom we seldom failed to smoke many pipes during
the day's ride.   The inhabitants were chiefly occupied
in weaving a coarse kind of carpet and in the manufacture of cotton, which, growing extensively about
Adana, would, if its cultivation were encouraged, yield
no inconsiderable supply for the European market.   At
present more is not grown than is wanted for actual
consumption in the neighbourhood.   Thousands of
acres lie waste, not only here, but in all the best places
of Asia Minor and Syria, offering a magnificent inducement for its cultivation, which ought, indeed, to become
a source of future wealth to the country.   The cotton
produced, to judge from the soft cloth made from it,
is of excellent quality.   But in these countries, unhappily, all agricultural enterprise is crushed by bad
administration.   The peasant and farmer are borne
down with taxes, which are always levied in kind, with
the exactness and proverbial hardness of a publican.
Sometimes three-fourths of their produce passes without recompense into other hands, or perishes from
delay in the harvesting, for the husbandman cannot
reap and gather in his harvest until the value of the

standing crops has been estimated by the receiver of taxes. It is not wonderful that, with such a system, thousands upon thousands of acres, which show traces of former careful cultivation, should now lie utterly waste. If the remedy be not applied in time, it will be found, when there are no longer virgin forests and boundless prairies to be possessed by our overcrowded populations, that these fine plains and well-watered valleys in Asia Minor and Syria will offer to emigrants all that they can desire in return for the sweat of their brow.

During these rambles we often met Circassians or Tartars from the Crimea, retaining still their national costume in the land of their adoption. They had received land, but did not trouble themselves much with its cultivation; at least the Circassians did not. I soon learnt by speaking with them that they were thoroughly disgusted at the change they had made. Two Circassians especially, who had been chiefs in their own country, and officers in the Circassian guard at St. Petersburg, entreated Admiral Shestakov to obtain them permission to return to Russia. This the admiral did, and they soon afterwards went back. It was not at this place only that the immigrants were disappointed. The fact was still more manifest at Smyrna a month or two afterwards.

During a long journey made in the following spring through the classic valleys of the Hermus, Caÿster, and

Mæander, I met with some hundreds, and talked with many of these noble but thoroughly barbarous men. I shall never forget how, one evening, after a long day's ride, our solitude was broken into by four pretty Circassian boys, who, hearing there were some Russians in our party, came to enquire about Schamyl, who they had heard was dead. In a mixture of Tartar and Russian they abused some of our company, saying that they would have the head of every Russian they met, if Schamyl was illtreated. When we told them that their hero was alive and well, they clapped their little hands, and ran off, to return soon afterward with some of their elders.

After the capture of Schamyl, a stream of emigration poured from the Caucasus into Asia Minor, chiefly of those tribes called Chechentsi and Tcherkessi. I was told there were more than two thousand in the province of Anatolia alone. They were to be met with in every part of the country, and could immediately be recognised by their national costume. Numbers had attached themselves to the households of the pashas and other great men. Plots of land had been given to many, but unlike the Tartars of the Crimea, who are industrious agriculturists, it was against their habits to cultivate it. They were now, it seemed, in bad plight, and wished to return to their native country. Seated one day on the stall of a pipe-cleaner in the little town of Odemisch, I was surrounded by a group of these men who spoke Russian. They said that they were in great distress. The Turkish authorities, having promised land and assistance, had given neither. The few who possessed any land were regarded as intruders by the Turkish peasantry, although they were their co-religionists, and one or two fatal conflicts had taken place between them. All were eager to hear about Schamyl, and listened with grave faces as I related what I knew. The veneration felt towards him by these men had been that of a family towards a father, of a flock towards a pastor, of an army towards a popular and fortunate general; and their grief was that of men who had lost all at one blow. 'Ah, nash bédnie Schamyl!' 'Oh, our poor Schamyl!' groaned one old man, when I finished, and turned away to hide or brush away a tear. During this trip, I had many proofs of the deplorable state to which these men were reduced. Many offered us for sale their silver-mounted daggers, and, when we returned to Smyrna, the bazaars were filled with these and other weapons, bought at a nominal price from their needy owners—a proof, indeed, of their want, for to a Circassian his arms are dearer than her wedding ring to a matron, and more highly prized than their wives and daughters, whom they still sell to the Turks for powder and lead. A few days after our return whole caravans came hastening into Smyrna, the women with their few chattels being packed on camels. Among them were many of the chief families of their tribes, while some had held the rank of officers in the Russian service. One man had been a colonel in the Circassian Guard at St. Petersburg. Some hundreds, all badly off, many starving, were waiting to embark. They had applied to the Governor, who had received no orders about them from head-quarters. Crowding the doors of the Russian Consulate, they received the same answer. In their despair they threatened violence, and strong patrols of troops were sent to control their movements. At last they were all shipped off to Constantinople, from which city they afterwards returned, as I heard, the Russian Government having refused to allow them to re-enter Russia.

During the last five years more than 300,000 Tartars and Circassians have emigrated to different parts of the Turkish empire. The Crimea, from a population of upwards of 300,000 Tartars on its cession to Catharine II., had in 1861 little over 80,000. These men, laborious agriculturists, seem everywhere to have been absorbed among the populations amongst whom they came. The Circassians, on the other hand, a brave and marauding race, who, in their native mountains, when not engaged in any expedition, pass their time listlessly on a mat, whittling a stick, while their women or slaves, when they have any, cultivate the ground, nowhere succeeded in establishing themselves as husbandmen; and all who could not find more genial employment in the households of the pashas wished to return to their own country.

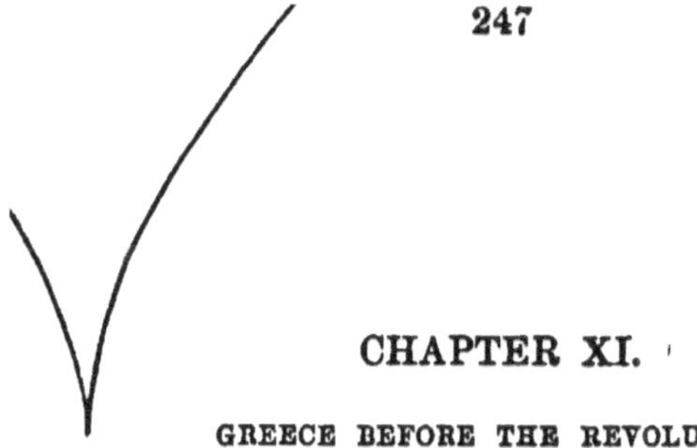

CHAPTER XI.

GREECE BEFORE THE REVOLUTION.

AFTER a couple of months' stay in the Bay of Smyrna, we proceeded to the Island of Lesbos, or Mytilene, and anchored in the beautiful port Hiero or Olivetta, one of the finest harbours in the east of the Mediterranean. The narrow and winding entrance rendered access somewhat difficult for a vessel so long as ours. From within, the port looks like a mountain lake. The hills around are covered with thick groves of olive trees, from among which peep small and miserable villages perched in difficult positions, which in former times secured them against the attacks of the Turkish or Frankish pirate. Around the shores of the bay are still to be found remains of Greek and Roman art, especially some marble baths in excellent preservation, built over hot mineral sources, but now seldom used except by the poor villagers or by travellers like ourselves. In an adjoining valley are the grand ruins of a Roman aqueduct on a double row of arches.

The morning after our arrival a party of us rode over the mountains to the town of Mytilene. After listening to many complaints from the Russian consul, of the bad treatment of certain villages by the Turks, who had desecrated the churches under pretence of searching for concealed arms—which were probably found there —we went up to the citadel to pay our respects to the Governor. This fortress, which we saw by order of the commanding officer, a negro, was evidently prepared to sustain a siege of any length. It had abundant munitions, an inexhaustible well, and large stores of food; but against modern artillery it could hardly stand twenty-four hours. Its chief use is to overawe the town below, and afford a refuge to a ruling minority in the midst of a native and secretly hostile population. The only object of interest in the fortress itself is the tomb of a former Pasha of Smyrna, who, having long braved the authorities of Constantinople, was decoyed on board a man-of-war under pretence of a friendly dinner. The credulous Pasha was decapitated, and his body afterwards buried with the greatest respect in the fortress at Mytilene.

During this visit a pair of tiny mountain ponies were brought for our inspection. These little animals, not much larger than a Newfoundland dog, are found wild in the remote parts of the island, and when tamed and well groomed, are very pretty creatures, and fetch a high price. Those which I saw were remarkably strong for their size, could trot with a light man on their backs, were full of spirit, and very intelligent. Admiral Shestakov wished to present a pair to the little son of the Grand Duke Constantine, but our stay was too short to await the return of hunters sent out to capture them.

It was on a glorious Sunday morning in the month of April that we anchored in the Bay of Marathon, where we passed the day rambling over the plain. It is a sad waste, and only interesting from its historical recollections. One or two wretched hovels, a few patches of barley, and a solitary peasant here and there, were the only visible signs of human life. A ragged shepherd offered his services as a guide, but his ignorance of the locality was only equalled by his stupidity. A quantity of bones had lately been dug up from the ground where the battle is supposed to have been fought. They were in good preservation although soft as chalk, the marrow bones being filled with white crystal. Before we returned a strong wind and heavy surf had arisen, so that it was necessary to swim off to the boats. When we came on board the frigate steamed over to a group of islands off the south coast of Eubœa, called the Petali Isles, where the frigate remained for some time for the sake of artillery practice. A day or two afterwards, having looked into Port Rafti, the ancient Prasiæ, we doubled Cape Sunium or Colonna, and the same evening were moored in Porto Leone, or the Piræus.

The sun setting behind Salamis was throwing its last rays over the plain, and lighting up the mellow ruins of the Acropolis, to which, as seen from a distance, ages and weather have given the warm ochre-like tint of the surrounding soil. The view of the Acropolis from the sea is always attractive, whether seen with the rising or the setting sun, when the hills which form the background are bathed in hues from the faintest yellow to the deepest purple, or in the calm repose of noonday, or, when, as I have sometimes seen it, the columns of the Parthenon stand out from the red disk of the rising moon, which they half obscure. During a prolonged stay in the Piræus, we had many opportunities of rambling over the still solid foundations of the walls and towers surrounding the old arsenal of Athens, and of making excursions to the most interesting places which are to be found in the islands or on the shores of the Saronic Gulf.

The railroad and the navvy have not as yet profaned the soil of Attica. A terminus is, indeed, to be seen at Athens, which bears the inscription of *Chemin de fer,* but there is no sign of a locomotive or a rail. Whether no one has been found venturesome enough to undertake the speculation, or whether the noble army of Greek coachmen resisted the proposed change, the reader may decide. Both reasons were given to me. A coach or an omnibus still carries the pilgrim to Athens.

The Temple of Theseus opens first to view on entering Athens. On one side is an English garden, on the other a parade-ground, where the modern soldier still exercises, as did the old Athenian Hoplite. Here, too, every Tuesday in Easter week, the young Athenians meet to perform the Labyrinth dance, which Theseus and the youths of Delos danced in commemoration of the Cretan expedition. Here, too, on the same day, nearly the whole population assembles to start on the one accustomed pilgrimage to the Acropolis, the Areopagus, the Pnyx, and other memorable spots; but except on that day, hardly a Greek, I believe, ever pays them a visit.

Rounding the Acropolis to the lately uncovered Theatre of Dionysus (or Bacchus), and passing under the Arch of Hadrian, the pilgrim stands beneath the gigantic columns of the Temple of the Olympian Jupiter. Passing the street of the Tripods, and skirting the north walls of the Acropolis, he enters the Propylæa, passing through which, he may survey all that Athens has still to show of the temples of her tutelary goddess.

Many days were spent in photographing these ruins from different points of view, but to give any description of them here would be an impertinence. Yet every traveller has generally some favourite objects in nature or art, which, more than others, he delights to contemplate, and sometimes to rant and rave about; so my special favourites among the beauties of nature are volcanoes and fountains. Of the former, I had already seen the most remarkable—Fusiyama in Japan and Hawaii in the Pacific, the latter in an active state. After these Stromboli and Vesuvius were molehills, and even Etna could not excite surprise. The beautiful fountains I had fallen upon in my travels were innumerable, but although as much the theme of song to the children of nature among whom they are to be found, they are little known elsewhere. The Fountain of Arethusa, in the island of Negropont, though long ago ruined by an earthquake, still preserves its celebrity. With the famous fountain at Athens, Callirrhoë or Enneakrounos, neither time nor man have wrought much change since the days of Pisistratus. Here, lying on a smooth-worn rock in the bed of the waterless Ilissus, the tourist, as he watches the well-known movements, and listens to the hoarse chatter of the ragged and bare-legged washer-women of modern Greece, may make comparisons between them and the damsels of old Athens coming with their pitchers on their heads to the well, when the Pelasgians rushed down on them from Hymettus.*

* *Herodotus*, lib. vi. cap. 137.

• One object may, however, be new, even to those to whom Athens is familiar. During the years 1861–3 the Theatre of Bacchus, on the east side of the Acropolis, was laid bare from the many feet of dirt and rubbish which had hidden it for centuries, and the vast space where the sublime dramas of the Greek poets were performed before 30,000 enraptured listeners can now be examined in every part. A few statues were discovered. The proscenium was almost intact, though most of the friezes which adorned it were either broken or defaced by remaining so long underground. The sedilia of white marble set apart for the magnates of Athens, and dating from the earliest times, were in good preservation. On the chairs could be seen inscribed the names of different priests—an addition of the Roman period. Of the higher rows of seats, cut into the rock of the Acropolis, which were occupied by the citizens, many stones had been displaced by the pick and the crowbar while digging. Around the pit was a marble parapet about three feet high, also dating from Roman times, when gladiator fights were more to the taste of the Athenian people and of their still less refined rulers than the tragedies of Æschylus or the comedies of Aristophanes.

Athens is the dullest town in Europe for a long stay. Once having examined the ruins, a visitor soon gets tired of the place. It is impossible to be always in ecstasies before mutilated marbles, even though a ' Victory without wings' be among them. Beyond these, Athens contains little that is interesting. Greek society is not very pleasant for strangers. The men are always up to their ears in politics, practising eloquence in the discussion of ideas for the good of their little country. The women, still retaining in some degree the exclusiveness of all Eastern countries, only come forth in the splendour of satin, jewels, and paint. Even then they have little to say for themselves ; and this is perhaps their least fault. Once or twice we had the chief society of the place on board the Russian ships to witness theatricals and to dance. One ball was given for the King and Queen. The King came dressed as a Palikari, was affable enough to speak to every officer on board, asking his name, putting to him some common question, then giving a smile, a hum, and passing on to the next. The Queen was most amiable in her haughtiness, and honoured nearly every officer with a dance, which quite eclipsed him in glory and crinoline. I believe they were quite satisfied with their reception on board—it was a break in the dull monotony of their lives—and when they left the ship at midnight, the illumination and glare of blue lights called forth from the Queen an exclamation of ' *Seh! Othon, wie wunder schön!* '

Many travellers were passing through Athens on their return from the Eastern tour. They were chiefly English and Americans, who had *done* the Nile, the Holy Land, Asia Minor, and Greece in a couple of months.

At the *table d'hôte* of the Hôtel des Etrangers, I found, one day, two masculine but kind-hearted spinsters who had by themselves braved all the inconveniences of the Eastern tour; a couple just married; several Greeks; and a Frenchman, who was writing his *'Impressions de Voyage,'* and who, if he understood English, might have secured the following anecdote to work up as an example of the eccentricities of *les belles Anglaises.* The conversation was between the two spinsters and the young bride. Supposing themselves the only persons present who understood English, they acted accordingly. The acquaintance had begun only that morning, when the bride in great distress had rushed into the room of the spinsters, and demanded her Pharaoh's frog. When the astonishment caused by this strange demand had a little subsided, a search was made, and the run-away frog was found under the ladies' bed, having hopped through the passage from the adjoining room. The conversation at dinner was explanatory. The young lady had brought with her from the Nile several frogs, the descendants (as she affirmed) of those which were the plague of Egypt, in order to propagate the species in Leicester-shire, where she had a park and a lake where they could breed. All had died except one; and she had been in agony at losing this last hope of her future race. The condolence of the two ladies was touching. They also had a loss to mourn, and could sympathise with the despair of their friend for her frog. The calamity had befallen them only the night before. Their more classic affections had been set on one of those wise little birds which flit by night round the ruins of the Acropolis; and this bird they called their Minerva's owl. In the middle of the night they had been roused from their dreams by a horrid rustling of the curtains, a crash of toilet-bottles, and thumps against the windows of their room. Frightened out of their wits they ran and opened the window, when the knowing little bird flew away to his old haunts in the Parthenon.

In the miserable village of Lepsina, on the site of the ancient Eleusis, I passed many hours one day in photographing the villagers among the ruins of the old Temple of Ceres (Demeter). Excavations had lately been made by the Society of Antiquarians, and several sections of columns, arches, cisterns, and subterraneous passages brought to light. We found great difficulty in arranging a group. The women would not *pose* at all; the men were so fanatical that they would not stand with two fine-bearded Jews; mothers would not let us have their children unless we paid for them. After a long parley and the bribe of a few drachmai, we overcame the bigotry of the men and the hesitations of the women, and made some tolerable impressions.

After a month's stay in the Piræus, M. Oserov, the Russian Ambassador, came on board to accompany us in a tour to the north of Greece. Steaming against a light Etesian wind, we coasted the round-topped mountain range of Euboea, and the next evening anchored in the Bay of Lamia, opposite Thermopylæ, with Mount Œta standing boldly forth at the bottom of the bay, and Parnassus, its sides still ribbed with snow, visible through a cleft in the irregular mountain outline. Before us was the plain of Trachis, and on our left that narrow path where a few resolute men opposed the onward march of the Persians.

Long before daybreak our Greek pilot had been despatched to look up all the horses in the neighbourhood, so that by six o'clock we were able to start upon our excursion. We found great difficulty in landing from boats, as the receding of the waters has left the south shore of the gulf shallow and marshy, and there was some chance of being half smothered in mud before reaching terra firma. Among the few clay huts of the village, the pilot had collected some stout horses with wooden pack-saddles, but without bridles. After an hour lost in dispute with their uncouth owners, and in arranging rope bridles, we succeeded in making a start. Striking inland, we soon came upon the ancient path which, skirting the base of the mountains, leads into Thessaly. This path is easily followed for miles, and, indeed, its traces must remain for thousands of years more, as in many parts it is cut out in the solid rock some six feet in width, here stretching in a straight line towards the defile, there curving round some little valley or watercourse. Following this road we soon came to those remarkable pools of reddish stagnant water, which are sure to attract the visitor's eye, and a little farther on, to the Thermæ themselves. Beyond these hot springs we quite lost all traces of the road, buried as it was in the rank vegetation and thickets of oak, oleander, and flowering brooms. Although the aspect of nature has here been so changed that rivers have been removed from their former courses, still the scene, as Pausanias and Herodotus describe it, may easily be identified. On the spot where so many Persians were drowned in the sea, which then washed the base of the defile, are now fertile corn-fields, over which, at the time of our visit, the heavy ears were drooping from their stems. In the midst of this wild but beautiful scenery, we picnicked by the ruins of an old wall. As soon as we returned on board, anchor was weighed, and late the same evening we were riding in the celebrated Euripus before the ancient town of Chalcis.

Kastro (the modern name of Chalcis) is a miserable place in spite of its admirable position, and has little or nothing left to remind the traveller of what it was when Aristotle inhabited it. Writers of his time describe the city as being eight miles in circumference, filled with temples, baths, and theatres, besides being one of the most important military ports in Greece. It is now a fortified town of about 7,000 inhabitants, the seat of a small coasting trade, and contains a central prison for the malefactors of Greece.   The bridges which connect the island to the mainland are the most interesting objects for a visit.

The acts of a capricious man were by the ancients likened to the irregular flux and reflux of the tides in the Euripus.   Tradition makes Aristotle find a voluntary death in its waters from despair at not finding out the mystery of their changes.   Other ancient writers represent this narrow channel as subject to continual storms, and tormented with currents as strong as torrents and whirlpools.   Modern science easily accounts for these effects.   A narrow channel between mountainous and broken coasts is especially subject to sudden changes of wind and tide, as well as to their continued and concentrated force; and both the Euripus and the Straits of Messina owe their celebrity only to this circumstance.   During the only day of our stay a gale was blowing from the NE., the hardest, the natives said, which had been known for years; but we had no difficulty in getting on shore, for the wind and current were both in one direction.

Eubœa was one of the most fertile territories of old Greece.   Now it is half a desert, and a disgrace to the people who inhabit it.   A few miles from the town of Chalcis is a little oasis, which shows what the country is capable of.   It is the property of Mr. B——, formerly the deputy for Chalcis, and a minister, who had now retired, disgusted, he said, with the manner in which public affairs were managed, to cultivate his little farm in peace. Having lost the rest of the party with whom I had started for a ride, I found frank hospitality and an agreeable afternoon's chat with him. Having shown me his well-ordered plantations of citrons and oranges, in the midst of which was the marble tomb of his father, he entered into an interesting description of the state of the country. Speaking of its unsettled state from bands of lawless men, he related to me an atrocious instance of brigandage, of which his own family were the victims. Two years before, a band of sixty-four armed men had, in broad daylight, entered the town of Chalcis, and carried off his son, daughter, and son-in-law to the mountains, where they were kept six weeks in suspense. The brigands demanded the sum of 30,000 drachmai for their release. But Mr. B——, acting with uncommon energy for a Greek, followed the band with a party of his friends and some troops, released his family, and took some fifty of the robbers prisoners, who were shortly afterwards executed. Brigandage is no common affair in Greece. The old, half-barbarous warriors of the war of independence are the chiefs of bands; disappointed officials (and their name is legion) fill up the ranks. Politics are conveniently combined with plunder, and a freebooting excursion does not much affect a man's position in society. He is only a patriot, whom the injustice of the laws and the ingratitude of Government have forced to extreme

measures for a livelihood. A few of the robber-exter-
minating heroes of former times would be of the
greatest use in Greece at the present day, though I
much doubt whether Theseus himself would not be
perverted and turn robber, if he had the misfortune to
be contemporary with the modern Palikari.

Just at this time there was a louder clamour than usual
for the union of the Ionian Isles to Greece, and our
conversation naturally glided into that topic. My host
was utterly averse to it, as the time had not yet arrived ;
and most of the influential men of Greece, he said, were
of his opinion. He explained that as the inhabitants of
the Isles were more civilised, better educated, and accustomed to a firm Government which understood its duties,
the chief Ionians, if the union were carried out, would
naturally find their level above the statesmen of Greece,
to the disgust and envy of the latter, and that a succession of plots and insurrections would be the consequence. According to his ideas the union was a matter
for time to bring about, when his countrymen should
show themselves capable of being not only good governors, but good subjects, neither of which he seemed
to think they were at present. In fact Greece and the
Greeks have everywhere become words of contempt,
even among those nations whose political and religious
instincts are the most inclined to them. This is as much
the fault of the restlessness and unstable character of
the people, as it is of a weak, vexatious, and incapable

Government.   During the last ten years the only progress which has taken place in the country has been in
those seaport towns which have a foreign trade, where a
few enterprising men have given an impetus to the sea-
going qualities of the people.   In the interior all is
blank and gloomy.   Ancient Greece contained within
the bounds of the present kingdom at least thrice its
present population; yet from land much of which is
proverbially barren, industry drew forth the means of
sustenance, while scanty mines became sources of
luxury.*   Now, however, all but the most fertile land
lies waste.   In Messinia and in the alluvial plains and
valleys of the north, where abundant harvests of the
finest grain reward the careless labour of the husbandman, not half the available land is under tillage, and
the method of cultivation is of the most primeval
kind.   So heedless are the Greeks and the Government
to agriculture as a source of wealth, so averse is the
peasant to the use of the plough and harrow, that every
year hordes of Turks from Thessaly and Macedonia
come into Greece for seed-time and harvest, and carry
off their wages from under the very noses of the native
peasants.   The land of Mr. B——, of whom I just
spoke, was entirely cultivated by these migrating labourers, as he found it impossible, he told me, to employ
Greeks.   This apathy seems the more strange because

---

* The population of Greece in 1862 was 1,067,216, about one-seventh
part of what the country could well support.

the Greeks in Asia Minor are everywhere acquiring and cultivating all lands bordering the sea coasts, thus gradually forcing the Turkish population farther and farther into the interior.

One cause of the present condition of the Greeks may be accounted for by their past experience. For centuries they were subjected to the ignominious Haratch, a poll-tax levied on Christians only under Mussulman rule. This tax was a brand on their nationality, their religion, and their persons: while its collection was accompanied by the most abominable abuses. Such degradation has it left, that even now that they are free, they cannot appreciate their position as freemen. All direct taxation becomes a loophole of abuse to the official, and a fair thing to be resisted by the subject.

Another cause must be looked for in the land-tax inherited from the Turkish administration, which, in all countries where it is in force, paralyses the energies of the cultivator. This tax is levied in harvest-time, in kind and not in money, according to the value of the crops.* The harvest is, therefore, at the mercy of the

* The Greeks themselves, after their revolution, did not wish to commute this tax into a fixed sum of money. The produce was always ready, they said, but the money would not be ; it would have, perhaps, to be borrowed at usurious interest, which would make their condition still worse. It may seem easy, in the retirement of a study, to find a remedy for this evil, but those best acquainted with the country have hitherto failed in finding one. Dr. Finlay's *Greece under Othoman and Venetian Domination*, and his *History of the Greek Revolution*, best trace the causes leading to the present condition of the Greeks.

tax-gatherer, and in order that he may not vexatiously delay the reaping and threshing, the poor farmer must pay another large portion of his produce as a bribe.* Against the extortions or dishonesty of officials he can have no redress. A Greek farmer's position, therefore, may be easily imagined. He cannot dispose of his crops until the land-tax is paid, bearing meanwhile all the risks of storm and waste; his proprietor then comes in for a large share; and often, when the man's barns and purse are three parts emptied, the official or the brigand appears to appropriate the remainder. He must consider himself fortunate if he can support himself and

---

* 'The farmer of the tax commands every agricultural operation: he fixes the time for reaping the fields, for cleaning the crop and preparing it for market. He compels the peasant to transport his share to market at the season when labour is most in demand. . . . . The farmer becomes the managing partner of the peasant, and the condition of the nine-tenths is subordinated to the profits to be derived from one-tenth . . . . The peasant cannot put a sickle to the crop without a permission from the farmer. He cannot thresh out his grain without a second permission. . . . . When the reaping is finished over the whole area hired by the farmer, he finds time to turn his attention to the threshing-floors. The operations of threshing and winnowing are conducted with primitive simplicity, and the ox that treadeth out the corn is not muzzled . . . . The object of the farmer is to get his share of the crop to market before the peasant can compete with him . . . . The peasant and every member of his family carry on a perpetual contest of deceit with the farmer, whom they consider they may defraud without dishonesty; and the farmers of the revenue, knowing that the law gives them every advantage in any contest with the cultivator of the soil, generally carry their exactions beyond the limits of strict justice.'—Dr. Finlay, in the *Daily News*, January 7, 1863.

family on coarse bread and olives during the year, and
afford to spare a lamb or two at Easter for the pascal feast.

A third cause is the insecurity of property. The
right in land is very indefinitely guaranteed by law,
and a proprietor neglecting to till his land for two or
three years would at the end of that time probably find
his field occupied by squatters and his title disputed.
This insecurity is the greatest bane to Greece, as it pre-
vents Greek capitalists from investing their money in
the soil of Greece. If they were enabled to do this
without risk, the prosperity of their country would be
far more advanced than by all their contributions in
money. With this insecurity of landed property is the
still greater insecurity of movable property. The
present Government scarcely understands the A B C of
its duty. Instead of waging, in the name of society and
civilisation, a stern war against the lawless men who
infest the country and rob the hard-working man of his
earnings, its system seems to be to debase the one and
exalt the others. The farmer may be dying from
ill-treatment and want among his marshes; the robber
is parading his booty in the halls of the palace.

In considering, therefore, the condition of the Greek
agriculturists, the member of a more civilised community ought not to be too harsh in his judgment. When
a man finds the whole produce of the sweat of his brow
fall into the coffers of others; when he sees no hope of
ultimately extricating himself from his liabilities, or of

bettering his position, all inducement to labour is at an end, and the most energetic nature sinks disheartened and crushed.   Great reforms in the systems of taxation and justice are an absolute necessity.   If such are not carried out, Greece will present the same aspect thirty years hence as she does now, and as she did thirty years ago.

Another drawback to the progress of Greece is the want of roads.   Not one-fourth part of that projected between Athens and Corinth has been finished.   A few roads cross the chief plains, but they are never extended further.   Between the Piræus and the capital, little over four miles, the ground is perfectly level, yet travellers must waste an hour on the journey, besides being either smothered in dust or drowned in mud, whereas a railroad might be made in two months, with little expense.   Many beneficial schemes for irrigating lands now barren from want of water have at various times been proposed, but the matter always ended in talk.   The cause of all this neglect lies patent in the miserable incapacity and dishonesty of the Government. Public moneys which ought to have been expended in public works have been grossly misappropriated.   Its behaviour towards foreign creditors has been such that Greece is now financially outlawed by the rest of Europe, and it will only be by some years of rigid honesty that she can ever hope to restore her credit. No foreign speculator will ever be found willing to risk his capital in public works with no better security than the protection and promises of the Government of King Otho.

Throughout the country there are everywhere traces of the incapacity of Government, of an indolent conservatism and lack of energy in the mass, and it has been the opinion of all intelligent Greeks with whom I conversed that only a thorough change in the Government and administration could give an impetus towards reform and a general improvement in the country.

After leaving Chalcis, we continued our cruise for a few days, and then sailed to the Cyclades.

CHAPTER XII.

GREECE DURING THE REVOLUTION, 1862.

Passage to the Piræus—Causes of the Greek Revolution—Political Parties—The Grand Idea—The Conspiracy of February 1862—At Athens—At Nauplia—At Syra—How the Insurrection was subdued—Compromise—State of Greece between February and October—The Hetairia—Whispers about Prince Alfred as King of Greece—Dinner at Argos—Stupidity and Dishonesty of the King's Government—Patriotism of Greeks of Foreign States—Their Aid to the Government—How recompensed—Departure of the King and Queen—The Revolution—The King's Return—The 22nd and 23rd October, 1862, in Athens—Chiefs of the Movement—Behaviour of the Troops and People—The Gensdarmes—Loss of Life—Provisional Government—Grivas—His Death—Enthusiasm of the People—Generosity of Greek Merchants—The Elections—Alfridos—Reasons for an English Alliance—Demonstrations in Athens and the Piræus—Obstinacy of the Greeks for Prince Alfred—Behaviour of the Townspeople and Peasants—Demonstration to the Three Protecting Powers—Opinions of the Press—Voting Lists—Russian Sympathies in Greece—Popular Logic on Alliances—Propositions of other Candidates—How received by the Greeks—Conceitedness of the Greek Character—A Republic for Greece—A King found at last—Ζητῶ Γεωργίος—His probable Career—Applications for a Kingship—A Descendant of the Comneni—Proposal of a modest Englishman—Letter of a Mr. Paget—The Palace at Athens—Revenue of the King and Queen—Apathy of the Greeks in Arts, Science, or Taste—Disposal of the King's Property—The Correspondence of Foreign Princes with Otho.

IN the autumn of 1862 the frigate was lying in the beautiful harbour of Villa Franca, near Nice, when the news of the outbreak of the Greek revolution reached us. Almost at the same moment came the order that we were to proceed at once to the Piræus. Instead of the anticipated charms of a cloudless winter and the pleasant society of Nice, we were once more to look on the barren hills and face the keen NE. wind of Attica. Fate seemed as adverse to our going thither as were the desires of those on board. After our departure it was as though the King of the Winds had centred on us his whole power from the mountain islands,* his fabled throne, towards which our prow was turned. The forces of uncontrolled nature, and of nature controlled by art, strove for the mastery;—and art won the battle, though hardly. As we passed Stromboli at early morn on the fourth day after leaving France, the air and sea were again calm, and the smoke was hanging around and lazily curling up from the crater on the north-west side of the island. A few hours later, on entering the Faro of Messina, hardly a ripple lapped the rocks of Scylla, and but a slight gurgle marked the spot of the whirlpool of Charybdis. After leaving Malta, where we stopped for two days, the fierce scirocco and our 3,000 horse-power had another combat, which so delayed us that we did not arrive in Greece till about three weeks after the breaking out of the revolution. I soon heard from different eye-

* The Lipari Islands.

witnesses the particulars of what had already occurred; of what happened subsequently I had opportunities of judging for myself.

A large and powerful part of the Opposition had for the last year been conspiring to upset the established Government. To this party was attached the whole of young Greece, consisting of some hundreds of talented, poor, ambitious, and therefore dissatisfied men. Their ruling star was the 'Grand Idea,' the overthrow of the Turkish power in Europe, and the establishment of a State which should include true Greek and orthodox, whether on the continent or among the islands. In league with the revolutionary party in Europe, and especially with the Italians and Garibaldi, who were only awaiting a fitting occasion to extend a helping hand to their mourning sister, as they styled Greece, a plot was already formed in January 1862, which should have had the intended effect of upsetting the Government. It was arranged that an outbreak should take place in the capital, and in two or three other places at the same time; and the fated day was named.

On the 6th February, the twenty-ninth anniversary of King Otho's landing in Greece was celebrated by official demonstrations and also by a certain manifestation of public enthusiasm. On the morning of the 13th the plot, which was to have been carried out in Athens that same evening, was discovered. A large ball was to be given in the palace, and the conspirators intended to surround the building at midnight, and to seize the persons of the King and Queen. Measures were immediately taken to counteract the plot, and the revolution was cut short, so far as the capital was concerned.

Nauplia or Napoli di Romania, an excellent port on the gulf of the same name, contains about 6,000 inhabitants, and is the naval station of Greece. From the natural strength of its position, it has, though somewhat inappropriately, been styled the Gibraltar of the Archipelago.   Situated only a few miles from the ancient Argos, it was always an important place under both the Greeks and Romans, as under their successors the Venetians and Turks.   Walled and fortified by the Venetians, besieged and taken by Bayezid II. in 1495, retaken by the Venetians under Morosini in 1686, and again by the Turks in 1715, it finally became the chief town of the pachalik of the Morea. After the war of independence, Nauplia was the seat of the provisional Government of Capo d'Istria, and here the President was assassinated by the famous brothers Mavromichaeles. Here also Otho, accompanied by his Bavarian troops, landed for the first time in Greece in 1833, to commence that reign which has been so abruptly and ingloriously ended. In 1862 the three forts which command the place were garrisoned by about 1,000 troops, a great part of which had been bought over by the conspirators. On the 13th February, at a given signal, this party, headed by Colonel Artemis and young Grivas, then a lieutenant, secured all who were not privy to their designs, released the prisoners, and appointed a provisional Government.   As soon as these events became known in Athens, the German General Hahn was sent with a force to beseige the town by land, and a few steamers were despatched to blockade it by sea.

At Syra a somewhat similar but less serious movement took place.   This town, the capital of the nomarchy of the Cyclades, is built, terrace upon terrace, on the steep side of the island.   Of its 7,000 inhabitants three-quarters are Roman Catholics, and among these French influence preponderates more than in any other part of Greece.   The chief place of trade in the little kingdom, its geographical position makes it a central depôt for the commerce of Europe, Asia, and Africa. The various steamboats of the companies which work the traffic of the Mediterranean keep up a constant stream of intelligence between its inhabitants and the rest of Europe.   Here, with a few private soldiers, three lieutenants, Leotsakos, Moraitini, and Canaris, gave the signal for insurrection.   Having plundered the Customhouse and established a provisional Government, the ringleaders betook themselves to the neighbouring Isle of Tinos to continue the good work.   But on their way thither the steamboat fell in with the corvette Amalia, and the chiefs of the insurgents were either killed or made prisoners.   Order was restored in Syra immediately after their departure.   At Chalcis in Euboea a like attempt was made, but beyond letting loose the 150 convicts confined in its prisons, order was not troubled.

Meanwhile Nauplia held out for two months, and its surrender on the eve of its bombardment is still shrouded in some mystery. The besieged when they capitulated were, it is said, in a better position for prolonging their resistance than ever they were. The truth seems to be that a compromise was made between Otho's Government and the revolutionary party in Europe. However strange such a statement may appear, its probability is well warranted. Emissaries of Garibaldi had been seen continually moving between Athens, Nauplia, and Italy, where the General was then making his preparations for invading the Austrian frontier. His aid seems to have been invoked and a compromise effected. An amnesty, with a few necessary exceptions, was offered to the defenders of Nauplia and accepted. The king promised to reconstruct his ministry more in accordance with popular feeling, to allow the organisation of the national guard, to which he had for many weighty reasons been averse; and to observe the articles of the Constitution better for the future. Behind all this was the promise that, when peace and order were once more restored, the *grand idea* of the holy crusade should at length be carried out. Young Greece was advised to harvest its energies and strength for the great conflict. At the same time many who had been obnoxious to the Government were released from prison, where they had been

T

detained in defiance of all law or right.   One gentleman, well-known in Greece and to foreigners who have visited Greece, M. Dimitrius Boudouris, who at the time I write is a member of the provisional Government, told me, that on his release from prison, when he desired to know the cause of his arrest, and demanded a public trial, the answer was, ' Hush! let the past be forgotten : we are just going to begin the great work-- let us be united and strong.'

From the surrender of Nauplia until October 22, the little kingdom relapsed into its usual state of half order, half anarchy, which has marked its new existence. During this time a vague rumour was spread abroad that a prince of the royal family of Great Britain might be hoped for as the future king of Greece.* The king and queen were henceforth looked upon in that contemptuous manner in which mankind are wont to regard objects about to be changed for better ones. The unanimity with which the revolution of October, in every way a military revolt, was seconded by the people, is more to be ascribed to this report than to any other cause; and as soon as it was accomplished

---

* ' On the 12th April 1862, just after the surrender of Nauplia, a banquet was held at Argos, at which some thirty of the conspirators were present. After all had taken a solemn oath to effect a change in the Government, the portrait of a foreign prince was presented and kissed by all present, as that of the future King of Greece.'—*History of the Insurrection at Nauplia*, by Spiros Kydonakis. This portrait is said by some to have been that of Prince Napoleon; by others, and with much more probability, that of Prince Alfred of England.

the eyes of all men naturally turned towards England, and Alfridos became the centre of the hopes of the statesman, the soldier, and the peasant.

An act of supreme stupidity on the part of the king's Government hastened the impending crisis. Greece is a small and insignificant country, but the Greeks are a widely spread and highly intelligent people. While at Athens political speculations and intrigue occupy the little world, thousands of Greeks living under foreign rule are honourably engaged in the pursuit of wealth. In all the seaport towns of the Mediterranean and Black Seas they are as numerous as the Jews, of whom in mercantile instinct they are worthy rivals. While the pious Jew may turn a sorrowful eye to the stony land of his forefathers, and rely with more or less faith on the fulfilment of prophecy, the Greek looks towards his fatherland with the conviction that its restoration to pristine vigour lies more within the scope of human means. His offerings have never been want-ing; a tithe of his wealth was never held to be misspent if it could advance the day of Greek regeneration. The sum of money which Otho's Government had received in this manner was immense; and fresh sums were every now and then solicited. This money, designed by the donors to be spent in improving the country, in organising a national soldiery, and in hastening the triumph of the national cause, was applied to the support of courtiers and ministers, who must have chuckled among themselves at the success of their duplicity. The king had doubtless a hard course to steer between the observance of treaties and the wishes of his subjects. In reality he has been made to bear the shame of his ministry. That he had not sufficient knowledge or a will strong enough to control his corrupt and turbulent ministers is a misfortune, but not a fault. But that he should wink at the deception practised in using this money, and beg for further supplies under such false pretences, was degrading kingly honour to what in a subject would be considered a misdemeanour and punished by picking oakum.

Such double dealing could not long remain a secret. The Greeks of Galatz and other towns on the Danube called the attention of the Senate to the fact. The Senate refused to entertain their petition as coming from Greeks who were not citizens of Greece, and who paid no taxes. The indignation roused by this conduct among the Greeks of foreign countries, who had long been giving their money, can well be imagined; in a moment the liberality, support, and sympathy of the most enlightened men of the Greek race were alienated from Otho's Government.

The petition was presented and refused at a time when a more serious conspiracy than the former one was impending. This time the conspirators were aiming not at a change of ministry, but a change of dynasty. So openly was it conducted that the party in power must have allowed it to come to maturity from sheer despair of finding means to crush it, or from an apathy akin to treason.   Coming events had cast their shadows far before.   The political clubs had been busy in their deliberations ; officers, who had never had half a dozen drachmai at one time, boasted of the comparatively large sums which they had received as the price of their own treason and for corrupting others.   It was well known that contributions had been received from the Greeks of England and the towns on the Danube for revolutionary purposes.   The king was informed of his imminent danger.   He was warned against making that tour to the Morea, to which his ministry had urged him in order to conciliate the chief men of the army and civil service in districts which he intended to visit. But he had so often heard the cry of 'wolf' that he either disbelieved the rumours or rashly braved the warning.   On October 13 (the very day on which, thirty years before at Munich, a deputation offered to him the crown of the newly-formed State) he embarked with his queen on the corvette Amalia, called after Her Majesty, and steamed from the Piræus, to which he was destined never to return.   During his tour he was received with every appearance of popular enthusiasm.   But on the 17th the revolution broke out in Patras and Missolonghi. Old Grivas had roused his wild mountaineers of Acarnania.   On the 22nd the work was accomplished in the capital, and on the king's return the next day he found the gates of his kingdom and the hearts of his subjects alike closed against him.

When the royal vessel anchored in the bay of Phalerum, and the ambassadors hastened on board to inform the king of the events of the preceding night, he was for a moment stunned by the tidings, and unwilling to believe that the Greek people had turned against him. But the open rebellion of the crew of his frigate, the excited crowds on the shore running wildly about, shouting insulting cries and firing their guns in the air, convinced him that his own person and that of the queen were no longer in safety on board the Amalia. On the 24th, therefore, he passed on board the Scylla, a British man-of-war, and in the more retired Bay of Salamis, two miles distant, dictated a proclamation to the Greek people. Almost the only one of his subjects, and the only one of his officers who accompanied him was the captain of the Amalia. His conduct throughout the whole business did him honour. While he remained on board, his resolute demeanour awed his rebellious officers and crew; and another officer sent by the provisional Government to supersede him was met on the gangway by a loaded revolver, and forced to depart again as he came. But no sooner had the king left the frigate, than the royal arms were torn from the national flag: the red colours were hoisted; officers and men pinned red cockades to their jackets; three shouts were given for *Eleutheria* (liberty), and a salute of fifty guns was fired in honour of the new Government. Shortly afterwards the name of the frigate was changed to Hellas, while that of a steamer bearing the king's name was also changed to Patris. The figure-heads, consisting of the superb bust of Queen Amalia and the king in Palikari costume, needed no alteration to represent Mother Greece and Fatherland.

Bulgaris, the chief of the Opposition, was the real head of this revolution, while an artillery officer, named Papadiamantopoulos, managed the troops, for which service he was made military Governor of Athens. The revolution was in reality a military revolt. Most of the young officers aud non-commissioned officers had been previously bought over; and an eye-witness described to me the approach of the cavalry and infantry to the spot where a few drachmai were distributed to each for breaking their oath of fidelity to Otho. Those officers who set a value on their dignity and military honour retired to their homes on finding it impossible to stem the tide, and thus young sub-lieutenants, the produce of political clubs, found themselves in command of regi-ments—a command they were afterwards very loth to resign.* I shall have to speak hereafter of the sad dis-

* One infantry battalion seemed disposed to make head against the insurgents. They were ordered to fire, and they did fire—but in the air. Their commander called out to them, 'You're a pack of scoundrels,' and then, turning to his officers with the words, 'And you, gentlemen, are little better,' he stuck his sword in its scabbard, and went home. The next day the soldiers hunted him out to kill him, but he contrived to escape from Athens.

orders resulting from this, as also of the rotten organisation of the Greek army in general.   Only one brigade, the gendarmes, the choicest of the Greek army, held aloof from the sedition, and, retreating to the marble entrance-hall of the palace, were soon besieged by the soldiery and mob.   General Hahn, who was with them, seeing that resistance would be of no avail, and that the soldiers were going to storm the palace, agreed to evacuate it, and the faithful gendarmes, fifty in number, retired unarmed to their barracks.   The mob and troops were then free to roam the streets, shouting their mottoes, singing revolutionary hymns to the motive of Viva Garibaldi, exacting contributions from citizens and even strangers, and exhibiting a wild and childish joy which could only be equalled in Port-au-Prince or any other negro state.   A few houses, especially those of Germans, against whom the bitterest hatred was manifested, were plundered, or ransomed for a sum of money.   Few lives were, however, lost, during either the revolution or the succeeding troubles, for the Greeks are not a cruel or a blood-loving people.   Only two gendarmes were killed during the night of the 22nd and 23rd.   One or two obnoxious men were afterwards shot, among these was the Governor of the Piræus, who wished to telegraph to Athens for aid to support the king.   No doubt many more political murders would have been committed during the heat of popular rage, but the objects wisely barricaded themselves in

their houses till the fury of the moment passed.   And
the rage of the Greek populace is like the white squall
of the tropics; it ceases as suddenly as it begins.

Meanwhile a provisional· Government had been
formed, comprising Bulgaris, Roufos, and the celebrated
Admiral Canaris, who on the same evening issued a
proclamation, exposing the backslidings of the past,
flattering the national and military pride, and promising
a golden age for the future.   The next few days were
occupied in administering the oaths to the army, navy,
ministry, and clergy, and in ordering a levy of the
National Guard. Adhesions to the new Government came
pouring in by telegraph and steamer from all the nom-
archies of the kingdom ; so that the first act of as complete and curious a revolution as any recorded in history
was wrought out with little bloodshed and in comparative order.   During the few days which followed, an
alarm was, indeed, raised of a grave impending danger.
Old Theodore Grivas, the chief of the democratic party,
whom some considered a patriot, while others called him
a brigand, but who in reality happily combined the two
characters, was said to be marching towards Athens at
the head of some thousands of wild Acarnanian mountaineers, in order to upset the new triumvirate.   The
old man had, no longer ago than in the preceding spring,
been prevented from joining the insurrection at Nauplia
by a present amounting to 20,000 drachmai.   Roufos
was immediately sent to gratify his predominant vice,

and to announce to the old Palikari that he was appointed Commander-in-chief of the Greek army, with a yearly pay of 40,000 drachmai. But death at this time put an end to the old man's ambition. He died from eating too much lobster, according to one account; or, as others said, from having made too long a march; and the Government, in gratitude or sorrow, ordered a state mourning during five days. In the meantime the persons implicated in the late troubles returned from banishment, and were received on their landing with rapturous welcome by their fellow-citizens. Most of them were immediately installed into good places.

While the enthusiasm of the people was chiefly shown by parading the streets, shouting *Zito Eleutheria*, firing muskets in the air, or disputing at the street corners, the more sensible part of the community manifested theirs in a more useful manner. Measures were taken for the security of property and the maintenance of public order by the rapid embodiment and training of a National Guard; and it was no uninteresting sight to watch the motley groups of men, grave professors, gay students, palikari, shopkeepers, clerks, peasants, and here and there a negro, learning the goose-step in front of the Temple of Theseus, or in any of the other open spaces of Athens. Hundreds of merchants sent in sums of money to the Government; many paid their taxes for years in advance; patriotic officials, in the enthusiasm of the moment, gave up half their salaries; while from

all the towns of the Mediterranean and Black Seas
contributions came pouring into the almost empty
treasury. The Greeks of Constantinople alone sent
$2\frac{1}{2}$ millions of drachmai in the form of a loan at two
per cent. Alexandria, Smyrna, Trieste, and other towns
did the same in proportion to their wealth and population. But all this money was spent much as patriotic
contributions had been spent before; it went into the
pockets of men in power and of their supporters.

From October until the National Assembly met towards
the close of the year, tolerable order prevailed throughout the little kingdom, with the exception of some paltry
squabbles at the elections. The whole Greek people were
on their best behaviour. They were courting *Alfridos.*
That name had now become noised abroad, and the
Greek imagination soared high in its dream of a golden
age to come. Alfridos meant to them freedom under a
strong Government, with the sympathies and assistance
of a people kindred to them in many qualities; it meant
a flourishing trade, a full exchequer, an iron navy, a
happy and united Greece, with the old city of Constantine for its capital. ' Our geographical position, our
traditions of liberty and glory, our commercial relations
by land and sea, our pretensions to the east and to the
civilisation of this part of the world, and especially our
firm resolution to be governed constitutionally and to
become a great people—all plead in favour of Alfridos.'
These words of a Greek writer represent the general

tone of the Greek press. So impatient were they to have their darling, that they would not wait for the meeting of the National Assembly, but demanded a universal suffrage, while the ministry and all classes of the people seemed so sure of their success, that the voting throughout the kingdom was but a matter of form.

Some of the demonstrations which took place in Athens were very curious. On entering Athens from the Piræus, the narrow street of Hermes leads up to the large open place where the palace stands, and which received after the revolution the name of the Constitution Place. The middle of this street is intersected at right angles by that of Æolus, which reaches from the celebrated Tower of the Winds under the Acropolis to the village of Patisia at the other end of the town. At one of the corners of these two streets is a coffee-house, called Ὡραία Ἑλλάς, where the motley groups of Athenians commonly assemble to talk over the affairs of their country. Here Saturday after Saturday, and Sunday after Sunday, the mixed mob of professors and palikari, soldiers and peasants, would join the processions which carried their hot homage to Mr. Scarlett, and, after his arrival, to Mr. Elliot. At one time it would be a carriage containing a horrid caricature of the prince, surrounded by Greek and English flags, and escorted by the mob of soldiers, civilians and priests, all carrying lighted candles, and headed by a band of music. There was at this moment no portrait of the prince to be had, but the occasion soon produced artists, and Prince Alfred was portrayed to the Greeks as an interesting little sailor boy, about ten years old, leaning on a cannon and looking very miserable. But in matters political, as in matters religious, it was necessary to speak to the mass pictorially. After a short time better portraits of him made their appearance, and then nobody was without his *carte-de-visite*; even the poorest peasant could have his portrait printed on the cover of his cigarette-paper for five *lepta*, or a half-penny. On another occasion the heart of the procession was an omnibus, containing a symbolical female figure, with the motto, Σύνταγμα Ἑλλάδος (Greek Constitution). As these processions passed through the streets, the gaily dressed women of the balconies clapped their little hands, showered down bouquets on the portrait, and strained their throats with screaming ' Zito Alfridos.' Even the guarded official replies received at the British embassy could not damp the ardour of the devotees, whose orators had employed their most touching eloquence in speaking of the prince and the hopes of the Greek people. Similar manifestations at the Piræus had the same serio-comic effect on a bystander. The English Consul had to receive divers deputations and listen to pretty speeches, wherein mention was made of Byron, Hastings, and other Philhellenes, and the amiable Consul returned the compliment with quotations in their own

language from the ' Republic of Plato.' Many provincial
towns, too impatient to follow the example of the
capital, proclaimed Alfridos without any delay at all.
Everywhere the elections went on with the most perfect
confidence of ultimate success; and at length Alfridos I.
was solemnly proclaimed second King of Greece by the
almost unanimous suffrage of the nation.   In Athens on
the day of his proclamation a solemn Te Deum was sung
in one of the public places, and at the opera the same
evening a portrait of the prince was put in the royal
box, and the same honours paid as though he himself
were present as King of Greece.

Long after the Provisional Government had received
official information that the protecting Powers felt themselves bound by the protocol of 1832, the enthusiasm continued unabated among the mass. Though the educated
part of the community now saw that the encouragement given to the desire of an English prince was but
a *ruse de politique*, and complained that they had been
unfairly trifled with, the faith of the common people
did not waver. Even when they began to doubt, an
unguarded word in the translation of one of Mr. Elliot's
speeches was sufficient to revive hope. ' You cannot
have Alfridos for the present' (ἐπὶ τοῦ παρόντος), and
those words were enough for them. The sanguine
youth who, overlooking the consent of father, mother,
or guardians, hastens to noise abroad his future union
with his beloved among all his connections and friends,

could never be more dismayed at the irrevocable veto of papa, than Greece was when her darling Alfridos was denied her. In her young passion she had overlooked parents, ministers, and treaties. 'She had been on her best behaviour, she had cunningly concealed her imperfections for a time, and sought with the glances of a siren to attract the young mariner to her bosom.

It was not only in Athens, but among the peasantry in all parts of the country that this strange enthusiasm prevailed. Wherever an Englishmen went, whether for a walk a short distance from the town, or for a shooting excursion in the interior, he was almost sure to be made the object of a demonstration in favour of Alfridos. In making an excursion with an officer of H.M.S. Queen, whose stay in the Piræus afforded an agreeable society to us, I had constant opportunity of observing this. The presence of two Englishmen in a village soon brought together all the population. The frequenters of the wine-shops by the roadside would press us to drink with them, would dance around us to some unearthly music, and shout Zito Alfridos, till we thought them either drunk or mad.

Before the elections were completed in the provinces, the last reasonable hope of having Alfridos had been taken away by the proposition of King Ferdinand of Portugal, and afterwards of the Duke of Saxe-Coburg. Still many people would not be convinced. They thought that obstinacy and a deputation to London, with a little manœuvering on their part, such as the threat of setting up a Republic, would result in annulling the treaties of 1831–2. 'We'll set all Europe in flames,' were the words of one young patriot in petticoats; 'We'll set all Europe in flames, if the Great Powers don't let us have what we want.' Even the press used such phrases as these: 'Palmerston only wants us to force him a little. What are treaties? Only like private promises made to be broken, as interest dictates.' The private feelings of the Queen of England, the political dispositions of the English Government, never entered their minds. Their interests were alone to be considered, even at the expense of a European war.

So exclusively were the Greeks taken up with their idea of Alfred, that they quite forgot that there were two other Powers besides England to which the country had been under some obligation. After a time, however, they remembered the fact, and made an honourable apology by dedicating one of their demonstrations to the three protecting Powers. Caricatures of Queen Victoria, the Emperors Alexander and Napoleon were paraded in a carriage through the streets, and homage was paid at the three embassies. Some of the newspapers also, fearful that all these demonstrations for Alfridos might injure them with the Russians and French, devoted many articles to recalling the benefits which Greece had received from all three Powers during the war of independence. 'You accuse us of ingratitude,' said one of them, 'in thus giving all our suffrages to an English prince. But we have not therefore forgotten that Russia in the days of our bondage was our best friend; that her hearths, her army, navy, and diplomatic service were ever open to our talented children, who had to flee from the land of their birth. Can we forget that Ypsilanti and Capo d'Istria were among their number? Do we not remember that she gave the signal of our war of independence, and supported us through it? Can we also forget the good offices of France, and the chivalrous aid received from French Philhellenes? But of England, what shall we say of her? She has lately abused us much, and laid bare the shortcomings of our nature; but the interest of Englishmen in our welfare can be read in the names of Byron, Canning, Hastings, Hamilton, Codrington, and others. Greece may be selfish in her demands for an English prince, because she is convinced that the policy and institutions of England are necessary to her progress, and most congenial to her people. And, moreover, she needs the material aid of England to work out her prosperity.' But while they paid their homage to the three Powers, the populace manifested their antipathy to the Austrians on every possible occasion, and it was a favourite recreation to row round the Austrian Commodore's ship in the Piræus and gratify those on board with a lusty chorus of ' Viva Garibaldi ! La Santa Libertà !'

That the political interests of Europe clashed with the wishes of the Greek people, is probably a happy thing for Prince Alfred. His occupation of the Greek throne could only have been useful to Greece, if Great Britain had maintained for some years a land and sea force to preserve order while certain indispensable reforms were being carried out. The Greek army, thoroughly and disgracefully demoralised, was a snare to the prince and a terror to the people. With a small force to back his executive, and supported as he would have been by the whole of the mercantile class, the most orderly though not the most honest in Greece, the rule of our young prince would undoubtedly have improved the country. But when he exercised his constitutional prerogatives against his turbulent estates; when he showed the most unprincipled of his leading subjects that popular liberty must not merge into treason; when he rooted out the robber clans of the Peloponnesus and hanged their leaders, he would probably have become for a time the most unpopular sovereign in Europe. If Otho had been for a time more inflexible and less merciful, he would have been reigning still. As it was, he was so bandied about from one set of ministers to another, that Athens contains at the present moment more ex-ministers than all the States of Europe put together. Alone and unaided from without, Prince

at a discount.   For the same reason, a king, who is not
of the national creed, can never hope for any length of
time to retain the sympathy of the people in Greece.*
The educated and governing classes seem, it is true, to
have abjured by their late acts all political tutorship by
Russia; but the priests and common people are more
conservative in their ideas.   The inhabitants of the
towns and seaports will never permit a religious interest
to clash with self-interest; and therefore all their ideas
will always be more or less in accordance with the
desires of those powerful nations whose fleets visit
their shores.   'We like the Russians very much,' said a
tradesman to me, 'to kneel side by side with them at
our common altar and perform our *oraisons*;—but
the policy of their Government does not suit us—our
political and private interests bind us to England and
France.'

After the hopes which the prospect of Alfridos had
invoked, and the subsequent disappointment, the candidates successively proposed were not looked upon with
any great enthusiasm.   The name of King Ferdinand
of Portugal was received with the greatest apathy by
all classes.   That of the Duke of Saxe-Coburg had
scarcely a better reception.   The newspapers tried,
indeed, to impress on the public the difference between
Austrianism and Germanism; that the duke was nearly

* Georgios I. seems to have been very wisely advised to become
Orthodox before his arrival in Greece.

allied to the Royal House of Great Britain; that their darling Alfridos was his next heir, and *might* come to Greece after all; and that the duke's reputation as a man and a sovereign was such as gave hopes of finding in him all those virtues which they had not found in Otho. It would not do. They would not be ruled by a German, rule he ever so wisely. The Greeks had by this time arrived at such self-conceit that they thought half the younger sons of royalty were ready to devour each other for the honour of being king over such noble and classic subjects. *Græci sua tantùm mirantur*, wrote Tacitus some 1700 years ago, and the vice is as bad as ever, only there are no opposing virtues to be lit up by it. The undeserved praise which they received from some of the English newspapers and even from British Legislators, roused their spirit of self-sufficiency to an unbearable point. The refusal of Ferdinand, followed by that of Duke Ernest, somewhat cooled their conceit; and as their revolution tended more and more to anarchy; when sensible men saw the ministers one after another giving proof of their incapacity and want of principle; when the army had trampled down all discipline; when the treasury was empty and brigandage approached the Acropolis; they began to whisper that even a bad king was better than no king at all. It also gave them some idea of what they might hope from a Republic.

Before we left the Piræus a king was at last found,

though not such a one as sensible men desired. The same demonstrations took place; high masses were celebrated in the open places; volleys of musketry shook the air; and *Zito Georgios* replaced *Zito Alfridos* as the popular cry, with a weaker enthusiasm. What his fate will be if he have not a body of foreign troops, is very doubtful. Not much dependence is to be placed on the affections of so fickle a people. Yet it will be better to trust in these, rather than in such an army as Greece has at the present moment. Perhaps the brother of a Queen of England, and it may be of an Emperor of Russia, may inspire the Greeks with a little more awe than the prince of a State buried in the midst of Germany. But that he is not the sort of ruler wanted by the Greeks at this crisis is certain. Just before leaving Athens, one of the leading men made the following remark in my hearing: 'We asked them (the three Powers) for a man of intellect, strong will, and political education; and they send us a beardless and inexperienced youth. Otho reigned thirty years, but without a body of foreign troops that boy will not stop in the country thirty weeks.' Whether this remark be fulfilled or not, time will show; meanwhile Prince Wilhelm will not find the throne of Greece padded with rose-leaves.

The vacancy of the throne called forth some amusing incidents. Many persons, some in joke, others in earnest, or rather as a satire, made applications for the post in much the same manner as they would have answered an ordinary advertisement in the public papers. One letter, written in French, came from a Comnenus, a pretended descendant of the Byzantine Emperors of that name. An Englishman, who wished for the present to remain unknown, also offered his services to the Greek nation. He was twenty years old, was a good mathematical scholar, had studied the language and literature of ancient Greece, was convinced of the superiority of the constitutional over other forms of government, and promised that if the Greeks would give him a trial, they should not be disappointed in him. He begged to inclose half his photographic *carte de visite*, divided lengthways ; adding, that if the Greeks accepted him, he would present the other half, by which they would see that they had the right man.

But the most curious of these applications, apparently made in perfect sincerity, came from an obscure village of West Canada. The writer, who signed his name Paget, began his letter by insisting on the improbability that an English prince could ever reign in Greece. Giving first a compressed account of the history, policy, finances, and general resources of the country, as they had been, and as they should be, he unfolded his plan of benefiting the country. 'His knowledge of our country, its history, and the character of the people was such as hardly one of the members and few of the ministers could show,' said a deputy who had read the letter. The remuneration required by Mr. Paget was only half a million drachmai a year, with the stipulation that his salary should be increased in proportion to the improvement of the country—so many thousands for every million increase of revenue. All these letters were laid before the representatives of the nation, and naturally caused roars of merriment. They were solemnly ordered to be preserved, along with many other as futile documents in the archives of the National Assembly.

On the night of the revolution a guard had been placed in the palace, and the property of the royal house was tolerably respected. A small farm belonging to the queen, a few miles from Athens, was completely sacked, the trees destroyed, and the cattle, even the fowls, stolen. But in the town itself there had been but little robbery or wilful destruction of property. The gentlemen and ladies of the court were permitted to take away with them whatever might be needed for the personal wants of their master and mistress. Seals were placed on all the doors, in order that the rest of the property might be intact when it should please the late king to give orders for its final disposal. The stud of horses was, however, taken for the use of the new Government, and about half its value paid to the king's agent. The only exceptions made with regard to the property were the king's correspondence and the various curiosities of ancient art, of which Otho had made a considerable collection. The former was sealed up and placed under proper guardianship for subsequent examination; the marbles and other antiques were claimed as national property, and placed in one of the museums. After a time orders arrived from Munich to forward thither all the furniture and nicknacks which had immediately surrounded the persons of the king and queen, and all the pictures and works of art; but to dispose of all the other articles in the palace, with the exception of the furniture and fittings of the state-rooms, which it was thought advisable to leave until the arrival of the future sovereign, who would probably occupy the palace.

The palace is a large unpretending square building, having a public garden and place on one side, and on the other a spacious terraced garden, filled with groves of oranges, tufts of palm-trees and shady walks, making it the most agreeable retreat in Athens, to the inhabitants of which it was always thrown open. The interior contains a handsome and well-arranged suite of state and other rooms, where pillars and slabs of marble from Pentelicus intervene between bright-coloured frescoes of the Bavarian school. In the entrance-hall and vast antechamber are painted scenes taken from the war of independence, with portraits of all the heroes of modern Greece and celebrated Philhellenes. Admiral Canaris and his fire-boats in the midst of the Turkish fleet are alone not represented there. A petty feeling of personal hatred had suppressed one of the most glowing tableaux which could have adorned the walls. This palace was the private property of the king, and, as I was informed, the whole of the fortune of his queen, about five millions of francs, had been spent in its construction and decoration. It has been unjustly urged against Otho that he did nothing to improve the city. This is not quite true. When Athens was made the capital, the city was in dust and ashes, and had for centuries been nothing better than a dirty Turkish town of the fourth rank. It can now boast of a few streets and buildings which would vie with those of the capital of any little German principality. Greater improvement might certainly have been made, but what has been done was mostly done by the king and queen. The king's income was small, consisting of one million drachmai from the state, and a private fortune of 80,000 *gulden*, in all about 43,000*l.* a year, and he seems to have done for the city as much as his means allowed. If there is any spot in Athens where the least taste has been displayed, the Greeks have to thank Otho and Amalia. Left to themselves they are singularly devoid of all that we consider taste. Unlike that celebrated people from which they derive their name, their bastardised language, and their pretensions, they seem entirely to neglect all that is graceful in art or in the common things that surround them. Instead of profiting by the presence and lessons of the many artists and artisans whom Otho called from Germany to decorate

his palace, and, as he thought, to instruct his new subjects in useful and lucrative industry, the Greeks con-
temptuously spurned both the art and the artist.   The
consequence is that wherever art or a display of taste is
needed, it must be sent for from Germany, France, or
Italy.

I went more than once to the palace to see the private
sale of the king's property, consisting of the carriages,
wines, and utensils of his establishment.   Only the light
carriages found a purchaser, and they were soon afterwards seen, with all their royal bearings, on the hackney-
coach stands of the town.   In one of the lower rooms of
the palace I found kitchen utensils, wines, large jars of
pickles and sweetmeats, and divers other odds and ends
for sale, with an old German servant of the king pre-
siding.   Some old port wines had been packed off to
Munich, and the stock of other sorts was but very
limited. ' Foreign wines,' said the old man to me, ' were
by Her Majesty's orders only put before her foreign
guests; the Greeks had only Greek wine. For when Their
Majesties first came, and fine old Bordeaux or Johanis-
berger cabinet were put before them, the old Palikari
turned up their noses, and called it vinegar. So Her
Majesty said they should get no more, and gave them
only Greek wines to which they were accustomed. Few
of the things there,' he continued, ' suited the Greeks,
who were too poor and abstemious; and purchasers
could only be found among foreign residents and hotel

keepers.' Nearly all the property, therefore, was forwarded to Munich.

The king's correspondence became the subject of diplomatic intervention. When the seals were broken in the presence of a commission, of which the ambassadors formed part, the contents were investigated, and the Greek Government declared itself willing to deliver up all that were strictly private or family letters. But with many which contained political matter from royal personages it refused to part, declaring them to be state papers. Against this Count Bludov, the Russian minister, protested, for, as it seemed, the most important of these letters were part of a correspondence between the Emperor Nicholas and King Otho. The affair was ultimately remanded until the throne should be again filled and the Government established. Even if they are finally kept, it is not probable that their contents will ever be published, although they were at the time pretty well known in Athens.

CHAPTER XIII.

Anarchy in Greece—Acts of the Provisional Government—Universal Suffrage—Greek political Men—Abuses—The National Assembly—National Guards– Greek Empire—Parliament of the Greeks—Its Character—Disproportion of the Institutions and Ideas of the Greeks to the Size of the Country—Pay of Members—Visits to the Assembly—Its Appearance—Behaviour of the Members—Character of the Modern Greeks—Imitation of the French—Cause of the Anarchy of the Country—Complete Disorganisation of the Army—Opinions of a Prussian Officer about the Greek Army—Incidents showing the prevalent Anarchy—Lieutenant Leotsakos and his Mainiots—The Government powerless against him—Brigandage triumphant.—Incapable Government—An Example—Rivalry of the Soldiers and National Guard—Murders and other Crimes unpunished—Coup d'Etât of February—Overthrow of the Ministry of Bulgaris—Aspect of Athens during the Three Days of February—The Carnival—Balbis President—Conspiracy for the Recall of Otho—The Cession of the Ionian Islands—Their History—Character of the Greeks displayed during the Revolution—Progress made since the War of Independence—Revenue—Army out of Proportion to the Wants of Country—Aspirations of the Greeks—Downfall of Mussulman Rule—Duty of the Greeks to be prepared for such an Event—A strong Government necessary—Extract from the 'Clio.'

WITH the new year, when the National Assembly assumed the sovereign power, a new phase of the revolution commences. Thus far the fixed idea of having Prince Alfred for their king had acted as a restraint, and been the means of preserving order. When that hope was finally taken away, the popular feeling threw off all disguise, and the country made rapid strides towards anarchy. In one short month the spread of brigandage made it unsafe to move out of the villages, while in the towns and the capital the ambition of individual citizens had divided the civilians and soldiers into adverse factions, which produced all the disorders of the middle ages.

One of the first acts of the Provisional Government had been to remove the mayors of towns, who were said to have been the easy agents of Otho, in order that the coming elections might be conducted in a more legal manner.* Yet the first act of the Assembly, when it met, was to revise the list of members, when it was found that nearly half of them had been brought in illegally. What could the Assembly do in the critical state of the country? It rejected a few of the worst and condoned the rest. In one commune, of which the whole

---

* In Greece the members of the Legislature are elected by universal suffrage; most of the local magistrates, on the contrary, are appointed by the executive, and are removable at pleasure. It is not necessary to point out the fatal effects of such an arrangement. The municipalities are thus under the thumb of the Government, and made use of by the executive of the moment in such a manner as to render universal suffrage a farce. This latter ought to be abolished, and the possession of property made the *sine quâ non* of voting. The municipalities ought to be reformed, and in local matters rendered independent of any control from the Central Government. The physical character of Greece is sufficient to show the necessity for this.

population does not exceed 6,500 souls, 7,500 votes were found in the urn. In another commune 216 electors placed 1,166 votes. The nomarchy of Sparta has from 6,000 to 7,000 voters, while no less than 36,000 votes were found in the box, the greater part, of course, for the Government candidate. In some places votes had been changed; in others, voters were prevented from voting at all. The worst case occurred in the Island of Hydra, where Dimitrius Boudouris was elected. Well educated and well informed, speaking many languages, of pleasing manners, and with the most elastic of principles, Mr. Boudouris would have been one of the leading men, if his countrymen could only have thought as highly of his moral as of his intellectual character. In contesting the election of his native isle, fifty of his partisans, dressed in the uniform of the National Guard, under the pretence of protecting the independent voters, kept out of the church all who were opposed to their patron. Yet his election not only passed muster, but when the *coup d'état* took place a few weeks afterwards, he became Minister of Marine, a post which he had the talent to retain for a fortnight. The new Assembly, which met in December 1862, was made up of new men without the least idea of business; some of them being mere youths, in the teeth of the law which made twenty-five years the legal age for sitting in the National Assembly. A few had filled the Opposition benches during the latter Parliaments of Otho's reign.   Into the hands of this Assembly the Provisional Government resigned its powers, although for a time it retained the executive.

It would be tedious to mention all the complete or partial changes of ministry which followed during the next six months.   The first ministry of Bulgaris was soon upset, and those which succeeded it sometimes contrived, by good management, to keep their ground for a month, and sometimes even more.   With every change of ministry came new alarms.   A fresh oath had to be taken by the military; men appointed to office during the former ministry lived in constant dread; the friends of the new men became boisterous in their expectations, and besieged the doors of their patrons; while the quiet people of Athens shrugged their shoulders, cursed all their rulers for a set of rascals, and prayed for Georgios, Ernest, Otho, anyone, in short, who might bring them peace and security.

The Provisional Government of Bulgaris kept up all the abuses with which it reproached the reign of Otho. Its only merit, certainly not a small one, was that it preserved tolerable order in the towns, thanks to the name of Alfridos at first, and afterwards to the National Guard.   But there was, at the least, as much corruption as before.   Arbitrary imprisonment and banishment became the fate of all who opposed its measures.   Whether writers in the press, officers in the army, or friends of the late king, they were hurried off between gendarmes

to the Piræus, and placed in confinement on board
the steamers until the Austrian or French packets
sailed. ' No Greek can be expatriated,' said an article
of the Constitution; but they could be baited by
a mob, put in fear of their lives, and then sent out of
the country by the Government, in order to protect
them. The long lists of pensions, gratifications, and
promotions which appeared in the official papers, revealed the way in which the Government rewarded its
friends, or rallied round it men whose opposition would
have been dangerous. On the breaking out of the
revolution, there were still two or three millions in the
treasury; a few millions had been received during
the Provisional Government. When Bulgaris and his
ministry fell, there remained, I was told, a few hundred
drachmai.

The National Assembly met in a low wooden building
which had formerly been a store-place for lumber. Near
it were the foundations of a more solid marble building,
the completion of which had been retarded for want of
funds. At the gates of the inclosure which contained both
was a mixed force of the army and civic guard; on one side,
the dirty, lounging foot-soldier; on the other a national
guard, a student perhaps, proud of his showy uniform,
blue coat, red trowsers and cap, or a Greek in Albanian
kilt, or a tradesman *en bourgeois*, all of whom tried to
look soldierlike, and performed their duty *con amore.*
It was a knotty point to determine which force should
have the honour of guarding the turbulent Assembly.

It was decided at last that both should enjoy the honour at the same time.   But as disputes among the deputies might end in violence, it was the duty of the guard to see that all arms were given up at the gates, and to search suspected or unknown persons for concealed weapons.   The interior of the building was of the simplest description.   On one side was the president's desk, immediately below it the tribune, and in front, reaching to the opposite wall, rows of benches rising one above the other for the members.   Two boxes were reserved for the diplomatic corps, and there were two small galleries for the public.

In accordance with ancient political traditions, it was determined that the National Assembly should receive delegates from bodies of Greeks in foreign countries. Whether in Manchester or Odessa, wherever from 100 to 1,000 Greeks could record their votes, one member was returned; from 1,000 to 10,000 two members, and so on.   The Grand Idea took thereby a wider meaning, and 'Parliament of the Greeks' was substituted for the Parliament of Greece.*   The Assembly numbered over 300 members, of whom 240 were for the kingdom, and the rest for Greeks living under foreign rule.   This may seem an enormous number for so petty and poor a country as Greece, but it is only on a par with their

---

* This idea has been further carried out by the title assumed by King George—King of the Greeks, subsequently changed to that of King of the Hellenes.

other institutions, whose numbers far exceed the wants and means of the country. Greece contains little more than a million of people, and yet requires half as many law makers as Great Britain, which has twenty times its population. In fact many wish to be governors, while few submit to be governed. There is no lack of men to make laws, but there is nobody to obey them ; fifty want to speak for one who cares to listen ; and a superabundance of theory is accompanied by little or no practice. Again, Greece, though protected by the strongest powers in the world, must have an army of 10,000 men to play at soldiers with, instead of having half that number employed as police to enforce order and protect property. In the civil service there are three men to do the work of one, and that work is badly done. Every man who has received any book education looks to the state to employ him ; and turns rebel and even brigand if it will not do so soon enough. Soldiers, lawyers, doctors, tailors, cobblers, and students, all neglect their immediate duties to provide for the good of the state. The soldiers are, therefore, a rabble, the doctors kill their patients, lawyers ruin their few forced clients, tailors make bad coats, cobblers bad shoes, while students get a superficial education, which is at bottom the real cause of the disgraceful state of the country. Meanwhile there are no roads, much less are there any railroads. There is no agriculture, and all the means of wealth and prosperity are neglected. Brigands are plentiful, and there is a universal discontent which at last ends in revolution. Thus, though they sent away their king laden with the burden of their own short-comings, the Greeks naturally find themselves in a worse state than before. Otho used to complain, ' For all that goes well the ministry takes credit; all that goes wrong is shoved on to my shoulders.'

During the late reign the members of the Assembly were paid 10 drachmai a day during its session ; and this increased the annual expenses of the country by 600,000 drachmai. For some time the new Assembly received no pay, but in the beginning of April a motion was made that the members should receive their 10 drachmai a day as before, and this at a time when the treasury was absolutely empty. When this became known out of doors, the people, roused to fury, mobbed the Assembly and the houses of the ministers. After much hot talking, it was decided, that in a democracy like that of Greece, all members of its Legislature ought to be paid ; but that rich members might be generous enough to refuse their salary. A voting list was, there-fore, laid by the President before the Assembly, that those members who wished to receive pay and those who did not might subscribe their names. But it was thought too hazardous to persist, in the excited state of the public mind, and the matter dropped for a time. Half the members were, in fact, too poor to live like gentlemen in the capital without an allowance, in spite of their abstemious habits: indeed many of them, (lawyers, doctors, and proprietors) would have done more service to their country by attending to their own business, than by playing at legislators for seven shillings a day. Many were officers and civil servants, with the pittance of pay derived from their place; while not a few were clever adventurers, who had no income but that which they made by their wits. One of these Bohemian members had for years regularly dined at one of the hotels in Athens, where he charmed the foreign society of the *table d'hôte* by his conversation, his amusing anecdotes, and his patriotic effusions against the despotism of Otho. He always promised to pay for his dinners when he became a minister. He became one at last after the revolution, and the hotel-keeper's hopes revived. But the minister had fallen upon hard times. There was no money to pass through his hands; the treasury was empty; he was himself soon shouldered out by another; and the trusting host must wait till his guest becomes a minister in the golden age of Georgios.

During our long stay at Athens I was frequently present at the sittings of the National Assembly, and though unable to follow the debates, always had a more or less faithful translation of them from one of the amiable secretaries of the Turkish embassy.* The

* Why do they not teach us Greek with the modern pronunciation at our schools and universities? It might then be of some little use in

greater part consisted of young or new men, quite un-
used to serious political discussion. It was at best a
good school for the practice of eloquence, and a few of
its members showed, by their modulation of voice and
attractive gesture, that their speech was likely to exercise some influence on their auditors. But the majority
indulged simply in violent gesticulations, wild waving of
hands, shaking of fists, and screaming defiance to adverse
orators. The sight of the group below from the gallery
was highly interesting. About one-fifth part of the
members were in the nationalised Albanian costume,
that is, in short white petticoats, red, blue, or crimson
vest embroidered with gold or silk on the back and hanging sleeves, red or blue gaiters, and the ordinary red fez or
skull-cap with flowing blue tassel. The rest were either
in military uniform or *en bourgeois*. Any old Nestor
ascending the tribune was sure to be listened to with
silence and respect, and a murmur of applause would
follow his words of wisdom. When old General Maccry-
janni, for example, entered the Assembly, every sound
suddenly ceased. He rose to beg that the few words which
he had written on paper might be read by some younger
voice, as his own was too feeble from age and weakness

listening to an Athenian debate. The learned in Greece do their utmost
to assimilate the written language to that of the ancients. The same
remark applies to the Latin language. With our way of pronouncing
the vowels, a man fresh from England, who quotes Horace or Cicero to a
German or Frenchman, is about as much understood as if he were talking
Sanscrit.

to make itself heard.   This was allowed, although contrary to the rules of the house.   He begged the assembly to confine itself exclusively to measures tending to preserve order in the country, and, without entering into stormy discussions, to maintain union and self-restraint until the new king should arrive to control and give validity to their deliberations.   His words failed to impress them for a quarter of an hour.   The greatest trifles were brought forward which could excite the venom of party spirit.   Every motion that was made led to at least a dozen risings for a personal matter. The voice of the member occupying the tribune was often drowned by a dozen voices in screaming chorus from the benches.   Insults were added to intimidations. ' You are a liar,' roared one member ; ' Do you not know that you are a cuckold ?' retorted his opponent.   Such is a sample of the language heard in the Greek National Assembly in the month of February 1863.   More than once was presented the undignified sight of two honourable members coming to blows.   It was not for nothing that all arms were given up at the gates.   Mr. Balbis, the President, an aged gentleman, was continually getting on his legs to enforce order, or vigorously ringing his bells, of which he had two beside him, the louder one to be tolled when the tumult became too uproarious. Even this had only a momentary effect, so that the poor President's time seemed to be wholly spent in getting up and sitting down again disheartened, ringing his two bells, and shaking his head in despair at his uncontroll-able charge.   Sometimes the turbulence of the Assembly went so far, that the President found himself forced to prorogue the sitting.

The character of the ancient Athenians, as we read it in the pages of their most celebrated writers, exactly fits the present generation of Greeks.   The satirical poets represented their countrymen as having all the qualities of an old man and of a child, the proneness to be deceived without danger as the former, the wish to be constantly amused as the latter.   By turns showing great and noble qualities, and then the meanest in human nature; adoring liberty without knowing how to appreciate it; quick to seize any project, but impatient of details; passing from hope to despair and from despair back again to hope on the slightest cause; rebellious to all authority; meek and insolent by turns; furious without being cruel; frivolous and fickle in the extreme—as their fathers were, so have the Greeks shown themselves during the late revolution.

In their feelings and habits the Greek people are as democratic as ever their ancestors were in the days of Pericles and Cleon, and the insidious speech of a demagogue as easily leads them by the nose.   Here and there may be found an oligarchic faction of some large landowner, surrounded by clients and clansmen, striving to obtain the mastery in the state.   The Greek character is indeed such a mixture of noble and frivolous qualities, that sometimes we scarcely know whether to admire or despise it. 'The French have had their revolutions; the English have hunted away their king—why should not we?' was a remark often heard. 'Look at our glorious revolution, what a model for other people! In Paris there would have been fusillades, barricades, bloodshed, and pillage: we hardly took away a life, and what revolution could be more complete?' But such expressions ignore the difference between Paris with its hundreds of thousands unknown to each other, and a little democratic city of a few thousands where everybody knew more or less of his neighbour. While boasting that English institutions alone were suited to their character, the *Greeks* aped everything French. They wore French uniforms, had a *mountain* in their National Assembly, and tried a little *coup d'état* now and then. In all public demonstrations there was a constant exploding of fire-arms, shouting, boisterous laughter—the antics, in short, of school-boys set free for a holiday. In the streets, young patricians, lawyers, professors, and sergeants vainly tried to deceive themselves and others that they were sprouting Alcibiades, Cleons, and Demosthenes. And to crown all, the chosen three hundred of the nation were playing such pranks in their Assembly as brought it to the level of a pot-house club; while out of the House many were intriguing, bribing, or fomenting sedition at the corners of the streets or, having been bribed themselves, were conspiring for a certain number of *zwanzigers* to bring back the very man whom they had just ignominiously expelled.   If a few had talent and good intentions, they lacked political education; while those who had the latter were mostly excluded from office by the late elections, and could only shake their heads in mistrust of the future.

And when that future became present, bad had become worse.   The anarchy of the country undoubtedly dates from the refusal of Prince Alfred.   As candidate after candidate was proposed, Greece sank deeper and deeper in the mire.   The national jealousies of the three protecting Powers must have been exceedingly virulent, if this little country could not be suited with a king in less time than nine months.   The blame lies with them for keeping up a state of uncertainty, by feasting the people with hopes which went no further than promises and flatteries, till the national character cast off all restraint.   In the first few months of the year the fruits of the acts which effected the revolution began to ripen.   The peasants could not or would not pay their taxes, and their levy could no longer be enforced by the soldiery.   The army, bribed to perjury, became a lawless and tyrannical mob.   Soldiers began to deliberate and discuss the orders of their superiors; non-commissioned officers petitioned for their promotion, and seconded their petition with threats.   They besieged the members on their way to the House, and threatened to burn the town if their desires were not granted. The Government, instead of shooting half a dozen, promoted them, and sent forth a proclamation extolling the fidelity of the army to the principles of the revolution. After a time the army broke up into two or three parties, some for, some against, the actual Government. One example will show the state of insubordination into which it had fallen. The few batteries of artillery pretended the utmost loyalty towards the National Assembly, to which they had just taken the oath of fidelity. The latter appointed a commander who did not please them, and what did this faithful body of troops then do? They appointed a commander of their own, and, in bravado, harnessed their pieces and marched round the town with their new leader at their head. The Government again flattered their military honour, and there was nothing else to be done. It tried indeed to disband the army altogether, but the army would not be disbanded. It gave the soldiers unlimited leave of absence, but they received their drachma a day, and would not go. To give them their due, they did less harm than soldiers in other countries would have done under similar circumstances.

A few facts will show that the organisation of the Greek army was thoroughly rotten, if indeed it had ever possessed any stability. A Prussian officer attached to his embassy in Athens, who has made the Greek army a subject of special study, says, with truth, that this army, of only thirty years' standing, lacks that prestige of former heroism which serves in other countries to bind soldiers to the path of honour or duty, and to create an attachment to their colours; that being born and brought up in the most democratic of societies, the Greek soldier never separates himself from the rest of the people, never acquires a thorough *esprit-de-corps*, and would never act against the people in case of revolution; that equality, which is nowhere so strong as in Greece, is hurtful to discipline, as the officers often live on terms of intimacy with their men; that there are too great facilities for rising from the ranks; that the officers themselves find in intrigue the best mode of advancement in their career; that even their education in the public schools is often interrupted by political demonstrations, which they afterwards continue in their clubs and coffeehouses; that as, in their many plots and conspiracies, officers and privates are privy to the same secret, insubordination and neglect of duty are naturally induced in the inferior; and, lastly, that the king, so far from taking pains to conciliate his army, showed his dislike and contempt for it. He further adds, that the regiments were split up into small detachments scattered over the country under hardly any control; that soldiers were used as police or tax-gatherers to bully the voters at an election, or sent, dressed in plain clothes, to vote for some ministerial candidate. Thus, concludes Lieutenant Rundstedt, had the Government, by using the army as an instrument for deceiving others, thoroughly demoralised it long before the revolution.*

A few instances, some of them hardly credible, of the behaviour of the Greek soldiery, will confirm these remarks. A week after the revolution, the troops were paraded to take the oath of fidelity to the Provisional Government. The greater part refused to swear. The officers vainly waved their sabres; the men remained stubborn. 'What is the use of swearing?' said they, with some wit; 'the Government will not last a week, and we shall have to swear again. We will swear when the new king comes.' Not knowing what to do in such a dilemma, the commander sent for Mavromichaelis, the minister of war. When that majestic personage arrived, he made a fine speech, called the soldiers his children, and promised them a good dinner after the swearing was over. This promise had the intended effect, and the refractory regiments took the oath. But the farce did not end here. The men waited two or three hours, but no dinner was forthcoming. Getting impatient, a party of them marched to the place where their officers were dining, and threatened to drive them away from table. The minister of war was again sent for, and told them that

* Die Griechische Armee und die Revolution, von R. von Rundstedt.

the cook had forgotten the dinner. This did not
assuage them. They threatened to kill the cook and
burn his house. Finding that they began to cock
their muskets, the officers retired; and the soldiers,
taking their places, began feasting, and finished the
evening by roaming drunk through the streets, screaming Zitos, and firing their muskets in the air.

Another scene, in which officers were the actors, followed some time afterwards. A young sub-lieutenant
of cavalry, who had just returned from Constantinople
with his pockets well furnished, gave a breakfast to his
comrades. In the heat of their wine, the thought struck
them that such a generous host would make a good
colonel for their regiment. So they promoted him to
that post at once, set themselves in carriages, and
mobbed the President of the Provisional Government
to confirm their choice. Mr. Bulgaris made his appearance on the balcony, and actually promised that,
if the rest of the officers agreed to it, he would confirm
their wish. This was not enough. He must be made
commander immediately. Superior officers tried in
vain to reason with them, and it was only when some
troops were sent for that they were arrested—but never
punished.

A battalion of the line, consisting chiefly of Mainiots,
and commanded by a certain Lieutenant Leotsakos, was
for months the astonishment if not the terror of all the
quiet people of Athens. Leotsakos first fortified him-

self in the lower apartments of the palace, and afterwards in the barracks behind it. When superseded by the Assembly, he refused to quit his command.* The minister of war then demanded full powers from the Assembly to turn him out, but the panic-stricken assembly refused. The minister resigned; the assembly would not accept his resignation. The minister appointed another colonel, but the soldiers would not have him. He next ordered the battalion to embark for Calamata, but it refused to move. Meanwhile, a conspiracy was discovered in the regiment itself. Some sergeants, envying the position of their commanding officer, seduced two companies to favour their interests, and these fortified themselves in a large room of the barracks. Thus was seen the curious sight of a regiment fortifying itself against the Government, and two companies in revolt against the regiment in the same barracks. Leotsakos, however, soon starved them to submission, and then expelled them. When we left Athens, he was still in command of the remaining eight companies, and was likely to remain so until the new king arrived. The Government had either not the means or the power to treat him as he had treated his rebellious companies. To give him also his due, he

---

* This was after the *coup d'état* of February. Leotsakos kept his position and command till just before the arrival of King Georgios. At the present time (January 1864) one or two garrisons are in open rebellion against the King's Government.

kept his men under better authority than the other troops in the town.*

Any Government worthy of the name would have considered the preservation of order and the protection of property its first duty. I am not aware that the Provisional Government exercised one single act of authority, by punishing the brigands and murderers who chanced to fall into its hands. Brigandage was common throughout the land. I do not speak of those turbulent clans in the mountains of the Morea. They were never better than freebooters, yet even these of late years had seldom ventured to the sea-shore. Now, however, they came boldly down from their hills, whither they carried whatever they could lay their hands on—and nothing was too worthless for them. Bands of marauders from one province made forays among their neighbours, and drove off their cattle.

---

* The outbreak of July 1 was only to be expected. The two parties had become more and more embittered one against the other. On that day Leotsakos was arrested by the Minister of War, but his soldiers seized two of the ministers as hostages, and Leotsakos was released. This officer and his soldiers still held out for Bulgaris; the opposite, or mountain party, of which young Grivas and Canaris were the leaders, had also become strengthened. For three days the two parties of troops and partisans, with the addition of a few brigands, fought in the streets and places of Athens, and about seventy lives were lost, young Canaris being amongst the slain. A compromise was at last made by forming a ministry of both the parties. During the tumult a party of English, Russian, and French sailors marched up to Athens to keep guard at the Bank.

In another part of the country a general's son, disappointed in his hopes, gathered around him a dozen men and became a chief of brigands. The Greeks, as much fitted for piracy as for brigandage, plundered not only Turkish but Greek ships among the Cyclades. But here they were within reach of the gun-boats of the power, who acted as the police of the blue waters. On shore, brigandage reigned supreme. Even the towns did not escape. One night the iron chest of the custom-house at the Piræus was cleared out. On another evening, within a stone's throw of Athens, a youth, the son of rich parents, was carried off by a band, who left a notice posted on the walls of the palace garden, that 70,000 drachmai were required for his ransom. Soldiers were immediately sent in pursuit, but the brigands had already concealed themselves in the marble quarries of Mount Pentelicus. Edmond About's ' Old Man of the Mountains' is no fiction. Of course the soldiers did not find the young man. The father paid 50,000 drachmai, and the Government promoted the leader of the band to sub-officer's rank in the army; and brigandage was not greatly discouraged. The National Assembly, to remedy the evil, offered to pardon all bands who should surrender before a certain day. A few old hands, tired of their trade, or disgusted at the rapid influx of new members, gave themselves up. At the same time, considering that the expectation of a general amnesty on the new king's arrival was an inducement to crime, the Assembly gave notice that from a certain date, all criminals should be excluded from such amnesty—a pretty state of affairs, where an amnesty is expected by gentlemen who follow the trade of highwaymen or pirates! Although the ordinary courts of law were suspended, surely the Government would have been justified in appointing extraordinary tribunals, and after due process, in hanging a few of these brigands on the tallest tree in the neighbourhood. But it was necessary first to catch them, and no reliance could be placed on the troops.

The capital meanwhile was kept in constant alarm by wild rumours, and every now and then by some terrible act of brigandage or murder. Fortunately, by this time, a patriotic National Guard had been formed, and to it was added a certain number of the more respectable soldiers, and these acted together as the police of the city. Yet between the National Guard and the mass of the soldiery, there soon arose a jealousy which more than once nearly brought about a conflict. As the discipline of the regulars became more and more lax, that of the civic guard became stronger. Like all volunteers, they took heartily to their work, chose a showy uniform, and generally turned out clean and smart. They even dressed their children in the same uniform, and it was a common sight to see little fellows armed and equipped like their fathers, toddling after them through the streets. On the other hand, the troops became every day more slovenly in their dress, dirty in their persons, and lawless in their actions. If the civic sentry sometimes called forth a smile by his anxiety to salute all passing epaulettes and by his minute observance of orders, the soldier on guard aroused a feeling of disgust as he was seen lounging or talking to his comrades, neglecting to salute passing officers, and sometimes even smoking, singing, or dancing in front of his box.

When, therefore, the capital saw itself threatened by the disorders which prevailed in the provinces, and after two or three barefaced robberies had been committed, strong patrols of soldiers and civic guards paraded the streets, visited all the drinking-houses and other low places of resort, and led off all suspicious characters in chains to the Piræus, where they were detained on board the ships-of-war in the harbour. Yet, in spite of these measures, the streets of Athens sometimes witnessed scenes of violence, the authors of which were allowed to escape. Returning one afternoon from Athens to the Piræus with Captain Stoffregen, of the Russian frigate General Admiral, we saw a soldier struggling with a national guard. The soldier had just run a man through with his bayonet. As he was a young and vigorous man he threw off the national guard, and casting away his musket, fled over the rocky ground of the ancient Pnyx. The citizen, a corpulent man, hampered with his musket, followed him till he was out of breath, while several people to whom he shouted to stop the soldier only stared after him.   Presently two mounted soldiers came up, and hearing the story, set off with tremendous energy, and rode to the top of the ridge, where they stopped.   Then, although we pointed the man out to them running a few hundred yards ahead, they coolly turned round and rode back to the town.   For fully ten minutes after they had retreated, we could see the soldier running along the slope of the hill, before he disappeared in the broken ground where Hymettus slopes down to the Bay of Phalerum.

The only two incidents of importance which marked the further progress of the revolution during our stay in Greece, were the *coup d'état* which overthrew the ministry of Bulgaris, and that mysterious conspiracy whose purpose seemed to be the recall of Otho.   Against the ministry of Bulgaris there were, in truth, sufficient grounds of grievance.   He was, therefore, invited to form another; but as he hesitated in doing so, the rumour that he was aiming at the dictatorship and the recall of Otho gained ground.   The crisis was hastened by Admiral Canaris.   This old man seems never to have been a conscientious member of the triumvirate, and his ambitious son was one of the chiefs of the plot about to be carried out.   A few restless sub-officers, who received orders from their clubs rather than from their superiors, bought over the greater part of the infantry in the town to the plot.   The younger Grivas was similarly employed. The battalion of Leotsakos which occupied the palace, and which was said to belong body and soul to Mavromichaelis, the minister of war, declared for Bulgaris and took measures to defend its position. The gendarmes, who from the first moment were always on the side of the Government then existing, loopholed their barracks.   The artillery declared against the President, but devoted itself to the National Assembly and the preservation of order. In other words, it did not interfere at all. At midnight of the 20th and 21st of February the *coup d'état* commenced. All the officers of the army who were not privy to it were locked up by their men in stables and other temporary strongholds. Canaris, with the troops devoted to him, occupied the open places, the Palace Square, the place before the Tower of the Winds, and that extensive ground near which was situated the old Academia. A detachment sent to seize Bulgaris found his house occupied by fifty or sixty resolute clients, and returned disappointed to the main body. In the Palace Square the troops mistook a party of their own for the force of Leotsakos, and a skirmish ensued, in which only one man was killed, though the upper windows and walls of the Hôtel des Etrangers, and the British consulate adjoining, were riddled with bullets. The soldiers had by this time become so accustomed to fire in the air for wantonness, that they continued to do the same even in a serious fight.

During the three following days the excitement was

as great as on the 23rd of October, and the town presented a curious though bewildering sight to a stranger not conversant with the Greek character.   On the 21st all the shops were closed; and those in the market which were opened for the sale of provisions were pillaged.   Some few resolute shopkeepers were national guards, in whose shops might generally be seen three or four loaded carbines, which somewhat awed the cowardly soldiers.   Some of these plundered the national stores; [*] others took forcible possession of the public carriages, and might be seen driving at a furious pace through the town, firing their muskets in the air, brandishing their naked bayonets and sabres, and shouting ‘Zito Grivas! Zito Canaris! Down with Bulgaris!’ &c. &c. The Assembly, meanwhile, was wrangling.   Bulgaris still delayed his resignation, although his colleagues had already given theirs.   He remained closely guarded in his house; and the houses of all the other chief actors in the movement were also little camps, between which mounted emissaries were continually moving to and fro.

No one looking at the palace would have thought that it was holding out against the town. The front doors were wide open, although videttes were placed all around in the gardens to prevent a surprise. Crowds

---

[*] Several chests with Minié rifles for arming the National Guard were forced open, and their contents, which had cost the country ninety francs apiece, were afterwards offered for sale for ten francs each.

of soldiers and palikari were continually passing to and
fro, and even a stranger met with no interference when
it was seen that he was a foreigner. I passed several
times through the gardens and palace to see what was
going on, and was everywhere received with civility.
On the second evening Leotsakos sent a messenger to
Canaris, who lived a short distance off, to know if it was
his intention to attack the palace that evening. Canaris replied courteously that he must be prepared for any
event. But no attack took place this time. The whole
affair gave one the idea of schoolboys playing at government, revolution, and *coups d'état*.

And as such, the state of Athens was regarded by not
a few of its light-minded folk. The people celebrated
the last three days of the Carnival as usual. Around
the few columns, and on that enormous basement where
once stood the Temple of the Olympian Jupiter, groups
of soldiers, peasants, men, women, and children were
dancing, singing, and making merry. The greatest
public anxiety, the uncertainty of what a few hours
might bring forth, a country without a Government, a
complete state of anarchy, could not damp their light-
heartedness.   While two of the triumvirate and all the
late ministers, except one, scarcely dared show their
faces, that one, Mavromichaelis, rode proudly round the
town, stopped under the old temple, encouraged the
people in their amusements, picked out an olive or
two from their messes, and flattered them with all those

little attentions which sometimes gain or recall popularity to a great man.

After three days the usual order was restored. The executive was vested in the Assembly, which commanded the troops to retire to their quarters. A day or two afterwards the army took its third oath of allegiance. An executive of seven ministers, with Balbis as President, was chosen, into whose hands the Assembly resigned the powers it had assumed on the emergency. During the whole of these days strong patrols of national guards and picked soldiers moved about the streets, and though unable to preserve order, at least protected property. Putting aside all political feeling, these men showed that there were, at all events, a few left who understood what their duties were as members of their little commonwealth.

Scarcely had the emotions of these three days subsided, when Athens was again alarmed by the pretended discovery of a plot to which many of the chief officers of the army were privy, whose intention was the recall of Otho. This was only a symptom of reaction naturally to be expected from a disappointed people. That Otho, after a twenty-nine years' residence in Greece, had many friends, no one can doubt; that many, seeing the state of anarchy which everywhere prevailed, and the difficulty in finding a sovereign from some powerful reigning house, would have welcomed his return, is equally certain. 'Otho,' it began to be said, 'was not so bad, after all; he was too weak and indulgent; at all events, what followed his deposition had been ten times worse than the worst part of his reign.   His return would be far better than a military despotism, and the national bankruptcy to which the country was fast hastening.'

When, therefore, intelligence was received that an extensive plot was on foot to pave the way for his return, and that the Bavarian Consul had distributed some thousands of Maria Theresa thalers and zwanzigers to oil the machinery of the counter-revolution, the Government was in dismay.   The consul was immediately arrested; some dozens of suspected officers were exiled to the neighbouring island of Ægina; many more were imprisoned among malefactors on board the vessels of war lying in the Piræus; domiciliary visits were made to all suspected persons, and all the carriages and passengers between Athens and the Piræus were searched for the Austrian silver, or for papers which would expose something further.   But I could never hear that anything was brought home to any of the persons suspected or arrested.

In sketching the events of this revolution, I have not spoken of one event which, though it caused great sensation and astonishment throughout Europe, raised but a slight excitement in the country whose interests it most touched.   I mean the cession of the Ionian Islands to Greece.   Though the offer of the British

Government took everyone by surprise, the disappointment by which it was accompanied, viz. the refusal of Prince Alfred, counterbalanced any enthusiasm which might have been aroused under more favourable circumstances. The usual demonstration of thanks was made through Mr. Elliot to the British Government; Te Deums were chanted in the public places (rather in too much of a hurry, many people thought); but more important events banished the subject for a time from people's minds. The little success of the candidates proposed by England, the opposition of one of the great Powers, the cautious wording of the Queen's speech from the throne, and the adverse expression of feeling in the Imperial Parliament, for a long while made the Greeks doubt if the annexation would be accomplished after all.

To a prosperous and well-governed kingdom, their cession would have been both honourable and advantageous, as the geographical position, race, and religion of the people make them naturally dependent on the adjoining continent. England would at the same time have got rid of a troublesome and ungrateful burden. But it seems, at the least, unfortunate that their cession should be proposed at a time when Greece was in such a state of anarchy as in the year 1863.

The supposition that these islands formed part of Greece under the modern constitution of Europe, is quite an error. One must go back to the Peloponnesian war and the Roman Empire to prove their political union with Greece. Like most of the favourable spots in the East, the Ionian Islands during the middle ages fell under Venetian rule. On the fall of that republic, they passed by the Treaty of Campo Formio to the French, who, two years afterwards in 1799, were driven out by the Russians, when the Ionian Republic was formed. The treaty of Tilsit restored them again to the French, who kept Corfu until the peace of 1814. The other islands had been conquered by Great Britain, under whose protection the whole Republic was eventually placed by the treaty of Vienna. Although most of the inhabitants are Greek in language and religion, many belong to the Latin race, being chiefly descendants of the Venetian settlers. Under British protection, a large military force has put a rein on the national turbulence, and the energies of the people have been more directed towards their little country. The contrast, therefore, between the Seven Islands and Continental Greece is as evident as it is favourable to the former.* The administration remained in native hands, and so sure were the Ionians of the inviolability of their institutions, that they could sometimes afford to be insolent to their protectors. It

---

* Dr. Finlay writes that 'the Ionians have not availed themselves of the liberty they have so long enjoyed for improving their moral condition, and for attaining a moral and intellectual superiority over the other Greeks who were subject to the Sultan.' Fifty years of British rule has, at all events, had the effect of making the Ionians far superior in wealth and political training to their countrymen on the mainland.

is true that for years cries have been heard for annexation with their brethren in Greece. Year after year came that inevitable petition to the Lord High Commissioner, who as often refused to receive it as contrary to the constitution. The offer of the British Government brought everybody to look on the annexation in an interested point of view, and to make a choice one way or another. As a rule, the merchants and moneyed class desired the continuance of the Protectorate. Proprietors and professional men of political inclinations, with the clergy and all under their influence, were for the annexation. This annexation is now being carried out; and the result can only be a great falling off in the prosperity of the country, leading to discontent, if not to something worse.

In these pages I have endeavoured to describe the state of Greece, and the behaviour of the people during their revolution. All who were in the country at the time will, I believe, allow that my account is not exaggerated. The time was undoubtedly an exceptional one; but these exceptional periods show most clearly the true character of a people. In fact, the revolution only exposed the condensed form of what had been going on for the thirty preceding years—a fearful laxity of political morality among the rulers, and an unbridled lawlessness among the mass.* For years, nothing has been heard from Greece but accusations

* Dr. Finlay well sums up the state of Greece under its new existence: 'The administrative organisation of civil and financial business remained

and recriminations; conspiracies on one side, and illegal imprisonments on the other; one series of disputes on the most futile of subjects leading to another, while the real interests of the country have been neglected. A few acts of constitutional authority by the sovereign might long ago have set all this straight; and unquestionably the country must be regulated before it can ever hope to realise its great idea. Another fault is universal corruption in the administration. The highest briber in money or promises gets his man ; and everyone has his price. With this must be taken the lax notions prevalent concerning the sanctity of property and the little severity exercised in the punishment of evil doers. The neglect by the peasantry of labour as a source of wealth, added to an unjust and vexatious system of taxation ; the proneness of the educated classes to attach themselves to liberal professions, and especially

practically the same in free Greece as in Turkey. No improvement was made in financial arrangements, nor in the system of taxation; no measures were adopted for rendering property more secure; no attempt was made to create an equitable administration of justice; no courts of law were established; and no financial accounts were published. Governments were formed, constitutions were drawn up, national assemblies met, orators debated, and laws were passed according to the political fashion patronised by the liberals of the day. But no effort was made to prevent the Government being virtually absolute, unless it was by rendering it absolutely powerless. The constitutions were framed to remain a dead letter. The National Assemblies were nothing but conferences of parties, and the laws passed were intended to fascinate Western Europe, not to operate with effect in Greece.'—*History of the Greek Revolution*, by George Finlay, i. 281, politics, as a means of living, causing a supply greater than the demand, are further causes of the backwardness of the country, and the instability of its moral prosperity.

It must not, however, be supposed that Greece has not improved during the past generation. In spite of bad government and worse administration, she has marched on with Europe, though with shorter strides. A few statistics will prove this. The population has been increasing during thirty years at the rate of 2·16 per cent. per annnm, thanks to a healthy climate and the absence of war. This increase is four times greater than that of France, and sixteen times greater than that of Portugal, two countries from which there is little emigration.* Her revenue in 1833 was only seven millions of drachmai; in 1847 it had doubled; in 1860 it was twenty-two millions. At first this revenue was derived from land and direct taxes, the customs and other indirect taxation being trifling. Now the customs far exceed the land-tax, and supply one-fourth of the net revenue. It is true Greece has incurred a debt of 112 millions,† which she is not willing to pay, but of which she might easily pay the interest, if her finances

---

* Block's *Puissances Comparées.*

† In this is included the debt of 1824, for 800,000*l*., which produced 300,000*l*. This, as has been satirically observed, 'was a small payment of the debt due by civilised society to the country that produced Homer and Plato.' As such, I fear, it must be considered.

were properly administered. In 1860 there was a balance of a million and a half in her favour, and it might have been much larger if she had had a smaller army. A Greek army of 10,000 men is an absurdity, and the cost of supporting it has consumed one-third of the revenue. England and France—states requiring large armies—spend on them respectively one-fourth and one-fifth of their revenues. Greece, placed as she is under powerful protection, might advantageously replace the army, which is only a nuisance to the country itself and a vain threat to its neighbour, by a national force, as in Switzerland, where the expenses of training a militia are only one-ninth of the revenue. The disposition of the Greek people would be admirably suited to such an arrangement, for the national guards of Athens and other towns behaved on the whole admirably during the most critical phases of the Revolution.* Two or three thousand of the most orderly troops might be retained as a royal guard and as gendarmes. The other seven thousand would become available for the industry of the country. The few millions of drachmai thus saved might be most appropriately applied in paying the interest of its foreign debts, and founding a national

---

* Under Venetian rule the Greeks were allowed to form local militia for the preservation of order and the protection of property, and the system seems to have answered admirably. The country was tranquil, and very few crimes were committed. See Finlay's *Greece under Othoman and Venetian Domination*, p. 250.

credit; in augmenting the little navy, which, from the geographical position of the country, is really wanted; in making common roads and railroads; in cutting through the isthmus of Corinth; in irrigating the land, much of which is barren only from long drought; and, generally, in giving encouragement towards the working out of the productive forces and manufacturing industries of the country.

The Greeks complain that their country is too small for them.   It is not easy to see how, if a small house or a small state cannot be well administered, a larger one would be better.   If the governing classes in Greece have not been able to maintain order, and regulate their money matters in so small a territory, would they manage better if they had half of European Turkey to govern in addition?   We have not to look far for the reason why the rule of the Sultan in Europe is so upheld by foreign Powers.   If the Sclaves of the north are not more advanced in political and popular education than their brethren in the south, the downfall of the Crescent is yet far distant.   Were either of the two states in the Eastern peninsula in the position of Piedmont, the Turks would not remain a year in Europe.   That the break up must come sooner or later, in the natural course of things, is evident.   The Mahommedan rule in Europe would fall at once if the support of foreign Powers were withdrawn.   Its glory is with the past, and its revival seems almost an impossibility.   The course to be followed by the Greeks is plain enough. Their wisdom is to remain quiet, and employ all their talent and energies in improving their country, in organising its society on a firm basis, and calmly to await the issue. The heritage is theirs. A large part of Turkey and the adjacent islands must fall to their lot. Without an effort, the fruit, ready and ripe, will tumble into their hands; and if they be prepared to receive it, Europe will hail with joy the solution of a question which has perplexed it for generations. But woe to Greece if the breaking up of the Turkish power come at a time when she can give no better guarantees than at present! The Christians of Constantinople and the islands would probably prefer to found a sovereignty of their own, rather than to unite their destinies with men who had learned no lessons of political wisdom from three centuries of servitude, and the freedom of the thirty years which followed it.

The more I consider the present state of Greece and the character of the Greeks, the more is my opinion confirmed that an intelligent absolutism, under popular forms, would be the best thing for Greece during the next generation. This opinion is also common to thousands of Greeks.* Exercised with all due feeling

---

* The *Clio*, a Greek newspaper published at Trieste, having a wide circulation among the Greeks of foreign countries, contains the following address to the King, in January 1864: 'Sire, the august Frederick, on your departure for Greece, gave you the wise counsel to "reign and not

for the national character, and especially allowing the freest local self-government, such a system would probably cure the country of many of the evils under which

to govern." Yet this country, Sire, wants a governing prince, because it does not possess any politicians capable of governing for him. Greece does not resemble either Denmark or Belgium; her people are good, but untrained—her soil is fertile, but cultivation is backward. Your mission, Sire, is to instruct the Greeks in sound public morality, to perfect the productions of the soil to the same degree as the intelligence of the people, so as to make Greece the model kingdom of the East. Nevertheless, however constitutionally you may reign, the country will never justify your efforts and purpose, unless you put an inflexible hand on the very centre of the evil.

'You found Greece plunged in anarchy, completely disorganised, and bent under a yoke of terrorism. An unbridled license had begotten a universal disorder; an unprincipled press had annihilated all morality, and provoked massacres among citizens and brothers. Save our country, Sire, by restricting its liberties until such a day when those who now abuse them return to a proper sentiment of their duties towards society. Put a curb on the intemperance of the press, and prevent honest consciences being led astray by those which are corrupted.

'Such men as are the refuse of our society will probably reproach you with violating the constitution; all who are honestly devoted to their country will bless you. For who would dare to say that there is any law superior to the safety of one's country?

'Remember, Sire, how, after the horrors of June 1848, when the streets of Paris were dyed with the blood of its citizens, General Cavaignac boldly repressed the sanguinary feud, and imprisoned or banished the most uncontrollable journalists and turbulent members of the Assembly. General Cavaignac saved his country. Turn your eyes to the most constitutional state of Europe, and see what took place there in April 1848. Ambitious partisans tried to assault the Acropolis of the Parliament; the Government did not then hesitate to propose to the Parliament the restriction of the liberties of the subject.

'So do you, Sire, not hesitate to strike down those who outrage the it is groaning. A strong central power is absolutely necessary to fix the civil and military administrations on a pure and firm basis; to introduce a good system of legislation, and especially of taxation; to restore the national credit; and, in general, to put the institutions of the country in such a channel that the progress and welfare of the people might be their result. If Otho had only been an intelligent despot, he might have accomplished this in the early years of his reign. The constitution which succeeded would then have included all the elements necessary for the prosperity of a people. The misfortune of Greece is, as the eminent historian of

purity of Greek honour, and prevent the moral and material progress of the nation. Put a strong bridle on selfish and ambitious passions; repulse from you that ignoble sloth, which causes the very soil to protest against the unproductiveness which is imposed on it. Restore harmony to the strings of society. Temper our disorderly liberty by a legal rigour.

'Two centuries ago Fra Paolo Sarpi wished to teach the Venetians the surest manner of maintaining their sovereignty over Greece, and recommended, *Pane e bastonate!* The demagogues of Athens, Sire, are worthy of being controlled by like means.

'Postpone then, Sire, until a happier time, your benevolent intentions. Crush under your feet the vermin who are devouring the public wealth. Imitate Cavaignac. Do not hesitate at imprisonment; apply a remedy to the cancrous sores of the country; purify her political atmosphere from its miasma of corrupted incense. Demagogues and adventurers will loudly cry against you, but they are only the tail, and not the head, of the nation.'

This article was read by the democratic factions in Athens with the fiercest rage, and several copies containing it were publicly burned in the clubs and cafés. Some such policy, however, as the writer recommends must be put in force before social order can ever be restored in Greece.

that country remarked, ' that the Greek revolution produced no man of real greatness, no statesman of unble-
mished honour, no general of commanding talent.'* The
present revolution has afforded the same barren result,
and Greece must abide her time until it shall please
Providence to send her such a man to command and
guide her destinies.

* Dr. Finlay.

CHAPTER XIV.

THE LEBANON, AND THE CHRISTIAN MASSACRES.

Beyrout in June 1861—Departure of the French—The Effects of
their Occupation—Reasons for a Tour in the Interior—Cause of
Disorders in Syria—Religion and Nationality—Orthodox and
Schismatic Greeks—Maronites—Druses—Sketch of the Maronites
—Their Country—A happy Valley—Nessaris—Metoualis—Ismaliens—Their Pagan Rites—Religion of the Druses—Their Fanaticism - Start on a Tour—Zachlé—It is sacked by Druses
and Turks—An Orthodox Village of Anti-Libanus—We cross
the Anti-Libanus—Character of Syria—The Ard Zebdani—The
Valley of the Barada, or ancient Abana—Its Charms—The Khan
of Damar—Arrival in Damascus—Strolls and Visits—The Christian Quarter—History of the Massacres—Loss of Life and Property—Visits to the Seraskier and Pasha Governor—His Conversation—The Hadj—The Minister of Police—Citadel of Damascus
—The Grand Mosque, or ancient Church of St. John the Baptist
—Interior of the Mosque—Fanatic Arabs—Tombs of St. John
and of Ali, Grandson of Mahomet—The Pilgrimages of our Guide
—The Minaret—The Tower—Visit to an Arab Gentleman—His
House — The Bedouin Chaik, Mohammed Duki—The rival
Chiefs—Policy of Turkish Government—Mohammed Duki in his
real Character—Pilgrimages—Deceptions on Pilgrims - Return—
The Ain Fidji—Baalbec—Ruins—The modern Village—Our
Visitors - Interest of the Valley of Cœle-Syria—We recross the
Lebanon—The Cedars—Maronite Valley—Tripoli—Return to
Beyrout.

THE town and roadstead of Beyrout on June 5, 1861,
presented a very animated appearance. A large

French fleet of transports and men-of-war was waiting to take on board the army of occupation. Six English line-of-battle ships and frigates, five Russian vessels of war, and a Turkish squadron were there to witness the embarkation. The old town had been completely transformed by its visitors. Notices in the French language directed the stranger to the different *bureaux d'administration*, and French names pointed out innumerable *cafés*, *restaurants*, and *cabarets*. Ragged, half-naked Arab *gamins* clung to the skirts of the stranger's coat as he landed, screaming *bon jour* and *bakshish* in a breath. From the ' Grande Place,' the omnibusses of a French company were conveying passengers every few minutes to a wood of cedars, which had been planted a century ago by the Emir Fakr-el-din to prevent the sand of the downs from choking the green mulberry plantations. In this wood, which had been their camp, the few remaining troops were packing up their chattels. The larger camp in the mountains had been abandoned some days before, and its men were now crowding the jetties in the order of embarkation. On June 17, the date of General Beaufort's departure, the only French soldiers remaining were the few unfortunate inmates of the military hospital.

The departure of the French troops took place, according to French newspapers, amid the tears of a mourning population: let me add also, amid the execrations of the Mussulmans, and the wailings of many hundred women who had amused the leisure of the red-breeched sons of Mars. Yet the occupation by the French was one of order and humanity, and their influence should have broken down many of those prejudices which blind Orientals to the civilisation of the West. But so stubborn, so unimpressionable are the people of these lands, that as soon as the external stimulus is removed, they return, like the sea after a storm, to their old insensibility and apathy. No sooner had the last company departed, than the Turkish authorities began to sweep away all traces of their presence—many of which, indeed, were no great honour to our civilisation. The low grog and wine shops were closed; the police rooted out the dens of abandoned men and women who had only been tolerated as long as the troops remained. Beyrout soon reassumed the look of former days; and the Frank in Syria was once more a page in history.

No time seemed fitter than the present for making a tour through those districts which had lately been the scenes of so many political and sectarian murders. It was said, indeed, that the departure of the French would be the signal for fresh atrocities; that skilful agents were ready to excite them in order to render a second occupation necessary, and to raise a howl of indignation throughout Europe against that Government which had been instrumental in putting an end to the first. But in the moral as in the physical world there is generally a lull after an outburst of passion ; besides, Fuad Pasha was there, and he knew too well the hazards of a second occupation not to do all in his power to prevent it.

'Our nation,' said an Arab gentleman to me in conversation—

'Your nation!' I replied with some surprise; 'what nation is that?'

'Orthodox,' he replied; and his answer is the clue to all the disturbances and fermentations in the country. Putting aside the Druses and other Mahometan sects, the Christians of the same blood and language, who live in the same village and observe the same traditions, make their religion their nationality. The three sects are the Maronites, the Orthodox, and the Schismatic Greeks.* Each of them, and with apparent cause, considers itself and its interests under the protection of some European potentate—the Maronites, or Roman Catholics, and the Schismatic Greeks becoming almost

* Orthodox Greek, looking up to the Patriarch of Constantinople as chief of the Church; Schismatic Greek, having the same liturgy as the others, but acknowledging the supremacy of the Roman Pontiff. Many of the Greek Schismatic bishops took part in the famous canonisation of the Japanese martyrs at Rome. If the French clerical journals are to be believed, Roman proselytism is everwhere crowned with success in the East. The Bulgarians, *en masse*, became Schismatics in 1861–2, owing to the vexations of the Byzantine clergy. In 1862, among the Islands, several thousand Orthodox, with their priests, went over to the Church of Rome.—*Journal des Débats*, July 1862.

the partisans of the French Emperor; the Orthodox, those of the Russian Tsar.   Even the Druses are fully persuaded that they are protected by the British Government, and so become its partisans.*   Unfortunately, travellers, both official and private, do much to strengthen these ideas in the native mind, forgetting that such sectarian favour has a most debasing influence in fostering prejudices which it should be the duty of every European, if possible, to remove.

The Maronites derive their name from one of those Syrian monks who, in the sixth century, buried their austerity in the holes and caverns of their mountains. At a later period, another monk, who assumed the name and dogmas of the former, was consecrated a bishop by the Roman Patriarch of Antioch, and became the chief of a military schism against Constantinople.   He and his followers settled themselves in the gorges of the Lebanon, whence for some time they opposed the inroads of the Arab conquerors.   Of the Crusaders they were alternately the allies and enemies.   When Selim II. conquered Syria, the Maronites and Druses were the best of friends; thus united, they long preserved their independence.   But the Turkish policy long ago severed those bonds of union, and has now nearly subdued both peoples.

* See reports of Messrs. Robson and Graham, missionaries, in Government despatches.   To both these gentlemen the Druses declared that they looked on themselves as doing a pleasing act to their friends, the English, in extirpating the Christians, i.e. French influence.

The Maronites inhabit chiefly the slopes of the Lebanon between Tripoli and Beyrout. South of Beyrout to St. Jean d'Acre, and in the interior from Mount Hermon to the once-fruitful Haouran, are to be found the strongholds of the Druses. Between the two the villages are composed of mixed Druses and Christian sectarians. But the chief home of the Maronites is in that large and remarkable valley which extends like a funnel from the sea-shore at Tripoli to the snow above the cedars of Lebanon. Many-villages are here seen in spots which seem wholly inaccessible. Perched on the borders of ravines, and within pistol-shot of one another, they are separated by hours of toilsome march. Monasteries overhang frightful chasms. The stony mountain sides and gorges are built up into narrow terraces, where vines, with rich crops of grain and inviting fruit trees, everywhere refresh the eye. Rude aqueducts bring down from unfailing sources the water which, regularly distributed in every direction, keeps up the appearance of perpetual spring. Nowhere except in Japan, where the mountains are terraced to their summits, have I seen such a picture of cultivation under difficulties as among these valleys of the Lebanon. Monks may be seen working in their common possessions. The small proprietor, surrounded by his sons and daughters, is hoeing his patrimony of mulberry trees or vines; or, reclining beneath the shade of a sycamore tree, is enjoying with them their frugal meal. Such is a poetical glimpse of life in this most beautiful of valleys. But, side by side with their praiseworthy industry, the Maronites have vices which, though only the necessary effects of oppression, leave the worst impression on the stranger. They are mean, cowardly, cunning, avaricious, and besotted with bigotry. Their hospitality is a niggardly calculation on the generosity of their guest, and they are the most confirmed beggars in the world. From the cedars to the sea-shore the tourist is pestered for alms by people who are ten thousand times better off than the peasants of his own country. His presence is a signal to everybody— monk, man, woman, and child—to throw down their implements of husbandry, and hold out a hand for charity. A handful of green barley for your horse, the first flower that comes to hand, or, as was once offered to me, a sprig of hemlock, afford an excuse and an apology for their importunate demands. Even the very dogs seem to howl *bakshish* at your horse's heels. Wherever the Druses and Maronites came into contact, the latter threw down their guns and fled to the fastnesses or the sea-shore. In fact, they suffered much less than the other sects of Christians, who sometimes endeavoured to defend themselves and their property.

The tribes which profess, or pretend to profess, the Moslem faith, are the Druses, the Nessaris, and the Metoualis, who are sectarians of Ali. Among all these, there is mixed up with Islamism much of the ancient paganism of the country. A sect of the Nessaris, called

the Ismaliens, still practise the rites of the old Phœnician adoration of Priapus or Astarte. 'The Druses,'
says Volney, who saw much of them at the end of the
last century, 'exhibit a wonderful facility of belief in
religious matters. Some of them believe in Metem-
psychosis; others adore the sun, moon, and stars; every
one follows his own religious ideas, which, from their
manner of life, are of the greatest simplicity. So little
bigotry have they, that among the Turks they act like
Mussulmans, prostrate themselves in the mosques, and
perform ablutions. If among the Maronites, they follow
them to church, and cross themselves with the consecrated water. Some, importuned by missionaries, have
allowed themselves to be baptized; then, requested by
the Turk, have submitted to the rite of circumcision,
and have died at last neither Christians nor Moslems.'
The Metoualis, who formerly inhabited the great valley
of Lebanon, are the most fanatic of all Mussulmans;
but they number now only a few tribes, having been
almost exterminated by Djezzar Pasha in 1790.

The Druses, and some of the Greek Christians, are
undoubtedly among the noblest races of the mountain.
Even their vices seem more amiable, because free from
the low taint of meanness and cowardice. Their pride
is the fitting dignity of independence, and their simple
hospitality is given without a second thought. A Druse
may plunder you, but he will never implore your charity. When once he has given you his word, his life is

guarantee for yours. The worst crimes with which they are reproached arise from that deep resentment of injuries, which, however repugnant to Christian ethics, has descended to them from their forefathers, and which many people regard as meritorious when they read of it in the Books of Moses or of the Kings. Chief actors in the late atrocious deeds, the Druses were but tools in the hands of the Turkish authorities,* and would have been their victims also if a just hand had not intervened to save them from indiscriminate slaughter. By these acts they have done much to rivet their fetters. Their strongholds have been occupied by Turkish troops, and their character has been vilified over all Europe. As to the Christian tribes, they have now obtained from the Porte a sort of autonomy; and perhaps for the future the Government will understand that its first duty is to protect the persons and property of all classes of its subjects, of whatever race or creed. It is, however, a slender hope, for Islamism knows nothing of tolerance, which can only exist in Turkey under a sort of hydraulic pressure from without. The Mussulman Arabs are fearful fanatics, and so are the Christian sects. The duty of the Government is to subdue the fanaticism of both. A strong body of police is needed every Easter at Jerusalem to prevent Christian fanatics of different sects from dyeing the stones of the Holy Sepulchre with

* Such was the verdict of the Commissioners of the Powers, assembled at Beyrout.

each other's blood; the same police might be usefully employed in towns where Mussulmans and Christians are found living together. Tolerance among these fanatics can be sincere only when steam, the railroad, and the printing-press become common among them, or when the whole country shall have fallen under some European and Christian domination.

Our proposed tour lay over the beaten track of a thousand preceding travellers. But the circumstances of the time may render a sketch of it not uninstructive to the reader. It was a half-official journey and a pleasure tour combined. Our party consisted of Admiral Shestakov, the Russian consul, and a few other gentlemen, with the usual train of servants, *moukres*, horses, mules, and donkeys bearing tents, hampers, &c. A small guard of dragoons had been added by the Governor of Beyrout. As the new French road from Beyrout to Damascus over the Lebanon was only completed for about fifteen miles from Beyrout, we drove over this distance to the station where our horses were awaiting us.

Six hours' riding brought us to Zahlé Zachlé, situated on the eastern slope of the Lebanon. It is one of the largest of the Christian villages, and was among the greatest sufferers in the late disturbances.* This village was always noted for the turbulence of its inhabitants, and Volney relates that a hundred years

* Damascus, Zachlé, Sidon, Daïr el Kamar, Rasheya, and Hasbeya, were the chief centres of the massacres.

ago it was the head-quarters of a large gang of coiners. Before the massacres it numbered 15,000 souls, and could bring 3,000 guns (i.e. all the able-bodied male population) to bear against an enemy. When the Druses first attacked it, they were driven back with some loss, and it was only on their second attempt, when the inhabitants had given up their arms under promise of protection from the Turks, and when they saw the uniforms of soldiers and a piece of artillery among their assailants, that the two bishops with their flocks fled to the mountain. The place was then pillaged, and the roofless and gutted houses were still much as the Druses had left them.

On the green sward of a hillock overhanging the village we found our tents pitched and dinner ready; after which, in the cool and mellow twilight, under the soothing charm of *chibouks* and *narguilés,* audience was given to the Orthodox and Schismatic bishops and the ancients of the village. The next morning, accompanied by the two bishops, who *brothered* each other in every phrase (and it is to be hoped acted up to their language), we rambled among the broken-down hovels, watching the inhabitants making their sun-dried bricks of mud and chopped straw, much in the same manner, probably, as the children of Israel made theirs for Egyptian masters. The rest of the day was spent on the carpets of the Orthodox bishop's dwelling (which consisted of only one room), partly in solemn conclave with the clergy and chief men, listening to the lamentable but somewhat exaggerated tale of their sufferings, and making arrangements that the money we brought should be distributed in the most equitable manner. When business was over, we partook of the cheer, good for the time and place, of our host. For the benefit of those who have never dined in an Arab family in Syria, I may mention that our dinner consisted of tiny pieces of mutton or goat's flesh roasted on a skewer, from which we gnawed it, pilafs of rice prepared with fat from the enormous tails of the Syrian sheep, sour clotted milk, and stinking goat's milk cheese. The bread, as eaten in the East, consists of large unleavened pancakes of meal, which at the same time serve as table-cloths, plates, and napkins. But the limpid water, the aromatic moka, and the white compressed snow from the summits of Lebanon floating in bowls of delicious sherbet, were real luxuries.

Having crossed the plains of Bequáa to a miserable orthodox village on the slope of the Anti-Libanus, we sat down beneath its only shady tree on a few ragged carpets, spread for us by their still more ragged owners. There were only a few wretched hovels, the roofs of which were covered with the dried dung fuel burnt in this country. Scarcely a fruit tree was left; and a few half-starved and moping goats and fowls seemed the only riches of the inhabitants, who had fled on the approach of the Druses. Having left them suitable assistance, we went on our way over the Anti-Libanus, through a singular scene of natural desolation. The limestone rocks on either side of the pass had been torn and split into a thousand fantastic figures, here shapeless or deformed, there resembling castellated towers, gothic decorations, or fine-pointed minarets. One enormous fragment of rock, detached from the mountain, looked like the figure of a woman, with drooping head and hand raised to her cheek, weeping over the desolation around. On the top of the ridge the view changed, and the eye looked down on that beautiful Alpine valley, the Ard Zebdani, lying surrounded by hot and tawny rocks, like a huge emerald in a setting of fire.

Syria is, indeed, a land of sudden and remarkable contrasts. In the morning the pilgrim may be gasping among sandy plains in a haze of heat, and gazing at the mirage and wonderful phenomena of refraction among the surrounding mountains; and at noon, he may be inhaling the cool air on the summit of that range on whose beauties the great lawgiver of the Jews sighed in vain to look before he closed his eyes.* As his horse's hoofs crunch the crisp snow, he may look down on one side on the grey hazy space of the desert of sand, while on the other the eye ranges over the blue 'desert of waters,' † where ocean and firmament are imperceptibly

---

* Deuteronomy iii. 25.

† When the Bedouins first came in sight of the Mediterranean at Gaza, they called the sea the desert of waters.

blended together.   Again, struggling through some dreary gorge amid the terrible monuments of volcanic strife, he suddenly emerges on the green oasis of a mountain spring, round which is a tiny Eden.   Here the eye grows dazzled and dim, and the head weary from the glare of the precipices which bound the valley; a little farther, and the eye reposes on the refreshing verdure of fruit trees, luxuriantly thriving amid the cool waters of torrents, fountains, and cascades. The wild and *bournoused* Arab of the plain, the still wilder kerchiefed mountaineer, ride proudly by on their prouder steeds; a few more minutes bring the sober merchant or the patient husbandman on the beloved mare, the sharer of his caresses with his wife and family. From a village threshold the white close-muffled figure of a Mussulman female will flee to the dark interior at his approach; while the half-naked Christian maiden will smile as he stops at her parent's door, and present him her offering of cool water or of fruit.   In no other country that I can mention is there such a sublime contrast in nature, such a degrading contrast in man.

The inhabitants of the village of Zebdani are chiefly Mussulman Arabs; the Christians numbered only eighty 'guns,' who were decoyed to Damascus, and on their return found that their houses had been sacked by their neighbours or the Druses.

Owing to its elevation, fertility, and distribution of waters, the Ard Zebdani is one of the pleasantest spots in all Syria. The village itself is completely lost in gardens of fruit trees, while at each end of the valley are open cornfields or well-irrigated pastures. Between the two we pitched our tents for the night.

From this valley to Damascus the path follows the winding course of the Barada or ancient Abana, which, leaping down from the high land in a series of cascades, passes by many branches through the city, and is absorbed in the desert beyond. The ride is one of the finest that can be imagined. At the entrance of the Suk Barada, or defile, are the remains of two Roman bridges, spanning a cascade, with some traces of the old Roman road. A little farther, and high up in the rocks, are some remarkable holes, which, having first served as sepulchres, became afterwards the abodes of hermits, and are now the home of bats and birds unclean. Just below these the broken columns of a temple are scattered about the defile. From this pass the traveller emerges into a lovely valley, winding along between the grey and yellow, the steep and naked precipices, which, whether sun-lit or overshadowed, are for ever varying their tints. Tall poplars and larch, the drooping willow and the sycamore, gardens of orange-trees, mulberries, and pomegranates, and, still more conspicuous, the golden *mishmush*,* mark the course of the torrent. Beyond these on either side is a fringe of

---

* The apricot. There are twenty species of this fruit known in Syria, the stone of one of which is much esteemed for its flavour and perfume.

vineyards. The tumbling water sparkles through the green foliage at every step, and where it is not seen, its presence is felt by its never-failing music. Art has everywhere assisted nature in beautifying this valley, and a whole network of aqueducts robs the volume of every waterfall. To a mind never insensible to the fixed or fleeting charms of nature in every clime, a ride through this valley on a cool day in June was invigorating and refreshing; and though not given to ecstasy, I must confess that the reality here presented far exceeded any poetical description. It seems the more beautiful, perhaps, from its contrasts with surrounding objects.

On reaching the Khan of Damar, an hour's ride from Damascus, we found a troop of cavalry, sent by the pasha, awaiting our arrival. Preceded by this guard of honour, we mounted the last hill, from which is obtained that remarkable bird's-eye view of the oasis of El Cham, its city, and the surrounding desert, which, although described already a thousand times in a thousand ways, it is hard to refrain from describing yet again. As we entered the city, a salute was fired from the citadel; but the welcome offered by a Turkish bath, with a comfortable bed in the only Frankish hotel of the place, was much more grateful, and of these luxuries we availed ourselves without delay.

Damascus is, *par excellence*, the country of fruits and roses, quantities of which are exported thence for Constantinople.

Our stay in the capital of Syria was short—only four days. Yet in that short time we saw all that strangers with the best introductions could see. Old Abraham Abou, whom many tourists will probably remember, showed us a few Jewish interiors, where Oriental luxury was seen in all its soft splendour, and led us one or two strolls through the interminable bazaars and narrow lanes of the Moslem city. But of course it was the Christian quarter which chiefly attracted our attention. Acres of ground, where a few months before had stood the dwellings of a peaceful population, were covered now with naked walls and heaps of rubbish. The scared inhabitants had fled to the sea-coast, and there only remained in Damascus the dregs of the Christian population. Between the gutted walls of churches and richer houses, broken fountains, columns, and arabesques were protruding from masses of plaster and dust. On the walls of the church the grotesque pictures of virgin and saint bore marks of insult from mud and bullets. In a hundred different places about this quarter some rude artist had drawn something which was meant for a steam-ship on four wheels, from the yard-arms of which hung figures with drooping heads, wearing the Turkish fez. The drawing probably intimated the punishment which the murderers were likely to receive from their Christian friends beyond sea. The solid cavern-like shops of the smaller tradespeople had resisted the fury of the assailants. The fountains were all choked up and dry. To heighten the desolation still more by the contrast, some trees which had been spared were. blooming, and a few flowers had sprung up on the ruins.

The manner in which the massacre began was described to me by an eye-witness.   Long before, there had been rumours of the rapine and murder perpetrated in the mountain, and the timid Christian population felt very much as sheep would do who were herding with wolves. Oval figures, with a cross in the middle, were found chalked on the doors of many of the Christians.   The traders in the bazaar had amused themselves by inciting their children to draw on the pavement crosses, which they spat on and effaced with their feet on the approach of any Christian.   On the 8th July, 1860, two children amusing themselves in this manner were suddenly arrested by the Turkish police, roughly handled, and put in prison.   This, it is confidently asserted, was done only to excite the fanatical mob.   At all events, it had that effect, for the mob easily released the children, and then immediately bore away with shouts of rage to the Christian quarter, situated about three minutes from the bazaar.   The Turkish guard not only failed to prevent the massacre and pillage which immediately began, but even encouraged, aided, and abetted the murderers. The superior authorities, it is known, took no steps for several days to stop the fearful tragedy, but even prevented the approach of those who would have done so. For this negligence or connivance the governor afterwards paid the penalty with his life, being condemned and shot in the citadel. On the fourth day, Ismael Atrash, with his Druses of the Haouran, entered the place, and completed the destruction and plunder. When Abd-el-Kader arrived with his Arabs, he saved all he could; among others the French Sisters of Charity. About 3,000 men were killed. One English missionary received eleven wounds before he died. The Russian dragoman, the brother of our guide, was mistaken for the consul, and killed. No women or children perished in Damascus from actual violence; their portion of grief, want, and suffering was reserved for the future. Twelve hundred houses were destroyed, one of which, with its contents, was valued at two millions of piastres. The whole loss of the Christians in the city and mountain, estimated by themselves, amounted to no less than 400 millions of piastres, or about 3,200,000*l.* Two Arab merchants, who had been spectators *only* of the massacre, assured me of what is now well known, that the mob would never have proceeded to such extremities, if they had not been convinced that they were forwarding the views of the Turkish authorities.

* An amusing incident of the valuation of losses was told me. Fuad Pasha, on referring to the lists of taxation, found that the whole value of the Christians' property, as declared by themselves, amounted to little more than half the sum which they professed to have lost. He declared that having so long made false returns to cheat the Government, he would keep them to their first valuation. It seems, however, that thirty millions of francs was decided on by the commission, and accepted by Fuad Pasha, as the indemnity; but not half this sum was ever paid.

One day was set apart for our visits to the Pasha Governor, the Seraskier, and bishops. The Seraskier, whom we visited first, was an old soldier, who had commanded a division on the Danube during the late war. All the troops which had been in Damascus at the time of the massacres had been changed, he said, and more disciplined regiments had taken their place. At that time there were three battalions in the city, and 6,000 men camped in various parts of the mountain. Amin Pasha, the governor, we found to be a young Turk, educated in Paris, who had made the round of European Courts, and whose Oriental nature had received a good coating of European civilisation. As he spoke French fluently, we had a conversation of more than two hours over our pipes and coffee, chiefly on the state of the country, and, to judge from his remarks, his mind was everything that was liberal and reforming. 'Under his rule,' he said, 'it would be dangerous to attempt any such horrors as stained that of his unfortunate predecessor.' He had that day been despatching a detachment of troops, with stores of biscuit, oil, and fruits, to meet the Hadj or sacred caravan on its return from the Holy City, where the pilgrims had been celebrating the feast of Bairam. 'The expense which attended these Hadj,' said the pasha, 'was enormous. The one for that year had cost twenty millions of piastres. Few pilgrims now joined it, except those who combined commerce with their devotional visit; the great body of pilgrims preferring the easier route by sea and through Egypt. Although the pilgrimage had fallen into comparative disuse, it was impossible for the Government either to stop or diminish the grant, which might be much more usefully spent in paying the arrears due to the troops and the civil authorities.' *

We were very anxious to visit the interior of the Grand Mosque. After some hesitation, the pasha consented and ordered the Police Minister, who was present, to accompany us. This person, an old man of a remarkably astute and cunning countenance, who by his familiarity might have been the favourite, by his fawning the slave, of his master, rose up immediately, said something in Turkish, which I suppose was, ' To hear is to obey,' kissed the hand or robe of the pasha, and signified to us that he was at our service. ' Allez,' said the pasha with a smile to the admiral, who was seated next him, ' Allez, ce garçon-là a de l'ambition.' Whatever may have been his ambition, he was certainly a shrewd and cunning rascal, who, had he lived a century ago, might have played with some success the part of slave, flatterer, spy, betrayer, executioner, and successor of his master. ' Beware of thy neighbour,' says the Arab

---

* A comparison will show how this Hadj is changing its route to Mecca. In 1757 the Bedouins plundered the caravan, when 6,000 pilgrims were slain or dispersed, the women being carried into captivity. In 1860 only twenty pilgrims from Syria joined the Hadj. In 1861 there were none at all.

proverb, 'who has made *one* Hadj; if he has made two, leave all thou hast and get thee away from near him.' Now our guide prided himself on having made three Hadj, and must have been a dangerous companion if there is any truth in the maxim.

From the residence of the pasha he led us into the citadel through a gateway which had been walled up for more than eight hundred years, and only just re-opened. In the courtyard of this fortress some hundreds of destitute Christian families had found a refuge during the massacres. The ancient Christian Church of St. John, now the Great Mosque, is so completely sur-rounded with buildings that it is impossible to obtain any complete view of its external architecture. So jealous were the Arabs of the admission of any Giaour, that a firman from Constantinople was necessary to obtain an entrance. In 1856 a Frenchman was nearly killed for attempting to enter it. At the present mo-ment there is less difficulty, and a large bribe will over-come any opposition either here or at Jerusalem and other holy places, which are interesting alike to Chris-tian and Mahometan pilgrims. As we shuffled about the interior, with the yellow Turkish slippers put on over our boots, we had a few sullen looks from some of the most fanatical worshippers, who, however, stood aloof and greeted us with only a growl or two. Some younger fanatics were much bolder. They kept close to our sides, and now and then, when none of our guides were looking, favoured us with a few significant grimaces, until one of them, caught in the act, received such a whack from one of the police as sent him howling away. This example had the effect of keeping his mischievous companions at a distance during the rest of our visit.

In the interior of the mosque there still remain, in spite of long neglect, many vestiges of its ancient splendour, especially the fragments of pictorial mosaic along the walls of the courtyard, and the marbles and tesselated pavement of the body of the mosque. But the edifice is chiefly interesting as containing the supposed tombs of St. John the Baptist and the unhappy Ali, son of Fatima, daughter of the Prophet. The tomb of the former is in the body of the mosque, standing out from the wall, and covered over with a monument; that of Ali is in a small apartment at one end of the building. In the corridor outside is a marble slab, embedded in the wall, with the name and qualities of the dead inscribed on it. Just inside the adjoining door is the stone sarcophagus containing the body. The only other things in the cell are two small and coarsely-coloured drawings, one representing the sacred place at Mecca, the other the Prophet's Tomb at Medina. Here our guide related to us how he had made his difficult pilgrimages, and pointed out in the pictures the spots where he had adored. After this he led us up the winding staircase of the Great Minaret, from which there is a magnificent view of the city, with the surrounding desert and mountains.   On descending he called our attention to the walls of the tower, covered from top to bottom with names in Arabic characters, and explained the popular belief that the Prophet Jesus Christ will one day pass down from heaven through that minaret, when all whose names are found written on the wall will be transferred to Paradise.   How they whose names become effaced would fare, he did not say; for the scribblings of many a generation have been effaced by the scribbling of those which have followed them.   After spending about an hour in this interesting building, we proceeded to pay our visit to the bishops.

Two or three of the most instructive hours of our stay in Damascus were passed on the carpets of Mohammed Aga Nouri.   His dwelling was situated in the most ill-famed part of the city, where, as the Arab proverb declares, the inhabitants also bear the worst of characters.   Yet in this district, though thickly settled with Christians, not a single murder took place.   The Mussulmans there seemed to have spared their immediate neighbours, while massacring the Christians in other parts of the city.   Our host had justly rendered himself an object of esteem to all Europeans, by having saved, concealed, and succoured more than one hundred Christians.   The large saloon of his house, whose ' beams were of cedar and its rafters of fir wood,' was hung with the rich tapestry and brocade, for the manufacture of which the city was once so famous.   On these hangings were suspended curious groups of guns and pistols, richly wrought sabres and daggers. Low divans were fixed around the walls, and on the floor in the centre were soft cushions of silk, among which we reclined, inhaling through rich amber and jessamine the fumes of the best of Latakia, and listening to another account of the fatal days of July. Presently a personage still more interesting joined our party. This was Mohammed Duki, a Bedouin Chaik, the lord of a district of vilages around Damascus, who, it was said, could bring 5,000 guns into the field. He, too, had been a great protector of the Christians: indeed, many hundreds of his tribe, he said, were Christians themselves. He was already approaching the city with a body of his followers to protect them, when he was met by a battalion of infantry, the commander of which ordered him back to his village. His only alternative would have been to have forced his way through them; but, not knowing how matters really were, he dared not resist the order, and so retired.

Like most of the chiefs of his race, Mohammed Duki was frail in person, of swarthy face, with small, sparkling, unsteady black eyes peering out from the folds of his kerchief; his one hand (the other had been cleanly amputated by a sabre-cut) and naked feet were small and delicate, and although well tanned were exquisitely clean, with the nails neatly cut and trimmed; his demeanour was full of vivacity; his arms graceful in action

while speaking, and his speech calm and well accentu-
ated, sometimes quickening into a tremor as he related
some of the wrongs he had suffered from a rival or from
the Turkish Government. His object in coming to
Damascus, he told us, was to make terms with and pro-
pitiate the pasha, who had been incensed against him
by his old foe, Ismael Atrash, the Druse chief of the
Haouran. The chaik and Ismael were the two most
powerful men in the pashalic, and continually in feud
one against the other. Ismael Atrash had been persuading the pasha and seraskier that the power of
Mohammed Duki was too great, and that it was the
interest of the Turkish Government to lower his influence by dividing the villages and tribes under his
command, or by dispossessing him altogether of his
chaikship, which had been inherited in his family for
more than 300 years. Mohammed Duki, who had
brought 3,000 Arabs with him into the city, had that
day had an interview with the pasha, to whom he
offered his services to annihilate the Druses altogether.
What the result of such extraordinary proposals was,
does not appear; it is probable that the wily pasha left
each party to meditate on his reputed wrongs; receiving with many thanks their presents and offers of service,
and secretly resolving to lower the pride and the power
of both. It has always been the policy of the Turkish
Government, in its remote pashalics, to untie the bundle
of sticks by sowing and fostering discord, and then to

crush them one after another when they have suffici-
ently weakened themselves. In doing this it is very
patient, but the result is infallible. *The Osmanli catch
hares in carts* is an Arab proverb, which well explains
the Turkish policy.

Mohammed Duki had seen much of Europeans, and
seemed to seek their society, for he fully understood the
influence exercised by them on the Turkish authorities.
He had lately been on board the great ships of the
English at Beyrout, and longed to pay a visit to the land
from which they came; but he could not face the risk
of leaving his country exposed to the intrigues of his
enemies. Yet he would come to Beyrout once more to
see his friend, the admiral; and, as he said this, he took
off his head-dress and presented it to Admiral Shestakov,
as a token of the sincerity with which he would perform
the promise. Four thousand years ago a patriarch
would have taken off his sandal, and presented it as a
pledge under similar circumstances. The naked-footed
Bedouin chief offered his head-dress instead. Mohammed Duki was the first and only specimen of those
interesting men that we had the good fortune to see;
for our tour ended on the borders of the desert, where
they dwell, as their fathers did before them, in all the
simplicity and insecurity of primæval times, beneath their
camel-hair tents beside the scanty stream of the oasis.*

---

* Such was the Bedouin chief in contact with civilisation, and on his
best behaviour. Let us look at him in his native desert and natural

El Cham, or Damascus, was the terminus of our journey. Before leaving, we, like good Christians, made a sort of pilgrimage to certain places of historical repute in the early days of our religion, such as the street called Straight, the Via Recta of the Romans, the spot where St. Paul is said to have been let down from the walls in a basket, and the house where he tarried while awaiting his Divine commission. There is, of course, nothing remarkable in any of these, beyond the memories that are associated with them. The Straight street, like all other streets in oriental towns, is narrow, filthy, and full of little shops: the other places it would be much more satisfactory to visit if the topography could be more relied on. Tradition and the intense reverence of orientals for the great men of old time, together with priestly cupidity, have found many a local habitation for the names which they love to recall. Travellers in Syria may have pointed out to them *two exact* spots, where Jonas was cast out from a fish's

character. In the report of Mr. Skene (August 1860), H.B.M. Consul at Aleppo, we read that Mohammed Duki, at the head of 2,000 horsemen of the tribe of Beni-Sachar, had just before devastated and unpeopled twenty-five villages in one incursion alone. He goes on to say, that in a large fertile district near Aleppo, which twenty years ago possessed 100 villages, there are now only a few fellahs to be seen ; that he had passed over towns in the desert, having well paved streets and houses still in good repair, but totally uninhabited; that thousands of acres of land, showing signs of former irrigation and extensive culture, now hardly afford a scanty bite to the Bedouin's sheep or camels. So much for the civilisation of Mohammed Duki and his fellows.

B B

belly ; * they may walk over the arena of the terrible conflict between St. George and the dragon ; may stand on
several spots where the ark rested ; behold the actual
tomb of the patriarch Noah ; bathe in the very part of
the Jordan where Christ was baptized.   It is the same,
though in a less degree, with places where events of a
less spiritual character have occurred, as every visitor of
' show places ' may have remarked, where exact localities
are assigned to events with the most consummate im-
pudence and the smallest possible probability.   The
lion-doing tourist should, however, be thankful that
there is a place assigned to them at all.

We retraced our steps along the green banks of the
Abana to its source in the Anti-Libanus, turning a little
aside to visit the Ain Fidji (eye or fountain of Fidji),
with the ruined temple which overhangs it.   Baalbec is
one-and-a-half day's easy journey from Damascus.   On
our arrival there we found our tents pitched under the
Acropolis, on which are the noble ruins of the Temples
of the Sun and Jupiter.   The only other objects of interest are, the circular temple among the hovels of the
modern village, and the Mosque of Saladin, in one corner
of which is shown a tomb, said to be that of the Emir.
The governor of the place, hearing of our arrival, despatched the greater part of his garrison to sweep away
the dust and dirt, and to water the space around our

* One near a large stone, a few furlongs from Alexandretta; the other
near Sidon, where a mosque has been erected over the spot.

tents.   One of his officers also brought a present of two sheep.   Soon afterwards the governor himself paid us a visit, as we were lunching under the magnificent columns of the Temple of Jupiter.

The period during which the mighty foundations of Baalbec were laid, has, I believe, never been decided by antiquarians.   That he who built the great Temple at Jerusalem, 'whose foundations were of costly stones, even of great stones, stones of ten cubits and of eight, sawed with saws,' may also have laid the foundations of the Temple of the Sun, whose largest stone measures in length 69 ft. 2 in., in breadth 12 ft. 10 in., and in thickness 13 ft. 3 in.—is not at all improbable.   The traditions of the country affirm that he did; and that the building he erected was a strong vault for concealing his gold and precious stones, to find which all the caverns under the building have been ransacked in vain.   Certain it is that long ages intervened between the laying of those huge foundations and the erection of the superstructure, the walls and columns of which excite as much admiration as the former excite surprise.   The Mussulman quarrying material for his mosque, the Christian for his church; the Bedouin rudely pulling down whole columns for the few pounds of lead which cemented their sections; the bigot destroying for the sake of destruction; the antiquarian disturbing in his pursuit of knowledge; and lastly, repeated shocks of earthquake have strewn the area with fragments of the stately temples which once rose proudly to the sky. The Cyclopean blocks which supported them in their splendour are still as they probably were 3,000 years ago.

The modern village is a miserable collection of hovels, built like all places in similarly classic positions, with fragments from the adjoining ruins. In 1861 it contained about 3,000 inhabitants, partly Metoualis, partly Christians, besides a garrison of two companies of troops. During the last century it was a place of much greater importance, having a population of more than 5,000; but the terrible earthquake of 1759, and the ensuing wars between Yousef and the notorious Pasha Djezzar, left in 1780 only 1,200. During the late massacres the Turkish garrison acted like the other troops, and its commander, who was afterwards a member of the Commission, was expelled from it, as having been an accomplice of those whom he was called upon to judge. Our encampment attracted the greater part of the village around us. Even the two Mahometan schoolmasters brought their pupils; and, seated near us on the banks of the neighbouring rivulet, with their feet dangling in the water, they smoked their chibouks; while their pupils, naked in the stream, jabbered verses of the Koran between their splashings. A beautiful moon-lit evening spent in wandering among the ruins, and the next day occupied in photographing them from their best points of view, served to fix on our memory the scenes of the ancient capital of Cœle-Syria.

The great interest to a thinking tourist in this ancient land is, that it was the chief scene of the combat of Judaism against idolatry. Throughout the earlier books of Jewish history, this plain of Cœle-Syria, or, as it is there called, the valley of Lebanon, is constantly coupled with the name of Baal.* There that great dogma of faith and reason, the sublime 'I am,' stern, unrelenting, even cruel, but accompanied by law, order, and morality, came into contact, and struggled through ages with the fascinating polytheism of Persia and India, which, despite its poetry, was bloody, corrupt, and frightfully obscene. How seductive these religions were to the Jewish people, worn out with toil and hope deferred, every reader of the Bible well knows. So insinuating and tenacious must these old religions have been, that when Deism came forth victorious from the struggle, it had received from their mysteries a taint which only another great reform could remove. In like manner Christianity, in its fight with other forms of the same polytheism, took an impression from them which fifteen centuries have not sufficed to wipe out.

From Baalbec we again passed the plain of Bequáa in a straight line for the Lebanon, to that group of trees which still represent those ancient cedars out of which the Phœnician fleets were hewn. Passing a solitary

---

* 'Baalgad, in the valley of Lebanon' (Josh. xii. 7). 'Baalgad, under Mount Hermon' (Josh. xiii. 5). 'The Hivites that dwell in mount Lebanon from Baal Hermon' (Judges iii. 3).

pillar still erect in the midst of the plain, we soon entered the spurs of the mountain. Droves of camels, on their way to Damascus, laden with ice packed in reeds, were descending from the summits, where snow still lay in abundance. One or two villages of the Metoualis and Maronites lay on our road, and our noonday halt on the banks of the pretty mountain lake of Ain Attar was passed in a long conversation with a Maronite priest, whose knowledge of the Italian language rendered him more successful than the rest of his fellows in the art of begging. On reaching the cedars our tents were already pitched beside them, and a ragged boy and girl were waiting, in the hopes of gaining a few piastres, to offer cones to any enthusiastic traveller who might wish to reproduce the exact species in his native land. A day's ride from the cedars down that remarkable valley inhabited by the Maronites, which I have already described, brought us to Tripoli, where, having spent some hours with the bishop and in visiting the female refugees from Damascus, we embarked on board a gunboat and returned to Beyrout, having made one of the most interesting of tours—a tour which I would recommend the reader to try when he makes his visit to these parts.

PRINTED BY SPOTTISWOODE AND CO., NEW-STREET SQUARE, LONDON

MOUNTAIN EXCURSIONS IN THE VENETIAN CARNIC AND JULIAN ALPS.

Early in the Spring will be published in One Volume, square crown 8vo. uniform with *Peaks, Passes, and Glaciers* illustrated by a Travelling Map of the District, a Sketch Map geologically coloured, 6 full-page Plates in Chromolithography by M. and N. Hanhart, and 26 Engravings on Wood by E. Whymper, price One Guinea.

THE
DOLOMITE MOUNTAINS:
EXCURSIONS
THROUGH
TYROL, CARINTHIA, CARNIOLA, AND FRIULI, IN 1861, 1862, AND 1863.

By J. GILBERT and G. C. CHURCHILL, F.G.S.

WITH A GEOLOGICAL CHAPTER, AND PICTORIAL ILLUSTRATIONS FROM ORIGINAL DRAWINGS ON THE SPOT.

Illustrations in Chromolithography.

1. The Langkofel and Plattkogel, from the Seiser Alp.
2. Monte Civita, with the Lake and Village of Alleghe.
3. Cirque of the Croda Malcora, near Cortina.
4. Castello Pietra, Primiero.
5. General View of the Rosengarten Gebirge, from the Sasso di Damm, Fassa Thal.
6. Sasso di Pelomo, from Monte Zucco.

Engravings on Wood.

1. Heraldic Dolomite, from the Arms of a Carinthian Nobleman.
2. Dolomite Mountains, near Lienz.
3. The Schlern and Ratzes Bath House.
4. Sasso di Pelmo, from Santa Lucia, near Caprile.
5. The Langkofel and Plattkogel, from Campitello.
6. Cortina, the Croda Malcora, and Antelao in the background.
7. The Kollinkofel, Valentiner Thal, Carnic Alps.
8. Barn in Styria.
9. The Mangert, and Sir Humphry Davy's Lake, Julian Alps.
10. Shrine, near Lengenfeld, Save Thal.
11. Lake of Veldes, Bishop of Brixens' Schloss.
12. Dragon at Klagenfurt.
13. Val Auronzo, the Drei Zinnen in the distance.
14. Titian's Birth-place, Pieve di Cadore.
15. Titian's Tower, Pieve di Cadore.
16. Monte Antelao, Ampezzo Road.
17. Sella Plateau, from Santa Maria, Gröden Thal.
18. Agordo.
19. Castello, near Buchenstein.
20. Marmolata, from the Sasso di Damm.
21. Count Welsperg's Jagd Schloss, Primiero.
22. View in the Sexten Thal, Puster Thal.
23. The Drei Schuster, Sexten Thal.
24. Stone Chair of the Zollfeld.
25. Monte Cristallo, and the Düren See, near Landro.
26. Monte Civita, from Caprile.

London: LONGMAN, GREEN, and CO. Paternoster Row.

LIST OF NEW WORKS.

GUIDE to the CENTRAL ALPS, including the BERNESE OBERLAND, EASTERN SWITZERLAND, LOMBARDY, and the WESTERN TYROL; being the SECOND PART of the *ALPINE GUIDE*. By JOHN BALL, M.R.I.A. F.L.S. &c. late President of the ALPINE CLUB. Post 8vo. with Maps.
[In the Spring.

GUIDE to the WESTERN ALPS, comprising DAUPHINÉ, SAVOY, and PIEDMONT; with the MONT BLANC and MONTE ROSA districts: being the FIRST PART of the *ALPINE GUIDE*. By the same Author. With Six MAPS and Two PANORAMAS of Summits .... Post 8vo. 7*s*. 6*d*.

SOUTH AMERICAN SKETCHES; or, a Visit to Rio Janeiro, the Organ Mountains, La Plata, and the Paranà. By THOMAS W. HINCHLIFF, M.A. F.R.G.S. With MAP and Illustrations .... Post 8vo. 12*s*. 6*d*.

EXPLORATIONS in SOUTH-WEST AFRICA: being an Account of a Journey in the years 1861 and 1862 from Walvisch Bay, on the Western Coast of Southern Africa, to Lake Ngami. By THOMAS BAINES, formerly attached to the North Australian Expedition, and subsequently to that of Dr. LIVINGSTONE on the Zambesi. 1 vol. 8vo. with a MAP and numerous Illustrations..*[In May.*

EXPLORATIONS in LABRADOR. By HENRY Y. HIND, M.A F.R.G.S. Professor of Chemistry and Geology in the Univ. of Trin. Coll. Toronto. With MAPS and Illustrations............. 2 vols. 8vo. 32*s*.

By the same Author, in 2 vols. with Illustrations, price 42s.

The CANADIAN RED RIVER and ASSINNIBOINE and SASKATCHEWAN EXPLORING EXPEDITIONS.

THE SEA and its LIVING WONDERS. By Dr. GEORGE HARTWIG. *Second Edition*, with numerous Wood Engravings and Chromolithographic Illustrations .... 8vo. 18*s*.

By the same Author,

The TROPICAL WORLD: a Popular Scientific Account of the Animal and Vegetable Kingdoms in Equatorial Regions. With 8 Chromoxylographs and 172 Woodcuts .... 8vo. 21*s*.

HOME WALKS and HOLIDAY RAMBLES. By the Rev. C. A. JOHNS, B.A. F.L.S. Author of 'British Birds in their Haunts,' &c. With 10 Illustrations .... Fcp. 8vo. 6*s*.

THE WEATHER BOOK: a Manual of Practical Meteorology. By Rear-Admiral ROBERT FITZ ROY, R.N. F.R.S. *Second Edition*, with 16 DIAGRAMS .... 8vo. 15*s*.

THE WEATHER SYSTEM, or Lunar Influence on Weather. By S. M. SAXBY, R.N. Principal Instructor of Naval Engineers, H.M. Steam Reserve. New Edition, thoroughly revised; including a List of nearly 100 dates which the Author foresees will be marked by unusual meteorological and atmospheric phenomena up to January 1866 ....*[Just ready.*

London: LONGMAN, GREEN, and CO. Paternoster Row.